Rave reviews for *AS ONE MUST, ONE CAN*

*****

For those who have wondered what happened to Havah and the others, an uplifting resolution is in store. As they did in *Please Say Kaddish for Me* and *From Silt and Ashes*, the characters shine in the third in Havah's trilogy, As One Must, One Can. The warm smells of the Jewish cooking kept me hungry during the process. It was tradition and a story of triumph over adversity, full of interesting historical facts that enriched the narrative and provided a sense of authenticity.

~~L.D. Whitaker, author of *Geese to a Poor Market*

*****

In *As One Must, One Can,* the third book in the Havah Gitterman series, Rochelle Wisoff-Fields once again takes readers on a historical and cultural journey, creating a world as seen through the eyes of her characters. Best of all, this story of love, joy, conflict and fear kept me turning the pages and taught me many things about Jewish culture I might not have known otherwise.

~~Jan Morrill, author of *The Red Kimono*

*****

Author Rochelle Wisoff-Fields captures the heart of the reader right from the beginning. *As One Must, One Can* is like moving prose and history through a time capsule. Kansas City, Missouri becomes the canvas from which the author paints. She weaves words and phrases with all the colors of the human emotional rainbow with gentle hands and a compassionate heart. I found myself enjoying the reading journey as much as the story itself.

As One Must, One Can is about never giving up hope and always finding that light at the end of the tunnel of life. This is about the importance of not going into the darkness when times go bad. This book is both inspirational as well as entertaining. Truly a Five Star Reading Experience!

~~Rev. Bill McDonald, author of
Alchemy of a Warrior's Heart

*****

The heartwarming—and heart wrenching—tale of life for pre-World War I Jewish society, *As One Must, One Can* is moving and carefully crafted. A culture facing prejudice and the struggles of being Jewish in America, are made painfully clear while drawing the reader in connections with various characters. Well-researched and a gem of a novel.

~~Caroline Giammanco, author of *Bank Notes*

*****

Having survived the savage pogroms in Russia that killed members of her Jewish family, Havah Cohen Gitterman now lives in Kansas City with her husband, Arel, and their blind daughter, Rachel. Though life is somewhat peaceful, the past plagues the present and threatens the future for Havah, her loved ones and friends who suffer physical and emotional scars. *As One Must One Can* is a story of determination, grit, and love—not just any love, but the kind that gives us wings and the power to overcome.

~~Diane Yates, author of *Pathways of the Heart*
and *All That Matters*

To Joyce Kay,

Thanks for loving Havah as much as I do.
A good read. Blessings.

Your sister(in law)
Rochelle

AS ONE MUST,
ONE CAN

Rochelle Wisoff-Fields

W & B Publishers
USA

W & B Publishers

For information:
W & B Publishers
9001 Ridge Hill Street
Kernersville, NC 27284

www.a-argusbooks.com

ISBN: 978-1635540-0-4-8

Book Cover designed by Rochelle Wisoff-Fields

Printed in the United States of America

Dedication

To Olive

Acknowledgements for As One Must, One Can

Some special people inspired my trilogy. My maternal grandfather Sam Weiner, a tailor, came to the US at the turn of the 20th century to escape the pogroms in Eastern Europe and built a thriving business in Kansas City. He and my grandmother Nettie Weinberg raised four children—Harry, Edith, and twins, Evalyne and Norman. My aunt, Edith Weiner Myers, my mother's sister, best friend and confidante, lived one backyard away. Like Havah and Shayndel, they were inseparable. My mother, Evalyne Weiner Wisoff, whose Hebrew name was Havah, instilled in me the desire to remain true to my roots and never forget. May their memories be a blessing.

I would also like to take the opportunity to thank those among the living who have encouraged me along the way.

A special thank you goes to Jeanie Loiacono, my agent who has worked tirelessly on my behalf. She's never stopped believing in Havah or her purpose.

To Lois Hounshel, my sounding board who patiently listened to almost every rendition of the manuscripts and insists she loved every one of them.

I owe much to the keen eyes of Lonnie Whitaker and his green pen.

Jean L. Hays, Mrs. Spears is smiling down on us. Thank you for all of your help, Taffy.

Muchas gracias to my cousin, Kent Bonham, for proofreading and giving good suggestions. Also a hearty thank you for lending your expertise as a videographer in the form of book trailers.

To Douglas M. MacIlroy for whom the bells clang

and whirling discs sail, I have one thing to say, "TYVMDM."

Many thanks to Susan Hawes who gave Pavel Trubachov his motive and mission in life. "It's what my Lord would've done."

A huge helping of hunky dory goes to Regina O'Hare who inspired Fruma Ya'el's character, compassion and stubborn strength.

A round of applause goes to my friends here and abroad in Friday Fictioneers. Who knew that a hundred words a week could build such a wonderful community?

Here's a resounding thank you to William Connor for putting Havah in print.

Last and never least, a huge thank you goes to my husband and best friend, Jan Wayne Fields. Without your love and belief in me none of this would have been possible.

PROLOGUE

SOLOMON'S LAMENT

"I've reported what I saw and heard, but only part of it," said Edward R. Murrow in his radio broadcast after the liberation of *Buchenwald*. "For most of it, I have no words."

World War II ended in 1945, the year I turned twelve. To celebrate, Dad treated my grandmother and me to a movie at the Uptown. Today—seventy years later—I can't recall what was playing. All I remember is the newsreel.

Emaciated men and women stared at me from the screen. Bodies were stacked like pencils in mass graves. Images of skeletons in brick ovens flashed before me. Nazi murder mills, the newsreel announcer called the death camps.

The stunned silence that filled the theater was broken only by scattered gasps and sobs.

My father, a doctor who had survived the atrocities of the Odessa pogrom in1905 and treated the wounded on the battlefields of WWI, turned ash white. He dropped his head into his hands. "The war's over, but it never ends."

Later that night, Dad had to rush to the hospital to perform an emergency C-section. Since Mom had gone to visit family in Oklahoma, and I was too young to be left alone, I spent the night with my grandparents.

I couldn't sleep. Every time I closed my eyes, I saw hollow cheeks and empty stares. I slipped on my bathrobe and padded to the living room where *Bubbe* sat at the piano and played Chopin's "Nocturne in C-Sharp Minor." She stopped and smiled. "You, too?" Curling up on the sofa, I nodded.

She looked younger than her sixty-two years. In the dim lamplight her brown eyes glittered. Her dark hair, too thick to pin up, cascaded around her slender shoulders and her ivory cheeks shone with tears. Sitting erect in her chair, she wheeled it to the couch and stopped beside me. She cupped her soft hand around my chin. "I wasn't much older than you—sixteen. The Cossacks burned our village and murdered my family before my eyes."

"That's the night you escaped in just your nightgown, right, *Bubbe*?"

"Mama kissed me and shoved me out the door. 'May the God of *Yisroel* go with you, Havah. Don't look back.' Her last scream behind me still makes my ears ache."

"Then you ran all night through the forest until you collapsed in front of the synagogue in Svechka. And your foot was so badly frostbitten and infected that your adopted mother, Great-grandma Fruma, cut part of it off. Then you ran away to Kishinev and—"

"I nearly died in that pogrom in 1903. Fifty people, some of them babies, died that weekend. What was their crime? They were Jews." She dropped her hand into her lap. "You've heard this a hundred times already. But I want you should never forget, Edith Gitterman." Her eyes were suddenly faraway clouds. "Czar Nicholas was cut from the same cloth as this Hitler monster. As King Solomon said, 'There's nothing new under the sun.'"

PART I

GHOSTS OF THE FALLEN

Chapter One

KANSAS CITY, MISSOURI

Afternoon sun streamed through the tall classroom windows and cast long shadows across the dusty floor. On the chalkboard in rigid script was written, "9 October 1907, Wednesday." Arithmetic problems in childish scrawls covered another blackboard on the opposite wall.

Behind her desk, the teacher sat with rawboned fingers clasped on top of her attendance book. Her hair was parted down the middle and pulled back from her face into a severe bun.

Under the teacher's spectacled glare, Havah fidgeted on the hard chair. "What did my Reuven do that was so terrible?"

"He gave another boy a black eye."

"Reuven says the other boy hit him first."

"I don't care who started it. Fighting will not be tolerated in my class, Mrs. Gitterman, and that is that."

"He says the other children are mean to him. They call him names. They call him 'Liar' and 'Gravedigger.'"

"Yes, they do. But he's partly to blame for this I'm afraid."

"Can't you make them stop, Miss Kline?"

"Please read these poems the children wrote, 'Autumn Comes to Kansas City.'" Miss Kline handed Havah a stack of papers. "Perhaps it will help you understand."

Havah picked up the first page, cleared her throat

and read the smudged writing.

'Autumn comes to Kansas City
Yellow leafs drop
My Pa rakes them into piles
Me and my bruther jump on them.'

"This looks like a cat wrote it. Miss Kline, what has this to do with my boy?"

"Keep reading, please."

"Very well." Havah smoothed out the wrinkled page and read aloud.

"'Autumn comes to Kansas City
Leves fall
Red and gold
I think they are prety
Sissy and me munch apples
An drink cider.'"

After Havah read another poem about golden leaves, delicious apples and Halloween, Miss Kline took one from a folder and handed it to her.

"And this is Reuven's. When you read it you will most certainly understand my concern."

"His handwriting is very nice isn't it? And he knows how to spell. We practice together every night."

"I have no quarrel with your boy's spelling abilities." Miss Kline folded her arms across her chest. "And his penmanship is the best in my class. As far as that goes, he's a talented writer. It's *what* he's writing that worries me."

Havah slowly turned her eyes back to Reuven's poem.

"'Autumn comes to Kansas City

Orange and golden trees make me sad
Far, far away in a graveyard
The dead girls can't see them.
They used to dance in the leaves
Now they lie ever so still in the dirt
and wait for snow.'"

The page blurred. Havah sniffed and dabbed her eyes with her gloved hand.

"Now do you see? I'm appalled a child would write such things. I fear he has a morbid fascination with death." Miss Kline leaned forward, rested her elbows on the desk and peered at Havah as she took another paper from the folder.

"I asked the children to write an essay about their hero. Most of them wrote about their mother or father.

"It's not unusual for boys to make up adventure stories, especially when the truth is less than exciting. One of my students writes his father is a cowboy. What an imagination. I know his father, a mild man who works at the meat packing plant. But what your son wrote is beyond adventure."

Miss Kline read in a low, strained voice.

"My Hero
"By Reuven Gitterman
"I will never forget the day my Papa the shoemaker saved my life. It was morning. We had just finished breakfast. My sisters were washing the dishes when some bad men pushed open the door of our apartment above the shoe shop.

"Bang! Papa shot two of them. They fell dead. But there were too many, and they killed my sister Leah, then they shot Papa. When I ran to him he grabbed me and made me lay down on the floor. Then he fell on top of me.

"He said, 'Be very quiet, Little Apple.'

"I pretended to be dead. I heard gunshots and the babies cried.

"Then they stopped and it was quiet. Dead people quiet. Papa stopped breathing. I could feel his warm blood on my back. The only ones left are Lev and Bayla and me.

"I will never forget Papa. My hero.

"The End.

"Terrible." Miss Kline shuddered, clucked her tongue and tossed the paper in Havah's lap.

"Yes," whispered Havah as she took the page in her hands and caressed the corners with her thumbs. "Terrible."

"You see why I urge you to have a talk with your son, Mrs. Gitterman? You and your husband are very much alive and he writes this?"

The paper fell from Havah's trembling hands. She stood, slammed her palms on the desk and leaned into the other woman's face until the tips of their noses almost touched.

"It is *you* who will have a talk with the children of your class. You will make them apologize to Reuven. He is no liar."

Chapter Two

Arel Gitterman grimaced at his reflection as he shaved and washed the soap off his face. Scars trailed from the corner of his left eye to his chin. Although he was only twenty-seven, his dark hair had already begun to gray at the temples.

Nonetheless, Havah insisted these things made him distinctively handsome. The thought of his pretty wife made him smile as he put away his shaving soap and razor.

He tiptoed from the bathroom to the bedroom to dress for work. Opening the armoire, he took out his clothes and gently shut the door, careful not to wake Havah. When it latched she rose up on one elbow and looked at the clock on the bed stand. "Arel? Why didn't you wake me? It's eight o'clock."

He sat on the bed, pushed her long black hair off her face and kissed her. "Let your mama take care of things."

Before he finished she yawned again, sank back into the pillows and closed her eyes, a half-smile on her face. He brushed his lips across hers one more time.

On his way down the hall he stopped to peek in on Rachel Esther, their three-year-old daughter. Her black curls fell across her nose and rosy cheeks. Overwhelmed by his good fortune, Arel knelt and kissed the top of her head.

She giggled and threw her arms around his neck. "Good morning, Poppy."

"Good morning, Rukhel Shvester." He scooped her up into his arms. "Shall we go see what *Bubbe*'s fixing for breakfast?"

Curled up at the end of the bed Kreplakh, Rachel's cocker spaniel, raised her head and yipped. She rose onto all fours, stretched and wagged her tail.

"Kreplakh's hungry, too," said Rachel.

"Then let's go."

He descended the stairs and made his way to the kitchen with the dog at his heels.

"Good morning, Arel." Fruma Ya'el, a buxom woman in her mid-fifties, pushed back a wisp of grey hair and looked up from stirring a skillet full of scrambled eggs and potatoes. She spooned some of the mixture on a plate, set it on the table and beamed at Rachel. "*Bubbe* has breakfast all ready for her big girl." She took the child from him and sat her atop a stack of books on a chair.

"Good morning, Mama," Arel kissed Fruma Ya'el's cheek. "Is Papa still at morning prayers?"

"You know how those old men are. *Shakharis* could last for hours the way they like to argue."

"That's one of the reasons I quit going. They made me late for work."

Despite sunlight bathing the kitchen, Arel shivered. "Does anyone else notice it's cold in here? This is what heaters are for."

He knelt beside the cast iron radiator and twisted the handle to open the valve. It hissed out a steamy burst, warming his cold cheeks.

"I don't trust it." Fruma Ya'el pulled her shawl around her shoulders. "What if it blows up and burns the house down?"

"It's steam, Mama, hot water. If it weren't for me you'd huddle in a corner and freeze to death."

"Nonsense. We have a fireplace."

Arel grinned at his stepmother. For all of her wisdom, she held onto many old world ideas and superstitions. When they had first arrived in America it took three weeks before she would go near a telephone.

Before marrying Yussel she had been Auntie Fruma to Arel and his sisters. As the most experienced midwife in Svechka, Moldova, Fruma Ya'el had delivered most of the villagers under the age of thirty. After Arel's mother passed away, Fruma Ya'el took the Gitterman children under her wing. Arel's heart swelled with love for her.

"Is Havah coming down?" she asked.

"No."

"I hoped not. I heard her cry somewhere around midnight. Her nightmares again?"

"And pain."

"Poor Mommy," said Rachel, with tears in her eyes. "Her legs hurt her almost all the time, don't they, Poppy? Can't Dr. Miklos make them better?"

"Doctors can't fix everything."

"You mean like he can't fix my eyes?" Rachel walked her fingers along the table until she came to a spoon. She used the spoon to search for the food on her plate. After she took a bite and swallowed, she tilted her head. "But my eyes don't hurt like Mommy's legs."

"My daughter's as smart as she is talented." Arel filled a plate and took the chair next to hers.

Fruma Ya'el poured two cups of coffee, gave one to Arel and sat.

"You missed Bayla and Reuven by minutes. He couldn't wait to get to school. I'm so glad Havah set that teacher straight. She gave him an A+ on his papa-my-hero story and now the other children think Reuven's a hero, too." Fruma Ya'el's brows furrowed. "Their brother Lev, on the other hand, didn't come home last night. I told you, you shouldn't have allowed him to quit school."

"He's seventeen and never cracked a book. What else could I do? He promised me he'd find a job."

***

Yussel Gitterman's world was one of sound, scent and touch. He breathed in the aroma of his coffee before taking a sip and listened to the rustle of Fruma Ya'el's starched petticoat. She hummed a tune as she washed the dishes. At his feet the dog snored and yipped in her sleep.

On Yussel's lap, Rachel read from her Braille book. He stroked her soft curls that felt like silk against his palm. Unlike him, she had been born blind. Although he loved all of his grandchildren, he shared a special bond with her. When she was an infant, he thought he would be the one to teach her. Instead, the teacher had become the student.

After so many years, a glimmer of light penetrated his darkness and the joy of the printed page, even a children's story, infused him. The raised dots under his fingertips became words, taking shape and form in his mind.

"*Zaydeh*, are you listening to me?" Rachel tugged at his beard.

"Sorry, Teacher. I must've been daydreaming."

"You mustn't do that, *Zaydeh*. How will you ever learn to read if you don't pay 'tention? Now read for *Bubbe*."

"Yes, ma'am." Obediently he skimmed his fingers across the page of McGuffey's *First Reader* and slowly shaped the words aloud, "'The boy has a bird. This...bird is on his...hand.'"

"It's a miracle!" Fruma Ya'el clapped her hands.

"My turn! My turn!" Rachel turned the thick pages. "'Come with me, Ann, and see the man with a black hat on his head.'"

"A genius, this girl." Yussel pinched her nose between his first two knuckles.

"Someone's coming up the walk, *Bubbe*," said Rachel.

"I don't hear anything," said Fruma Ya'el.

Yussel tilted his head. Dry leaves crunched under heavy footsteps on the pavement. A few moments later the doorbell chimed.

Fruma Ya'el held her breath and exhaled. "I swear you could hear dust moving in Russia, Rukhel Shvester."

The dog barked, and as she ran to the front door her claws clicked along the floorboards. Fruma Ya'el's skirts swished as she followed her. The door opened and shut. The smells of witch hazel, licorice, and pipe tobacco filled the air.

"Rabbi Zaretsky." Yussel set the book on the table and Rachel on her feet. He stood and extended his hand. "What brings you here this fine morning?"

The young rabbi cleared his throat with a loud cough and lowered his voice to a whisper. "May I speak with you alone, Rabbi Gitterman?"

Yussel pulled back his hand. "Why the secrecy?"

"It's a matter of deep concern, not for women's ears."

"The study then."

He touched Yussel's shoulder. "Let me help you, sir."

"I can find my way in my own home, thank you. Follow me, but please try to be quiet. Our Havah didn't sleep well last night."

Yussel shook off the proffered hand, picked up his cane, and sliding the tip along the floor, made his way to the other room without bumping into furniture. Once he found the desk, he sat in the chair behind it.

The other chair groaned under Rabbi Zaretsky's considerable girth. Clearing his throat again, he drew a querulous breath and let it out slowly with a soft whistle. "I'll come to the point. Are you aware of your daughter-in-law's Hebrew and *Humash* classes for *girls?*" He spat out the last word.

"Right here, in this very room."

"Surely you see the harm, Rabbi Gitterman. Women are supposed to take care of the home, teach their daughters to keep kosher. What kind of example is she setting? What kind of example are *you* setting by allowing it?"

"Look around you, Rabbi. I dare you to find a cleaner house or children who are better cared for. I warrant there's not a woman in the congregation who can bake a better *holla*. And on top of all of this, she reads and teaches the holy language. Besides, your predecessor had no objections to her classes as long as she didn't hold them at the synagogue."

"But *Humash* itself—Torah forbids—"

"Show me where, chapter and verse."

Rabbi Zaretsky gasped and coughed several times.

"Rabbi Gitterman, our laws have preserved our people through persecutions and—"

"What do *you* know of persecution?"

"My parents came from Poland in 1870. And I read about the Kishinev pogrom in *The New York Times*."

"You *nebbish*! You overgrown ignoramus! My Havah nearly died in Kishinev!"

Chapter Three

Injuries she had suffered at the hands of the Cossacks left Havah with little resistance to sickness, so Fruma Ya'el fretted over her every cough or sneeze. On the way to America, Havah became quite ill and could not keep anything down. Dr. Florin Miklos, a fellow traveler aboard the ship, came to her aid. After examining her, he gave the Gittermans the good news that Havah did not have a disease but was with child.

A portly man with fiery hair and moustache to match, Dr. Miklos filled the long journey with friendship and laughter. He refused any payment for his services saying, "All I did was give the little lady bicarbonate of soda for her morning sickness."

Fruma Ya'el's heart went out to Dr. Miklos, a widower, who had lost his only son in Kishinev. His eyes glittered as he spoke of him. "Petru always wanted to be a physician like his Papa. He felt a calling on his life to your precious people. Alas, he was only fifteen and never had a chance. The police tried to convince me 'those treacherous Christ Killers' in the Jewish Quarter beat him to death. I didn't believe them for one minute. No, not even for a second."

When the Gittermans and Dr. Miklos parted in New York, Arel gave him his sister Sarah's address where they would live until they found their own homes. Dr. Miklos stuffed the paper into his vest pocket and shook Arel's hand. "If you're ever in Minneapolis, Minnesota, I'll be working at Asbury Methodist Hospital."

Fruma Ya'el never expected to see him again, but less than a year later at Passover he showed up in Kansas City. She marveled at his timing. After the Seder meal, when the children went to the door to open it for the prophet Elijah, there stood Dr. Miklos.

In many ways, Fruma Ya'el considered him their Messiah for he had appointed himself their personal family physician. When the children all came down with chicken pox he was there. Even as his practice grew he found the time to treat their tiniest cuts with iodine and lollipops. Fruma Ya'el believed he had been blessed with a sixth sense, especially when it came to Havah. He had an uncanny way of showing up when she needed him most. At the same time, he refused remuneration of any kind save an occasional home cooked meal or cup of coffee.

***

Fruma Ya'el pressed her palm against Havah's clammy forehead. "No fever."

Although she had slept until ten, long after Arel had gone to work and the children to school, Havah seemed more fragile and tired than usual. She sipped her hot chocolate and picked at a bowl of raisins.

"I'll be fine, Mama. I just need a nap." Havah's pallor and puffy eyes betrayed her.

"Just the same, I'm calling Dr. Florin. I think he should take a look at you." Fruma Ya'el lifted the earpiece from the telephone on the kitchen wall and reached for the crank to ring the operator.

Havah rolled her eyes and popped a raisin into her mouth. "He's taken more looks at me than Arel."

Before Fruma Ya'el could utter another word, the doorbell rang. She dropped the earpiece back on the hook and hurried to the door. Swinging it open she smiled up at the doctor. "*Nu?* What took you so long?"

***

Florin sat on the sofa, coffee cup in hand, transfixed as Havah and Rachel played a duet on the piano in the front corner of the living room. Afternoon sun poured through the windows bathing mother and daughter in a halo of gold.

When they finished, Rachel slid off the bench, turned, and curtsied. Then she took hold of Kreplakh's halter and the dog guided her to Florin. Kreplakh sat on her haunches, staring at him with her soft brown eyes.

"Smart pup, this one." Florin pulled a treat from his pocket, held it out to her and patted her silky head with his free hand. Her tongue tickled his palm.

Rachel climbed onto his lap. "Poppy says she's my other eyes."

"Yes, she is. She certainly is. Someone's trained her well."

"No one," said Havah. "Kreplakh took it upon herself to take care of Rachel. Arel designed the halter to give Rachel something to hold onto besides the dog's fur."

"More comfortable for both of them." Florin scratched Kreplakh behind one of her droopy ears. Ingenious."

After she swallowed her treat, Kreplakh trotted back to Havah, licked her skirt, whimpered, and curled up under the piano bench.

"Rachel's not the only one she cares for." Florin sat Rachel down and slid onto the bench beside Havah. "I share the puppy's concern."

"You shouldn't listen to Mama. She worries too much."

"Is that so? Then you tell me, dear lady. What can this old doctor do for you?"

Havah's dark eyes, almost too large for her delicate face, brimmed and her lower lip quivered. "Make me well."

Chapter Four

Between her daughter's painful cries, her husband's snoring, and her own swirling thoughts, Shayndel Abromovich had given up on sleep. She laid her slumbering baby in her crib, shut off the lamp beside it and backed out of the room on tiptoe.

She turned only to bump into Itzak who stood in the doorway. He wrapped his arms around her and whispered, "Her tooth?"

"Yes, it finally poked through about an hour ago." Shayndel leaned her head against his bare chest. His hair tickled her nose and cheek.

"It's half past two. You need sleep, my golden flower." He scooped her up into his arms and headed across the hall to their bedroom.

Once they nestled under the feather comforter, Itzak nibbled at her ear. Ignoring the shivers he sent through her, she turned in his embrace. "I'm worried about Wolf."

With an audible groan, Itzak rolled onto his back. "Why? He's finally acting like a human being again."

"It's so sudden."

When her sister Sarah succumbed to pneumonia a little over a year ago Shayndel feared her despondent brother-in-law would find a way to join his wife. It was months before he slept a full night, bathed, or ate a decent meal. Arel and Havah took in his twins, Jeffrey and Evalyne, to save them from unintentional neglect.

In June, four months before, Wolf received an invitation from an old friend in St. Louis. Everyone agreed a change of scenery would be good for him and the twins, who were delighted to be reunited with their father.

Who would have suspected Wolf's friend of acting as a matchmaker for his widowed sister? By the time he and the kids returned to Kansas City two weeks later, Wolf was engaged to be married.

"I'm worried about Havah, too," murmured Shayndel.

"You're not happy unless you have something to worry about."

"You don't care."

"All right already." Itzak sat up. "Why are you worried about Havah this time?"

"She's so attached to Jeffrey and Evalyne, and now Wolf's taking them away."

"It's St. Louis, Shayndel, not Siberia, and it's not as if Havah doesn't have four other children to take care of."

"That's true...Lev alone is one big pill."

"If she gets really lonely, I'll send our four over to keep her company."

***

Havah lit the Sabbath candles, circled her hands around them three times, pressed her fingers against her eyelids and recited the blessing. *"Barukh asah Adonoi, Eloheynu, Melekh ha Olam,...*Blessed are you, *Adonoi* our God, King of the Universe...*asher kidshawnoo b'mitzvosahv, v'itzivanoo l'hadlik ner shel Shabbes,* who sanctified us with His commandments, and commanded us to light the Sabbath candles."

After saying "amen," she opened her eyes to see her family's faces aglow in the candlelight. To have cheated the angel of death more than once and now to be surrounded by life infused her with joy. At the same time twinges of sorrow mingled with her happiness. She would always see the ghosts of those she had lost for she would never allow them to leave.

Arel stood and blessed the wine, his cup upraised. Everyone clustered around Havah's dining room table and took a sip from their own cups. Then he held up the *holla,* a braided egg bread and recited the traditional prayer. He broke off a piece of it and passed the loaf around the table.

"Amen." Itzak ripped off a chunk of *holla.* "It's about time. I'm starving to death."

"Take heart, my teddy bear." Shayndel patted his rounded belly. "Relief is as close as the kitchen." She left the room followed by Fruma Ya'el.

Although Shayndel and Havah continued the family tradition of taking turns hosting the *Shabbes* dinner every Friday night, it did not seem right without Sarah taking her turn. In fact, she had left such a void, Shayndel and Havah honored her memory by setting a place for her at their Sabbath tables.

"I wish we didn't have to move." Nine-year-old Jeffrey frowned. "I don't like dumb old Dora. She's nothing like Mama."

"She looks like this." His twin sister Evalyne puffed out her cheeks and crossed her eyes. "And she smells like lemons and mothballs."

Evalyne left her chair, made her way to Havah, and wrapped her gangly arms around her. With her frizzled black hair and huge brown eyes, she bore an uncanny resemblance to Sarah.

"I'm gonna miss you, Auntie Havah."

Havah brushed a tear from the girl's cheek with her thumb. "The next time I see you, I'll have to look up at you."

"That's not saying much, Havaleh," said Itzak. "Our Elliott's only three and he's nearly as tall as you."

"Who will give me Hebrew lessons in St. Louis?" Evalyne tightened her arms around Havah. "Who will teach me *Humash*?"

"I will," said Wolf softly, his gaze fixed on Havah. "But I might not do it as well as your auntie."

Havah returned his gaze with a raised eyebrow. "You didn't always think so."

Two years ago the idea of girls learning Hebrew angered him. Almost every family gathering ended with an argument about traditions and Torah until the night he heard Jeffrey ask Evalyne for help. To Wolf's amazement, his daughter was farther along in the lesson book than his son.

Havah cherished the memory of the day Wolf went down on one knee, kissed her hand and said, "A true scholar admits when he's wrong."

"*Oy yoy, meyne mishpokhah,* my family." Yussel trembled and rocked back and forth in his chair. His wrinkled cheeks and white beard glistened with tears. "*Meyne* Sarah."

All conversation ceased. Even Tikvah in her high chair stopped her chatter and crammed her fingers into her mouth. Yussel wiped his eyes with his napkin and held out his arms.

"Jeffrey. Evalyne. Come here."

Evalyne let go of Havah and Jeffrey, sucking on his lower lip, slid off his chair. Eyes on Yussel, the twins slowly approached his end of the table. He curved an arm around each of them and drew them into a strong embrace.

"Since when are you afraid of your old *Zaydeh*?"

"You sounded all mean," said Jeffrey.

Yussel kissed the top of Evalyne's head. "May Adoshem bless you and guard you." He kissed Jeffrey's forehead. "May Adoshem make his face to shine upon you and give you shalom, peace." He turned toward Wolf.

"Take care of my grandchildren. And take care of yourself, my son."

***

Looking up from his sewing machine, Arel gazed out the shop window. A little boy raced by, his mother close behind shouting at him to slow down. Arel grinned when she caught the boy and applied paddle to bottom. Then he returned his attention to the pair of trousers under the machine's presser foot. It needed to be his best work.

Wolf squeezed Arel's shoulder. "I don't know anyone who sews a straighter seam. Sarah couldn't have done a better job."

Arel winced at the mention of his sister's name. "Thanks, Wolf. That means a lot coming from you."

"You've become quite the tailor. Tell me, are you ever sorry you gave up being a rabbi?"

"Nah. Havah would make a better one than I in any case."

"That she would." Wolf pointed to the sign painted on the window glass that boasted, *Tulschinsky's Fine Tailoring.* "You'll have to change it to Gitterman. The shop's all yours now."

Standing in front of a full-length mirror, Wolf stretched out his lanky arms in the suit jacket that matched the trousers on the sewing machine. He turned one way and then the other, admiring his reflection. "Perfect down to the last stitch. Add a top hat and a necktie and I'll make a fine bridegroom."

After he put the finishing touches on the trousers, Arel handed them to Wolf. "Try them on."

Wolf sat and slipped his long legs into them, stood and fastened the fly. He walked from the back of the shop to the front and stared out the window for a few moments. With one slender finger he wiped off a smudge.

"I'm going to miss this cow town."

"Why can't Dora move here?"

"I'll bet you think I'm a terrible father for uprooting the kids."

"Does it matter what I think?"

"They need a mother and they love Dora."

"So I heard."

"Okay, maybe not, but they'll learn to love her." Wolf turned away from the window, his eyes welling up. "Not a day goes by I don't think about and miss my beloved. Don't you see, little brother? I could never allow another woman to live in Sarah's house."

Chapter Five

Like Havah, Arel had narrowly escaped with his life in Kishinev. Pogromists beat him with crowbars, mutilating the left side of his face. Havah would never forget the sight of him lying unconscious and unrecognizable for all the blood, certain she had lost him forever.

His scars never seemed to bother him as much as Havah's embarrassed her. He appeared to take everything in stride. However, since Wolf left the tailor shop to him, Havah noticed a change in Arel, a self-consciousness she had never seen before. More than once she caught him snarling at his reflection in the bathroom mirror.

Tonight Havah and Arel cuddled on the sofa in front of the fireplace as everyone had gone next door. With a houseful such as theirs, it was a rare treat to have the living room to themselves.

Leaning her head against one of the arms of the couch, she stretched out on her back and propped her bare feet on Arel's lap. A delicious wave of sleep swept over her as he massaged her deformed foot with his thumbs.

"Do you still have feelings for Ulrich?"

Arel's voice startled her and she snapped open her eyes. "Why do you ask?"

"He's a very nice looking man."

"And he's madly in love with Catherine."

"Are you so sure he didn't marry her on the rebound?"

"I was his housekeeper."

Arel's grip on her foot tightened and his thumbs dug deep, striking a tender spot. "His housekeeper with whom he took the time to teach English, piano, and whatever else you might've cared to learn."

"Ouch! How can you think such a thing?" Havah jerked her feet off his lap and scooted to the opposite side of the sofa. "Ulrich Dietrich's the reason we're here. He pulled us out of the fire and paid for us to come to America first class instead of steerage like so many others. On top of that, he's shown you nothing but friendship and respect."

"You haven't answered my question."

"Nor will I."

"In Kishinev, after the pogrom…when you were finally well…" Arel's stormy eyes sent electric shocks through her. "I saw the two of you, in the ballroom…alone at the piano…"

"He was helping me limber up my hand." Havah studied the long scar from a knife wound on her right palm that went from her thumb to her pinkie. "Dr. Nikolai said playing the piano would exercise it."

"Did that 'exercise' include Ulrich's kissing it to make it better?"

"What do you want me to say?"

"You're the lucky one, Havah." Arel turned his head and gazed into the fire. The flames cast flickering light on his cheek, accentuating the tangle of scars. "I can't hide my face in a shoe."

***

Ulrich Dietrich, a concert pianist and wealthy heir to an Austrian banker, made it his daily habit to take long walks at sunrise. He relished the solitude of the early hours. Often he would peruse the closed shops of downtown Kansas City, taking in the grandeur of the growing number of skyscrapers. Other times he would walk through the parks or residential areas.

This morning he returned home from a brisk walk, invigorated by the cold air. He hung his coat on a hook in the kitchen and set a pot of coffee on the stove to brew. Whistling a few bars of "The Entertainer" he went upstairs to look in on Catherine. He stopped whistling, tiptoed to the chaise lounge beside the bed, and watched her sleep.

Bathed in sunlight, her auburn curls blazed across the pillow. A sprinkling of freckles on her cheeks and upturned nose gave her a childlike appearance, but her attributes, visible through her thin nightgown, said otherwise. Unable to contain his desire, he reached out to caress them.

"Professor Dietrich." She caught his wrist in midair and opened her luminous green eyes. Her melodious British accent tickled his ears. She pulled his hand to her lips and kissed his palm. "You naughty boy, you're going to be late for school."

"Not so, my delicious firebrand, it's Saturday."

Clutching his hand, she held it against her cheek. "Ulrich, dearest. May I ask you a silly question?"

"For you," he snuggled against her, breathing in her lavender perfume. "the answer's always yes."

"Do you still have…feelings for Havah?"

Chapter Six

"Frederick Chopin succumbed to consumption on 17 October 1849 with his sister Ludwika at his side." Nikolai Derevenko's voice echoed about the half empty auditorium.

He shut his textbook, rose from the bench by the grand piano and observed the vacant expressions of his students. Clenching his teeth, he turned to the piano and hammered out a mélange of sour chords. All but one of his seventeen pupils snapped to attention in their chairs.

Nikolai stepped off the platform and walked around them until he came to a student in the back row. Head back, mouth open and legs stretched in front of him, the boy's snores reverberated throughout the hall. When Nikolai tapped his shoulder he opened his eyes and bolted upright, nearly upsetting his chair. "I'm awake!"

"Mr. Gelbart, is my class that exciting?"

"It'll do." The boy flushed and shrugged his shoulders. "I'm here to become a concert pianist. Why bother about a bunch of moldy old composers?"

A few of the other students voiced their agreement. Nikolai bristled. "Tell me, Mr. Gelbart, how old was Chopin when he composed his first Polonaise?"

"I dunno. Twenty maybe?"

"Guess again."

"I know, Dr. Derevenko," cried a skinny young man in the next chair. "He was seven."

"Bravo." Nikolai clapped his hands three times. "So I haven't bored all of you into oblivion. By the time he turned twenty, Chopin was a recognized composer and accomplished pianist."

Mr. Gelbart folded his arms across his chest. "So what?"

"How can you play one of his nocturnes or mazurkas and not care about the man himself?" Nikolai waved his pencil like a conductor leading an orchestra. "To know Chopin, the loves of his life—his pain, his passion—is to know the very depth and soul of his music."

Prepared to expound further, Nikolai realized a hush had fallen over the classroom. Seventeen pairs of eyes riveted on him. He pivoted and walked back to the platform. "That will be all for today unless there are any further questions."

"I have a question." Mr. Gelbart leaned forward. "Where did you study music, Doctor?"

"St. Petersburg Conservatory in Russia. Why?"

"Professor Dietrich says you play the flute."

"That is correct." One of the boys on the front row snickered. Nikolai scowled. "I beg your pardon, but did I say something funny?"

Squirming under Nikolai's glare, the student stammered. "No, sir, it's just that flute…well…it's…"

Nikolai pursed his lips in an effort to maintain his composure and returned to the piano. "An old lady's instrument?"

Before he could pile his papers and books into his open satchel, Mr. Gelbart walked up behind him and lifted out Nikolai's flute case.

"Would you play something for us, Dr. Derevenko? Please?"

Angry words rushed to Nikolai's tongue, but something in the youth's eyes changed his mind. He took the case, sat on the piano bench and opened it. "What would you like to hear?"

"Bach."

"*Da,* Bach. He's a favorite of mine, too."

Nikolai pressed the flute against his chin, closed his eyes and played Bach's "Partita in A Minor." The Conservatory of Music in Kansas City disappeared as the lilting melody filled the hall and carried him back to St. Petersburg, to the first time he played with the Philharmonic Orchestra. His father beamed and twelve-year-old Nikolai's chest swelled with joy.

Playing the last few notes, he opened his eyes to see his students circled around him. Tears streamed down Mr. Gelbart's cheeks. For several moments, no one dared to speak.

Nikolai bowed and cleared his throat. "Monday we will discuss the turbulent life of Franz Schubert."

He laid his flute in the velvet lined case. Still no one spoke nor moved.

"One more question, sir," whispered Mr. Gelbart. "Is it true you're also a surgeon?"

"I suppose Professor Dietrich told you this, too."

"Yes, sir."

"Class dismissed."

***

Although Nikolai's modest salary at the conservatory could only buy a simple one-story house, his wife Oxana could not have been more pleased. Compared to the dingy apartment in Odessa they had shared with her brother Pavel, it was a palace. Nikolai could not deny it. With her ability as a seamstress and her eye for décor, she had turned the house into a comfortable home.

In all the rooms, pastel or white lace curtains graced the windows for Oxana abhorred dark colors. She even insisted on painting the kitchen yellow.

"There's been enough death," she said when he questioned her choices. "We've seen too much darkness."

"We'll have to wear sunglasses at breakfast," said Nikolai's sixteen-year-old son, Vasily.

A cheerful fire warmed the parlor and cast random light and shadow on the flowered wallpaper. Outside, the wind blustered and rain pelted the windows. Nikolai glanced at the grandfather clock in the corner of the parlor.

"How late did Vasily say he would be?"

"He went out with friends." Oxana stood at the dining room lighting candles on a cake with scrolled icing borders. "You know how boys are. He said they were going to grab bite to eat after they go to the library. He said to save him a piece of your birthday cake."

Nikolai envied his son. After a trying day, he had looked forward to relaxing with his family. Instead he came home to a surprise birthday party. While he hated being fussed over to begin with, he detested it on his birthday even more.

Before he removed his coat, Ulrich and Florin greeted him with slaps on the back and off-key singing. Catherine set a birthday hat on his head. With heat rushing to his cheeks, Nikolai forced a smile.

In the excitement, Oxana forgot about dinner in the oven until it was too late to save it. The chicken was black and the potatoes had turned to cinders.

An hour later, after a makeshift supper of scrambled eggs and toast, he picked up his plate and stood. He took a deep breath and slowly exhaled. The air reeked of burnt chicken. "Let me help with the dishes."

"Guest of honor should not clean up." Tears trickled from Oxana's pale blue eyes behind her wire-framed spectacles. She took his plate. "I'm sorry for *ushasnyy*—terrible supper."

He took the plate back, set it on the on the table and wrapped his arms around her. "No one starved."

"I want your—*den' rohzdeniya*—birthday to be…how you say…perfect."

Even after two years, Oxana struggled with English. Although Nikolai encouraged her to speak it, in private they spoke Russian. Tonight, for Catherine's sake, she made a special effort.

While Oxana was three inches taller than he, she weighed at least twenty pounds less. A long flaxen braid formed a crown around her head. Her lips, almost too full for her narrow face, coupled with angular cheekbones and long neck, gave her an exotic appearance. For a moment, he forgot about his ruined supper and entertained other ideas.

Instead he brushed away her tears. "The eggs were delicious and I love *holla*. It's the tastiest bread in the world."

"I didn't make. Havah did. She say to tell you she is sorry they cannot be here for party. She is not well and Rachel has sniffles so Reuven bring it by with birthday card."

Havah had tried many a time to teach Oxana the finer points of baking, yet the dough never cooperated with her. How his wife could create masterpieces with her needle, yet could not grasp the simple concept of boiling an egg, Nikolai would never understand.

He glared at Ulrich. "I begged all of you to forget this birthday nonsense."

"Poppycock," said Catherine with a shake of her ungovernable auburn curls. "Have some cake. Oxana told me chocolate is your favorite."

"How rude of me. It's a masterpiece, Catherine. Thank you."

"How could we let my best friend's day slip by without acknowledgment?" asked Ulrich.

Nikolai glowered at him. "Force yourself."

With his matinee idol looks the tall German was the most sought after piano instructor at the conservatory by female students. He sat on the stool in front of the upright piano in a corner of the room.

"Let's see if this brand new, secondhand spinet of yours produces anything that sounds like music."

Nikolai picked up his flute from a stack of unopened presents on top of the piano. "How about the duet we're playing for our concert next week."

"Good choice, Kolyah."

Assuming a stance beside Ulrich, Nikolai positioned his flute against his chin. He counted as Ulrich played the opening measures. Pachelbel's "Canon in D" embraced him like a safe cocoon until the antiphony between flute and piano lilted to conclusion.

Florin jumped to his feet and applauded. "Bravo, Kolyah!"

Jarred from his brief escape, Nikolai sank down on the sofa and laid his flute across his knees. "The credit goes to the pianist. He merely allows me to accompany him."

"Never underestimate your ability, Kolyah." Turning from the piano, Ulrich flexed his fingers. "Your performance in music history yesterday afternoon is all Stephen would talk about when he came for his session."

"Stephen?"

"Stephen Gelbart. He's an up and coming virtuoso. I have high hopes for him."

"Ah yes, the young man who's more interested in my personal history than music history...thanks to one Professor Dietrich."

Dr. Miklos raised one bushy eyebrow. "You know what I think?"

Nikolai gazed at his distorted reflection in the flute. "I've heard it a hundred times before, Doctor."

"Then you shall hear it a hundred and one times. Yes, you shall hear it again. Have you forgotten it was I who taught you in Heidelberg and worked with you in Kishinev when you were but a lad?"

"You won't let me forget."

"I will not. No, I won't. Such skill in a surgeon I've not seen before or since."

"It's behind me, now, Florin. Leave it there, please."

"Behind you, is it, Doctor? Half the physicians in this country aren't fit to practice veterinary medicine and you throw away your gift to blow into a...a tube."

Ulrich pulled the cover over the piano keyboard and draped his arm across it. "Leave him be, Florin. He's a consummate flautist and his students admire him."

"What will you do with your medical diploma, Dr. Derevenko? Wrap fish?" Florin clamped his fingers around Nikolai's wrists. "These hands were meant for surgery."

"Remember, Doctor, our Kolyah was groomed to be a musician long before he chose medicine. Leave us not forget, music has charms to soothe the savage breast."

Florin's steel-blue eyes flashed and his grip tightened. "With a scalpel, Doctor Derevenko could remove a tumor from that savage breast."

Chapter Seven

Two years ago, Dr. Miklos had offered Nikolai a position as his partner in his thriving private practice. At the time, Nikolai lived in Odessa, Ukraine where he worked in the Jewish hospital. Due to political turmoil and rising anti-Semitism, he readily accepted Dr. Miklos' offer. However, he put off the move until his Jewish friends could join him.

In an effort to expedite travel plans, Ulrich sent money for their passage. Two short weeks later, the telegram came. Only three of the Gitterman children survived the bloody pogrom.

Ulrich remembered the night he and Arel went to the depot to meet their train. He barely recognized the man whom he had known since their university days.

"I'm giving up medicine," Nikolai announced one night soon after. "I quit."

"Why, Kolyah?" asked Dr. Miklos.

"I failed." Nikolai's eyes, dark and hollow, pierced Ulrich's heart.

Nothing anyone said could convince Nikolai to change his mind. Disappointed, Dr. Miklos posted an advertisement in the *Kansas City Times* for a partner. Dissatisfied with all applicants, but increasingly desperate, he finally hired Wilhelm Huber, a recent immigrant from Nuremberg.

Although Ulrich did not care much for this new doctor, he was the only one in the office while Florin was out on an emergency house call. Ulrich watched the stocky man with a receding hairline and waxed blond moustache look down the eighteen-month-old girl's throat.

"Open wide, *liebling.*"

The child gagged on the tongue depressor and whimpered. Turning her head, she hid her face under Ulrich's arm.

"All done, little *fräulein.*" Dr. Huber patted her blonde curls and pinched her nose. "I see no sign of infection. It's nothing more than teething on her two-year molars. She's a fine healthy girl of good German stock like her papa." He took her in his arms and kissed her forehead.

"I wish she were my daughter, Doctor. You see, my wife and I can't have children. Catherine and I are tending to her and her brother for some friends of ours. Catherine was beside herself when she woke up from her nap with a fever."

"I understand. Look at those blue eyes, *sehr schöne.* She's the perfect picture of an Aryan child."

Ulrich bristled. "Florin tells me you received your medical degree in Heidelberg. What brought you to Kansas City?"

"Why does anyone come to America? For the money of course! Tell me, Professor, is it true you used your wealth to bring the Gitterman family here from Eastern Europe?"

"*Ja.* They're my friends. Why do you ask?"

"You're an educated German and a celebrated musician. Haven't you read Wagner's *Jewishness in Music* or Treitchske's historic essays?"

"Unfortunately I have—pure rubbish."

"I wouldn't be so quick to dismiss them, *Herr* Dietrich. Take young *Frau* Gitterman and her daughter for example: a cripple and her blind spawn."

At the mention of Havah, Ulrich's mind traveled to the day she came to work for him. Brokenhearted and angry when Arel married her sister Gittel, Havah had come to Kishinev to start over. In spite of her limp and often losing her balance, "cripple" was the last word he would ascribe to her.

Not only her delicate beauty, but also her brilliant mind captivated him. He went out of his way to nurture her latent musical talent and feed her avid desire to learn. When she found he spoke English, she begged him to teach her.

"Only if you will teach me Hebrew," he had answered, going down on one knee.

"Why? You're a—"

"A *shaygitz*? A gentile pig?"

"Yes." Her flawless skin reddened and her dark eyes flashed. "I mean no."

He took her hand in both of his. "Hebrew is the Holy Language. The original tongue of the Old Testament."

In a little over a year, she spoke, read, and understood English well enough to hold her own at Ellis Island. Even after five years, he could not say the same for himself when it came to his grasp of Hebrew.

"Professor Dietrich?" Dr. Huber's strident voice jolted him back to the present. "Don't you agree?"

"Agree with what?"

"I said, clearly the Jews are a lesser species." Dr. Huber kissed the little girl's forehead. "Would you want this *schönes mädchen* to marry one?"

"I suspect she will someday."

"*Ich vershtehe nicht.*"

"Then let me help you understand, *Herr Doktor*." Ulrich took the child from Dr. Huber and sat her on treatment table to put on her coat and bonnet. "Allow me to introduce *Fräulein* Tikvah Abromovich, Rabbi Yussel Gitterman's granddaughter."

Chapter Eight

For the most part, Havah did not regret one moment of the past two years. She had always dreamed of having a houseful of children, and believed, given their own experience, she and Arel were the best parents for Lev, Bayla, and Reuven. However, Lev, the eldest of the three, presented one challenge after another.

The November wind blew through the cracks between the window panes as she searched the street for him. He told her he was going to take a walk around the block to get some fresh air...three hours ago.

In the front yard, seven-year-old twins Mendel and David tossed a baseball back and forth. Mendel squealed when it went over his head and he fell on his bum trying to catch it. Havah grinned. Those two boys held a special place in her heart. Not only had she helped Fruma Ya'el deliver them, but Shayndel and Itzak honored her by naming them after her brothers who had been murdered only months before.

It seemed to Havah that Mendel and David Cohen lived on through their namesakes Mendel and David Abromovich. Dark-haired Mendel was already a scholar and the joy of his second grade teacher, while golden-haired David preferred athletics. Unlike Mendel, David enjoyed teasing the girls in his class or disrupting arithmetic lessons by making up silly songs about numbers.

Havah started and turned from the window in time to see her daughter pick up a wooden building block and throw it at her cousin Elliott. Havah hurried to the coffee table to stop the fight, but was not quick enough to keep him from sweeping the rest of the blocks to the floor.

"You're such a dummy!" cried Rachel.

"It's a stupid book," said Elliott. "It don't has no pictures. Just bumps."

"And you're stupid 'cause you can't read."

"Am not." Elliott stuck out his tongue.

"Stop it," said Havah.

"Why? She can't see."

"Wanna bet, noisy mouth." Rachel stuck out her tongue.

Havah pinched her daughter's ear lobe. "And you, Miss Rukhel Shvester, tell him you're sorry."

"I'm sorry you're stupid, Elliott."

"If you two can't play nice, Elliott will have to go home."

"Huh-uh. Auntie Shay said he has to stay here 'til Tikvah wakes up from her nap."

"Maybe I'll put you two down for a nap."

Not waiting for a response, Havah rose from her knees and went back to the window to resume her vigil.

"Where could Lev be?"

"No doubt he's found another way to get into mischief." Arel peered over his newspaper. "That boy's going to end up in a detention home."

"Maybe you should spend more time with him; teach him to be a tailor."

"I tried. Remember? He spilled machine oil and ruined three yards of expensive linen." Arel bunched the paper in both hands. "If that wasn't enough, he had a temper fit and broke my best dress form. And did he so much as apologize?"

"Please, Arel, a *bissel* patience. He's lost so much."

"Haven't we all? Why must you always defend him?"

Seven-year-old Bayla who had been singing to her doll, clapped her hands over her ears. "Please! Please, don't! Don't! You're hurting Miss Tova's ears."

'Havah went to her and collected her, doll and all, into her arms. On the other side of the long couch Reuven looked up from his book with brimming eyes. Havah understood his concern, for in the aftermath of the bloody massacre Bayla had been trapped under her sister Leah's body. When Dr. Nikolai rescued the child she had changed from a vibrant chatterbox to an expressionless mute.

When the children first arrived, the ladies of the synagogue collected a box of toys and clothes for them. Bayla found the porcelain doll with black ringlets right on top of the pile. In Miss Tova, Bayla rediscovered her voice.

Havah had hoped Miss Tova would stop speaking for Bayla, but even after two years, it seemed the doll "spoke" more now than ever. Despite Dr. Miklos' assurance Bayla would stop relying on it when she felt safe, Havah had her doubts. This family quarreling certainly would not make any child feel secure.

Havah hummed a lullaby in Bayla's ear until her sobs subsided.

After a few moments, Bayla raised her head. "Miss Tova says we're fine and dandy, just like sugar candy."

"How many times do I hafta tell you? Dolls don't talk." Reuven looked back down at his book with a relieved smile, and muttered, "Girls."

***

Afternoon faded into evening and Itzak had come for his sons, but still no Lev. Heat from the oven warmed Havah as she took a chicken from the oven and set it on top of the stove.

"Golden brown, exactly like the recipe says. Mama would be proud." Havah poked it with a fork. "On the other hand, Mama never needs a cookbook."

Most of the time, Fruma Ya'el tended to the bulk of the cooking and Havah assisted. But today, Yussel and Fruma Ya'el had gone to a concert at Willis Theatre and dinner with friends afterward. At first Fruma Ya'el resisted the idea of such frivolity saying, "What if you should need me with all the children, Havah?"

"Arel's here, Mama, and Shayndel and Itzak are one house away."

"And the police are a phone call away," said Arel. "Unless they're busy arresting you."

"What?" Fruma Ya'el's mouth dropped and her eyes widened to twice their normal size.

"If you read the *Kansas City Journal*, you'd know about Judge Wallace, champion of the Blue Law. He wants to make going to the theater on Sunday a crime, punishable by hanging."

Arel could no longer keep a straight face. He chuckled and kissed her cheek. "Enjoy the concert, Mama. We'll be fine."

Havah grinned as she stood on tiptoe and took a platter from the cabinet. She studied the floral pattern. Ulrich and Catherine had given it to her and Arel for their fourth anniversary. With its gold edge, it was almost too fine for everyday use, but it cheered her on gray days like this one.

The minute she turned to set the platter on the table, her right ankle twisted and her knees hit the floor. Holding tight to the plate, she shut her eyes and clinched her teeth until the pain eased. When she opened her eyes, she found herself face to face with Reuven.

"It's worse, isn't it, Mama?"

"No worse than usual, little apple."

His sad expression told her he did not believe her any more than she believed herself. He took the serving dish from her and offered her his hand. Clutching his shoulder, she leaned on him for support and stood.

Barking came from the living room and the doorbell rang. The door opened and a familiar woman's voice said, "Good evening, Mr. Gitterman. Is Reuven here?"

Reuven's reddish cheeks blanched. "What's Miss Kline doing here?"

***

Reuven's teacher did not appear to be nearly as austere and threatening to Havah as she had weeks before behind her school desk. Her light brown eyes shone in the candlelight and she had a pleasant smile.

"Thank you for such a lovely supper, Mrs. Gitterman," said Miss Kline. "I usually eat a sandwich on Sunday evenings while I grade papers."

"Don't you have any kids?" asked Bayla.

"No, dear. It's just my Oscar and me."

"Is he your husband?"

"He's my cat."

"Don't be such a busybody, Bayla," said Arel.

"Nonsense, Mr. Gitterman. She has an inquisitive mind, that's all." Miss Kline pulled a leather-bound book from her bag beside her chair and handed it to Reuven. "I've enjoyed your hospitality so much I almost forgot the reason I came in the first place."

"Thank you." Reuven opened the book and his forehead puckered into a puzzled frown. "The pages are empty."

"It's a journal. The pages are blank so you can write on them."

"Such a fine present for our son," said Havah, "but why would you come out on such a cold night? Couldn't you give it to him at school?"

"Oh my, no. Not in front of my other students." She switched her gaze to Reuven. "You are a gifted storyteller. Fill these pages to your heart's content."

"May I see the book?" asked Rachel.

Miss Kline glanced at the girl, and quickly looked back at Havah. "She's…"

With her black hair and pale complexion, Rachel looked like a smaller version of Havah. However, one of her dark eyes turned inward toward her nose while the other seemed to stare into space. She inclined her head toward Miss Kline.

"I'm blind. Dr. Miklos says I don't have any floppy nerves."

"Optic nerves," said Havah.

"My, what a precocious child. How old are you, Rachel?"

"This many." Rachel held up three fingers and then raised another. "I'll be this many in March. Wanna hear me play piano?"

Miss Kline pursed her thin lips. "If it's all right with Mommy."

"Always," said Havah. "Play something pretty."

Kreplakh rose up on all fours beside Rachel's chair as Rachel grabbed her collar. The dog led Rachel to the upright piano in the living room and laid down next to it. Using Kreplakh as a stepstool, Rachel climbed onto the bench, sat on her knees, and lifted the lid.

"Surely you don't allow her to bang on that lovely instrument?" whispered Miss Kline.

Havah smiled but said nothing until Rachel danced her tiny fingers across the keys in a playful melody.

Miss Kline's mouth dropped open. "Bless my soul, it's…it's…Bach's 'Musette'."

Chapter Nine

In Kansas City, motorcars were rapidly replacing the horse and buggy. Automobiles went faster and did not eat their weight in hay and oats. Even so, Nikolai preferred the clip-clop of horses' hooves on pavement to the grinding noises and choking exhaust fumes of modern transportation. It did not matter for he could afford neither car nor carriage. Even if he could, walking, even in winter, would always be his preferred mode of travel for physical stamina. Ducking his head, he pulled his hat down and his coat collar up to shield his ears from the frigid wind.

To add to the cacophony that made his head throb, bells clanged as streetcars hummed by on steel rails. If the city's hubbub was not enough, he had spent the better part of the afternoon auditioning students for the chamber orchestra. The final entrant was a violinist hopeful who raked his bow across the strings with the gentle timbre of an animal caught in an iron trap.

A familiar voice from a nearby alley woke him from his musings. He turned to see a boy with dark red hair shake his fist at another boy.

"You want I should punch you in the nose, you dumb Irish Mick?"

The other boy took a swig from a whiskey bottle and pushed him. "Not if I bust your Yid beak first."

Nikolai sprinted toward them. "Lev, stop!"

With a raucous laugh, Lev dropped to his knees, his speech slurred. "Jamie Flynn from County Crock, meet Doc-tor Draykopf-venko, the dizzy doctor from Russia."

Jamie, a round-cheeked boy with turned up nose and orange freckles, wiped drool from his chin on his sleeve. "Like I told ya and told ya, Lev, me boyo. It's K-O-R-K. County Cork." He offered the bottle to Nikolai. "Care for a drinky, milord?"

Lev seized it. "Meet my other buddy from County Cork, Irish whiskey. *L'khaim.*" He took a drink and coughed.

"Your parents are worried sick about you." Grasping Lev under his arms, Nikolai helped him to his feet. "Let me take you home."

"My parents are dead."

"Havah's called me four times this week asking if I've seen you and Arel is ready to call the police."

"What do you care?" Lev pulled away from Nikolai and staggered off the curb into the path of an oncoming automobile.

"Watch out!" Nikolai chased after him, shoved him out of the way, and tumbled headlong, to the pavement.

***

Cold rain beat against Nikolai's eyelids and the icy pavement underneath him poked his back. Drifting in and out of consciousness, he sensed the throng around him.

"Is he—is he dead?"

"Doctor, remember, you gave me your word," whispered Gavrel.

"He ain't dead, kid. Just knocked cold."

"Another death won't bring them back," said Nikolai.

"Idiot ran out in front my car, him and the kid."

Hyram held the gun to his own head. "I'm dead already."

"Could'a got his dang fool-self killed."

"Dr. Nikolai, I was going to be a ballerina," said Pora. "Why didn't you save me?"

"My wife's smelling salts oughta wake him up PDQ."

The pungent ammonia mixed with alcohol and perfume made Nikolai gasp. The little girl with honey hair pirouetted down Grand Avenue and disappeared like steam from a samovar. He groaned and rubbed the painful bump on the side of his head. Holding his other hand above his face, he opened his eyes to see blood dripping from his fingertips.

A stout man wearing bib overalls and a straw hat knelt and slipped his hands under Nikolai's arms. Nikolai cried out as pain shot through his left shoulder. The man pulled back. "I ain't no doctor, but I'd say you wrenched that there shoulder good and proper when you fell."

"Just an old war wound. I'm okay."

"Cracked your skull. That an old war wound, too?"

As Nikolai struggled to his knees, the street swerved and streetlights spun in a dizzying haze. He pitched forward and his stomach emptied itself. He laid his cheek on the cold cement to catch his breath.

"Yep, you're just hunky-dory, Mister." The man curved his hands around Nikolai's arms. "Here, kid. Let's get your buddy to the hospital. I reckon he's gonna need a stitch or two."

Lev helped the man lift Nikolai into his wagon. Taking a greasy rag from his back pocket, the man handed it to Nikolai. "Hold this against your head so's you don't bleed all over my fresh hay."

The wagon lurched and Nikolai held his breath. Beside him, Lev sniffed and wiped his mud-streaked face with the back of his hand. He took a bullet from his shirt pocket. "This was meant for me, not you."

"Get rid of it," said Nikolai.

"No." Lev slipped it back into his pocket and held his hand over it. "I'll keep it forever to remind me that those *goyishe* pigs meant to shoot me not you. You saved my life twice."

"Maybe they had bad aim."

"What about Dr. Pavel? Was that bad aim, too?"

Nikolai covered his eyes with his arm. "How many second chances do you need, numskull? Make his sacrifice count for something. Don't throw it all away."

"You mean like *you* did?"

Chapter Ten

Thanks to bloomers, petticoats, and long skirts, Havah had been able to hide her swollen legs and increasing pain...until tonight. On her way upstairs to tuck the children in, a sharp pain caused her foot to buckle under her. She tripped and tumbled to the bottom of the steps, knocking herself unconscious. When she came to she found herself in bed surrounded by worried family.

She squirmed and fiddled with the edge of her blanket. "How long have I been out?"

"Over an hour," said Fruma Ya'el.

Arel, sitting on the end of the bed, glared at Dr. Miklos, then at Fruma Ya'el and then at her. "Why didn't you tell me your legs were getting worse?"

Havah twisted a lock of hair around her pinkie. "It never came up in conversation."

"I'm your husband."

"With all the stairs, this house is a death trap." said Dr. Miklos. "Yes, it could be a death trap for you, my dear lady. This doctor's prescription is a house on one level."

"I don't want to move away from Shayndel." Havah gingerly fingered the stinging lump on the back of her head.

"It's not like we'd be moving back to the old country," said Arel. "There are lots of nice houses without stairs. Shayndel can come and visit anytime, every day if she wants."

"With four kids?"

"So she won't be next door."

"Papa and I could switch rooms with you." Fruma Ya'el turned to Dr. Miklos. "Would that work, Doctor?"

"Only if the young lady behaves herself and stays away from the stairs."

"My furniture..." Havah blinked and chewed her bottom lip. "...and my window."

"Itzak and I can move the furniture," said Arel.

Gray light poured through the lace curtained window highlighting the flowered wallpaper. Filigreed tile adorned the ceiling and the polished hardwood floors shone.

When the Gittermans had first moved into the house, Havah chose this room for its view. Beside the four-poster bed that made her feel like a queen, there was a rocking chair and round end table next to the window where she could read and watch the sun set.

From the second story, she could observe people going about their daily business. Her favorite was watching the milkman in his wagon, drawn by a dappled mare, usually arriving right around sunrise. After he made his final deliveries on her block, he would reward his horse with an apple and pat her flank. She, in turn, whinnied her gratitude and nuzzled his ear.

On stormy nights Havah beheld magnificent lightning that illuminated the neighborhood. Sometimes, when sleep eluded her, she would curl up in the rocker and study the moon. Mama and Papa's downstairs room may have been twice the size of Havah and Arel's, but it only had a view of the house next door.

In a last ditch effort, she said, "But Papa's blind."

Moving his cane from side to side, Yussel tapped the doorframe as he entered the room. "And I thought it was my little secret."

"But, Papa, what if you should trip and—?"

"Listen to me, young lady, my legs are healthy and I've been blind since you were in diapers. Understand?"

"Yes, Papa. I understand."

***

Havah turned her head to see a familiar young woman in the chair beside the bed. A crown of light encircled her long red hair as she sang a lullaby to the newborn in her arms. She stopped and smiled at Havah.

"I thought you were going to sleep all day, lazy bones. Hershel and I have been waiting and waiting for you to wake up. I named him after my poor dead papa. Do you like it?"

"Gittel, is it really you?"

Without acknowledging Havah's question, Gittel continued to chatter. "Why aren't you cooking supper for our husband, little sister? Does he miss me? Does he ever speak of me? I still love him, you know."

"But, Gittel you're dead." Havah reached for her.

"Of course I am, silly girl." Gittel dodged Havah's hand and went through the wall to a spring meadow. Havah swung her legs over the side of the bed and ran after her. The grassy path ended abruptly and she lurched forward.

Just as the rocks rushed toward her someone grabbed her shoulders and slapped her face. She opened her eyes to find herself on the edge of a stair; Arel's hold preventing her from toppling again.

"Did you have to hit so hard?" Rubbing her stinging cheek, Havah collapsed against his chest.

"I'm sorry I didn't realize—"

She looked up into his worried gray eyes. "I understand."

"Off to bed with us." He swept her up into his arms and headed for the bedroom. Entering the room, he shut the door with his foot. "Tomorrow we move downstairs."

"My poor beloved. I'm such a bother."

"Never."

He laid her down and tucked in beside her. She snuggled against him, relishing his warmth. "Gittel was here. With your son."

"It was a dream."

"Of course it was, but she seemed so real I could almost touch her." Havah closed her eyes; her mind refusing to rest. Arel's breathing slowed, a sign he would soon be sound asleep. She nudged him. "Do you still think about her?"

"Who?"

"Gittel."

"Of course. She was my wife."

"Promise me something, Arel."

"Anything, Havah, if you'll let me sleep."

"Promise me you'll marry again after I die."

Chapter Eleven

After two days of Florin's examinations and interrogations, Nikolai luxuriated in his own feather mattress and pillow. He suspected his friend of keeping him in the hospital longer than necessary for a mere concussion and a simple cut. In Nikolai's educated opinion, a stitch, aspirin powder, and a bandage were all he needed.

The commingled aromas of burning wood, pinecones, cinnamon and black tea from the kitchen whetted his appetite. He breathed them in as he slipped on his bathrobe over his pajamas. Russian tea was one of the few culinary delights Oxana had mastered. Spurning the American tradition of morning coffee, she made a ceremony of tea preparation.

He padded to the kitchen where the barrel-shaped brass samovar sat on the table like a king on his throne. An ornate teapot perched atop the steaming chimney. Both were belated wedding presents from Sergei Derevenko, along with a set of matching brass cup holders. Nikolai thought it strange his father would acknowledge his marriage or even know about it, since the two of them had not spoken in several years. The sight of the large urn and the fragrance of tea sent Nikolai's mind back through time.

Wielding a leather strop, Sergei loomed over twelve-year-old Nikolai and pointed to a dent in the side of the samovar. "Do you know anything about this?"

"I'm sorry, Tatko. I think I did it in my sleep, I dreamed Bodrik—"

Sergei took a drag from his Meerschaum pipe and blew the smoke in Nikolai's face. "Never speak that name again, do you hear?"

Vasily's cheerful voice snapped Nikolai out of his musing. "Good morning, Tatko."

"Good morning, *Solnyshko*."

"I'm nearly seventeen, must you call me that?"

"You'll always be my 'little sun.' Even when you're seventy." Nikolai tousled his son's pale blond hair. "It's getting rather long, don't you think?"

"I'm an artist." Vasily tucked his sketchbook under his arm and headed for the living room.

"Where are you going in such a hurry?" asked Oxana. "It's Saturday."

"I'm meeting friends. We've started a weekend sketch club."

Nikolai stirred blackberry jam into his tea. "There wouldn't be a young lady amongst those friends, would there?"

On his way out, Vasily peered over his shoulder and stuck out his tongue.

Standing behind Nikolai, Oxana leaned over and wreathed her arms around his neck. "Why do you tease him so?"

"Because I can." Nikolai turned in her embrace and pulled her onto his lap.

Oxana had not yet dressed for the day. Her hair hung over her shoulders and fell to her waist like a silken cape. He lifted her spectacles from her nose, set them on the table, and unbuttoned the first three buttons of her dressing gown. Gathering her up in his arms, he headed for their bedroom.

As he lowered her onto the bed, she skimmed her fingertips across his bandage. "Kolyah, what if I hurt your head?"

"Yes, my poor, injured head." He lay beside her and continued to unbutton her dressing gown. "It needs some tender loving care, Nurse Derevenko."

***

Oxana brushed her hair and watched her slumbering husband's reflection in the mirror over the bureau. Florin had warned her that with a head injury such as his, Nikolai would tire easily for a few days.

Even though Florin assured her he would make a full recovery, she worried. His health had been precarious since their wedding day. Her eyes welled up at the memory of what should have been a crowning moment in her life.

Against her better judgment, he had insisted on adhering to the ridiculous Russian tradition of the groom coming from afar to claim his bride. Since he shared the apartment with Oxana and her brother Dr. Pavel Trubachov, Nikolai prepared for his wedding at the hospital a few blocks away.

Flanked by his groomsmen, Lev and Vasily, he began the short trek. Halfway home, anti-Semitic vigilantes with guns rushed them, shouting curses. By the time they reached the apartment, Nikolai, who had taken a bullet in the shoulder, could hardly stand while Lev kept repeating, "It should've been me! It should've been me!"

Instead of exchanging their vows in a candlelit service, Nikolai and Oxana pledged their troth as he drifted off under the ether.

If that was not bad enough, the increase in patient load at the Jewish hospital compelled him to return to work sooner than he should have. Despite his desperate efforts, he could not protect the Wolinskys from the slaughter. He took their deaths to heart. Between grief, insomnia, and lack of appetite, his health declined.

Pneumonia nearly took him from her shortly after they came to America. To this day, Florin could not explain Nikolai's sudden deliverance from death.

"God had his hand on him," said Florin. "Most assuredly He did."

God's hand or not, Nikolai still caught cold easily. Sarah Tulschinsky's death, a few months after Nikolai's miraculous recovery, made Oxana more solicitous than ever. He might not be so lucky next time.

She opened the bureau drawer to put away her comb and brush. Leah Wolinsky had given them to her as a wedding present and they were among the few valuables she managed to recoup after the pogrom. Other treasures salvaged from the ravages of their apartment included their wedding photograph, tattered pages of Pavel's Bible and the cross he gave her for Christmas five years ago.

"It will keep our Savior close to your heart," Pavel told her when he clasped the chain around her neck.

"Your Savior, perhaps." She muttered as she fingered the broken necklace.

Her ears ached to hear his gentle teasing, and even his incessant preaching.

Why did he insist we dwell in squalor among the Jews in Moldavanka? We were neither poor nor Jewish. Where was Pavel's Savior in the midst of the massacre? Why did my brother sacrifice himself like that? Why did he have to be so damned unselfish?

To his final breath the answer to those questions never changed. "It's what my Lord would have done."

***

Well into the afternoon, before Nikolai awoke for the day, the sound of the crackling fire in the fireplace lulled him. He fought to keep his eyes open. He focused on

Oxana in the rocking chair, her needlework on her lap. Her long hair gleamed in the flickering light.

Vasily, Nikolai's mirror image, sat on the hearth rug and hunched over the sketchbook propped on his knees. While Vasily sometimes protested the frequent comparisons, neither of them could dispute the fact that their uncanny resemblance had reunited them.

Twelve years ago, in Kishinev, to heap hurt upon injury, Nikolai's unfaithful wife Ivona left him and took their six-year-old son with her. After seven years of fruitless searching, Ivona's body turned up in a house of ill repute in London. She had been strangled to death, leaving the boy in the care of a colleague.

Nikolai would never forget the night Mary Alice, in all of her brightly feathered glory, showed up on the doorstep of the house he shared with Ulrich.

"I shoulda knowed it the first time I seed ya in the artist shop." She nudged the sullen boy forward. "It's your daddy, Dodger. Ya looks just like 'im, ya does."

"You should go to bed, Tatko." Vasily's voice startled him. "You're already nodding off."

Nikolai rubbed his eyes and yawned. "What are you drawing?"

"You tell me."

Vasily flipped the pad around so Nikolai and Oxana could see his sketch. The little girl hugging her teddy bear seemed to jump off the page. Her dark curls framed her smiling face.

"It could be a photograph of Rachel," said Oxana. "You even captured her poor blind eyes."

"Don't ever say poor anything around Havah," said Nikolai. "She'll scratch *your* eyes out. And for all that, Rachel's one of the most contented children I've met."

"And talented. Don't forget talented." Vasily brushed eraser crumbs from his sketch, his eyes taking on a faraway look. "She gets it from Mrs. Gitterman, I think."

"I don't know where you get yours. It certainly wasn't from me."

"It wasn't from Ivona, either." Vasily smirked as he closed his sketchbook. "She had one talent and we know what that was, don't we, Tatko?"

"Vasya, this is no way to speak of your mother," said Oxana.

"*You're* my mother."

"Thank you, *Solnyshko*." She went to the piano, and picked up a gift-wrapped package that had been on top of it for nearly a month. "Kolyah, you really should open Florin's present."

"I already know what it is."

"Open it anyway." She dropped the gift onto Nikolai's lap. "I want to see it."

Nikolai ripped off the paper and opened the oaken box. Scissors, tweezers, and scalpels on a bed of red velvet shone under the lamplight. Each instrument's handle had been engraved with his initials. *Why won't Florin leave well enough alone?*

Oxana sank down on the sofa beside him and brushed her fingertip over a scalpel's sharp edge. "Pavel would have given his right arm for tools like these."

"He was a great doctor. The world suffered a terrible loss."

"He said you were the best surgeon he'd ever known. It's why he begged you to work with him in Odessa."

"What made us think we could right centuries of wrongs? It's like trying to capture the wind in a butterfly net." Nikolai shut the box. "What good came of it?"

Like snapshots, images of Kishinev and the Abromovich children's broken bodies flashed through Nikolai's head. Perhaps it had been Arel and Havah's need for him afterward that kept him from going mad. Two years later, when the Wolinskys suffered the same fate in Odessa, there were no wounds for him to bind...only friends to bury.

He reopened the box, lifted out a shiny amputation saw and held it to the light. "How can I ever cut into flesh again?"

"I understand, Kolyah, but—"

"Do you agree with Florin, Oxanochka?"

"It is true you make people happy with your music," she placed her hand over his heart, "but sometimes I think you are not happy in here."

Chapter Twelve

"I don't get it, Lev." Jamie fished a licorice stick from a small paper sack and handed it to Lev. He rubbed a dark bruise on his cheek. "You lives in a nice house, with nice people."

Lev bit off a piece of the candy and crunched it between his teeth. The bitter taste stung his tongue. He spat it out and stared at the black puddle on the pavement. "Ick! You couldn't steal peppermint, too?"

"Beggars can't be choosers, me boyo." Jamie took the last stick and crumpled the bag. "You could be home eating eggs and bacon you know."

"Eggs, yes, bacon, no."

"You should be going back home whilst ya still can, eejit." Jamie sucked on his candy. "Count yourself lucky you don't live in McClure Flats like me."

Lev tilted back his head to see the turrets of Union Depot. A flock of pigeons perched on the ledge of the four-sided clock tower reminded him of the nattering old women in Svechka.

Svechka, dear Svechka.

Does the village of my birth still exist? Do little boys still study their Hebrew lessons, cheek by jowl, at long tables in heder? Does the synagogue still stand in the midst of the town or have the Cossacks destroyed it?

"My father did this to me when I was nine." Lev pointed to the diagonal scar across his lips that went from his cheek to his chin, "He used a whip."

"Just like me dear old dad." Jamie whistled. "No wonder you don't want to go home."

"Nah, it's not that. He's dead. I live with my aunt and uncle and my grandparents."

"Do *they* beat you, too?"

"Never. My *Zaydeh* and *Bubbe* are the kindest and wisest people you'll ever meet. Aunt Havah's as smart as she is beautiful. Sometimes I think she's the only one who understands me."

"Then why don't you go home?"

"I don't deserve them."

***

Lev wandered alone downtown. His empty stomach growled. Feeling faint, he sat on the curb. Jamie's words exploded in his head.

"You're lucky...you're lucky..."

Lev closed his eyes and saw Mama, great with child, huddled in a corner of their squalid shack. She curved a protective arm around two-year-old Reuven to shield him from Papa's cruel whip. Nine-year-old Lev cupped his hands over his ears to block out her plaintive cries as she begged for her children's lives.

"No, Papa." Lev tugged at Papa's sleeve and kicked his spindly leg. "Don't!"

Papa walloped the side of Mama's head with his knuckles. She collapsed on top of Reuven. Then Papa spun around, grabbed Lev's arm, dragged him out of the house, and knocked him to the ground. Rocks stabbed Lev's shoulder blades through his thin shirt. Lying in the snow, he looked up into Papa's rheumy eyes half obscured by his grimy eyeglasses.

"You little *momzer*! I'll teach you!"

Papa's pinched face contorted with rage as he lashed the whip across Lev's mouth. Choking on his own blood, Lev covered his lips with his hands and rolled over in the dirt to protect himself, but the whip sliced into his back and legs.

Bayla was only a few days old when they found Papa's mutilated body in the woods. The synagogue elders guessed Cossacks had killed him, but no one really cared. Neither Lev nor his sisters, Leah and Devorah, or even Mama, shed a tear.

During the peaceful time that followed, the orphaned Havah Cohen who lived with the Levines, caught his attention and captured his imagination. They said she had escaped her burning village half naked. Rumor had it she had gone to *heder* like a boy. Lev believed the rumor for no other girl in Svechka had the audacity to ask the questions she dared to ask. She was indignant when Mama betrothed sixteen-year-old Leah to Gavrel the shoemaker, a man old enough to be her father.

One particular spring morning Lev happened on Mama and Havah washing clothes by the river near the rabbi's house. Hidden behind a bush, he stifled his laughter as he watched the two of them go at each other. Havah threw a wadded diaper into the water and doused Mama. Mama slapped Havah's bottom with Lev's wet knickers.

Havah hollered. "You're selling your daughter for shoes."

"How dare you judge me?" Mama shoved Havah and turned on her heel. Plodding up the hill, she did not see Havah lose her balance and fall backward into the river clinging to her basket of laundry.

Lev ran to rescue her, but Uncle Arel, who had been reading under a nearby tree, beat him to it. Lev held his breath as his uncle fished the limp girl from the water and laid her on the ground. He exhaled with relief when Havah coughed up a mouthful of water and opened her eyes.

After that day, Lev noticed their stolen glances. The night before Uncle Arel's arranged marriage to Gittel

Levine, Lev saw him kiss Havah by the river. Suddenly, she slapped his face and shouted, "Drop dead!"

As he trudged up the hill, head down, Uncle Arel stumbled into Lev. His eyes, red and swollen, narrowed as he leaned into Lev's face. "What are you doing here, you little spy?"

"Why don't you marry Havah?"

"I made a promise to Gittel and her parents."

"But you love Havah."

"You'll understand it when you're older."

"I understand it now, Uncle Arel. You're a *schlemiel*!"

Havah ran away right after the wedding. Lev suspected Aunt Shayndel knew where she went, but when he asked her she merely frowned and said, "Mind your own business, little boy."

One day, Lev overheard her tell Mama that Havah lived with Uncle Itzak's brother Evron and his family in Kishinev. She even worked for a rich German musician who gave her piano lessons.

Mama's gray eyes twinkled. "Throw a cat wherever you want, she always lands on her feet."

***

Stiff with cold, Lev rose from the curb and stuffed his hands into his pockets to warm them. Snow had begun to fall. He hunched his shoulders against the wind, and as he walked he studied his footprints on the sidewalk.

A warm bath and a soft bed would feel nice. Maybe Bubbe *made bagels. They would taste so good with a glass of cold milk.*

Lev's hollow stomach agreed.

What will Uncle Arel say? The same thing he always says, "Get a job, Lev. Do something useful, Lev. You're wasting your life, Lev."

He stopped and stared at his reflection in a store window. Under his cap his deep red curls grazed his upturned collar. Dark circles framed his eyes and his cheeks were as sunken as his father's.

Why was I born?

Once more memories of Svechka flooded him. He tried to focus on the few happy ones: Mama's voice in the night as she sang to Bayla; Reuven's laughter when Gavrel tickled him.

Lev's happiness was short lived. As always, the ugly memories crept in and overshadowed the good ones: Mama's untimely death, the news of the Kishinev pogrom that stunned everyone in Svechka, and Gavrel's fateful decision to move to Odessa.

Guilt plagued Lev. *If only I had been respectful of Gavrel. If only I had been a better brother. If only I had not run away that horrible day, Leah might have agreed to seek refuge in the Jewish hospital courtyard instead of waiting for me.*

If only...if only...

No matter how hard he tried to blot out the sights and sounds—Gavrel's death rattle as he lay amid broken dishes and torn bed linens; Leah's empty eyes and the stench of decaying flesh—they would never leave him.

A resonant voice startled him. "Are you Lev Gitterman?"

He turned and looked up into the ebony face of a uniformed police officer.

"Who wants to know?"

"Officer Lafayette Tillman and your mother. She's worried about you, son."

"She's not my mother." Lev squared his shoulders and frowned. "And I'm not your son."

Chapter Thirteen

Lev woke to the sound of singing. The night before, when Officer Tillman picked him up, Lev pleaded with him not to take him home. It was after midnight and he did not want to disturb Aunt Havah. Moreover, he feared Uncle Arel's wrath.

"I'll let you stay at my house this time. But, keeping company with that Irish boy is bound to land you in the detention home. Is this what you want?"

"No, sir."

"Your aunt tells me you dropped out of school."

"Yes, sir."

"Please heed my word of advice. Go back to high school and get your diploma." Officer Tillman's dark eyes flashed. "Education, young man. Education is what sets a man apart."

Rubbing his eyes, Lev burrowed his head into the soft pillow and listened to the baritone voice resonating from another room.

"Amazing grace, how sweet the sound that saved a wretch like me,

I once was lost, but now I'm found, was blind, but now I see..."

Lev stood and stretched. He found his clothes neatly folded on the bureau. Soap and a pitcher of warm water sat on the table beside it. Gratefully, he scrubbed and slipped on his shirt and trousers. He wet his kinky hair and tried to comb it, but decided it was a lost cause.

Padding to the parlor he was met by Officer Tillman and a younger man. Lev felt shabby next to their rich brown skin and fine suits.

With a proud smile, Officer Tillman put his hand on the other man's shoulder. "Mr. Lev Gitterman, I'd like to introduce you to my son, Dr. Lon Tillman."

Lev tried to hide his surprise. "You're a...a physician?"

"Admit it. You wanted to say 'Negro physician.'" Lon held out his hand. "Does that offend you?"

Visions of Odessa rushed to Lev's mind. He still felt spittle running down his cheeks and heard cries of "Kill the Jews." *How many fist fights have I won and lost, simply because of what I am?*

"Not at all." Lev clasped Lon's hand. "Pleased to meet you."

***

"'The house whirled around two or three times and rose slowly through the air.'" Bayla, sitting cross-legged on the hearthrug, read in a clear voice, annunciating each word with crisp accuracy. "'Dorothy felt as if she were going up in a balloon.'"

A strong wind rattled the windows and shook the walls until Havah feared her own house would be ripped from its foundation. She gently rocked in her chair with Rachel asleep on her lap. Havah warmed her stocking feet on the hearth while another storm raged inside her head.

Where is that boy? He should have been home last night. What are we doing wrong to make him run away?

"Mama, you're not listening." Bayla tugged at Havah's skirt.

"You're missing the cyclone, Havaleh." Fruma Ya'el peered over her knitting needles.

Beside Fruma Ya'el on the sofa, Yussel cocked his head. "It sounds like there's one right here on our street."

Bayla jutted out her lower lip. "Miss Tova's annoyed."

Arel sat next to her on the floor, his gray eyes locked on Havah. "Keep reading, little sister, the rest of us are all ears and I'm sure Mommy's listening with her heart."

"Please read on, chatterbox." Havah tweaked Bayla's pigtail. "We can't have Miss Tova angry at me, can we?"

"She's just a doll," said Reuven who laid on the floor using the dog to prop up his journal. He rolled his eyes. "Girls."

"Reuven Gitterman, what have I told you?" Havah gave him a warning frown. "Bayla, read already."

Bayla turned the book around so Havah could see a picture. In it Dorothy held onto Toto by his ear as the house flew through the air. She turned the book back around and read, "'It was very dark and the wind howled horribly around her, but Dorothy found she was riding quite easily. After the first few whirls—'"

The doorbell startled Havah. She went to the door, opened it, and greeted the tall dark man on the porch with Lev at his side. "Officer Tillman. Please come in."

"No thank you, Mrs. Gitterman. We're on our way to church. I just stopped by to deliver your boy."

"Where on earth have you been?" Arel scowled at Lev. "What kind of trouble have you gotten into this time? Have you any idea what you've put us through? Your aunt and your grandmother didn't get a wink of sleep last night. Think about somebody else for a change, use that *kopf* of yours!"

"Don't be too hard on the boy, Mr. Gitterman." Officer Tillman put his hands on Lev's shoulders. "He's had a rough night, too."

***

Uncle Arel's office smelled of bay rum, peppermint and musty books. It reminded Lev of *Zaydeh* Yussel's library in Svechka; Lev's oasis in the desert. There his grandfather would sit Lev on his lap, feed him peppermint sticks from a jar he hid in the bottom desk drawer and tell him stories of his boyhood in Kishinev.

After the other kids and Aunt Havah went to bed, Uncle Arel summoned him to the office for a talk. Lev could tell by his expression it was not to share happy memories. Head down, Lev counted the knots in the fringed rug under the desk and listened to the trees bang against the outside of the house in the wind.

Finally, Uncle Arel's voice assailed Lev's ears. "It's time we talk, man to man." While Aunt Havah spoke almost perfect English, Uncle Arel had not lost his thick accent.

Lev raised his head. "Bawl me out in Yiddish if it's easier, Uncle. I still understand it, but I have something to tell you."

"Tell me later." Uncle Arel gritted his teeth, doubled his hands into fists and crammed them into his trouser pockets. His soles squeaked as he paced back and forth. "First I talk. You listen."

"Uncle Arel, please listen to me. What I have to say is important."

"Nothing is more important than what *I* have to say."

"But it will make you happy."

"You want to know what will make me happy? Some respect from you, my sister's son, my father's oldest grandson." Halfway through his tirade, Arel switched from English to Yiddish. "Simple respect. You owe us that much. But do we get it? No! I've given you my name and this is the thanks I get?"

"Gitterman was my mother's name before *Zaydeh* sold her to my father."

"He did not sell her. She was expecting Leah."

"So?"

"Would you want your sister to be a bastard?"

"It would've been better than my mother being shackled to one."

"You're missing the point." Uncle Arel looked up at the ceiling as he paced. He stopped and leaned into Lev's face. "You are legally my son."

"So, you want I should call you Papa?"

"Call me what you like." Arel took his hands out of his pockets and shook his fist under Lev's nose. "You live under my roof. If you're not going to school, you'll get a job and earn your keep. Do you understand?"

Feivel suddenly stood in Uncle Arel's place, his teeth bared like a crazed wolf.

"Don't, Papa!" Lev cowered and covered his face with his arms. "I—"

"*Guten Nacht!*" Uncle Arel turned, shut out the light, and slammed the door behind him.

***

Hours later, still stunned by Uncle Arel's outburst, Lev sat in the darkened office and listened to the wind. A mixture of fear, anger and sorrow welled up in his chest. Never had he seen such rage from his uncle. *Uncle Arel was always the one who stood up for me against Papa and his demon whip. Where will I go if Uncle Arel throws me out?* Lev doubted he would be welcome next door at Uncle Itzak and Aunt Shayndel's. Perhaps Dr. Nikolai would take him in. A hundred thoughts tumbled through Lev's mind.

The lights switched back on and Aunt Havah entered the room, her dark eyes awash with concern "Lev? It's well past midnight. You should be in bed."

"I…I couldn't sleep."

She scooted the desk chair next to his and sat. With two fingertips she brushed tears from his cheek. "What's really bothering you?"

Lev dropped his head into his hands. He felt Aunt Havah's warm, accepting hand on his back. Once his tears stopped, he wiped his eyes with his palms.

"Uncle Arel wouldn't let me talk."

"Then talk to me."

Lev lifted his head and gazed at his aunt, unsure of what to say first. She was only seven years older than he and, no matter what the law said, not old enough to be his mother. Her hair hung past her waist like an onyx waterfall and accentuated her flawless complexion. She smelled of rosewater and her robe did not hide her slender, yet full, figure.

Mentally berating himself for his unwholesome thoughts, he swallowed and whispered, "I tried to tell Uncle Arel he's been right all along. This is my chance. I'm going to finish high school and then I'm going to medical school."

"Lev, that's wonderful. What brought this on?"

"Did you know Officer Tillman used to own a barber shop?"

She ruffled Lev's neatly trimmed hair. "I see he used his talents on you."

"He's done it all. He went to college, owned a restaurant, and was even a lieutenant in the army in the war. Not only that, his son's a physician."

"*Nu?* What's so special about that? You know plenty of doctors—Dr. Miklos, Dr. Nikolai."

"Don't you see, Aunt Havah? They're white. They didn't have to fight to go to medical school in Russia. The Negroes aren't treated much better in this country than we were there. If Dr. Tillman can do it, so can I."

Chapter Fourteen

Havah ladled hot chocolate into three cups. After she gave one to Fruma Ya'el and another to Shayndel, she set her own cup on the table. She itched to tell them about Lev's decision to go back to school after the holidays, but he had sworn her to secrecy. He wanted it to be his Hanukkah surprise. If only she could tell Arel, perhaps he would stop nagging the boy so.

Sitting at the table, she took a potato from a burlap sack on the next chair. Since it was the Friday before Hanukkah and her turn to host *Shabbes* dinner, Fruma Ya'el decided they should prepare latkes. The traditional pancakes consisted of shredded potatoes, eggs and flour. These would be fried in hot fat to commemorate the oil that miraculously lasted in the temple menorah for eight days in ancient times. Anticipation of the savory treat made Havah's mouth water.

As a child, Havah looked forward to her mother's flaky fried pastries loaded with raisins and crispy latkes. Even though Hanukkah only lasted eight days, Miriam Cohen usually started cooking her special treats several days before. She loved celebrations and said a mere week was not long enough.

Each night of Hanukkah, Havah and her brothers took turns lighting the candles. Her father, Rabbi Shimon Cohen, led the recitation of the blessings. To this day, when she heard thunder, Havah imagined it to be Papa's resonant voice chanting prayers in heaven.

One year, her brother David, then twelve, ate so many latkes he spent half the night in the outhouse.

The next morning, fourteen-year-old Mendel, the quintessential teacher, seized the opportunity to expound on the evils of gluttony. David's green-tinged cheeks flushed while six-year-old Havah giggled into her napkin.

Ten years later, when Mama brought home potatoes from the market, a month before Hanukkah, Havah, who hated grating them, groaned. "We've never started this early."

"Why wait, Havaleh?" Mama cupped her hand around Havah's cheek. "Who knows? This could be the last time it will be just the five of us."

There was an urgent plea in the way Mama said, "last time," that chilled Havah even now. Sometimes Mama dreamed things that came true. Did she know Natalya, their peaceful village, would go up in flames and smoke in less than two weeks? Did she hear the gunshots, shattering glass, and screams in her sleep? Had she already seen David and Mendel lying on the frozen ground in their blood-spattered nightshirts?

Havah blinked and shook her head as if she could shake off her sorrow. "I've nearly shredded my fingers off. How many of these do we need?"

Shayndel muttered under her breath. "Not nearly as many as we used to."

Havah stared at the golden-haired woman who was not only her sister-in-law but also her best friend. Shayndel's sunny disposition could almost always shine a light into Havah's darkness. However, a pall that refused to lift seemed to have settled on Shayndel in recent weeks.

Havah took a sip of from her cup and savored the creamy chocolate before swallowing. "Shayndel, you haven't touched your cocoa. You're usually on your second cup by now. You don't want to hurt my feelings, do you?"

Stony silence answered.

Havah continued to chatter hoping to brighten Shayndel's mood. "I can't believe our little Bayla's going to be eight already. Isn't it sweet her birthday falls on Hanukkah again?"

"What's sweet about it?" Shayndel flung a potato to the floor. "My sister cursed our family when she named her baby after our evil sister."

***

Letting the ethereal strains of Chopin's 'Nocturne in C-Sharp Minor' waft over her, Shayndel sat in the rocking chair beside the piano with Tikvah asleep on her lap. While Shayndel did not know many musical pieces by name like her sister-in-law, she always recognized this one. When Havah was sad or needed time to think this was the piece she chose to play.

Shayndel ached with remorse. "Forgive me, Havaleh. We're supposed to be preparing for a celebration and I've turned the day into a *Shiva*, a day of mourning."

Havah's fingers stilled. "What was your sister Bayla like? Arel refuses to talk about her."

"I'll never forgive her. Never. She committed the most horrible sin—suicide."

"So you think Tova was wrong to honor her with a namesake?"

"Bayla was Tova's best friend. Like you two girls, they were more than sisters." Fruma Ya'el entered the living room with a basket of mending and sat on the sofa. "Shayndel, tell Havah the whole story and then decide who really killed Bayla."

Havah leaned forward. "Yes, please. Tell me."

Tikvah squirmed, slid off Shayndel's lap and toddled to Fruma Ya'el. "Want *Bubbe*."

Setting her basket aside, Fruma Ya'el helped the child climb onto her lap and gave her cheek a gentle pinch. "This one's a double for her Aunt Bayla."

Shayndel drew up her knees and wrapped her arms around her legs. "Bayla was the prettiest of us."

"She was only fourteen and already had the curves of a woman." Fruma Ya'el clucked her tongue. "Such a tomboy she was. Always climbing trees and challenging the boys to foot races."

"She used to beat them, too," said Shayndel. "We went for a walk—Bayla, Arel and me—to pick berries..."

Murky images, long forgotten, filled Shayndel's mind. She saw Arel, a weedy four-year-old in knickers with a thatch of black hair, and Bayla, her knee-length braid gleaming in the afternoon sun. Bayla stopped beneath a tall mulberry tree, took off her shoes and stockings, tucked her skirt into her bloomers and shinnied to the lowest branch. Curling her bare toes around it she stretched to pick the purple berries.

Shayndel craned her neck to watch Bayla fill her pail. "Be careful big sister, don't—"

Suddenly a rough hand covered Shayndel's mouth and nose and a voice behind her said, "What shall I do with this little *Zjid* puppy, Grigory?"

Her lungs burned as she tried to scream.

"Squash her like the insect she is, Fedor," growled Grigory who did not look much older than Bayla. He slammed Arel to the ground and pulled down his knickers. With a leering grin, Grigory took a dagger from his belt. "Let's circumcise the little Christ Killer."

Arel whimpered. "Please...don't..."

"Wait! You're already circumcised." Grigory brandished the knife over Arel's lower extremity. "I'll just cut it all off."

"Let go of my brother and sister, you Christian *khazers*!" With a shriek Bayla leaped from the tree and landed on Grigory's back. "Pigs!"

Losing the knife, he staggered and weaved as he tried to pry off her stranglehold. Fedor released Shayndel and yanked Bayla's braid. Bayla pitched and landed on her back in the dirt. Like a vulture descending on its prey Grigory dropped down and pinned her to the ground.

Bayla thrashed beneath him. "Arel! Shayndel! Run! Go to—"

Fedor jabbed his boot into her side with savage force. "Shut up!"

Grigory pressed his mouth against hers. Bayla pulled back and spit in his face.

"Come on, Shayndel." Arel tugged at her hand, but her feet refused to move. "Please, Shayndel."

Paralyzed, she watched the frenzied boys tear at Bayla's blouse until there was nothing left of it. Bayla writhed and fought. One of them, Shayndel could not tell which, picked up the knife and slashed Bayla's face.

Blackness swallowed Shayndel. She awoke a day later to a silent stranger who bore a faint resemblance to her sister. Shorn hair, scraggly and unkempt, replaced her golden braid. A red scar streaked across the mouth that never again chased away clouds with a song...

Tikvah patted Shayndel's cheeks bringing her back to Havah's living room. "No cry, Mommy."

"Shayndel, you look like you're going throw up," said Havah. "Are you ill?"

"She's not ill, she's remembering something she forgot, aren't you, Shayndeleh?" Fruma Ya'el beckoned Shayndel, patting the cushion beside her.

Trembling from the inside out, Shayndel stumbled to the sofa. "All this time I've blamed Bayla for killing herself. Why didn't you remind me?"

"You weren't ready to remember."

"But the horrid, selfish way I berated Tova when she named her baby...Why didn't she set me straight?"

"Tova knew you'd understand some day. We agreed to let you remember in your own time."

"I feel like such a fool."

Fruma Ya'el curved her arm around Shayndel's shoulder and continued to intone the rest of the story for Havah. "Bayla never spoke again. As the months passed no one needed to ask what happened…"

Once more Shayndel saw Bayla perched on a high branch of a tree in the yard, naked.

Five-years-old again, Shayndel put her hands on her hips and stamped her foot. "Come down from there right now, big sister or I'll tell."

Bayla patted her swollen belly and lifted her arms like wings. "Goodbye, little sister."

Chapter Fifteen

After a dinner of savory roasted chicken and latkes, Havah leaned back in her chair. She grinned at Ulrich across the magnificent Austrian table that had followed him from one end of the earth to the other. In Kishinev, it would often be piled high with delicacies. For no matter how insignificant the occasion, he saw it as an excuse to throw a party. Nothing pleased her more than to see that after years of being a lonely widower, he had married a woman who shared his enthusiasm for celebration.

Tonight, being not only the first night of Hanukkah but also Bayla's birthday, Ulrich had spared no expense. Catherine made latkes according to Fruma Ya'el's instructions. To go with them Catherine made applesauce loaded with raisins. If that was not enough, the main dish was roast lamb with mint jelly.

There were party favors—chocolates, raisins, and Hanukkah *gelt* (silver dollars)—for all of the children and a few wrapped presents for Bayla. Havah popped a piece of chocolate and a raisin into her mouth at the same time. "You've gone to way too much trouble, Ulrich."

His blue eyes sparkled. "What did I tell you way back in Kishinev? We've no other family but you."

Yussel leaned back in his chair, let out a hardy belch and groaned. "Catherine, I won't be able to eat again for a month."

"Poppycock." Catherine pointed to the cake in the middle of the table next to Yussel's silver menorah. "There's still dessert."

"Oh, I could not eat another thing." Oxana leaned her head on Nikolai's shoulder. "I will be so—how you say it?—fat like hippo-pata-moose."

"You need to gain weight, Mother." Vasily shoveled the last of his latke into his mouth. "May I have the recipe for these, Aunt Catherine?"

"You'll make a wonderful husband someday, Vasya" said Havah.

Lev poked Vasily's side with his fork. "Or wife."

Vasily's pale cheeks reddened. "Thanks a lot, friend."

Itzak rubbed his ample stomach. "Which shall we do first, sing happy birthday and have cake or light the menorah?"

"I think the birthday girl should decide," said Lev.

Like a princess on her throne, Bayla sat on his lap. "Miss Tova says 'cake.'" In the crook of Bayla's arm, Miss Tova's porcelain face bore no expression to indicate a preference. Bayla yawned. "But then we need to light the menorah before she gets too sleepy."

Havah noticed that Lev had dressed in a suit and tie for the event. His burgundy hair, recently cut short, gleamed in the candlelight. "You look quite handsome tonight."

"Thank you, Aunt Havah." Lev planted a loud smooch on Bayla's cheek. "Nothing's too good for my baby sister."

Havah marveled at the three-tiered cake trimmed with icing scrolls. Eight yellow roses with a candle in the middle of each cascaded from top to bottom. "That cake's too pretty to eat."

"It's fit for our Princess Bayla, named after my sister of blessed memory," said Shayndel, whose sunny smile had returned. "I would love to learn how to decorate cakes like that."

"Beware, my love." Itzak put his arm around her. "You're liable to find forty little helpful fingers in your frosting bowl."

"And ten big ones, I suspect."

***

Itzak Abromovich had a way of filling a room that had nothing to do with physical stature. Shorter than most men, with his rounded midsection he reminded Havah of an unruly bear cub. He adored his children and always had time to roughhouse with his sons. Even in the face of the greatest tragedy, that of losing his brother Evron in Kishinev, Itzak maintained his sense of humor.

Havah remembered Evron Abromovich, the tailor, with fondness. Like Itzak, he had an infectious laugh and an open heart. No matter that his dilapidated home swelled from wall to wall with children, he and his wife Katya made room for Havah when she had nowhere else to go. After Arel lost Gittel, as well as his desire to be a rabbi, Evron took him under his wing as an apprentice.

At first Arel protested the invitation to live with them. "You have so little for yourselves. I'll rent a place."

Evron folded his arms across his chest. "No you won't. To me this is a greater mitzvah than welcoming the *Shekhinah,* the Divine Presence."

Havah's favorite times when she lived with the Abromoviches had been evenings when Evron would assemble everyone for prayers. Each of his five children, from the youngest to the oldest, would read from the Book of Psalms. After kissing each of their foreheads, Evron would play a lullaby on his clarinet.

With equal affection, Havah remembered Katya Abromovich, who found her treasure in her babies' smiles.

If one of them should fall and scrape a knee, Katya would kiss it and say, "A child's tears rend the heavens."

When forced to witness the murder of that saintly woman and her babies, Havah imagined the heavens being ripped to shreds.

Havah often wondered what happened to Evron's precious clarinet. Then one unseasonably warm afternoon last February, Mendel appeared at Havah's back door clutching a velvet bag in both hands.

She crouched to his eye level. "Mendel, why aren't you at the park with your mama and the other kids?"

With his intense dark eyes and reserved nature, Mendel seemed older than his twin brother David. At the tender age of seven, he spoke with the conviction of a sage.

"Mama says you can help me with this." He took the battered clarinet from the bag and handed it to her. "It belonged to Uncle Evron."

Havah caressed it with her fingertips. She recognized every nick on the faded black surface, including marks left by teething babies on the bell. Longing to hear its dulcet tones and to see the serenity on Evron's face as he played it flooded her.

"Can you teach me to play, Auntie?"

"Why don't you ask your papa?"

"Oh, no. He told me and David not to ever, ever touch it and then he got a funny, sad-mad look on his face."

"But if Papa told you not to touch it—"

"Mama says that maybe Papa would be happy if I learned to play it real good even if *he* doesn't think he would be."

Havah twined one of Mendel's black curls around her pinkie finger. "Mama's a wise woman."

"Then you'll teach me, Auntie? I want to play it for Papa's birthday."

In all the time she had known the Abromoviches, Havah could not recall Itzak's birthdate or a celebration for it. "When is it?"

"It's December first, like Bayla's. But Papa says it's a secret on accounta he doesn't like all the fuss and 'cause Uncle Evron won't have any more birthdays."

Havah's eyes smarted. "And he told you this secret?"

"No, I heard him whisper it to Mama. Can you teach me? Please."

"I can't, but I know someone who might."

That afternoon she telephoned Dr. Nikolai who agreed to help. So for the past ten months Mendel had come to Havah's house every Thursday afternoon for lessons.

***

After dinner, Ulrich threw two logs onto the fire. A fountain of sparks shot up from the flames in the marble fireplace. Light from the crystal chandelier cast rainbow patterns onto the domed ceiling and wood-paneled walls of the great room.

Among his favorite pieces of furniture, a set of matching chairs with wooden frames and scrolled armrests sat in front of the hearth. Their oval backs and padded seats were upholstered with crimson brocade. He cherished the memory of Havah sitting in one with her feet on the other while she studied her English lessons or indulged in one of his many books. She claimed she felt like a queen on her throne.

He dusted off the bench and sat at his grand piano. Itzak stood beside it with violin at the ready and his bow poised over the strings. "What shall we play first?"

Nikolai positioned his flute. "How about '*Khosid Dance*'?"

Ulrich grinned and set his fingers on the keys. "Like old times." He sighed. "But it won't be the same without Evron's clarinet."

"Play it loud and lively so he can hear us in heaven and dance with the angels." Itzak counted. *"Eyn und Zvay und Dray!"*

Closing his eyes, Ulrich let his fingers cavort across the keyboard with gleeful abandon. He imagined the Abromovich children skipping and giggling in his Kishinev ballroom. So lost in the memory and the music, he could have sworn he heard Evron's clarinet in the mix until a loud squeak jarred him.

Opening his eyes, Ulrich saw not Evron but Mendel Abromovich, a miniature version of his uncle in every detail, including the selfsame clarinet. Despite his apparent embarrassment, the boy continued to play without missing another note.

When the song ended, Mendel's lower lip quivered and he mumbled, "I'm sorry, Auntie Havah. I ruined Papa's birthday surprise."

Itzak, his ruddy cheeks wet with tears, knelt and pulled his son into a tight embrace. "No, my little tsaddik, it's the best birthday surprise I've ever had. You brought my brother back to life."

Chapter Sixteen

Nearly every Monday started the same way during the school year in the Gitterman household. Bayla misplaced one or both of her shoes or Reuven could not find his pencil box. Once their lost articles were found, they noisily wolfed down breakfast. Arel shushed them as he read his morning newspaper. Kreplakh's claws clicked along the tile floor as she barked at the kids until they left for school.

On the days George Weinberg could not take him to morning prayers, Yussel enjoyed the sounds coupled with the aroma of coffee. The chaos spoke life to him.

This morning Lev's voice entered the mix.

"Hey everyone. Guess what? I'm going back to school."

Yussel trembled with joy. Rachel bounced up and down on his lap and clapped her hands.

"Adoshem be praised!" cried Fruma Ya'el.

"Miss Tova's so happy," said Bayla.

"Have you nothing to say, Uncle Arel?" asked Lev. "I thought you'd at least smile."

"Try not to make a mess of it this time," muttered Arel.

A lengthy silence followed.

At last Havah spoke. "I'm proud of you, Lev."

"As am I," said Yussel.

Lev kissed his cheek. "Thank you, *Zaydeh*."

Reuven's rapid footsteps resounded across the kitchen tiles. "Come on, Bayla. We'd better hurry or we'll miss the first bell."

After the front door shut, Arel folded his newspaper and downed the last of his coffee. "Why'd you do that, Havah?"

"Do what?"

"You undermined my authority."

"Undermined your authority?" Yussel shook his head. "You dizzy *vantz*. What gives you the idea you can curse someone to success?"

***

In the wake of Arel's angry exit, Yussel held Rachel close and prayed under his breath for peace between his son and his grandson. Rachel's fingers, as delicate as butterfly wings, brushed his cheeks and lips. With two fingers she pressed the corners of his mouth upward.

"Don't be sad, *Zaydeh*."

"How can I be sad with you in my arms?"

"Tell me a story." She turned and settled back against his chest. "Tell me about your very, very old menorah."

"But I've told you."

"Tell me again."

Every year on the morning after Hanukkah, Yussel insisted on cleaning and polishing the menorah himself. He skimmed his fingers along the table to search for it, being careful not to knock it over. Once he found it, he scooted his chair closer to the table and took Rachel's hand.

"You see the doves on the vines, Rukhel Shvester?" He guided her fingers up and down the branches. "Your great-grandfather, my papa, Rabbi Arel Gitterman, crafted it out of the finest silver money could buy. He engraved it with '*Heenakh yafah, ahynayeem yoneem,* Behold, you are lovely, your eyes are like doves.'"

"*Zaydeh* Arel wrote it there for *Bubbe* Suri who died, right?"

"I was your age when it happened. In the street—"

"Stop, old man!" Fruma Ya'el cried. "She doesn't need to know the details."

Yussel started. His world of shadow and sound was sometimes a narrow one. He had forgotten that he and Rachel were not the only ones in the room. He nodded toward the sound of his wife's voice.

"Your *Bubbe* Fruma's a wise woman. I wish I had not seen it. But I did. Angry with Adoshem, I was."

"Tell me about the miracle."

"Patience. I'm coming to that. Now where was I? Oh yes, the first night of Hanukkah came. Papa begged me to say the blessings over the candles."

"But you wouldn't."

"Papa and I went to bed and cried ourselves to sleep. But when I woke up in the morning, what do you think?"

"Did *Bubbe* Suri really come back from the other world, *Zaydeh*?"

"*Feh*! You fill the child's head with nonsense," said Fruma Ya'el. "It was a little boy's dream."

"Nonsense, you say? I ask you, does a boy remember a mere dream for sixty years like it was yesterday?"

***

That night Havah waited until the children went to bed to clean up after supper. This way there were no little ones underfoot and the job went faster.

Humming a Hanukkah melody, she placed the last dish in the china cabinet. She lifted the menorah from the dining room table and admired it once more before storing it on the top shelf until next year.

She smiled at Yussel, who sat at the table reading. "The children love your story, Papa."

He lifted his fingers from the page. "Why shouldn't they? It's a true story."

"Is it now?"

He grinned like a naughty little boy. "I would lie to my own grandchildren?"

"Of course not. It just seems that you remember a little more every year."

Havah stood on tiptoe to put the menorah away. The unique candelabra still fascinated her even as it had the first time she saw it, the night she met Arel.

Feeling Arel's hot breath on her neck, she shivered and set the menorah back on the table. He slipped his arms around her waist. She turned in his embrace. "Remember, Arel? It was love at first sight."

"I wasn't such a hideous sight back then."

"Miss Tova says Bayla has the prettiest Papa in town."

"Havah, do you have any idea how ridiculous you sound?"

"You know what I mean."

As he opened his mouth to reply, Lev rushed into the dining room with an armload of books.

Arel dropped his arms to his sides. "Where have you been?"

"Didn't Aunt Havah tell you I'd be late?"

"She didn't say you'd be this late."

"It's only eight-thirty."

"Well?"

"I went to Vasily's to study." Lev set his books on the table. "He's a year ahead of me so he gave me his old textbooks."

"Have you had supper?" asked Havah. "How was school?"

"School was great and Oxana invited me to eat with them."

"Oh dear, you must be starved."

"Not to worry, Auntie mine." Lev playfully pinched Havah's cheek. "Vasily cooked."

"Vasily is younger than you." Arel thumbed through a book. "Shouldn't you be ahead of him?"

Lev's jaw tensed. "I've missed a lot of school."

"And you're proud of this?"

Lev crimped his lips together.

Havah's stomach kinked into a knot. "Arel, listen to him for once."

"Damn you, Uncle Arel!" Lev seized the book. "Nothing I do pleases you."

In one heart-stopping motion Arel slapped Lev, hitting the menorah. It toppled to the floor and broke in two at Havah's feet. The ground listed beneath her. The color drained from Arel's face. Lev held his book to his chest, Arel's handprint bright on his cheek.

Yussel dropped to his knees and searched for the menorah with trembling hands until he found it. His shoulders sagged as he pressed the two pieces against his heart. Sitting on the floor, he rocked to and fro. Tears soaked his beard as he chanted, "'*Gahm kee elekh b'gay tzalmavet*...yea though I walk through the valley of the shadow of death...'"

"It's only one branch, Papa." Havah knelt beside him. "Surely it can be fixed."

"Once a limb is severed can the tree be made whole again?"

PART II

FROM EVERY DEPTH OF GOOD AND ILL

Chapter One

Kansas City's weather tended to be full of surprises. When it snowed last May, Havah's neighbor Mrs. Hutton wagged her head from side to side and said, "Didn't I tell ya? If ya don't like the weather here, jest wait a minute."

Havah learned the most sporadic weather came between winter and spring. Even in January it could be sunny and spring-like one day and snow the next. This January morning had been one of those snowy ones, and since there was no school, the children could not wait to play outside. Reuven wanted to try out the new sled Ulrich and Catherine had given him for his tenth birthday the week before.

He gulped down his eggs, stuffed a piece of toast in his coat pocket and before Havah could even give him a peck on the cheek, he ran out the door. She stood at the window and watched him greet two of his schoolmates.

Throughout the morning snow continued to fall until it reached Havah's ankles. By mid-morning, Bayla and Rachel abandoned their snowman. They sat side by side on the sofa wrapped in a blanket in front of the fireplace and took turns reading to each other from their respective books.

Bayla closed her eyes and grazed her fingertips across the page of Rachel's book. "I don't know how you read these bumps and read gooder than me and Miss Tova."

"Better, not gooder." Havah picked up the doll that was propped up on the couch next to Bayla. "Tell her, Miss Tova. 'You read *better* than Miss Tova and me.'"

"Yes, ma'am." Wrinkling her nose, Bayla opened her eyes and grinned at Havah. "Miss Tova says we'll do *better* next time."

Havah set the doll back down between the girls. "You girls are both good readers, but we're going to have to have a talk with Miss Tova."

"Where can Reuven be?" Fruma Ya'el looked up at the mantle clock. "Doesn't he know it's almost lunch time?"

"He's probably having so much fun with his buddies he's lost track of time." Havah tried to sound reassuring, but growing apprehension gnawed at her. The snow showed no signs of letting up. The wind kicked in and blew the flakes sideways. Havah could not even make out the light pole at the end of the yard.

"I hear Reuven." Rachel tilted her head. "He's crying."

***

On his way home from the library, Lev had happened on Reuven and his playmates. Waving to Lev, Reuven slid down a steep hill on his sled and collided with another sled. The other boy flipped over, stood and shook the snow out of his hair. Reuven rolled onto the ground clutching his left arm. By the time Lev reached the boys Reuven's wrist had already swollen to twice its normal size and turned purple.

Two and a half hours later, Lev sat with Aunt Havah in Dr. Miklos' waiting room. Reuven curled up in the chair between them holding his wrist. *Bubbe* had put his arm in a sling before they left the house, saying she could not set a broken bone.

Lev offered to bring Reuven to the doctor by himself, but Aunt Havah insisted it was her place as the boy's mother to be there. He wished she had not been so headstrong for he could tell Reuven was not the only one in pain. After trudging through the snow and enduring the cold streetcar ride, her face was drawn and pale.

He reached into his pocket and pulled out the watch Gavrel had given to him. *"Be sweet, Lev. Anger is a waste of time," said Gravrel when he placed it in his hand.* Nonetheless, Lev's anger mounted with each tick. In Dr. Miklos' absence, Dr. Huber had taken at least three patients before even acknowledging Reuven's presence.

"I'll be with you in a moment." The doctor looked down his nose as if Reuven was a bug to be squished beneath his fine leather boot. "Be a good boy, now."

Another twenty minutes passed. Lev watched the receptionist, an attractive young woman with coifed hair. "How much longer?" he asked. "My brother's badly hurt."

She gave him a disdainful look and turned back to the compact in her hand. "The doctor is with a patient. You'll just have to wait."

Lev gritted his teeth.

The treatment room door opened. A girl with ribbons in her blonde curls skipped out with a sucker in her hand. Dr. Huber patted her head and smiled. "Now there's a *gut kleine madchen.*

After the girl and her mother left the office, Dr. Huber looked around the room. "Next."

"That's us." Lev leaped from his chair. "My brother's wrist is broken."

"Oh, are we a doctor now?" Dr. Huber glowered at him and glanced at Havah and Reuven. "*Juden.*"

While Lev did not understand German, he did not need a translator. He recognized the tone he'd heard many times in conjunction with words like *Zjid, sheeny,* and *kike.*

"I want Dr. Miklos." Reuven wailed.

"He's delivering a baby," said Dr. Huber in a low condescending voice. "That takes time."

"Dr. Huber will fix you as good as new," Aunt Havah leaned forward on her cane, "or Dr. Miklos wouldn't leave him in charge would he?"

"Stay where you are, *Frau* Gitterman." Dr. Huber's lips stretched into an ingratiating smile. He gestured toward a buxom blonde entering the waiting room. "*Fräulein* Potter is ahead of you."

"This is an emergency." Havah thumped her cane on the floor. "Dr. Miklos would never—"

"Tut-tut, your little burst of temper won't help. *Fräulein* Potter has an appointment. The boy will have to wait his turn."

Dr. Huber pivoted on his heel, ushered *Fräulein* Potter into the treatment room and shut the door behind them.

Aunt Havah growled. Raising her nose, she mimicked his clipped accent. "'I assure you, *Frau* Gitterman, dees is a dire emergency. Dees poor, afflicted woman—who is not Jewish, I might add—is suffering from a severe hangnail.' Appointment, my eye."

Lev paced back and forth, clenching and unclenching his hands. "I should break his *goyishe* nose."

Another fifteen minutes passed. Reuven tugged at Aunt Havah's sleeve. "Mama? I feel funny."

His face blanched ash-white and his eyes rolled back in his head. He slid off his chair. She fell to the floor beside him and cradled his head in her lap. Lev ran to the treatment room door. He pounded it with his fist.

Dr. Miklos exploded through the front door. "What on earth!?" He knelt beside Reuven and held his fingers against Reuven's neck. "This boy's in shock. What happened?"

"He fell off his sled this morning," said Lev, "and broke his wrist."

"Good call, doctor. It is broken. No doubt it's fractured." Dr. Miklos gently prodded Reuven's distended wrist. "Why did you wait until this afternoon to bring him?"

"We didn't. We've been here for over two hours."

Wrapping his overcoat around Reuven, Dr. Miklos swept him up into his arms. With the force of a raging bear, he kicked open the treatment room door. *Fräulein* Potter and a rumpled Dr. Huber rolled off the examination table. She groped for her cloak on a nearby chair, hastily covered her exposed breasts and pushed past Lev.

With no sign of remorse, Dr. Huber clicked his heels and bowed to Dr. Miklos. "I hereby tender my resignation."

Dr. Miklos laid Reuven on the table, grabbed Dr. Huber's lapels with both hands and leaned into his face. "If this child dies, I'll see to your execution personally."

Chapter Two

"I hope you don't mind an audience." Havah leaned over Vasily's shoulder as he placed a row of colorful tempera jars on an old newspaper on the kitchen table.

Beside her, Arel patted Vasily's back. "He'll have to get used to it if he's going to be a famous artist."

"I don't mind." Vasily sat across from Reuven and swirled his paintbrush through a cup of water.

Lev leaned his chair back on two legs. "Ha, don't let that 'shy boy' routine fool you. He loves the attention."

Arel frowned at Lev. "Set that chair down."

Folding his arms across his chest, Lev sat up straight and set the chair on all four legs with a loud thump. "Yes, sir."

Arel averted his scowl from Lev and smiled at Reuven. "What kind of picture do you want on your cast?"

Like a scholar lost in thought, Reuven twisted his lips and looked up at the ceiling, extending his arm. "I know. Paint a picture of Papa."

Vasily looked over at Arel, held his brush at arm's length and shut one eye. Havah remembered how her brother David would do the same thing. He said it was so he could attain the right angle or perspective.

Reuven shook his head. "Not *that* Papa. I mean Papa Gavrel."

With a nod, Vasily dipped his brush into one of the jars and let the color drop onto a crumpled pie tin he used for a palette. "He was a good man. I miss him."

Arel's shoulders sagged as he turned to leave the room. Havah held her breath, let it out, then followed him to the dining room. She grabbed his arm. "He didn't mean it like that and you know it."

"Didn't he?" He pulled away from her and kept walking. "Who'd want to wear this face on his arm?"

Heaving an exasperated sigh, Havah went back into the kitchen. As she walked past Yussel, he reached for her hand. "Let him have his little conniption."

"I'm worried about him."

"Don't break your head. All he needs is a good stiff *potch en tokhes.*"

"Yussel!" Standing beside him, Fruma Ya'el dropped open her mouth. "He's your son."

"And my son is acting like a…a *schlemiel.*"

"He's not the only one."

Sudden pain in her legs sent Havah to the chair beside Yussel, hoping no one heard her muffled groan. Yussel said nothing; just squeezed her hand. The expression on Fruma Ya'el's face told Havah that she had also heard.

"Wait 'til the kids at school see this." Reuven pointed to his cast where Vasily had rendered an uncanny likeness of Gavrel surrounded by shoes of all sizes and colors.

"Amazing." Fruma Ya'el clasped her hands across her chest. "The Almighty has given you such a gift."

"Yes, ma'am." Color rose in Vasily's cheeks.

"It's nice of you to come over and do this for our little apple," said Yussel. "This is one time I wish I could still see."

"It's okay. Besides, Tatko has a terrible cold. He's a grouch when he's sick."

The doorbell rang. Before Havah could stand, Lev jumped up nearly upsetting his chair. "I'll get it. You need to rest, Auntie."

Havah marveled at the change in Lev since he had gone back to school. Every night he poured over his mathematics and science books. His chemistry teacher had already sent home a note to congratulate Lev for his perfect score on his first quiz.

Dr. Miklos' laughter preceded him as he and Lev entered the kitchen. With his hat in one hand, the doctor pointed to Reuven's embellished cast. "I shall have to be very careful not to damage the lad's masterpiece when the time comes to saw it off.

"Now it's *my* turn to share *my* artwork." He took a large envelope from under his arm, pulled out a thick sheet of film and handed it to Lev. "Tell me what you see, Dr. Gitterman."

"It's an x-ray." Lev held it up to the light. "Hey, little apple, this is what your wrist looks like under your skin."

The sun shone through the film revealing Reuven's wrist bones, including the fractured one. Havah could not stop staring. "We are, as King David wrote, 'wonderfully fashioned.'"

***

Steam rising from the samovar on the kitchen table helped clear Nikolai's clogged sinuses. He breathed it in as he poured a cup of spiced tea and took a sip. The hot liquid soothed his raw throat.

He padded to the parlor, eased down on the sofa and watched Oxana sew. Sitting in her rocking chair next to the fireplace, she propped her feet on a padded hassock and crossed them at the ankles. Her needle glinted in the light streaming through the front window.

A pleasant drowsiness washed over him. He had all but drifted off when the rumbling of a motorcar shook him from his stupor.

Oxana set her embroidery hoop on the end table beside her chair and walked to the door. "Were you expecting company?"

"I was expecting to go back to bed after I finished my tea."

Nikolai shut one eye, peered outside and groaned. Glare from the sunlight reflecting off the snow aggravated his already pounding headache as he watched Florin saunter up to the porch, medical bag in hand.

"What's he doing here on a Sunday morning?"

"He's our friend. Maybe he's only come by for a visit." Oxana curved her hand around the doorknob. "Should I let him in?"

Nikolai rose from the couch and cinched his robe. "By all means, let him in."

A frigid gust blew in as Oxana opened the door.

"*Dobrayah utra*, Doctor. Won't you come in?"

"Good morning, dear lady. I hope I haven't interrupted anything." Florin bowed, took off his hat, and stepped over the threshold. As he hung his coat on the hall tree by the door, he eyed Nikolai and frowned. "You don't look at all well, Kolyah."

"It's nothing more than a common cold. Did my wife call you?"

"Your son asked if I'd come by and look in on you. Vasily's worried about his Tatko." Florin raised an eyebrow. "And I must say, Kolyah, I've seen cadavers that looked better."

Fishing his handkerchief from his dressing gown pocket Nikolai sneezed into it and coughed. "It's good to see you, too."

"I don't like the sound of that." Florin took hold of Nikolai's arm. "To the bedroom, Squire."

"It's a cold, nothing more."

"Is that your clinical diagnosis, Doctor?"

"Yes."

Entering the bedroom, Florin motioned for Nikolai to sit on the bed. He set down his bag and took out his stethoscope. "Open your shirt and lie back." He pressed the bell against Nikolai's chest and listened. "No congestion." He poked a thermometer between Nikolai's pursed lips and shoved it under his tongue. After three tense minutes, he pulled it out and read. "Ninety-eight-point-three. I'd say it's nothing more than a common cold."

With an angry snarl Nikolai sat up and buttoned his nightshirt. In the process, a sharp twinge burned his shoulder. He flinched.

"That wound's still bothering you after all this time?"

"It's a little sensitive, that's all."

"When you're up to it, come to the office for an x-ray."

"Why? So you can play with your new toy? Nerve injury won't show up on an x-ray."

"Just the same, I'd like to see how your scapula healed."

As Florin stuffed his stethoscope into his bag, he picked up a magazine from the bed stand. "Do my eyes deceive me or is that a medical journal, open to an article about nerve injury? I thought you were quite finished with the medical profession."

"Personal research."

"I see." After he finished thumbing through the pages, Florin cast an almost pleading gaze on Nikolai. "Dr. Huber is gone."

"Lev told me."

"I've taken out an ad in *The Times* for a new associate."

Nikolai put on his robe and headed for the kitchen. "I hope you find one."

Following him to the table, Florin said, "It's been many a year since I've seen one of these." He picked up the teapot from the samovar's chimney and filled his cup halfway with dark tea, then repositioned the pot. After adding hot water from the spigot, he stirred the tea. "And this is a beautiful one. Yes, it truly is."

Oxana handed Florin a small dish of sugar cubes. "It was a gift from Kolyah's father."

"From your father, Kolyah? Does this mean there's been a truce?"

"Not to my knowledge. The samovar came with a card that had nothing but his signature." Nikolai plopped a spoonful of jam into his tea and stirred. "Most likely it's Tatko's way of assuaging his guilt without the distasteful business of an apology."

"Perhaps you judge him too harshly." Popping a sugar cube into his mouth, Florin took a drink from his cup. He crunched the sugar and swallowed, his blue eyes staring off into the past. "Good Russian tea. It reminds me of home and my beautiful Amelia. Those were happy times. How she doted on our little Petru. They both died too young."

Nikolai remembered Petru Miklos as a shy youngster who often shadowed him in surgery. The boy's greatest desire was to help people. It had saddened yet not shocked Nikolai to learn that Petru died shielding a Jewish child from the Cossacks' blows.

Florin's laughter snapped Nikolai out of his musing. "Dr. Derevenko, you haven't heard a word I've said, have you?"

Heat rushed to Nikolai's face. "What did I miss?"

"He's offering me a job, Kolyah." Oxana's thin cheeks flushed as she wound a stray lock of hair around her finger. "What do you think?"

"Doing what?" Nikolai sniffed in an attempt to breathe. "I thought you were looking for a doctor, Florin."

Florin poured himself another cup of tea and diluted it with hot water. "Alas, I need a secretary who can double as a nurse, too. Never hire a pretty young actress to do office work."

"My wife has never worked in an office nor is she a formally trained nurse."

"Perhaps not, but she has some nursing experience, yes?"

"Her brother taught her well."

"Then it's settled."

"She doesn't read or write English well."

"She has a quick mind, and you forget I read and write Russian. I don't want another child almost dying in my waiting room due to ignorance or negligence."

"I understand your concern, but my Oxana—"

"Stop it!" Oxana clanked her spoon against her cup. "Stop haggling over me like I am a...a piece of fish at market." She smoothed back her hair and squared her narrow shoulders. "When do I start, Dr. Miklos?"

Chapter Three

Holding Rachel's hand in hers, Havah paused in front of the tailor shop to admire the newly painted window. "'Gitterman's Fine Tailoring.' Vasily's quite the artist. Poppy's sign is magnificent."

The bell on the door clinked when Havah opened it. Leaning on her cane, she limped to the sewing machine where Arel hunched over a pair of trousers. When he looked up, she could tell something troubled him.

Rachel reached for him. "Poppy!"

He slipped off the chair and knelt to pick her up. She giggled as he nibbled her ear with a playful growl. He stood, and kissed Havah's lips.

"To what do I owe the pleasure of this visit from my favorite ladies?" His voice sounded flat.

"We missed you something terrible, Poppy." Rachel curled her arms around his neck. "So we come'd on the streetcar since it's a sunny Sunday."

Tears welled up in his gray eyes and he repeated, "Sunday."

"Arel, what is it?" asked Havah.

He tightened his arms around Rachel. "Mommy and I need to talk, Rukhel Shvester." He set her back on her feet and patted her bottom.

Havah fished Rachel's book from her bag and led her to Arel's desk in the back room. Rachel climbed up on the chair and opened the book. "I wish Poppy had a piano here."

Once Rachel had settled, Havah went back to the front of the store. Outside on the sidewalk two boys about Reuven's age, wearing suits and neckties, pointed and stuck out their tongues. Arel winced and looked away.

Havah rushed to the window and made an ugly face at them. An elegantly dressed woman grabbed their hands and scowled at her. The boys giggled and made faces at each other.

Havah fumed as she turned back to Arel. "Nice churchgoers."

With his elbow on the counter, he rested his chin on his hand, which he used to cover his left cheek. He waved his other hand over an official looking sheet of paper in front of him.

"What's that?" she asked.

"It's an indictment from His Honor Judge Wallace. I could go to prison."

"What crime did you commit?"

"I've opened my shop on Sunday instead of Saturday."

"And this is a crime?"

"According to him and his Sunday labor law, we're required to observe the Christian Sabbath or pay a penalty. We may open our shops, but if we sell anything we are in violation."

"I don't understand this man. Ulrich and Dr. Florin call themselves Christians and go to church on Sunday. They are kind and gentle, nothing like that judge." A lump formed in the pit of Havah's stomach. "Arel, you don't suppose..." She envisioned the police smashing the window. They beat Arel with their clubs while he pled for mercy. Next they came after Rachel.

Havah shook off her grisly daydream and remembered her chance meeting with President Roosevelt at Ellis Island. Imagine the ruler of the United States taking the time to speak with a Jewish peasant girl from Moldavia. Such a man would never allow another Kishinev or Odessa to happen in his great country.

She took the indictment in her hand and crumpled it in her fist. "Every ass likes to hear himself bray."

Chapter Four

Sitting at the kitchen table, Havah settled her stocking feet onto another chair and gazed out the window. An hour before, she had awakened to find herself cowering in a corner of the living room. Rather than go back to bed, she brewed a pot of coffee and heated a saucepan of chocolate milk to help calm her nerves.

The dregs of her nightmare clung to her like a shroud as she sipped coffee-laced hot chocolate. She tried to concentrate on the sunrise, but the strips of red, orange, and amber that streaked the sky served only to remind her of the fire that flared from the dragon's mouth.

"Sabbath on Sunday or die," he hissed through charcoal billows of smoke. Lightning shot from his yellow eyes. He wrapped his copper-scaled wings around her, his putrid breath searing her face.

"*Ai dee dai...lai.*" Yussel sang as he scraped his cane along the floor to maneuver his way through the kitchen. "Good morning, Havaleh. You're up early."

Grateful for the diversion, Havah swung her legs off the chair. When her feet hit the floor, fiery pain coursed through her right leg. She fought the urge to cry out.

"Let me get you some coffee, Papa. Would you like some toast? An egg?"

"Just coffee. George is bringing cinnamon buns to prayers this morning."

"Nettie shouldn't be baking."

"He's stopping by the bakery." Yussel cocked his head to one side. "If you'd like to talk about your nightmare, I'll listen."

"Did I wake you?"

"No, my little scholar. I hear it in your voice."

Pouring cream into his cup, she watched white swirl against the black. After she stirred it, she set the cup on the table in front of him and guided his hand to the sugar bowl beside it.

Stinging pain wracked her left leg. Biting her lower lip, she eased down onto her chair.

Yussel dumped two spoonsfuls of sugar into his coffee. "It's very quiet when Bayla and Reuven are at Shayndel's house. Have you ever noticed that our little Rukhel Shvester snores louder than Arel?"

Arel, dressed for the day, went to the stove. He poured a cup of coffee and sat beside Havah. "Your talking in your sleep gets pretty loud sometimes, Papa."

Yussel's mouth disappeared under his moustache. Palms on the table, he rose and grabbed his cane. "If you'll excuse me, Havaleh. I'll wait for George on the porch."

In the doorway, Fruma Ya'el frowned at him as he stopped to kiss her cheek and continued to walk. She raised her eyebrow and looked at Havah. "You're still in your nightgown and you don't look well."

Fruma Ya'el went to the stove where she buttered six slices of bread and stuck them in the oven. After that, she broke half a dozen eggs into a bowl and whipped them with milk. "Why don't you go back to bed?"

The dragon's face came to Havah's mind. She shuddered, shook her head and tried to stand. "Let me help you with breakfast, Mama."

"You're very pale." Arel reached for her hand. "Maybe I should stay home."

"No. It's Monday and you have a business to run."

"You're more important, Havah."

"Sit, Havah," said Fruma Ya'el, her brown eyes awash with concern. "I think I should call Dr. Florin."

"Please don't. As Catherine would say, I'm in fine fettle."

All through breakfast Havah picked at her toast, avoiding Fruma Ya'el's scrutiny and Arel's anxious gaze. Finally, he pushed back his empty plate and swallowed the last of his coffee. Dabbing his mouth with his napkin, he stood.

"Are you sure you don't want me to stay with you?"

"Yes."

"If you call the doctor let me know what he says, okay?"

"No one's calling the doctor."

He kissed her and left the room. Wishing she had told him how desperately she wanted him to stay, Havah listened for the door to open and close. She collected the dishes and headed for the sink. Both of her legs blazed with pain and she collapsed on the floor, the stack of plates shattering around her.

"Mama," she moaned. "Call Dr. Florin. Now!"

***

Fruma Ya'el's stomach roiled at the sight of Havah's red and swollen calves. Neither poultices nor willow bark tea did anything to ease the pain. Sweat ran down the sides of Havah's ashen face. Her teeth trenched her lower lip.

Sitting on the bed, Dr. Florin pressed Havah's legs with his fingertips. "How bad is it?"

Havah winced. "Not...bad."

He pulled the blanket over her. "I see."

Fruma Ya'el raised her hands and looked up at the ceiling. "'Not bad,' she says. Some days she can hardly move. And does she listen to me when I tell her to rest?"

Havah rose up on her elbows. "Listen to *her*, Doctor. Nag, nag, nag. 'Sit, Havah. Don't do that, Havah. Be a good little *cripple*, Havah.'"

Fruma Ya'el slumped in the chair beside the bed. "I *never* said that."

Havah fell back against the pillows. "It's just that I...it hurts so much."

Dr. Florin took a small glass vial from his medical bag. "Morphine will bring a bit of relief so you can rest." He filled a syringe and flicked it with his finger. "Rest is what you need. Watch closely, Mrs. Gitterman," he said to Fruma Ya'el. "You shall be giving the next dose, just enough to ease the pain, not make her dependent."

How much was enough? As he injected the hypodermic Havah squeezed Fruma Ya'el's hand until it throbbed. Havah's eyes closed and her erratic breathing steadied, slowed and gradually became soft and rhythmic.

Fruma Ya'el slipped Havah's hand under the covers. "She hates me."

Putting his instruments into his bag, the doctor frowned. "How could anyone hate you?"

Fruma Ya'el lifted the corner of the blanket and pointed at Havah's foot. "Those two toes and nearly half of the rest of it were so frostbitten and infected. What choice did I have? But look at it now." Fruma Ya'el grimaced. Havah's three remaining toes, in an effort to compensate, had spread and looked like claws. "Wouldn't you hate someone who did this to you?"

"You must stop blaming yourself for what those animals who murdered her family did. They're responsible for this nerve injury, not you."

"I crippled her."

"Gangrene would've killed her. You performed lifesaving surgery, my dear lady. You did exactly what I would've done."

"He's right, Mama." Havah opened her eyes for a brief moment. "I love you."

Chapter Five

By Wednesday morning Havah's pain had subsided to the point she did not need morphine and felt well enough to resume her normal tasks. That afternoon, she held her weekly Hebrew class, numbering anywhere from ten to fifteen girls, given the season or family activities. Her eager pupils, aged six to twelve, sat in a circle of chairs in the study.

After their lessons, the girls sipped tea and munched on the miniature sandwiches Havah had prepared for them.

She picked up an envelope from the desk and held it out for the girls to see. "I have a special treat, a letter from St. Louis."

Taking it from the envelope, she unfolded it and studied her niece's handwriting. Every *y* swooped beneath the lines. Evie had even drawn flowers with smiling faces in the margins. Havah smoothed the paper and read aloud.

"Dear Auntie Havah and my friends in Talmud Torah class,

"I miss you so much, even if I do have new friends in public school. I think it is dopey that girls can't go to Hebrew school. Papa reads with me every night just like he promised. He says maybe when I'm older enough we will have a secret *Bas Mitzvah* like you did in the old country, Auntie Havah.

"Auntie Dora gives me piano lessons and I really like her. She wants me to call her Mama. I wish I was in Kansas City with you and my real mama was not in heaven.

"Hugs and XXX,

Evalyne Grace Tulschinsky"

Bayla sat up straight in her chair and shot her hand into the air. "Miss Tova says Bar Mitzvah means 'son of the commandment' so *Bas Mitzvah* probably means 'daughter of the commandment.'"

"Right you are, Miss Tova," said Havah.

In her mind, Havah was twelve years old again and it was Friday night. Wrapped in the prayer shawl her mother had fashioned for the occasion with purple and pink stripes instead of blue, Havah chanted the blessings and read the Torah passages.

After their clandestine ceremony in the parlor, her brother Mendel, who had spent hours tutoring her, puffed out his chest. "She had a great teacher."

David punched his arm. "Remember what Solomon said about pride."

Havah melted into her father's embrace, his whispered blessing tickled the top her head. "Many daughters have done great things, but you have done far more. Someday women will read from the scrolls beside their men. Maybe not in my lifetime, but perhaps in yours, my brilliant daughter."

Nine-year-old Wendy Mayer's shrill voice jolted Havah from her reverie. "My mommy says when I'm twelve, we're going to have a big *Bas Mitzvah* in our ballroom with lots of food and presents. My *Zaydeh* was a rabbi and Mommy says he would be really proud. Isn't that so, Miss Havah?"

Havah put her finger to her lips. "Use your indoor voice, Wendy, please. Yes, your *Zaydeh* would be proud."

Blushing, Wendy, the daughter of a wealthy businessman, shook her glossy curls and lowered her voice to a whisper. "Sorry, Miss Havah. I didn't mean to boast 'cause we have lots of money. Mommy says it's unladylike."

"Your mommy is a wise lady."

Malka Berkovich, a skinny eight-year-old with sandy braids and freckles, raised her hand. "My papa says there's no such thing as a *Bas Mitzvah* and he'd whip me and Liba's *tokheses* raw before he'd ever let us do such a *meshuguna* thing even if we have learned some Hebrew." She stuffed a sandwich into her mouth and crammed another into the pocket of her pinafore.

A hundred words came to Havah's mind that she wanted to use, but she thought better of them. She had seen Zalman Berkovich at the synagogue on rare occasions. When he did come for services, it was always alone and he left halfway through without a word to anyone.

Little was known about the Berkovich family other than where they lived and that Zalman refused charity of any kind. So it surprised Havah that he allowed his daughters to come to her classes, and that neither of them had mentioned him until now.

"It's as they say, 'a free country.' Your papa has a right to his opinions."

Sitting beside Malka, her sister broke down in choking sobs. Malka rolled her eyes and heaved a melodramatic sigh. "Oh stop it, Liba. At least you won't have to worry about your arithmetic grade anymore."

Liba's sobbing changed to wailing. With her thin arms wrapped around herself, she rocked to and fro while the other students watched in stunned silence. Havah grasped the girl's skeletal shoulders and whispered, "*Vas iz mit dir?*"

Sucking in her lips, Liba hushed, sniffed and mumbled in Yiddish. "I have to quit school."

"Why?"

"To work."

"Where? You're only twelve."

"The canning factory with Papa."

"He knows this is illegal?"

"He knows."

"I'm going to have to talk to him."

Liba raised her head, terror in her huge golden-brown eyes. Her gaunt cheeks shone with tears. "No, no, please don't. If he finds out I told you, he'll beat me...or worse."

Chapter Six

Leaning back in his chair, Ulrich propped his slippered feet on his desk. After a Saturday morning of tutoring with a few less-than-talented piano students, he was ready for a respite. He lifted a cup of wassail to his nose and breathed in its fragrance.

Eyeglasses on top of his head, Nikolai stretched out on a chaise lounge near the desk and sipped from his cup. "The distiller's daughter hasn't lost her touch."

Emptying his drink, Ulrich relished the slow burn in his chest. "It's Daddy's tried-and-true recipe: cinnamon, cider, cloves, ale, and more than a little brandy. Fiery and delicious, like my bride."

Nikolai patted his stomach. "Thank you for lunch. Catherine hasn't lost her touch in the kitchen either. I wish my wife…" His voice trailed off. "I hope Catherine isn't coercing her into spending her first week's wages on anything too frivolous."

"Oxana seems pretty sensible to me."

"She's still a woman."

"How does she like working for Florin?"

"She loves it. However, with our schedules, it seems that one of us is always rushing out the door."

"Florin's ad is still in the paper. He hasn't found a partner yet."

Nikolai settled his eyeglasses on his nose and smoothed back his lank white hair. "Shouldn't we be rehearsing for tomorrow's concert?"

Despite Nikolai's claims of contentment in teaching music, he seemed restless and unsettled. Ulrich could not dispute his friend's musical ability or dedication to it as a concert flautist. However, something was lacking. Whereas Nikolai had been passionate about medicine, the sentiment did not carry over into his music classroom.

Ulrich swung his feet off the desk and took two envelopes from a stack of books and papers. "Before we start, let me share what came in the post yesterday. The first is from Francis MacMillen."

"The young violinist you met in London last summer?"

"The virtuoso himself."

"What does he have to say?"

"He's scheduled to do a concert at Willis Wood Theater here in Kansas City April 12th this coming year and he's asked a certain Austrian to accompany him."

"You're going accept, of course."

"I've no choice. He's going to be our houseguest. Perhaps we can host an impromptu concert here, if he's amenable to it."

"I look forward to meeting him. Who's the other letter from?"

"My manager."

Ulrich took the letter he and Catherine had read that morning over breakfast and handed it to Nikolai. "Read it for yourself."

Scanning the paper, Nikolai peered at Ulrich over his spectacles and raised one eyebrow. "Have you discussed this with Arel and Havah?"

***

Standing on the front porch, Vasily watched Lev stroll down the sidewalk, a stack of books under his arm. Before turning the corner, he stopped and waved. "Thanks, Vasya, I appreciate the help."

Vasily waved back. "I'm not sure who really helped whom. You're way ahead of me in mathematics and science."

Once Lev had made the decision to finish high school, he hardly did anything besides study or write papers. In only a few weeks, Lev caught up to the rest of the junior class and passed most of them by, even in English grammar.

Vasily went into the house and shut the front door. He peeked out the window and looked up and down the street, but saw no sign of Tatko and Mother. He grinned and headed for his bedroom. It was not often he had the house to himself.

After undressing, he put on his nightshirt and crawled into bed, fluffing a couple of pillows against the headboard. He took a piece of parchment stationary and a fountain pen from a box on the bed stand. Settling back, he propped a drawing board on his knees as a desk.

He put pen to paper and wrote,

"Dear *Dedushkah*,
"Tatko and Oxana are pleased with the samovar; Oxana more than Tatko. She says coffee tastes like—"

"I can't write that." Vasily crumpled the paper and tossed it in the waste basket beside the bed. Taking another piece of paper, he started another letter.

He looked up to see Oxana and flipped the paper over. "I didn't hear you come in, Mother. Did you and Tatko have a good time with Uncle Ulrich and Aunt Catherine?" He hoped his smile looked natural.

"Your father's still there. Aunt Catherine brought me home." Oxana pointed to the paper. "This is homework?"

Vasily handed it to her. "No ma'am, it's a letter."

"I see you writing a lot of them lately." Her mouth dropped open. "It is in Russian. This is to—"

"My grandfather."

Chapter Seven

A group of angry, bearded men shouting in Yiddish crowded the butcher shop. Between the yelling and arguing, Fruma Ya'el felt as though she had never left Svechka. Dodging shaking fists, she and Yussel scuffed their way across the sawdust-covered floor, past the pickle barrel to the counter. Earthy smells of raw beef and chicken mingled with those of dill weed, vinegar, and onions.

"Judge Wallace should buy a big hotel and be found dead in every room," said one man.

"He's a piece of meat with eyes," said another.

"His brain is the same size as his—"

"Hold your tongues, all of you. There's a lady present." Behind the counter, George Weinberg, the shop owner, raised his cleaver over his head. With a single stroke he sliced through a large chunk of meat. "Can I interest you in a pot roast for *Shabbes*, Mrs. Gitterman?"

She eyed it and shook her head. "Better a chicken for the Sabbath."

George held one up by its feet. "Killed it this morning."

"Did you kill maybe two? The Dietrichs and Dr. Miklos are joining us."

"Dr. Miklos and his appetite? I'll throw in a third. No charge."

"George, how do you expect to make a living?" Yussel asked. "And you with another mouth to feed on the way?"

Mopping the top of his bald head with a rag, George shrugged. "It's what friends are for."

"All right," said Fruma Ya'el, "but only if you'll accept half of it cooked with noodle kugel and string beans for your *Shabbes* dinner."

George's dark eyes shone. "Thank you. My Nettie will appreciate it after having to gag down my cooking. Our Benny, on the other hand, will eat anything that isn't nailed down and cry for more."

"Such a handsome boy. He should live to see his children's children." Fruma Ya'el leaned forward and lowered her voice. "Tell me the truth, Georgie, how is Nettie, really?"

"She's a little crabby perhaps. But after four months in bed, who wouldn't be?" George wrapped three chickens in brown paper and handed them to her. "Dr. Miklos says any day now, and it's going to be a big one. His heartbeat is loud and strong. The kicking in her belly keeps me awake all night." George lowered his voice. "If it's a boy, we're going to call him Bernie after my father of blessed memory. If it's a girl, we'll call her Bernadette. But it's a boy, I know it."

Although Fruma Ya'el wanted to share his enthusiasm, she could not—not yet. Had not her own daughter, Gittel, died after giving birth to a stillborn son? A big boy who had kicked day and night in the womb, he came feet first and strangled on the cord before taking his first breath.

Nettie was no stranger to *tsuris*. On the way to America, in ship's steerage, she lost her first husband and son to cholera. She found love again with George Weinberg and hoped to start a family right away. However, before the Weinbergs adopted Benny three years ago, Nettie suffered five miscarriages, the last one in her sixth month. The tiny boy, who fit in the palm of Dr. Miklos' hand, lived less than ten minutes. Fruma Ya'el prayed this time would be different. But until she held Nettie's healthy baby in her arms, she would not tempt the Evil Eye by even speaking of it.

She pointed to the meat on the chopping block. "I'll take that after all. Would you mind cutting half of it into small pieces? A little meat would taste good in my *Shabbes cholent*, then I'll cook the rest of the roast Sunday. It will keep in the icebox, yes?"

"As long as it's close to the ice." George cut the meat into small squares. "Tell Havah, when she's feeling up to it, not to be a stranger. Nettie misses her."

One of the men fished a pickle from the barrel and laid a nickel on the counter. "Will you be coming to George's Purim opera at the Shubert Theater next month, Reb Gitterman? It will all be in Yiddish. Easier for us old folks to understand."

"If His Honor, the judge, allows it, Reb Kaminsky," Yussel replied. "According to Arel, the paper says Mr. Wallace might not give his permission since the play is scheduled on a Sunday, God forbid."

"We have his written permission. After all, it's for a worthy cause. Our new synagogue needs new furniture." Pickle brine ran down Daniel Kaminsky's chin. He wiped it off with the back of his hand. "It's a pity your Havah hasn't been up to it. With her looks and voice, she'd have been the best choice for Esther, next to my Rose of course."

"So Rose is playing the part?"

"No, she's busy preparing for her marriage to Dr. Abraham Miller from Ohio. Of course, you're all invited to the wedding."

Yussel grinned. "Wouldn't miss it."

Fruma Ya'el bundled her purchases into her basket and took Yussel's arm. "Good day, all. George, you'll call us when Nettie's time comes, yes?"

Once outside, she breathed in the crisp air. Looking up and down the street, she noted the growing number of new businesses and skyscrapers. Sunlight glinted off their windows.

"It's such a nice day, Yussel. Why don't we drop by the tailor shop and visit Arel?"

Yussel's smile vanished. "No."

Chapter Eight

Having spent the early morning assisting Fruma Ya'el in delivering Nettie Weinberg's baby, Florin ached with exhaustion and happiness. After a mere two hours' labor, she gave birth to a nine-pound boy with a full head of black hair and as lusty a cry as the doctor had ever heard. Never had he experienced such joy. George broke into song, Nettie's laughter filled the room and Fruma Ya'el danced with the infant in her arms.

Florin pushed open the clinic door and entered his waiting room where Oxana sat behind the desk with the telephone receiver to her ear. When she saw him, she held her hand over the transmitter. "This woman, she is speaking so fast I am troubling to understanding."

"Good English practice for you." He took the telephone. "Is that a new blouse?"

Oxana's taut lips relaxed into a smile. "Catherine picks it out. You like?"

"Lovely. White lace suits you." He handed her a dollar. "My dear Mrs. Derevenko, if you would go to the corner restaurant and get me some coffee and toast, I will be forever in your debt."

"I will get it for you now."

Following five minutes of natter through static, Florin answered the woman's frantic questions. "I'll be happy to lance your son's boil, Madam, but you'll have to take your ailing Fluffy elsewhere."

Dropping the receiver on its hook, Florin shook his head. "Can you believe it? She wanted me to treat her cat! Do I look like a veterinarian?"

"I should say not," said an unfamiliar female voice.

He turned to see a statuesque woman wearing a gray pork pie hat. He estimated her height at six feet, for he could look directly into her penetrating sorrel eyes.

Heat scorched his cheeks. "I beg your pardon, Madam. I didn't hear you come in. This way, please."

When they entered the treatment room she tossed her hat onto the examination table. Her taffy-colored hair, sleek and center-parted, shone like China silk. Taking off her coat, she laid it beside her hat with the confident air of a politician.

"Are you Dr. Miklos?"

"Who else would I be?"

Running her gloved hand over the top of the medicine cabinet, she bent down and peered at the rows of bottles. "Then I'm in the right place."

She went to the table where his instruments were laid out on a tray. Picking up a pair of scissors, she held them up to the light. "I assume you sterilize. I insist on everything being as clean as humanly possible."

"You're not here as a patient, are you?"

"I'm here to answer your ad."

"Oh dear, I'm sorry you've wasted your time. The nurse-receptionist position has already been filled."

Extending her hand, she held her head high. "I am Eleanor Whitaker Turnbull, *MD*. Now, shall we commence the interview or have you filled that position as well?"

Florin led her to his office and sank into the chair behind the desk. "No I haven't. But—"

"I was born and raised in Philadelphia. I come from a long line of physicians." She opened her bag, lifted out a framed diploma, and set it on the desk directly in front of him. "As you can see, I graduated from the New York Medical College for Women, class of 1892. Suma Cum Laude. I served my internship at Johns Hopkins in Baltimore, Maryland. Perhaps you've heard of it?"

"Very impressive." He took his handkerchief and wiped perspiration from his forehead. "I'm most certainly impressed."

"I'm thirty-eight years old and own my own automobile."

He twirled the edge of his moustache with one finger. "How does Mr. Turnbull feel about this?"

"My father passed away a little over a year ago. I'm not married."

Florin's heart raced. "I'm sorry to hear that…about your father, I mean. What brings you to—?"

"Kansas City? I needed a change of scenery. I've applied in a few towns and cities between Philadelphia and here, but you know how antiquated male doctors can be…too set in their ways to give even the most educated woman a chance. I'm glad *you're* not that way, Dr. Miklos."

He loosened his tie and unbuttoned his collar. "No of course not, but I—"

"Good. Everything seems to be in order. I'm prepared to start Monday unless you have need of me sooner. Do you have any questions for me?"

Regaining his composure, he cleared his throat. "Only one. How do you feel about treating Jewish people?"

"What kind of question is that?"

"Just answer, please."

She folded her arms across her chest. "I became a doctor to care for *people*. My father was a doctor *and* an abolitionist. He never turned a patient away for *any* reason and neither, Dr. Miklos, shall I."

"Welcome aboard, Dr. Turnbull." He stood and held out his hand. "You're just what this doctor ordered."

Chapter Nine

Lev would never forget his tumultuous introduction to Vasily Derevenko in Odessa. Gavrel, who did not approve of Lev's Marxist companions, hoped the two boys would become friends. Vasily, who was thirteen at the time, and appeared to be much younger, crammed his hands into his pockets.

Lev sneered. "What's the matter, *shaygitz*? You're too good to touch a Jew?"

At that, Vasily doubled over and vomited. Gavrel swept him up in his massive arms and carried him to Lev and Reuven's bed where he stayed for the next two days. Although Leah worried Vasily might be contagious, Dr. Nikolai assured her it was food poisoning.

Lev's gorge rose at the memory as he tried to focus on his science homework. Perhaps it was the yellow walls in the Derevenko's kitchen, but tonight his mind insisted on wandering. He tried to bite into one of the buns Oxana set on the table for the boys before she went to bed. While her cooking had improved somewhat, the roll had all the appeal of a rock.

Dunking the bun into his coffee, he glanced over at Vasily's easel. With deft strokes of his brushes, Leah appeared on the canvas. She held her hands over her eyes and her face glowed in the aura of the *Shabbes* candles. This was how Lev wanted to remember his sister.

Sometimes when he had trouble falling asleep, he envisioned her as an eleven-year-old with crimson braids. He missed the days when he was the baby brother she adored. If he skinned his knee, she would kiss it. If he had a bad dream, she would sing to him. If Papa raged after him, she would hide him.

Lev could not take his eyes off her portrait. "How do you do that?"

Without a trace of arrogance, Vasily shrugged. "I don't know. I just do it."

"You're going to be famous someday."

Vasily squinted at Lev's book. "You're in the senior textbook? You're really smart."

"My teachers say, if I keep working at this rate, I could graduate this year instead of next."

"Great. We'll graduate together, after all. That should make your uncle happy."

"He'll remind me I should've graduated last spring."

"Don't fret. He'll eat his words when you become a great doctor." Wielding his paintbrush, Vasily grimaced and pointed at the bullet between the pages of the science book. "Why do you hang on to that thing?"

"Your father took it in the shoulder for me. I owe him my life."

Flute case in hand, Dr. Nikolai entered the kitchen and set it on a chair. Taking a bun from the plate, he thumped it on the table twice and tossed it into the wastebasket under the table. He picked up the bullet. The light limned it as he held it between his thumb and forefinger. "You owe me nothing."

Dropping it into Lev's hand, Dr. Nikolai sat next to him. "Heroes aren't always what they're cracked up to be. I hope someday you can forgive me for falling off your pedestal. Maybe you'll be the physician I could not be."

"Why'd you trade your scalpel for a flute?"

"Why do you have to ask? You heard what I heard and you saw what I saw."

Protracted images flashed before Lev's eyes like intermittent lightning. The stunned look on Dr. Pavel's face when the knife meant for Lev plunged into his chest...Seconds later he lay in the street, his blood soaking Dr. Nikolai's lap. The ransacked apartment over the shoe shop. Leah's glazed eyes. His other sister Devorah's naked body sliced open; her infant son still attached to the umbilical cord, his head severed from his tiny body. Lev's nieces, toddlers, Pora and Tova, their arms rent from their sockets and legs hacked to bits.

Until that moment, Lev had all but forgotten the helpless despair in Dr. Nikolai's eyes. Rolling the bullet around his palm, Lev let it drop into the wastebasket. "You're forgiven, Kolyah."

Chapter Ten

Neither of the Berkovich girls had returned to Hebrew class since the day Liba wept so bitterly in Havah's arms. *What can her parents be thinking? Little girls like Liba should be skipping rope and studying their lessons, not slaving in factories.*

"Let it go, Havaleh," Fruma Ya'el had said. "Don't you have enough of your own *tsuris* already?"

Try as she might, Havah could not forget the terror in the child's eyes. *Has her father beaten her...or worse?* Havah shuddered to think what that meant.

Holding her handkerchief over her mouth and nose did not block the stench of McClure Flats. Havah linked her free arm with Lev's and limped beside him, careful to step over or around puddles caused by last night's rain. From the smell, she doubted that they were filled with water only.

They passed a row of brick hovels with lean-tos serving as porches. Some had tin roofs, while others were covered with scraps of lumber or oilcloth. Everywhere Havah turned she saw unkempt children whose noses leaked slimy trails to their lips.

A woman with pock-marked cheeks and sunken eyes sat beside a shanty. Her blouse hung open so her toddler could suckle from her shriveled breast.

A little girl chased a small animal crying, *"Kit-kat! Kit-kat!"*

The creature scurried under Havah's skirts before disappearing between the cracks of a dilapidated wall. The ground swerved beneath her when she realized it was neither cat nor dog, but a large rat.

Lev's arm tightened around hers. "Let's go home, Auntie. If you get sick, Uncle Arel will blame me."

"I have to see the Berkoviches and talk some sense into them."

"Do you even know which shack is theirs, Aunt Havah?"

They had not gone much farther when Liba, wearing a kerchief over her dark blonde hair and a stained smock, emerged from the closest dwelling. "Miss Havah? What are you doing here?"

She drew Havah into a crushing embrace. A bruise ringed one of her swollen eyes. She flinched and jerked back when Havah touched it.

"What happened, Liba?"

"I'm such a klutz. I...I fell in...in the bathhouse. It's slippery."

Lev scowled. "My mama used to have those kinds of accidents, too."

Havah's pulse thudded against her temples. "Where are your parents?"

"Please don't come in. I haven't made the beds and—" Liba stumbled backward when a man with a grizzled beard and greasy hair yanked her arm.

"Get back to your chores." He glowered at Havah. "This must be the cripple who fills my daughters' heads full of *mishegoss* about women scholars."

Writhing in his clutches, Liba gasped. "Papa!"

Despite the fear swirling in her stomach, Havah used her most authoritative tone. "Reb Berkovich, let go of that child."

"Who's going to make me?"

Lev doubled his fist and waved it under the older man's nose. "I am." Zalman Berkovich laughed, releasing Liba, who ran splashing through puddles as she went under a clothesline full of tattered garments.

He snarled and walked past her, splattering mud on her skirt. "Good day, *Froi* Gitterman."

"Let me break his face," whispered Lev.

Clenching her own fists, Havah entered the tenement. As her eyes adjusted to the dim light provided by the stove, gall burned her throat. The only furniture in the single room was two beds, a table and three chairs. Crusty dishes overflowed the sink in one corner that was hardly big enough to hold two at a time. The place reeked of stale booze and spoiled food.

In one of the beds, covered to her nose with a thin blanket, Malka shuddered and coughed. "Mama, is that you?"

Havah rushed to her and felt her hot forehead. "This child is burning up. Where *is* her mother?"

Zalman folded his arms. "She died in steerage, in her own filth, on the way to the 'Land of the Free.'" He spat on the floor, his bloodshot eyes boring through Havah. "*We* didn't have a rich goy to pay first class fare like *some* people. So go home, Princess, and mind your own business."

"Your daughter needs a doctor."

"Who's going to pay for him? *Kayn gelt.* No money."

"You made Liba quit school to go to work. What do you do with her salary? Drink it?"

Liba bent over a pot of soup at the stove. Zalman took her by the shoulders and shoved her toward Havah. Placing a knobbed hand on either side of Liba's stomach, he stretched her smock tight to show Havah the telltale bulge. "You see how the little tart has managed to avoid going to work."

"Mama, help me." Malka groaned and writhed on the bed. "I hurt."

Lev gathered her, blanket and all, into his arms and headed for the entrance.

Zalman chased him, shaking his fist. "Where do you think you're going with my kid?"

"To the hospital, you old *shtoob.*"

Havah followed them outside with Liba clinging to her, wailing, "Take me with you. Take me with you."

"Go, you little whore. Don't ever come back." Zalman kicked Liba's backside so hard she and Havah both tumbled into a puddle.

Blinking back angry tears, Havah struggled to stand. Muddy water dripped from Liba's hair into her swollen eye as she scrambled to her feet. "Hurry before Papa changes his mind."

True to Liba's prediction, they had not passed three houses when Zalman hollered, "Kidnappers! Somebody stop them!"

A crowd clustered along the dirt road watched in silence, ignoring his pleas for help. The child who had chased the rat waved. An old woman with rotted teeth blew Havah a kiss and cried, "Good health on your head, Angel."

***

In the emergency room a woman wearing a white coat over her simple brown dress took Malka from Lev. She laid her on a gurney and tossed the blanket into a garbage can. "Ugh. Fleas."

Havah had never seen such a tall woman. She would even tower over Ulrich. Placing her stethoscope's earpieces into her ears, the woman held the bell against Malka's bony chest.

Lev watched her every move. "Is it pneumonia or typhoid? What's her pulse? How high is her fever?"

Looking down at him the woman pursed her lips. "I'll have those answers for you in due time, 'doctor.'"

Exhausted and aching after the long trek from McClure Flats in wet clothes, Havah tried to find a comfortable position in a straight-backed chair. Her muddy hair hung around her face, stinking from the fetid water. She longed for a hot bath and a warm bed.

Liba sat erect in the next chair, hands folded in her lap and eyes fixed on her sister. "Is Malka going to die?"

"If the pneumonia doesn't kill her, malnutrition will." The woman frowned at Havah. "Are you her mother?"

Havah rose to the full extent of her four feet, eleven inches. "If I were her mother, she wouldn't be in such sorry condition. Is a doctor ever going to look at her, Nurse?"

"I am *Doctor* Eleanor Turnbull, Miss—?"

"*Mrs.* Havah Gitterman."

"The one and only?" Dr. Turnbull's expression softened. "Dr. Miklos holds you in highest regard. I'm his new partner."

Offering her hand, Havah noticed how grimy it was and crammed it into her coat pocket. "What about Malka?"

"I'm admitting her. She's a very sick little girl." Dr. Turnbull turned to Liba. "You're her sister? How old are you, sweetheart?"

Trying to hide her belly, Liba blushed and hung her head. "Twelve."

"Let's take a look at you." The doctor helped her up onto the treatment table. "Malnutrition can cause abnormal bloating, which is nothing to be ashamed of. You're a tad young for menses."

"The baby, he kicks inside of me night and day."

Dr. Turnbull's brow furrowed as she pressed her stethoscope against Liba's stomach. "When was the last time you...how do I put this...bled into your bloomers?"

Liba wove the folds of her skirt between her fingers. "You know about it? I didn't tell anybody. It only happened once, honest. It was September, I think."

"A baby having a baby." The doctor clucked her tongue. "She's at least six months along. The boy who did this to you should be hung from the highest tree. Where is he?"

Cupping her hands around the doctor's ear, Liba whispered something Havah could not make out. Dr. Turnbull's lips turned white. "Sweet merciful God in heaven!"

***

Havah woke from a nightmare with a start. Blinking open her eyes, she rose on her elbows and surveyed her surroundings. Besides hers, there were three other iron-framed beds in the hospital room. Despite the antiseptic odors, Havah relished the feel of clean sheets.

After she sent Lev home in a taxi, Dr. Turnbull had ordered Havah and Liba out of their wet clothes. Once they had bathed, she provided them with gowns.

"They'll never make the pages of *Harper's Bazaar*, but they're warm and dry," she said. "I can't have two more pneumonia patients on my hands. I'm a firm believer in preventive medicine."

Dr. Turnbull sat on Malka's bed. She stroked the girl's hand and sang a soft lullaby. "Her fever broke an hour ago."

"Miss Havah?" Liba moaned and sat up. "My tummy hurts."

Deep concern replaced Dr. Turnbull's jubilant smile. "Does it hurt all the time or off and on?"

Lying back, the girl whimpered. "Off and on."

"I'm a midwife," said Havah, throwing off the covers. "Let me help."

"This is a hospital. I can't allow a nonprofessional—"

"He's coming!" Liba arched her back and screamed. "Miss Havah! Help me!"

"But in this case, I'll make an exception."

Dr. Turnbull left the room and, in less than five minutes, returned with two nurses and a gurney. She tossed a cap and an apron to Havah. As the nurses lifted Liba onto the wheeled cot, her water broke.

Chasing them down the hallway to the operating room, Havah tried to cover her hair with the cap. By the time she caught up, the baby's head had crowned. Liba squeezed Havah's wrist, and with a grunt followed by a shrill scream, pushed him out into the doctor's waiting hands.

Dr. Turnbull's face blanched. "Put her under, *now!*"

The nurse muffled a gasp as she placed an anesthetic mask over Liba's nose and mouth. Liba's eyes rolled back in her head and she went limp.

Once she cut the umbilical cord, the doctor wrapped the newborn in a blanket and handed him to Havah. "How could I allow her see this?"

As Havah opened the blanket, she choked. Although the tiny infant's features were perfect in every detail, he had no arms and his heart had formed outside of his chest. She counted eight valiant beats before it stilled.

***

"Papa, don't! Please don't!"

Malka's cries beside her woke Bayla. Shaking Malka, she whispered, "Malka, wake up."

"Where am I?" Malka sat up, rubbed her eyes and looked around.

"You're here in my bed, silly, with me and Miss Tova." Bayla turned on the lamp on the bed stand. "Don't you remember? Dr. Turnbull brought you here from the hospital yesterday insteaad of taking you home so you'd have a clean bed to sleep in."

Hugging her pillow, Malka burrowed her face in it. "It's so soft and smells nice."

"*Bubbe* puts cinnamon in her washing soap."

Lying back, Malka fingered Miss Tova's black curls. "She's pretty. Bayla, does your papa ever hit you?"

"Sometimes he spanks my bottom when I'm naughty."

"No, that's not what I mean. Does he ever punch you and make purple marks on you?"

"My first papa was mean, but he got killed when I was just born." Bayla sniffed and a tear rolled down her cheek. "My second papa in the old country, he was funny and made me laugh. No, he never hit me, not even soft. He...he died, too." She curled up beside Malka. "Poppy's nice, but he's sad and doesn't laugh much."

"My papa was always angry, even in the old country." Malka lowered her voice. "But when Mama died on the boat, he got really crazy mean." Her eyes widened and filled with fear. "Do you think God will punish me because I hate my own Papa?"

Malka's words made Bayla's stomach hurt. Although she missed Papa Gavrel and her big sister Leah, she remembered how much they loved her. Where she had always known kindness, poor Malka had only known cruelty.

Even though she was getting better, Malka still looked sickly and way too skinny. Bayla wanted to do something to make her friend happy. Smoothing Miss Tova's dress, Bayla kissed her porcelain face and laid her in the crook of Malka's arm.

"Miss Tova says she needs to stay with you, Malkie."

***

The morning after his daughter gave birth, police arrested Zalman Berkovich, charging him with neglect and assault. News of his incestuous relations with Liba ignited a firestorm in the Jewish community. Zalman's trial date was kept secret from the public to avoid any possible repercussions.

Guards escorted Havah to a chair in the courtroom. Malka, holding Miss Tova in the cradle of her elbow, huddled against Nettie Weinberg in the next seat. Judge McCune, a wiry man with dark hair and a thick moustache, leaned back in his chair as Dr. Turnbull took the witness stand.

"It's my opinion as a physician, Your Honor, that Mr. Berkovich is psychopathic and certainly unfit to raise two young ladies. I shudder to think what would've happened to them had it not been for the intervention of Mrs. Gitterman and her son."

"Where is the older girl, now?" asked Judge McCune.

Dr. Turnbull cast a lethal glare on Zalman. "Liba Berkovich is still recuperating from an ordeal no twelve-year-old *child* should ever have to go through. She's in Mercy Hospital under my care."

From the other side of the courtroom, with chains around his wrists and ankles, Zalman glowered at Havah. Lev squeezed her hand and whispered. "I hope they stick the old bum in front of a firing squad."

After listening attentively to each testimony, the judge ordered Zalman to approach the bench. "I cannot think of a more heinous crime than a father impregnating his own daughter. I should sentence you to the penitentiary for life, but, because I believe you to be in an irrational state, I'm ordering you to the Osawatomie State Treatment Asylum for a period of no less than twenty years."

As the two guards led Zalman through the courtroom doors, he spewed venomous epithets at Havah. "You've not heard the last of this, Princess. You miserable busybody!"

In the ensuing hush, Nettie made her way to the bench with her newborn son asleep in one arm and Malka clinging to her free hand. "What will happen to these precious children, Your Honor?"

"Unless there's a better option, I'll assign them to a children's home, Madame," said Judge McCune.

"I have a better option."

He winked at Malka. "Do you now?"

Chapter Eleven

Havah admired Daniel Kaminsky who, like her, had lost his parents in a pogrom in Warsaw when he was only in his teens. Being a resourceful boy, he earned enough money to pay his way to America by sweeping floors, chopping wood...and picking a few pockets. With only the threadbare clothes on his back and the worn shoes on his feet, he hitchhiked from New York to Kansas City. In twenty-five years, he had built a thriving grocery business. The children loved Daniel, for he filled them with penny candy and stories.

He unscrewed the lid to a jar of red and white candy. "You're coming to Rosie's wedding tonight, yes?"

Havah took a peppermint stick. "I wouldn't miss it."

"It's going to be a magnificent affair. You know my Carla and her love of parties. She and her buddy Zelda have been sewing, cooking, and planning for a month. Nothing like weddings in the old country, eh, Havah? In those days, we were lucky if we got piece of herring and a slice of dry bread."

"Were you really poor, Mr. Kaminsky?" asked Bayla.

"Was I poor?" He handed her a licorice stick and slipped another into Reuven's pocket. "I was so poor I couldn't afford to pay a compliment." The grocer adjusted his skewed *yarmulke* on his thick auburn hair. "And so hungry, oy, I was hungry enough to...to eat ham."

"How do you spell compliment, Mama?" Taking his pencil from over his ear like a newspaper reporter, Reuven opened his journal, which he kept under his arm in case of sudden inspiration. Mr. Kaminsky never disappointed. "You wouldn't really eat pig meat, would you?"

"Who cares from Kosher when you're starving to death? I would've eaten your Rachel's puppy." Daniel took a dented tin from under his cash register. "If it hadn't been for this, I'd still be penniless or in the penitentiary."

"Oh, this oughta be good." Reuven grinned. "Tell me more."

Obviously pleased to have an audience, Daniel continued, his eyes gleaming windows to the past. "There I was, ready to take it from the shelf when a hand grabs mine. Like a vise, it was. I thought my wrist would break."

"Was it a policeman?" asked Bayla.

"No, Princess, it was none other than grocery owner, Harry Kaminsky of blessed memory. Instead of throwing my scrawny *tokhes* in the clink he adopted me." Daniel dabbed his cheeks with the hem of his apron. He scooped flour onto the pan of his scale and poured it into a sack. "Five pounds exactly. Eighteen cents. For the candy, no charge."

***

Candles held by guests illuminated Daniel and Carla Kaminsky's great room that had been cleared for the wedding. Everyone circled the bride and groom beneath the canopy made of a prayer shawl tied to four poles. Rose's face shone under her lace veil as young Dr. Miller slipped a gold band on her right index finger that she would switch to her left ring finger later. The affection in the young man's eyes was evident. No old country *shadchan* had arranged this marriage.

Surveying the crowded room, Havah noticed a well-dressed man she did not recognize. From stalwart forehead to majestic chin, his face had the appearance of chiseled marble. Head erect, he peered at her with shadowy eyes and his square jaw tightened. He nodded and returned his piercing glare to the ceremony.

She nudged Arel. "Who is he?"

"Don't you know? That's Judge William H. Wallace himself."

Switching to Yiddish, she asked, "Didn't he indict Mr. Kaminsky for selling an apple, God forbid, on Sunday? Why on earth would he invite such a *shreklekh*?"

"To heap coals of fire on his head." Itzak situated his violin, his brown eyes twinkling. "You're a learned woman, Havah, think about it. Doesn't the Holy Book say, 'If your enemy is hungry, give him bread—in this case, wedding cake—to eat'?"

Havah cast a sidelong glance at Judge Wallace. "Burning coals should descend on him and burn his evil head off."

Cheers went up from the guests as Dr. Miller crushed the wine glass under his foot to signify the shattering of a wall and the uniting of two souls.

Daniel raised a silver cup. "Please share our joy as our Rose is now clipped from our parental stem and given in matrimony to *Doctor* Abraham Miller. May he always keep her freshly watered. *Omayn!*" He took a sip and handed it to the closest guest.

Each one drank from the cup and spoke a blessing over the happy couple until it reached Judge Wallace who refused to even touch it. His high-boned cheeks flushed. "I...I've an important engagement to attend. If you all will excuse me..."

Without another word, he made his way to the door and took his hat from the hall tree. In the hush that fell, Havah's ire boiled in her chest. She hurried through the wide berth left in his wake and followed him outside. Supporting herself with her cane, she half-hopped, half-ran along the sidewalk to catch up to him.

"Your Honor, might I have a word with you?"

He stopped abruptly, turned, and gave his head a curt nod. "Madame?"

Clutching her cane, she squared her shoulders. "Who do you think you are?"

"I beg your pardon?"

"Do you fancy yourself to be God? The Messiah?"

"I'll not stand and listen to such blasphemy."

"My father was a rabbi. May the Almighty strike me dead if I speak one false word."

The judge's jaw rippled and his nostrils flared. "Go on."

"You are the rudest man I've ever had the displeasure of meeting. I can't believe you would insult such a kind man as Mr. Kaminsky. Why? Because he's Jewish?"

"Listen here, young woman, I'm a good Christian and I'm bound to uphold the law of the land."

"No, *you* listen." Havah raised her cane and shook it under his nose. "So called good Christians robbed me of my legs, murdered my family and slaughtered babies before my eyes. You, Mr. Honored Judge, are no better than the Cossacks in Russia who, as you say, 'upheld the law of the land.'"

Chapter Twelve

The Shubert theater stage came alive with George Weinberg's Yiddish production, titled *Aster di Malki,* in English, *Esther the Queen.*

"I'm so glad Judge Wallace changed his mind," said Shayndel. "After the way he acted at Rosie Miller's wedding, I didn't think he would."

"I have a sneaking suspicion I know what changed it." Arel squeezed Havah's knee. "Or rather, who. You really should've been Esther. Everyone knows you're the true queen."

Smiling inwardly, Havah shrugged her shoulders. "Maybe he had a change of heart, that's all."

"According to an article in the paper, he stipulated that he'd never again have such a change of heart concerning Jews in the theater on Sunday. But to be fair, even to one as unfair as the judge, it's not just us. Some local theater managers sent a petition against him to the Supreme Court."

Shayndel tapped Havah's shoulder. "The moment we've been waiting for. The grand finale."

One by one, the cast members walked out onto the stage. George, who had portrayed wicked Haman as a bumbling buffoon, swept off his three-cornered hat and curtsied. With a triumphant smile, he turned a summersault, jumped to his feet and skipped off the stage.

Havah clapped her hands. "I didn't know George was so agile. He's kind of...um...chubby."

In the seat in front of her, Malka giggled. "Dad's funny, isn't he, Mommy?"

Nettie winked at Havah. "It's a good thing we have plenty of liniment in the medicine cabinet."

Two stagehands pushed a grand piano to the center of the platform. Havah grinned at the Dietrichs and Derevenkos in the row behind her.

Vasily, sitting between Nikolai and Lev, leaned forward and squinted.

Nikolai took off his spectacles and handed them to Vasily. "Care to borrow these, *Solnyshko?*"

"I don't need glasses, Tatko." Vasily put them on and frowned. "On the other hand…"

"I thought so, you've been squinting an awful lot. The next Rembrandt needs his eyes to be in proper working order." Nikolai lifted his eyeglasses from his son's nose and put them back on.

Catherine fluttered her fan. "It was a lovely play, even if I didn't understand a single word of it. I wish I spoke Yiddish like the rest of you."

"You'll have no trouble understanding this part, my firebrand." Ulrich pointed to the stage. "Here come our star pupils, Kolyah."

Nikolai grinned. "Mendel's worked very hard. He could teach my conservatory students a thing or two."

Rachel and Mendel walked out on stage, hand in hand. In her new frock trimmed with white lace, Rachel was the epitome of fashion. Mendel looked almost grown up in his tuxedo with long pants. Evron's clarinet, in Mendel's free hand, shone like new.

He led Rachel to the piano and helped her climb onto a stack of books on the bench. Dark corkscrew curls framed her face offset by a huge pink bow. Once situated, she poised her hands over the keys.

Catherine leaned forward. "She looks so teeny next to that huge beast of piano, doesn't she?"

Ulrich beamed. "Just watch my little virtuoso tame that beast."

After he moistened the clarinet reed with his tongue, Mendel wreathed his lips around the mouthpiece and played the first few bars of '*Khosid Dance.*' The corners of his mouth turned upward as he swayed to the music.

Rachel joined in, her hands a blur on the keys, her curls bouncing in time. Some people clapped their hands to the beat while others danced in the aisles. As the children brought the music to a rousing conclusion, Rachel threw her hands in the air and yelled, "Hey!"

The audience exploded in thunderous applause.

***

With no streetlight outside her bedroom window, nights seemed darker than ever for Havah. She longed for her upstairs room. Most of all, she missed tucking her children into bed at night. Although she and Arel assembled them for nightly prayers and story time, it was not the same as watching them drift off in their beds.

Snuggling against Arel's back, she counted the stars over her neighbor's roof. "Mendel looks like his uncle when he plays that clarinet, doesn't he? Evron would be so proud."

Arel grunted, but made no reply.

"When Rachel and Mendel played tonight couldn't you see Ruth and Rukhel skipping and giggling? How those twins loved to dance! Two heads, one heart, Mama used to say. I used to have trouble telling them apart, didn't you? I can just see Katya with Baby Velvil on her lap—"

"Enough!" Arel rolled over, his breath hot on her face. "What good does it do to talk about them? Evron and Katya are *dead* and so are their children. Tend to the living, Havah. I have six pairs of pants to alter in the morning. Let me sleep."

Chapter Thirteen

Drowsy from a sumptuous dinner, Havah settled back against the chair cushion. She felt like an empress as Catherine catered to her every whim.

"Nothing's too good for the birthday girl." Catherine flounced toward the swinging kitchen door. "Time for that special dessert."

Havah took a sip of wine and savored it before swallowing. "It's kind of nice to eat a meal without having to stop to mop up spilled tea or break up a fight."

"My wife needs to get out more," said Arel with a mischievous grin. "Did you notice how she tried to cut my steak?"

Catherine burst into the dining room carrying a cake. She placed it in front of Havah. Like the one she had decorated for Bayla's birthday, it dripped with flowers.

Havah dropped open her mouth. "Daffodils are my favorite. How did you know?"

"You might say a little Austrian bird told me. Oh dear. I forgot the cake knife." Catherine turned and disappeared through the kitchen door.

At the end of the table Ulrich raised his glass. "Happy birthday, Havah."

Through most of dinner, he had been unusually quiet and hardly ate. Earlier that afternoon, during Rachel's piano lesson, he seemed oddly withdrawn, too. A sudden fear gripped her. *He did say he had come from seeing Dr. Miklos. Did the doctor diagnose him with some grave illness?*

"Ulrich?" Her voice caught in her throat. "Is something…wrong?"

"Not exactly, but I've a favor to ask of you." His focus switched from her to Arel. "Of both of you, as Rachel's parents. If you say no, I'll understand, but it's an opportunity I'd like you to consider."

Havah took a deep breath and exhaled. "You're not ill then?"

"Ill? Me? *Ach!*" Ulrich smacked his forehead with his palm. "I suppose I have been acting rather strangely."

"Strange?" Catherine entered the room and cut into her creation. "Positively barmy is more like it." She laid the cake slices on dessert plates and put one at each place setting. "All because he's fretting over whether or not you'll let him take Rachel with us on his next tour."

Arel dropped his fork in his lap. "What?"

Catherine's freckles suddenly stood out like ink spots on white parchment. "I thought—you didn't—oh blast, I've gone and mucked things up, haven't I?" Covering her mouth with her hand, she rushed from the room.

"Please excuse me." Ulrich rose to follow her. Before he reached the door, he pivoted and returned to his chair. "This wasn't how I'd planned it, but now that the cat's out of the bag, let me explain."

Arel shoved his plate away and folded his arms across his chest. "Go on, *Herr* Dietrich, please do explain yourself and where you want to take *my* daughter."

Ulrich folded his hands. "*Herr* Gitterman, your daughter—"

"If she is indeed my daughter."

Springing up from her chair, Havah stamped her good foot. "Arel! How dare you?"

Arel's eyebrows knit into a fierce scowl. "We did all live in the same house—*Ulrichs* house—in Kishinev, how do I know?"

Lowering his voice, Ulrich leaned into him. "I'll take into consideration that you've had too much to drink and ignore your *indiscretion* this time."

Havah blinked to stem her angry tears. "Please, Ulrich, what were you saying about *Arel's* daughter?"

Ulrich's iridescent blue eyes pleaded with her. "She has a talent, a gift from God. It would be a sin not to share it with the world."

Returning his gaze, Havah sat. "What part of the world?"

"So far, my agent has lined up concerts in Frankfurt, Vienna and London, contingent on your permission, of course."

In sullen silence, Arel poured a glassful of wine and downed it in one gulp. Leaning forward with his elbow on the table, he rested his chin on his hand. All the while, he fixed his eyes, like cumulating storm clouds, on Ulrich.

"Arel, you saw her Sunday night." Ulrich wrung his hands. "She's a natural performer. They'll adore her."

"I've never been apart from her for more than a few days." Havah twirled the fringes of her shawl around her pinkie finger. "How long will you be gone?"

"Only three months, from June to August. You both have my solemn promise that I'll lay down my life for her if necessary."

"It won't be necessary, if she stays put," said Arel.

Ulrich took a folded sheet of paper from his inside jacket pocket and indicated a fountain pen on the table beside his plate. "I've drawn up a contract that states all of her earnings shall go into a trust fund for her college education."

"And if I refuse to sign?"

"She doesn't go."

Havah envisioned Rachel performing for the King of England. *What mother would not desire that for her daughter?* Pride surged through her.

She picked up the pen. "Arel, you know Ulrich and Catherine will take good care of her."

"Should you give permission," said Ulrich, "I plan to take out a life insurance policy on her."

Arel wrenched the pen from her hand. "A life insurance policy? You want me to trade *my little girl* for a life insurance policy?"

Havah stared at the stinging scratch on her hand. "Stop it, Arel."

"You don't see it, do you, Havah?" Color rose from his long neck to his forehead. "*Herr* Moneybags bought you in Kishinev and now he lays claim to Rachel. He pulls the purse strings and his pretty puppets perform." Arel doubled his fist and slammed it into his cake. "Insurance policy be damned!"

***

The clock on the mantel chimed twice. Ulrich shivered. The fire had dwindled to embers hours before. No matter how vigorously he played them, neither Mozart's "Turkish March," nor Scott Joplin's "Maple Leaf Rag," could blot out Arel's spiteful words.

He saw a flame out of the corner of his eye. "Did I wake you, Cate?"

"I couldn't sleep." Setting her oil lamp on the end table, she sank down on the bench beside him. "I feel so bad about…everything."

"It wasn't your fault, *liebling*. I don't think he would've reacted any differently if I'd broached the subject in a gentler manner. Something's agitating him. I only hope he won't take it out on Havah."

"Surely you don't think he would?"

"I've never known him to be a violent man," Ulrich hammered out the opening chords of "Nocturne in C Sharp

Minor," "but I've never seen that look in his eyes before either."

Catherine snuggled against him and placed her hand over his. "Ulrich, please come to bed."

His throat constricted and his head throbbed. "His accusations—"

"To tell the truth, dearest, I used to wonder..."

Ulrich stopped and pulled Catherine closer. "If I were Rachel's daddy?"

"She does have an amazing musical talent."

"Which has nothing to do with me. If Havah had been given the chance, she would've been a child prodigy herself. She was barely eighteen the first time she laid a finger on the piano and in six months she could play Chopin."

"You were in love with her, weren't you?"

"I confess I would've married her in a heartbeat, but I never stood a chance. Her heart belonged to Arel. He needs to wake up and see that it still does." Ulrich tucked his fingertips under Catherine's chin and raised her head. Her green eyes, almost yellow in the light, gleamed with unshed tears. "Now and forever, my heart belongs to you."

"Arel's allegation that you've purchased their souls is what's really vexing you, isn't it?" She pressed her cool palms against his enflamed cheeks. "It's pure tommyrot and he doesn't believe a word of it himself."

"You think not?"

"Not for the briefest moment."

"I've always been wealthy, Cate. For this I should apologize?"

***

A loud shriek woke Havah. Arel writhed beside her.

Havah grasped his shoulders and shook him. "Wake up."

Wresting from her hold, he smashed his fist into her face. "Never again, you child murdering bastard!"

Bursts of light flashed behind her eyes and she reeled backward. Her shoulders hit the floor with painful force. Stunned, she sprawled on her back, pressing her fingers against her throbbing cheek.

The overhead lamp went on and Arel knelt beside her. He choked as he pulled her hand from her cheek. "God in Heaven, what have I done?"

Chapter Fourteen

The Gittermans' front door opened and Fruma Ya'el greeted Ulrich like a long lost son. "Professor Dietrich, since when do you ring the doorbell? Come in."

A sense of relief flooding him, Ulrich stepped over the threshold. Before he could take off his hat, Kreplakh scampered to him with Rachel holding tight to her halter. He took a piece of last night's pot roast wrapped in waxed paper from his pocket. The dog sat up on her hind legs and waited for him to unwrap it. As he held it out to her, she took it in her mouth. Her soft muzzle tickled his palm.

"You spoil that little beast," said Fruma Ya'el. "She eats too much as it is."

"*Bubbe* should know." Rachel scratched the dog's floppy ear. "She just fed her a whole bowl of scrambled eggs for lunch."

Like a little girl caught rummaging through her mother's jewelry box, Fruma Ya'el's cheeks flushed. Her good-natured smile with slight overbite and small gap between her front teeth always put Ulrich at ease. Still attractive in her late fifties, he had no doubt she had been a ravishing young woman.

The yeasty fragrance of fresh bread hung in the air. Ulrich breathed it in. "Ah, Havah's baking her famous *holla*."

"Today, *I'm* the baker. It must be ready to take out of the oven." She took an envelope from her pocket and handed it to him with a worried frown. "Havah's napping, but said to give this to you."Fruma Ya'el turned and headed to the kitchen.

Heart pounding, Ulrich slipped the contract from the envelope and unfolded it. As he had hoped, Arel's signature scrawled across the bottom of the page, followed by Havah's almost decorative one.

Rachel climbed up on the piano bench. "Lesson time, Uncle Uri."

"As you wish, your majesty." Ulrich hung his hat and coat on the hall tree and sat beside her. "One of these days you'll be giving me lessons, Rukhel Shvester."

With an impish grin, Rachel placed her hands on the keys. "And for your first lesson, we must practice our scales. Middle C is where it all begins, right?" Without waiting for an answer, Rachel ran her fingers up and down the keyboard, singing, "C, D, E, F, G, A, B, C." She stopped, her smile diminished and she cocked her head to one side. "Can we play Chopin for Mommy? She doesn't feel good."

Ulrich looked up to see Havah. For Rachel's sake, he squelched the expletives rushing to his lips. Her unpinned hair could not hide her eye, almost swollen shut, or the deep purple bruise on her paste-white cheek.

With obvious discomfort, she eased down on the sofa. "Play something pretty, Rachel."

"Don't be sad, Mommy." A tear trickled from Rachel's eye. "Listen to me play your favorite."

The child's depth of perception never ceased to amaze Ulrich. No one was more in tune with Havah. Perhaps separating them, even for three months, would be a grievous mistake.

After the hour's lesson that consisted of pieces by Chopin, Mozart, and one by Brahms, Ulrich kissed the top of Rachel's head. "*Wunderbar,* my little Beethoven."

"I can't be Beethoven. He was deaf not blind." She slipped off the bench and caught hold of the dog's halter. Kreplakh yawned and stood, her tail thumping the bench legs. "Mommy, may we go outside to play?"

Lying on the sofa, eyes closed, Havah murmured her permission. Once he was certain the child was out of earshot, Ulrich knelt beside her. "Did Arel do this to you?"

Havah opened her good eye and sat up. "Yes."

Ulrich's stomach knotted as he sat beside her. "Did you call the police?"

"He didn't mean to hit me."

"Don't make excuses for him. How could he not mean to?"

"He was asleep."

Visions of Havah cowering in the shadow of Arel's unprecedented rage the other night rushed to Ulrich's mind. "Are you sure?"

Chapter Fifteen

Sitting on the porch swing, Havah watched white wisps of clouds against bright blue. She drank in the fragrance of hyacinths and looked out on her front yard. Daffodils, like maidens with yellow bonnets, circled a young oak tree. Next door, in Shayndel's yard, a matching tree boasted early spring buds. Instead of daffodils, purple crocuses made a ring around it. Havah remembered the day she and Shayndel had planted the trees.

"I'm home at last," said Havah as they pressed the last scoop of moist dirt around her tree.

Shayndel entwined her fingers between Havah's. "We're home at last."

By the following week, both of them had given birth. Elliott squalled his way into the world on a Friday night and Rachel made her appearance hours later.

In four years, the trees had grown taller than the children.

Havah closed her eyes and allowed the gentle breeze to lull her to sleep. Beethoven's "Für Elise" wafted through the open window behind her where Rachel practiced at the piano in the front corner of the living room.

***

"Mind if we join you?"

Shielding her eyes from the sun, Havah looked up to see Shayndel with Tikvah on her hip. Both of their heads shone like spun gold. Shayndel sank down on the swing and sat the child on Havah's lap. "It's just us girls this morning. Itzak took Elliot with him on a cabinet delivery."

The music stopped and Rachel came out the front door, holding Kreplakh's harness. "*Al fin.* That's music talk for 'finished.' Hi, Auntie Shay. Did you come to my house to play?"

Kreplakh sat on her haunches as Shayndel patted her head. Tikvah slid off Havah's lap and wrapped her plump arms around the dog's neck. Rachel reached out and took her cousin's hand. "*Bubbe*'s baking a cake. Let's go see if we can lick the spoon."

Havah watched the dog lead the girls back into the house. "It's going to be awfully quiet without her."

"What a clever child she is," said Shayndel. "I can't believe she and Elliott are the same age. He makes motorcar noises and she's already making rhymes. But quiet? You still have three other kids at home." She touched Havah's cheek with her fingertip. "It looks better. Does Arel know you're with child?"

***

Exhausted from retching into the commode half the night, Havah whispered a prayer of thanksgiving for the miracle of indoor plumbing. She imagined how it must have been for her mother. Perhaps Miriam had not been so ill during her times. Havah hoped not. Even though she had been gone nine years, Havah could not bear the thought of her mother suffering.

After washing her face, she padded to the kitchen to fix a cup of tea to settle her stomach. She watched the crescent moon through the window over the sink as she filled the kettle with water. When she turned to put it on the stove, she saw Arel hunched over the table. His head rested on his folded arms with only the unscathed side of his face visible.

She limped to him and bent to kiss his cheek. "Arel, my beloved. Please come to bed."

He raised his head. "'You are altogether lovely, my sister, my bride.'" Cupping his hand around her face, he leaned in for a passionate kiss. Then he pulled back. "What if I should strike you again? Or worse, injure our child? No, Havaleh. You're better off without me."

Chapter Sixteen

Although she reminded herself that Dr. Florin had seen worse than her misshapen foot, it still embarrassed Havah when he examined it.

"It's so early in the morning. I wish Mama hadn't called you," whispered Havah.

"Nonsense. It so happens I was going to bring my new partner by to meet the rest of the Gittermans." Dr. Florin turned to Dr. Turnbull. "You see what I mean?" His touch tickled as his fingers followed Havah's scars. "Fruma Ya'el did a masterful job."

Dr. Turnbull laid a gentle hand on Havah's enflamed leg. "I wouldn't be surprised to hear that she had some professional training."

"I did." Fruma Ya'el entered the room carrying a tray with hot compresses and a plate of dry toast. "Many years ago, a young doctor named Charles Rosenthal came to Svechka and filled my girlish *kopf* with dreams. He promised if I'd marry him, he'd take me to America and send me to medical school."

"Why didn't you?" Dr. Turnbull applied the compresses to Havah's painful shins. "He was certainly correct about your aptitude."

"We were almost betrothed when my sister and I had a wagon accident." Raw pain filled Fruma Ya'el's eyes. "She fell under the horse's hooves and died of her wounds later that night. Her husband Hershel went crazy and blamed Charlie for her death."

"I don't understand. How did that stop you from marrying Dr. Rosenthal?"

"Hershel went to my grief-stricken father and demanded my hand. My punishment for living, I suppose."

Havah could almost hear Dr. Turnbull's teeth grind. "And your father agreed?"

"Perhaps Papa saw it as a way to keep me from moving away. I don't know. Within a month, I married Hershel Levine and my heartbroken Charlie left forever."

"That's awful!"

"It's true that not all that comes from a cow is butter, Doctor, but I learned to love Hershel, and I think, in the end, he cared for me. He was a good father, and when Hershel passed away, Yussel proposed. I've had a good life with three beautiful children, two from my womb and one from my heart."

A flutter, like butterfly wings, just above her hip startled Havah. She pointed to the spot. "My baby is kicking."

"You're only three months along according to our calculations." Dr. Turnbull stuck the earpieces of her stethoscope in her ears and pressed the bell against Havah's lower left side. "It's a bit early for you to feel it, but as tiny as you are, it's not impossible." After a few moments, she grinned. "That's one strong heartbeat."

Rachel, still in her nightgown, entered the room, holding tight to Kreplakh's harness. "May I listen, too?"

"This must be the little pianist I've heard so much about." Dr. Turnbull held out her hand until Rachel found it. Sitting the child on her lap, the doctor stuck the earpieces in Rachel's ears. "Tell me what you hear."

"Thumpty-thump-thump-thump." Rachel cocked her head to one side and guided Dr. Turnbull's hand so she held the bell against Rachel's chest. "Thumpa-thumpa-thump. Mine's not as fast as the baby's is it?"

"You have a very bright daughter, Mrs. Gitterman."

"Please call me, Havah."

"Only if you call me Eleanor."

"*Doctor* Eleanor then. Even in this so-called free country, men still expect women to be housemaids and mothers. You deserve to be addressed with respect."

The doctor put her stethoscope aside, opened her bag, and took out an instrument Havah recognized. Dr. Florin had used one when he gave them the sad news about Rachel's blindness.

"Would you mind if I examined her eyes? There are new advances being made every day." Dr. Eleanor gave the instrument to Rachel so she could feel it. "This is an ophthalmoscope. It has mirrors, and when I hold it in front of the light, I can see right inside those pretty brown eyes of yours."

Rachel rolled it around in her hands and held to her nose. "It feels like a lollipop, but smells like Poppy's watch."

Taking it from her, Dr. Eleanor held it up to Rachel's eye. She looked through the center at one eye and then the other. "Florin Miklos. Why didn't you tell me?"

Dr. Florin laughed aloud and winked at Havah. "I wanted you to see for yourself, Doctor." He took a peppermint stick from his pocket and handed it to Rachel.

Before the girl could take one lick, Fruma Ya'el nabbed it and stuffed it into her apron pocket. "Breakfast first, Rukhel Shvester."

The smell of onions and coffee caused Havah's empty stomach to growl and roil at the same time. "Ugh. I hate this part." She munched on the toast Fruma Ya'el had left on the bed table. After a few bites, Havah kicked off the compresses, grabbed her cane and hobbled as fast as she could to the toilet.

***

Havah brushed her fingertips across the eagle's head adorning the handle of her cane; the rest of which was embellished with flowered vines twining around it from top to bottom. Had Itzak not made it for the specific purpose of helping her walk, she would be tempted to put it on display. Many times she noticed strangers admiring it rather than pointing out her infirmity. *"Solid oak like our Havah," said Itzak when he presented it to her in Kishinev.*

Dr. Florin took the cane and handed it to Dr. Eleanor. "When it comes to woodcarving, Itzak Abromovich has no equal."

Sitting in the rocking chair beside Havah's bed, Dr. Eleanor laid the cane across her knees and rolled it over to inspect every detail. "I've never seen anything quite like it. This is certainly not going to break under anyone's weight, although you don't have much weight to speak of, Havah."

"It's not doing me much good these days, is it?" Havah settled back against the pillows and tried to swallow mortified sobs. "I can't even make it to the water closet without stumbling and throwing up all over the floor."

"We're going to have to face it. It's getting worse." A sad frown shadowed Dr. Florin's brow. "Eleanor, are you familiar with Dr. Silas Mitchell and his papers on Causalgia—nerve injury?"

"I'm better than familiar," said Dr. Eleanor. "My father worked with him during the Civil War. Brilliant doctor, but a bit of an old coot."

"I'm going to have to stay in bed until my baby's born like Nettie, aren't I?"

"I should say not!" Dr. Eleanor scowled and thumped the cane on the floor. "No woman should be confined if it's not necessary. Surely you don't ascribe to Dr. Mitchell's 'neurasthenia rest cure,' which is merely a means of keeping a woman shackled to her bed, completely isolated with no means of stimulation." Dr. Eleanor waved the cane, missing Dr. Florin's head by inches. "Promise me you won't do that to Havah unless it's absolutely necessary."

"Of course not. No indeed." Dr. Florin ducked. Plucking the cane from Dr. Eleanor's hand, he turned back to Havah and laid it on the bed. "The truth is that complete bedrest could be necessary. Your health was severely compromised. A bad fall could be devastating to you and the little one. So, for the time being, I'm prescribing a wheelchair. You'll still be able to go on outings…"

He continued his cheerful speech, but the only words she heard were, *"Wheelchair…helpless… wheelchair… feeble… wheelchair…cripple."*

Chapter Seventeen

Florin's neck ached and his feet throbbed. It had been a never-ending day with one emergency after another. Having a partner he could trust did make things easier. While he made house calls, Eleanor handled the office appointments.

The sun had set and night had fallen. Steering his automobile around the corner, he looked forward to a chicken sandwich on fresh-baked sourdough bread, a gift from a grateful patient, a frosty beer, and sleep. When he pulled in front of the clinic, a new sign greeted him. Under the porch light, skillfully hand-painted, it read, "Dr. F. D. Miklos and Dr. E. W. Turnbull."

He parked the car, slid out, and made his way to the porch. Opening the door, he scratched his head as he looked around the waiting room. He peeked outside and reread the sign. "I guess I'm in the right place."

Eleanor took his hat and hung it on a hook by the door. "Welcome to our new office."

Crisp curtains, ruffled and bleached white, adorned the windows. A basket of toys sat in one corner. End tables had been stacked with books and periodicals.

Two framed paintings hung on the walls. One was a picture of a vase with purple and yellow flowers, and the other was of a young mother with a little girl on her lap. They bore a striking resemblance to Havah and Rachel. Florin read the signature in the right-hand corner. "V. Derevenko."

"He's a very talented young man." Eleanor led the way up the stairs that went from the office to his apartment. "And he's quite taken with Havah, isn't he?"

"If I were twenty years younger, I would be too, Eleanor. I thought you'd have gone home by now. From the looks of my waiting room, I'd say you've been quite busy."

"Oxana helped. It's more inviting, don't you think?"

"Indeed."

"After supper, I'll show you how I've reorganized the clinic."

"You didn't have to do—"

"I wanted to. Besides, I only had four patients the whole day. Actually, there were a few more…but they said they'd come back when the 'real doctor' was in." Her mouth twisted and her eyes narrowed. She spun on her heel. "I made beef stew. Let's eat while it's still hot."

He followed her to the kitchen. "You'll prove to them what a fine physician—"

"How can I prove anything if they won't allow me do what I've been trained for?"

"Give it time, Doctor. People were skeptical of me at first. Kansas City gentry didn't 'cotton to no foreigner' treating them."

"You mimic the Kansas twang very well." She lit two candles on the small wooden table and then shut off the overhead light. After ladling two bowls full, she set one in front of him and sat down. "I've never heard it with a Romanian accent before."

"Candles? A fine dinner? What's the occasion?"

"I find candlelight aids with digestion." Her hair and eyes shone like satin and stars. "And I detest incandescent lights." Her low-pitched voice, pleasant as gentle rain after a long drought, soothed him. "Do you like the stew?"

"It's delicious. The most delicious stew I've ever tasted."

"Liar. You haven't taken a single bite."

He hoped the flames obscured the crimson heat rising to his cheeks as he brought a spoonful to his lips and swallowed the mixture of beef, onions and string beans. "Mmmmm."

"It's my mother's recipe. It has a little bit of everything: meat, potatoes and plenty of vegetables. She was a nurse, and she used to remind Father that a good doctor took care of himself first. There's plenty. It'll keep for a few days in the ice box."

"Is your mother—?"

"She passed away when I was ten. Childbirth. My brother came breech. His oxygen supply was cut off so he didn't make it either."

"Eleanor, have you ever performed a Caesarean section?"

"Not I. Too risky."

"I've witnessed three. All of them were successfully performed by Nikolai Derevenko."

"Oxana's husband? Isn't he a musician?"

"Musician? Ha! Those hands—don't get me started on that subject." Florin's spoon clanked on the edge of his bowl. "When Ulrich's first wife, Valerica, died in childbirth, God rest her sweet soul, Nikolai was devastated. Yes, he took it personally. So he dedicated himself to learning the procedure. He's meticulous."

"Admirable traits for a surgeon." Eleanor laid her hand over Florin's. "Why'd he quit?"

"He lost friends in the pogrom in Odessa two years ago. Despite his best efforts—"

"He couldn't save them. Where do we doctors get the idea that we're supposed to be gods? Father said every man has his breaking point. During the Civil War, he saw more than one doctor quit or go mad as a result of the carnage."

"Tell me, Eleanor—"

"Why did I become a doctor? It's all I ever wanted to be."

"Actually, I was going to ask if there's a man in your life."

"There was once." She pushed her empty bowl aside. "We met in medical school. But he—"

"His ego was too fragile to bear up under a relationship with a woman who was his equal or, worse, his better."

"How did you know?"

"I'm a man."

Chapter Eighteen

"*Unglaublich!*" Ulrich dropped the earpiece onto its hook and slammed the candlestick telephone down amid the papers on his desk, sending them in all directions. "Outrageous. Unbelievable."

"Ouch!" Catherine dropped her sewing. She popped her index finger into her mouth and held it out for him to see. "Please don't yell when I've a sharp needle in my hand. Look what you made me do."

Oxana, busily stitching beside her on the love seat, grinned. "At least the material is red so the blood she won't show."

After he tossed his renegade documents back on the desk, Ulrich picked up the cushion Catherine had been working on. He poked the needle into it and set it on her lap.

Amused by Ulrich's fit of temper, Nikolai knelt to help him retrieve the rest of the scattered letters. "What's the matter, Ulrich?"

Sinking down on the piano bench, Ulrich rested his hands on the keys. "This Sunday's concert's off." He played "Marche Funèbre" as he spoke. "That was Mr. Woodward on the telephone. Francis McMillen, the violinist, telegraphed to say he couldn't endure the indignity of arrest."

"That's six hundred admissions Mr. Woodward will have to refund." Nikolai took off his spectacles and wiped them with his handkerchief. "Is it any wonder Judge Wallace has so many enemies?"

Ulrich rubbed his hands together. "So now we concentrate on our next concert for Vasily's commencement ceremony. Are you ready for that one, Kolyah?"

"Oh yes, he practice day and night." Oxana held up her embroidery. "And I make new blouse for the occasion."

Catherine leaped off the sofa and grabbed Oxana's hand. "I have the perfect lace trim for it. Come with me. Nikolai's dad is going to be positively enchanted with you."

Settling back in his chair, Nikolai linked his fingers behind his head and followed them with his eyes as they flounced from the room. "Are you sure this sudden Derevenko family reunion was really my father's idea, Ulrich?"

"Care to see the telegram?" Ulrich went back to his desk and rifled through the pile of papers. "It was here this morning. Perhaps it fell underneath."

"Forget about it, I'm pretty sure I know where it went." Nikolai dismantled his flute and set the sections in the case. "At least Tatko should be happy that I've come to my musical senses, as he's so often put it."

Taking a decanter from the table in front of the fireplace, Ulrich poured two glasses of sherry. He sat in the chair across from Nikolai and held up his glass. "I propose a toast to the father and son reunion."

Nikolai raised his glass. "May it be painless and swift."

"Oxana's quite excited about meeting your father."

The sound of female laughter floated overhead. Nikolai gulped his sherry. His eyes watered and he coughed. "I hope she isn't disappointed."

"Have you ever told her about your brother?"

"Why should I?" Nikolai poured a second glass of sherry and downed it. "He's dead."

Chapter Nineteen

Arel tripped over a cracked tombstone that crumbled under his feet. Brambles with thorns snagged his nightshirt and slashed his ankles. Evron rose from an open grave and hollered curses.

Arel's own cries jolted him awake. Tumbling off the sofa, he dropped to his knees. The clock in the living room struck four. He tiptoed through the quiet house to the kitchen. To stave off the chill, he grabbed his coat from the hook by the back door and put it on over his nightshirt. As he stepped outside, the sound of singing and hammering rang out close by.

Wanting to remain close to his family, Itzak had built the small structure behind his house so he could run his business from home. So far, his Sunday money exchanges had escaped the notice of Judge Wallace and his henchmen.

Trudging through the wet grass, Arel wished he had remembered his shoes. Mud oozed between his toes and something skittered across his instep. He picked up his pace until he reached the shed and pulled open the roughhewn door.

"Daisy, Daisy, give me your answer do. I'm half crazy—speaking of crazy, look who's here!" Itzak peered over his hunched shoulder. "Can't you sleep either, little brother?"

"I had the most bizarre dream."

"You didn't slug Havah this time, did you?"

"You don't believe I did that in my sleep, do you?"

"As surly as you've been lately, let's say, I've had my doubts." Itzak pointed to a stool. "Sit."

"I've been that bad?"

"Do chickens have beaks?"

Arel shuddered and sat. "I'd rather lop off both my hands than harm her."

Easing himself into an oak chair with large and small wheels attached to each side, Itzak used his hands on the large ones to roll it across the floor. "I just finished putting the wheels on. Let's see how it works." He maneuvered it backward and in circles. "It should be easy for her to steer. Pretty nifty, eh? The design was Ulrich's idea."

"Of course." Arel's back stiffened. "Who else?"

"Along with a few suggestions from Catherine who, incidentally, went out of her way to find the fabric for the cushions."

Arel could not deny it was some of Itzak's finest work. The chair with its oval back and cushioned seat was almost an exact replica of the chairs in the Dietrichs' living room. Itzak embellished it with carvings of vines and flowers to match Havah's cane. To ensure her comfort, he had added padded armrests, a footrest, and designed it to recline to three different positions.

Shayndel's voice startled Arel as she stepped into the shed. "Itzak, do you have any idea what time it is?" She frowned. "I didn't know we had company."

"I had a nightmare," said Arel.

"Beat your wife again?"

Chapter Twenty

Itzak would never forget the winter of 1886. Brain fever, as he'd heard it called, swept through Svechka. No one left their homes. *Heder* classes had been cancelled indefinitely. The synagogue was dark and shuttered.

Papa, Itzak, and his older brother, Evron, had been spared, but Mama and their newborn sister had not.

One bleak morning, eight-year-old Itzak looked up into Evron's tearful eyes, black with sorrow. At nineteen going on twenty, he was almost an adult and Itzak's hero. It frightened him to see his brother cry.

"Little brother," Evron whispered as he knelt and embraced him, "the fever—Mama and the baby are gone."

Soon afterward, Itzak's papa told them that the rabbi's wife died. Although the rabbi recovered, the disease left him blind. For weeks he refused to leave his house. He would not even venture from his rocking chair.

"Rebbe Yussel's afraid to walk," said Evron one night over supper. "Perhaps it would help if he had a cane like Reb Shmuel, the blind beggar. Have you ever noticed how the old man uses it like feelers? It keeps him from running into things."

"Good idea," said Papa, who was the village carpenter. "I'll start on that in the morning."

"May I make it?" asked Itzak.

With Papa's guidance, Itzak had been carving animals from wood scraps. The prospect of making something useful for his rabbi made him happy, and happiness was something he had known little of since Mama died.

Itzak worked on the cane day and night for a week, stopping only to eat. The carving had to be perfect. Once he finished it, he sanded it smooth and varnished it.

The next day, anxious and excited, Itzak knocked on Reb Yussel's door. Shayndel let him in and led him to her father's darkened bedroom. He sat in a chair in the corner, hands folded in his lap.

"Rabbi? It's me. Itzak."

"What do you want?"

"I made a present for you."

"*Feh*! What need have I for presents I can't see?"

"It's a cane. To help you find your...your way. I carved a candle on it. Let me show you."

Reb Yussel smirked as Itzak put it in his hands. Standing, he scraped the cane along the floorboards. He took a halting step and another until he walked to the other side of the room. A slow smile spread his lips.

"Itzak, your candle has shined a light into my darkness."

Chapter Twenty-One

Resting his chin on his violin, Itzak doubted tonight would be cause for celebration. He drew his bow across the strings while fingering the chords. The fiddle's silken melody, coupled with the pulse of Ulrich's piano, and Nikolai's flute, filled the room. On cue, Mendel joined in.

Itzak glanced at the wheelchair in the corner behind Ulrich's desk. Covered with a bedsheet, no one seemed to notice its presence. Despite Yussel's encouragement, Itzak could not keep his apprehension at bay. *Will Havah say I've shone a light into her darkness?*

Presently, the ladies converged at one end of the expansive room. Like clucking hens, their heads bobbed as they shared mothering tips and gossip.

On the sofa, Catherine and Shayndel dwarfed Havah who sat between them. Unlike Shayndel, who blossomed like a healthy rose after conception, Havah had been ill for weeks. Her unborn, at a little over four months, had already thickened her waistline and thrown her off balance.

"May I have everyone's attention?" Lev rolled the covered wheelchair to the center of the room. "Uncle Itzak, the best woodcarver in Kansas City, probably the whole world, has a presentation to make."

Itzak whipped off the sheet and bowed. "Queen Havah, your chariot awaits."

Havah's wan cheeks colored and her mouth dropped open.

Itzak offered her his arm. "May I?"

Standing, she curved her hand around his elbow. Her tight-lipped silence hammered Itzak's temples as she lowered herself onto the chair. She brushed her hands over the red brocade padding on the armrests.

He went to his knees in front of her, unsure of what she might do or say next. "Forgive me, Havaleh. I had to do it."

"It's—it is—" She threw her arms around his neck and pressed her cheek against his. "—magnificent."

Chapter Twenty-Two

A festive air permeated the elementary school gymnasium, which doubled as an auditorium. Arel pushed Havah's wheelchair across the basketball boundary lines painted on the polished wooden floor. On Havah's lap, Rachel swayed and sang, "'Come away with me, Lucille, in my merry Oldsmobile...'"

Havah looked over her shoulder at Yussel. "Someone's been listening to Billy Murray records with her *Zaydeh*."

"'Down the road of life we'll fly, Automo-bubbling you and I...'" Rachel giggled. "That's my favorite part."

With concern clouding his grey eyes, Arel rubbed Havah's neck. "Are you sure you're okay?"

"Stop fussing over me."

Fruma Ya'el curved her hand through the crook of Yussel's arm. "It's huge, this school. Nothing like the tiny shack the boys went to in the old country."

"Maybe not," said Yussel, "but my boys learned without a lot of nonsense."

"Good thing we're early. The place is filling up fast." Arel rolled Havah to the eighth row and moved one of the folding chairs aside to make room for her wheelchair. "I hope you'll be able to see Reuven get his ribbon from here. The first six rows are reserved for the classes."

"Mrs. Gitterman, I'm so glad you're here." Miss Kline, dressed in a lacy white blouse and black skirt, made her way through the growing crowd and clasped Havah's hand. "Reuven told me that you're..." she lowered her voice "...in a family way and haven't been...well."

Miss Kline's sidelong glance behind her glasses did not escape Havah. Squeezing the teacher's hand, Havah smiled. "Isn't it the most beautiful wheelchair you've ever seen? My brother-in-law is an artist."

As if divested of a heavy weight, Miss Kline straightened. "He certainly is. In any event, I'm so pleased you could be here for Reuven's big night."

"A penmanship award is nothing to sneeze at," said Yussel as Miss Kline went to join her class in the fifth row. "But *this* makes it a big night?"

Shayndel and Itzak winked at Havah. While Reuven had been secretive about what, he had let it slip that he had a big surprise for them, "especially *Zaydeh*."

"Attention. May I have everyone's attention, please?" The principal walked out onto the stage and clanged a cow bell to hush the crowd. "Our Washington Elementary spring awards program is about to begin. Places everyone."

The audience rose and Havah's heart swelled as Reuven marched down the aisle carrying the American flag. Keeping his arms straight and his hands tight around the pole, he fixed his eyes on the flag. His hair, parted down the middle, was plastered down with Pomade. Despite his best efforts, a few unruly strands insisted on curling around his ears and forehead.

He ascended the stage steps and posted the flag in its stand. A uniformed gentleman with white hair and a handlebar moustache to match limped onto the platform, leaning heavily on his cane. He shook Reuven's hand. "Thank you, young man."

Havah nudged Arel and indicated a scar that went from the man's thick eyebrow to his chin. "I'll bet he got that in the American Civil War."

"Right you are, young lady," said a silver-haired woman who stood nearby. "That there's a genuine hero. He done took a minié ball in his leg, too. Major Frederick Porter, Eighteenth Indiana Calvary." She beamed. "Freddy ran off to join when he was jest sixteen."

"Are you his wife?"

"Nah. I'm his baby sister."

Turning toward the flag, Major Porter raised his right hand to his forehead in a salute. Beside him Reuven placed his right hand over his heart.

In an authoritative voice that resounded through the auditorium, Major Porter said, "All rise for the 'Pledge of Allegiance'."

Clutching Arel's arm, Havah struggled to her feet. He wrapped his arm around her waist. "We all understand if you sit for the pledge."

"As long as I am able I *will* stand."

The combined voices of men, women, and children reminded Havah of the sound of ocean waves and wind from the ship that had brought them to America. With visions of the Statue of Liberty at Ellis Island, she delighted in the words as she recited them. "'I pledge allegiance to my Flag and the Republic for which it stands, one nation, indivisible, with liberty and justice for all.'"

"You may be seated." Major Porter bowed to the audience, clasped Reuven's hand, and they slipped behind the curtain.

The principal returned to the stage. "The sixth grade choir will now sing 'My Country 'Tis of Thee' accompanied by our own Mary Beth Franklin on the piano."

A girl with two long braids secured by a jeweled comb at the nape of her neck strutted onto the stage. She curtsied and sat at the upright piano. While the students on risers behind her sang, Mary Beth picked out the notes, hitting some and missing others.

"Mommy, somebody needs piano lessons." Rachel held her hands over her ears and wrinkled her nose. "Ugh."

The odor of chewing tobacco assaulted Havah as a portly woman with a bleached pompadour leaned into Rachel. "I suppose you can do better, Missy."

"Yes, ma'am, but my name is Rachel."

"Rachel don't be rude," said Havah. "Apologize to Mrs. Franklin."

"I'm sorry your little girl doesn't play very good, Mrs. Franklin."

His lips quivering, Mr. Franklin curled his slender fingers around his wife's shoulder. "Now, Myrtle, little Rachel don't mean nothing." He winked at Havah. "She's just a baby."

With a sneer on her face, Mrs. Franklin fell back in her chair. "Blind little bat."

Havah muttered in Yiddish, clenching her hand into a fist. "If I weren't with child, I'd…"

The song came to a merciful end and the children filed off the stage. For the next forty minutes each teacher took center stage and handed out awards to their students for various achievements.

Once all the ribbons had been given out, Miss Kline walked out onto the stage, her narrow face aglow. Reuven stood beside her, wearing a gold medal on a lanyard around his neck, holding a brown folder.

She put her hand on his shoulder. "I asked the principal if we could save this moment for last. This year the Kansas City Board of Education sponsored a short story contest. Out of over two hundred entries at the elementary level, from first through sixth grade, my fifth-grade pupil Reuven Gitterman placed first. When he reads his story, I'm sure you'll agree the prize is well deserved." She stepped behind Reuven.

Opening his folder, Reuven cleared his throat. "This is a story about my grandfather when he was a little boy in

Svechka, Moldavia, where I was born. 'Suri's Heart' by Reuven Gitterman."

Havah glanced at Yussel who raised his trembling hand to his mouth. Reuven looked up from his paper and grinned. "Surprise, *Zaydeh*."

"Read already, little apple," said Yussel. "I'm tired of waiting."

Laughter rippled through the audience. Reuven blushed, licked his lips, and read aloud. "'Yosi, speak to me!' Papa pounded the table and spilled hot tea into Yosi's lap."

Reuven stopped reading to say, "Papa in the story is my great grandfather, Arel Gitterman. And Yosi is my grandfather when he was only five."

Yussel blew his nose into his handkerchief and his cheeks glistened with tears. Beside him, Fruma Ya'el sniffed and blotted her eyes on her sleeve.

Swallowing, Reuven continued to read in a clear voice.

"Even though his blistered legs hurt very badly Yosi clamped his lips together. Why should he speak? Had the Almighty listened to him when he begged him not to let Mama die? No! Not even one word.

"'Forgive me,' said Papa and picked him up.

"Yosi laid his head on Papa's chest and listened to his heartbeat that went ka-thump-thump.

"'Silence won't bring her back. If it would, I'd cut out my own tongue,' said Papa and set Yosi down. 'I have a Hanukkah surprise for you. It's only two nights away and I can't wait.'

"Papa opened his dresser drawer and took out a silver menorah that looked like a shiny tree with nine branches. Below the branches and above the trunk was an oval-shaped space. In the middle of it sat a pair of doves like two sweethearts. A vine with flowers twined around the trunk. On the bottom part of the oval Papa had engraved a verse from *Song of Songs*.

"'Go on, Son, read it. I know you can.'

"But Yosi wouldn't read.

"On the first night of Hanukkah, Papa lit the candles on the new menorah and chanted the blessings. His voice sounded flat and hollow. Dinner tasted like sand. The quiet settled like dust in the corners and made Yosi's ears hurt.

"The next morning, he smelled breakfast cooking and heard pots clattering. *But how can this be? Papa is still sound asleep.*

"Yosi threw off the blankets and ran to the kitchen where he saw a woman by the stove.

"She held out her arms. Her hair was long and black and her eyes were as gray as clouds. She was even more beautiful than he remembered.

"'Papa, Papa, Papa, come quick!' cried Yosi.

"'Yosi, you spoke!' Papa ran out of the bedroom and swept Yosi up into his arms and shouted, 'Adoshem, be thanked.'

"'Arel.' Mama's voice sounded like a song from heaven. 'My husband.'

"'Suri?' Papa dropped to his knees with surprise and Yosi toppled to the floor.

"She sat beside them and gathered Yosi onto her lap. 'Yes, my love.'

"'What cruel trick is this?' Papa's hands shook when he touched her cheeks. 'My Suri died.'

"Yosi wrapped his arms around her waist. She felt like Mama, warm and soft. She sounded like Mama. She even smelled like Mama. Who else could she be?

"He laid his head on her chest and listened. A melody, like tinkling bells and whispered prayers, was all he heard.

"'Where's your heart, Mama?' he asked.

"'Right here in my arms,' she said and brushed her hand across his legs. Like magic the blisters popped and melted like soap bubbles.

"For the next seven days, Papa and Yosi only went outside to visit the outhouse. Mama fried latkes every day. While Yosi and Papa did lessons after breakfast, Mama would sit in her rocking chair and knit from a big blue ball of yarn.

"On the last night of Hanukkah, Mama's face glowed, but her eyes were sad.

"'Goodnight, my Yosi, my heart,' she whispered and kissed him.

"The next morning, he skipped to the kitchen. Papa sat alone at the table polishing the menorah.

"Yosi blinked and rubbed his eyes. 'Where is Mama?'

"'She went back to the Garden of Eden.'

"'Was she really Mama or was she an angel?'

"'Papa wrapped a blue scarf around Yosi's neck and whispered, 'Yes.'"

***

Hours later, unable to sleep on the lumpy couch in the office, Arel sat at his desk and read Reuven's story a third time. How many versions of it had Arel heard growing up? The two pieces of his grandfather's menorah lay beside the lamp and taunted him.

Brushing his fingertip over the doves, he remembered Hanukkah 1899, the year his carefully mapped out destiny took a detour; the night he met Havah Cohen. Up until then, he considered his future sealed. He would marry Gittel. His father and Hershel Levine had signed the betrothal agreement years before when he and Gittel were children. Gittel was winsome, pretty, and good natured, but Havah's eyes, black diamonds in the candlelight, captivated him and held him prisoner.

Yussel entered the office and sat on the sofa. "How long has it been since my son has read to me? I miss him." He made a fist and pounded the cushions. "Like a sack of potatoes. You'd be more comfortable in your own bed, don't you think?"

"I should never have married Gittel."

"What's done is done."

"If I'd married Havah to begin with—"

"If, if. If a cat laid eggs, it would be a hen."

Arel rolled the severed menorah branch between his fingers. Letting it drop, he hung his head. "I'm sorry, Papa. I won't blame you if you never forgive me."

"I'm the one who needs to be forgiven. I've been a selfish old fool who's put more importance on a hunk of silver than his own son."

PART III

POMP AND CONSEQUENCE

Chapter One

The odors of ammonia and alcohol made the muggy air in the chemistry lab less than breathable. Dust particles floated on sunbeams pouring through the windows. Lev's collar chafed his neck. He counted the minutes on the clock above the blackboard.

Mr. Smith, the chemistry teacher, strolled down the narrow aisles looking every bit as uncomfortable as Lev. Perspiration collected along his receding hairline and stained his suit under his arms. He stopped at each student's chair to hand out report cards and test results.

"I hope your plans for next fall include college." He took a discolored handkerchief from his jacket pocket and mopped his forehead. "As President Roosevelt says, 'Believe you can and you're halfway there.'"

Lev's heart thumped against his ribs. Mr. Smith had told the class he would give out the results of the final exam on the last day of school. Lev had studied hard for it, but it proved to be more difficult than he anticipated.

"Mr. Gitterman," said Mr. Smith as he handed a grade card to the girl who sat next to Lev. "Could you remain after class?"

Lev's lips tingled and his throat went dry. "Yes, sir." *What could the teacher possibly have to say to me?* Perhaps he did not wish to embarrass him in front of his peers when he told him how miserably he failed. Lev considered science and chemistry his most important subjects. To fail either of them could keep him out of medical school.

After what seemed a fortnight, the bell rang. The shrill sound made the hair dance across the back of Lev's neck. One by one, his classmates filed by his desk and proffered farewells and best wishes.

"See ya at commencement, Gitterman, you ole highbrow."

"Twenty-three skidoo, Lev."

"Thanks for all the help with my homework, Gitterman."

"Ring me up sometime, handsome," said one pretty girl whose name Lev could not remember.

"You're a good egg, Lev...for a Jew."

Lev watched the blond youth swagger through the door and into the hallway. Mr. Smith followed him with narrowed eyes. "*Doz hitl iz gut nor der kop iz tsu klayn.*"

Lev's mouth popped open. "'The hat is fine, but the head is too small'. You speak Yiddish, Mr. Smith?"

"Simanovich, actually." The teacher's jaw relaxed and he took off his jacket. "Please excuse the shirtsleeves. Feel free to do the same." Sitting at his desk, he gestured to a chair next to it. "Come closer. My voice has had it."

Lev removed his jacket and stiff collar. A slight breeze cooled his back through his wet shirt. Keeping his eyes on his teacher, Lev sat and braced himself for what he might say next.

Mr. Smith handed Lev an envelope. "Open it."

Lifting the flap with trembling hands, Lev slid out his final exam. He felt the color leave his face as the red ink blurred across the top of the page.

"I pride myself on giving rough exams." Mr. Smith chuckled. "No one, in all my years of teaching, let alone a student who moved ahead two grade levels in one year, has gotten a perfect score, until now."

Tears stung Lev's eyes. "I don't know what to say."

"Don't swoon on me yet, Lev." Mr. Smith handed him a second envelope. "In light of your achievements, I recommended you for a scholarship to the University of Kansas School of Medicine. Mazel tov, Dr. Gitterman."

Chapter Two

Standing on Union Depot's platform, Nikolai shielded his eyes from the setting sun. Stench from the nearby stockyards made his eyes water. A whistle sounded and the ground rumbled underneath his feet.

Over twenty years had passed since he had seen his father. Nikolai's head jumbled with memories as he awaited Sergei's arrival. He still saw the fury in the older man's eyes as he made a last ditch effort to persuade his son from his folly.

"You'd rather slice people open and wallow in their blood and bile than delight thousands of patrons with your talent? You're a flautist not a surgeon." Sergei had seized Nikolai's shoulders. "I don't understand you, Kolyah."

"You never have, Tatko. Why start now?"

The likeness of Sergei shaking his fist as his train pulled away from Heidelberg's railway station would forever be etched in Nikolai's mind.

After that, only occasional correspondence passed between them; a number Nikolai could count on the fingers of one hand. Among them was a brief note of congratulations on Vasily's birth and an invitation to a Russian philharmonic concert in London, which Nikolai ignored.

In light of those things, Sergei's sudden reappearance mystified Nikolai. Sergei had never shown an interest in his grandson. Why was he coming all the way from Russia to play a single piece at Vasily's commencement ceremony?

"There!" Vasily pointed and hopped up and down like a little boy greeting Father Christmas. "That has to be *Dedushkah*'s train. Aren't you excited, Tatko?"

Without cracking a smile, Nikolai watched the train come to a stop. "Delirious."

Oxana patted Vasily's shoulder. "With the new eyeglasses your *Dedushkah* will think you are your father. Almost you are twins."

Her words sent an unexpected shiver down Nikolai's spine as Sergei descended the train. His goatee and curled moustache were as flamboyant as his ubiquitous Meerschaum pipe. However, he seemed thinner than Nikolai remembered. His narrow shoulders stooped and his back bowed. It was apparent that he used his brass-handled cane for more than appearance these days.

Sergei went first to Vasily and embraced him. "*Solnyshko*, I'd know you anywhere. If I didn't know better, I'd swear you were Kolyah." He kissed each of Vasily's cheeks. "Or your Uncle Bod—"

"Tatko." Nikolai tapped Sergei's shoulder. "Remember me?"

"Dr. Derevenko." Sergei's grey-blue eyes welled behind his spectacles and he pulled Nikolai in for a tight embrace. "*Sinoychek moy*—my son, my precious son."

***

Ulrich cut slices of succulent lamb for his guests. His stomach rumbled in anticipation as he breathed in rosemary and garlic. "Cate, you've outdone yourself tonight."

Catherine set a crystal bowl of mint jelly on the table and said in halting Russian, "*Ya nadeyus, vam ponravitsya vash uzhin, Gohspodyin Derevenko.*"

Sergei took a puff from his pipe and winked at Ulrich. "I'm sure I'll enjoy my dinner very much, *Gezha*

Dietrich. But you mustn't be so formal. To you, I am Sergei, dear lady, and I do speak English. How do you come to speak Russian?"

She took the chair next to Oxana. "When your best friend is from Russia, you learn. And she's a brilliant teacher."

"Cate is good teacher, too," Oxana's cheeks flushed, "but I am not so good English student."

Sergei threw back his head and laughed. "How fortunate am I to be in the company of two such ravishing young ladies?"

"You must be exhausted from your travels, Sergei." Ulrich handed him a plate with two slices of meat. "We don't have to rehearse tonight."

"Nonsense. I've waited my grandson's whole life to make music with his father."

After the serving dishes had been passed around, Ulrich raised his glass. "I propose a toast to the three generations of Derevenkos at my table. *Nahzdarovyah!"*

Sergei emptied his glass in one swallow, coughed, and took a drag from his pipe. "I trust you've been practicing for our piece, Kolyah. I'd hate to embarrass our *Solnyshko* at his own graduation, especially after he went to all the trouble to convince his old *Dedushkah* to come."

Nikolai flinched and nearly upset his water glass. "What's he talking about, Vasily?"

Vasily slunk down in his chair. "I...I wanted to meet my grandfather, Tatko. Uncle Ulrich found his address for me and I wrote a letter. *Dedushkah* answered it and we've been writing to each other ever since."

"How long has this been going on?"

"Since last summer."

"That explains the belated wedding present." Nikolai shot a glare at Oxana that would reduce glacial ice to steam. "Did you know about this?"

"Not until two months ago." She returned his look with a defiant scowl. "But what is so wrong with a boy wanting to know his own grandfather?"

"Nothing at all. But why the secrecy?"

Vasily straightened. "I was afraid you'd get mad, Tatko."

Something in Nikolai's eyes went beyond anger. Ulrich tried to shake the uneasiness welling in his chest. "Does any of that matter? We're all here now. How many years has it been, Sergei? Remember the week you visited Kolyah in Heidelberg?"

Sergei who, aside from the facial hair, was an older version of his son, slouched in his chair. "I remember it all too well. It was a fiasco. Kolyah would have nothing to do with me. You see, he never forgave me for killing Bodrik."

"*I* never forgave *you*, Tatko?" Nikolai jumped up and flung his napkin onto his plate. "*You* never forgave *me* for living."

Oxana's gaze darted from Sergei to Nikolai. "Who is this Bodrik?"

Sergei raised his head and stared at Nikolai with a look of disbelief. "You've never told your wife about your own twin brother?"

Oxana blanched. "He had a twin?"

"Not just a twin, my daughter, an *identical* twin."

Chapter Three

Lev combed Pomade through his frizzled locks. He felt fortunate to have a friend in Officer Tillman, a former barber who understood the frustrations of kinky hair. When he presented Lev with the tin, he shook his head. "Lev, I suspect there was a Negro in your family's closet somewhere along the line."

"I would be honored, sir."

Setting down his comb, Lev picked up the letter on his desk and read it for the fourth time since the mail came.

"Dear Lev, my friend and future colleague,

"I appreciate the invitation to your commencement ceremony, but feel it's within both of our best interests if I decline. I trust you will understand. However, I extend my most heartfelt congratulations on your scholarship to medical school, or as you would say, 'Mazel tov.' Pop and I are pleased you didn't let that brilliant mind of yours go to waste.

"Perhaps one day you and I will work side by side as we discover a cure for the common prejudice.

"Sincerely,

"Lon M. Tillman, MD"

***

Fruma Ya'el knocked on the bedroom door. "Are you dressed yet, Lev?"

"Yes, *Bubbe*. Come in."

Leading Yussel through the doorway, she surveyed the bedroom Lev shared with Reuven. It was a good size room for two boys. Each had his own bed, bureau, and study table.

Reuven's bed looked like it had been ransacked by Cossacks. Among his collection of treasures piled on his bureau was the colorful plaster cast from his sledding accident. Dr. Miklos had removed it carefully to preserve Vasily's artwork.

Atop a heap of dirty clothes sat the shoes he had long since outgrown. When Havah had tried to convince him to pass them down to Elliott, Reuven hugged them to his breast. "No, Auntie, no. Papa Gavrel made them for me with his own two hands. I'll never part with them, never ever, *ever*."

In contrast, Lev's side of the room was well ordered. His bureau and desk boasted stacks of books arranged in alphabetical order. The bedspread did not have a wrinkle or a crease. *Does he ever sleep? On the other hand, do I need to ask?*

When Fruma Ya'el woke in the middle of the night, for one reason or another, more often than not, light streamed under the boys' door. Sometimes she would press her ear to it and listen. Pages rustled, Lev recited his mathematical equations or chemical formulas while Reuven snored.

Standing in front of the full-length mirror in his graduation gown, Lev put on his cap and turned. "How do I look?"

A lump formed in her throat. *How does he look?* Although he had inherited Feivel's red hair and brown eyes, the resemblance ended there. His eyes shone with intelligence, kindness, and determination. Still a youth of eighteen, Lev's shoulders were already broader than his father's and, in the last year, he had grown taller by at least three inches.

"Like a scholar," she clasped her hands together, "and a handsome future doctor."

Her mind traveled back to Svechka, to the day Tova's time came. Fruma Ya'el could still see the girls, hand in hand, on her doorstep.

"Mama's getting a baby." Four-year-old Devorah hopped on one foot.

Already too old for her seven years, Leah wept and tugged at Fruma Ya'el's skirt. "Hurry, Auntie. Papa's angry and Mama—please, *hurry.*"

"Stay here with Gittel and Uncle Hershel." Grabbing her birthing basket, Fruma Ya'el tried to calm the girls and herself. "Everything will be fine, you'll see."

When Feivel met her at the door of their shack, he snarled. "What took so long?"

"How close are the pains?"

"Who knows? The cow's been bawling all day." He shoved her aside and spat out a glob of tobacco. "I'll be at the tavern. Don't bother me if it's another girl."

At first Feivel doted on his son. He stopped his visits to the tavern and took regular trips to the bathhouse. Even the townspeople marveled at the change. However, by the baby's second month, the reality of another mouth to feed set in and Feivel reverted to his old ways. Instead of Lev being the answer to Feivel's prayers, he became the recipient of his rage. Fruma Ya'el lost count of how many of the boy's wounds she dressed.

Returning to the present, she traced the scar across his lips with her fingertip. Lev squeezed her hand and kissed it. "It's okay, *Bubbe.* He made me strong. I'm going to make you proud of me."

"I've never been prouder than I am at this moment."

"Nor I," said Yussel.

Outside an automobile horn blasted and startled Fruma Ya'el. "*Oy*, that *fershtunkenah* noise. I'll never get used to it."

Lev slipped off his gown and folded it. "That's Vasily. Can you believe it? His grandfather bought him a car for graduation. It's not new or anything. Just a used 1905 Buick. It's still pretty nice, though." Tucking his cap and gown under his arm, Lev headed for the door. "See you at the school."

Yussel thumped his cane on the floorboards. "Lev, wait. I have a graduation present for you."

"Later, *Zaydeh*. Vasily's waiting on me."

"He can wait a little longer."

***

Zaydeh's tone allowed no room for argument. Lev turned and set his bundle on Reuven's desk. Sitting on the bed, Yussel took a pendant on a chain from his neck. Lev's breath caught in his throat. He had never seen his grandfather without it, even in the bathhouse.

"My father, your great-grandfather, Arel Gitterman of blessed memory, gave this to me the same year he crafted the menorah. Leftover silver, he said." Yussel patted the mattress. "Come, Lev."

Sinking down beside him, Lev stared at the round medallion, the size of a milk bottle cap. Intricate vines circled the outside forming a graceful border. In the middle of it *Zaydeh* Arel had engraved, *"Shiviti HaShem neg'di tahmeed."* Lev read the words aloud.

"So you do still read Hebrew." Yussel placed the necklace in Lev's hand and curved his hand around it. "But do you remember what it means?"

"I have set *HaShem* always before me."

A satisfied smile spread Yussel's lips. "*Heder* wasn't wasted on you, after all. Papa told me it would keep the Almighty close to my heart. Now it will keep Him close to yours, yes?"

Lev's tongue turned to sawdust in his mouth. The pendant weighed more than mere silver. His heart raced and he made no attempt to stem his tears.

With a chuckle in his voice, Yussel whispered, "I'm sorry we couldn't afford a Buick."

***

Nikolai climbed into the back of his father's new car and set his flute case on the seat beside him. "Beautiful night for a graduation, isn't it, Oxana?"

In the front seat, she neither replied nor turned her head. Nikolai heaved a frustrated sigh and settled back.

Sergei rotated the crank on the front of the car, starting the motor, and climbed into the driver's seat. "It's a Ford, Model N, made in 1906," he shouted over the noise of the engine. "Tomorrow you learn to drive it, Kolyah."

"Thank you, but no thank you, Tatko. God gave us legs and there are streetcars if those get too tired to walk." Nikolai leaned forward. "With all of your frivolous spending you won't have enough for your fare back to Russia."

"I'm not going back."

***

Electric chandeliers and sconces on the walls between the windows cast a warm glow over Central High School's auditorium. The sultry breeze blowing through the open windows did little to cool Havah.

Sitting behind her, Shayndel leaned over her shoulder and patted her stomach. "Are you sure you're not having twins, Havaleh? You're awfully big for four months."

Arel glared at his sister. "That's not funny."

Havah fidgeted in her wheelchair in an attempt to find a comfortable position. "Dr. Eleanor thinks we miscalculated and I'm closer to five months."

Fanning herself with her lace fan in one hand, Catherine pointed to the stage with the other. "Oh look, our three men are getting ready to perform."

"Who cares? I hear them rehearse day and night for two days," said Oxana.

"Haven't you spoken to Nikolai yet?"

"*Nyet.*"

On the stage, Ulrich sat at the piano with ceremonious aplomb. Nikolai took his place behind his music stand and positioned his flute. Sergei, violin in hand, stood center stage.

"Ladies and gentlemen, it is my very great pleasure to be in your wonderful country. At the piano is the distinguished Professor Ulrich Dietrich. For this grand occasion, we offer you Johann Sebastian Bach's 'Double Violin Concerto.' As you can see, we have but one violin, so a flute, skillfully played by my son, Dr. Nikolai Derevenko, shall replace the second violin."

Sergei played the opening bars. He bobbed his head in time to the music as Nikolai and Ulrich joined in. Havah could not help but notice the sparks that flew between father and son as the spritely melody engulfed the crowded hall.

Across the aisle, Vasily pushed an errant lock of shoulder-length hair under his cap. He slouched in his chair. Tears stood in his eyes as they met hers.

A few hours before, while he waited for Lev, he bemoaned his blunder. "They hate each other, Miss Havah."

"You did the right thing, Vasya. Blood against blood is never a good thing. Whatever it is between them must be settled."

When the music came to an end, the musicians bowed to a standing ovation. Nikolai offered his hand to Sergei who gripped it and drew him into an embrace. Vasily's taut lips relaxed and he grinned at Havah.

"Bravo!" cried the principal as he took the stage and waited for the applause to subside. "Next on our program is the Valedictorian's speech. This year's most outstanding student took us all by surprise. I'm sure you'll agree the faculty made the right choice in Mr. Lev Gitterman."

***

A group of students bunched up around Lev in the high school corridor, exchanging backslaps and accolades.

"Hey, Red, good job!"

"Straight A's, no wonder your head's bigger than the rest of you."

"I can see it now: Lev 'Smart Fella' Gitterman, the first Jewish president."

Lev's laughter rose above their comments and jests. "I'll settle for Lev Gitterman MD, thank you."

Arel could not remember seeing his eldest sister's son happier. *As far as that goes, what in Lev's life has ever brought him anything but misery? How have I helped him?* Certainly, he had opened his home to his nephew, but never his heart. Arel demanded Lev's respect, but what had he done to earn it?

Hanging his head, he turned to leave.

"Uncle Arel, don't go." Lev rushed to him and threw his arm around his shoulder. "I want you to meet Mr. Smith."

The slender man with thinning hair and wire-framed glasses extended his hand. "Mr. Gitterman, your nephew has told me so much about you. You've been most influential in his academic success."

Taking Mr. Smith's hand, Arel swallowed and cast a sidelong glance at Lev. "I dare say his accomplishments are in spite of me."

"I believe Lev's exact words were, 'I'll show him.'"

Chapter Four

Colorful balloons and ribbons festooned the Dietrichs' great room. A banner stretched over the fireplace on which was painted in bold blue letters, "Congratulations Vasily and Lev, Class of 1908."

"It's not nearly as artistic as Vasily's work, but it's legible," said Catherine.

"It's wonderful, Aunt Cate, all of it," said Vasily through a mouthful of cake.

Although the room was not as big as Ulrich's ballroom in Kishinev, it was spacious enough to accommodate twenty people, a baby grand piano, and four sofas. Havah stretched out on one of them with slumbering Tikvah curled up beside her. Mendel, David, and Bayla took turns giving each other rides up and down the adjacent hallway in her wheelchair.

Across the room, in Havah's favorite chairs, Lev and Arel seemed to be lost in conversation. *What could Lev say to Arel that actually made him laugh?* It had been months since she had seen her husband crack a smile let alone laugh. Havah strained her ears to eavesdrop but to no avail.

With Rachel in his arms, Ulrich sat at the piano. "What party would be complete without music?"

Sergei Derevenko fascinated Havah. The resemblance between father and son ended at physical appearance. Whereas Nikolai was quite reserved, Sergei enjoyed an adoring audience. For most of the afternoon he had regaled everyone with stories of his boyhood in Russia. His dramatic gestures delighted the children.

All conversation ceased as Sergei situated his violin. "In honor of the graduates I give you 'Pomp and Circumstance, March Number One,' first played three years ago at Yale University's commencement." He pointed his bow at Itzak. "Are you up to joining us, Mr. Abromovich?"

"Does President Roosevelt sit tall in his saddle?" Itzak poised his bow over the strings. "You lead and I'll follow."

True to form, Itzak did not miss a beat. As they came to the end of the march, Nikolai set down his flute. "What did I tell you, Tatko? Natural talent."

Sergei nodded. "I can't believe you've no formal training, Itzak."

"Nary a lesson." Itzak shrugged. "Unless you count my father's instructions, and he didn't read a note of music either."

"You, my friend, are as proficient as any trained violinist I've encountered. I admire musicians such as yourself and Sir Edward Elgar, who incidentally wrote the piece you so brilliantly followed. I had the pleasure of making his acquaintance four years ago in Covent Garden at the Royal Opera House in London."

"Does this orchestra take requests?" asked Dr. Eleanor.

"But of course, Mademoiselle."

"Do you know anything by Johann Strauss?"

Rachel rose on her knees beside Ulrich. "'Vienna Waltz Number Four.' Can we play it, Uncle Uri? May we, please?"

Havah enjoyed the surprise in Sergei's eyes. Up until then she could tell by his expressions that he regarded Rachel as the poor little blind girl. With a flourish he bowed at the waist.

"The stage is yours, *zaichik*."

"My little Mozart and I have been rehearsing this one for our upcoming concert in Vienna. Feel free to join us, *Herr* Derevenko." Ulrich placed his hands on the keyboard. "Shall we, *Fräulein* Gitterman?"

"*Ja, ja, sehr gut, Herr* Dietrich." Rachel giggled. "That's German talk."

Shaking his head and smiling, Sergei played the violin portion, while Nikolai's flute rounded out the rich piece.

Taking Dr. Florin's hand, Dr. Eleanor rose from the couch. "May I have the honor of this dance, Doctor?"

"Beware of these big clodhoppers." He bowed. "They are dangerous indeed."

She curtsied and twined her slender fingers through his. "I'll be careful to keep my dainty size tens out of their way."

Flushing as red as his hair, he wrapped an arm around her waist.

"They make a handsome couple, don't they?" whispered Shayndel.

Although Arel told her he altered some of the doctor's trousers, Havah did not realize until that moment how much weight he had lost. His face glowed and Dr. Eleanor's eyes sparkled as they danced cheek to cheek. Havah chided herself for thinking like a matchmaker, but never had she seen two people more suited to each other.

So intent on watching them waltz, lost in each other's embrace, Havah did not see Lev approach. He offered her his hand.

"May I have this dance, madam?"

His smile eclipsed his scar and his new suit accentuated his maturing torso. "Surely you've better things to do than dance with a fat old cripple."

"In a 'family way' isn't fat, it's beauty to the highest power, Auntie dear, and you're only seven years older than I." With his right arm firmly around her disappearing waist, he held her right in his left. She shut her eyes and followed his lead. For a few minutes she forgot her lame foot until it buckled underneath her, shooting pain through to her knee. Tightening his arm around her, Lev whispered in her ear. "Someday I'm going to find a cure for Causalgia."

The music ended with a rousing crescendo. Rachel clapped her hands. Sergei set down his violin, lifted her off the bench, and kissed her cheek with a loud smack. "A symphonious miracle sent from the Master Conductor Himself. Can't you hear the angels' joyful chorus?"

"You talk funny, *Dedushkah*." Rachel nuzzled her head on his shoulder and sniffed. "Mmm, Bay Rum. You smell like Uncle Uri only different. That's because he's him and you're you."

"You are a marvel, child. Is there anything you can't do?"

"See."

***

After a full afternoon and evening of celebrating the graduates' accomplishments, the crowd dissipated. In a corner of the semi-darkened room, Lev and Vasily engaged in a chess match by candlelight. Ulrich played a lullaby on the piano. Bayla and Reuven slumbered on blankets on the floor. Between the breeze blowing through the windows and the music, Havah struggled to keep her eyes open.

She snuggled against Arel on the sofa. "If we don't go home soon, I'll have to spend the night right here on the couch."

"You'll do no such thing," said Catherine who sat at the piano, her head on Ulrich's shoulder. "We've fresh beds upstairs and plenty of room for everyone."

In a rocking chair near the piano, Rachel sat on Sergei's lap and nestled her head against his chest. He rubbed her back and whispered, "Cherish these days for they are shifting sand; the tide rolls to shore at midnight and leaves little trace at daybreak. Hush, little Bodrik. Hush little Kolyah. Your Tatko's here and he will never leave you."

"Who is Bodrik?" asked Rachel.

"Only my husband's identical twin brother," said Oxana who had been unusually quiet most of the day.

Stretched out on one of the divans, Nikolai sat up. "Oxanochka, not now."

"If not now, when?"

Suddenly wide awake, Havah looked over at Nikolai whose angry glare shot lightning bolts at his father. "You have a twin brother, Dr. Nikolai?"

"Had," said Sergei, his voice laden with sorrow. He pulled a gold watch from his vest pocket and popped it open to show a faded photograph of two little boys. "They were the same age as your Rachel. Their own mother couldn't tell them apart."

"What happened to my grandmother, *Dedushkah?*" asked Vasily.

"Your father and uncle were not yet two. I woke one morning to find a note pinned to her pillow. 'My dearest Sergei…' Oh cruel prelude. She went on to say she never loved me and had tired of diapers. If that wasn't heartless enough, she left me for a French horn player; a mediocre one at that."

"Tatko, please," whispered Nikolai through clenched teeth.

For the first time that night, Oxana smiled. "What were they like, Kolyah and his brother?"

"They were two sides of the same ruble, identical faces but different personalities. Bodrik was a chirping bird, a magpie. You always knew what he was thinking. Nikolai, as you could guess, was the shy one. Quiet. Introspective."

"Did Uncle Bodrik play the flute, too?" asked Vasily.

"Oh my, no. He used to tease your father for choosing an old woman's instrument. I can still see Bodrik at the age of seven, trying to wield that big cello.

"Every night before prayers, we three would conduct our own private concert. One night it would be Schubert, the next Chopin. We laughed. We sang. We dreamt of the day we'd be the world renowned Derevenko Trio."

Havah felt like an intruder as he lowered his voice to almost a whisper, his eyes as distant as Russia itself. "December1880. Bodrik and Nikolai had just turned twelve. We celebrated their birthday with music of course. Always with music. I even secured solos for them with the Philharmonic. Kolyah chose Bach's 'Partita in A Minor' and Bodrik chose Bach's 'Cello Solo, Suite Number One.' They each gave splendid performances. Why shouldn't they? They *were* Derevenkos."

He drew a rasping breath and twisted a strand of his beard around his finger. His lip quivered. "How fleeting is happiness. A week later, Bodrik was dead. At the vigil, Kolyah was inconsolable. He climbed into Bodrik's coffin. It took three of us to wrestle him out."

Chapter Five

*"Slowpoke! Slowpoke! Kolyah is a slowpoke and an old
lady flautist." Bodrik's singsong taunts rang in Nikolai's
ears. No matter how fast he skated, he could not catch up to
Bodrik. The farther behind he fell, the louder Bodrik
laughed.*

*"Come back, Bodrik, come back," Nikolai
screamed until he crashed into a wall and Bodrik shattered
into shards of ice.*

"No!" Nikolai bolted upright in bed, clapping his
hands over his ears. He turned to see if he had disturbed
Oxana. She did not stir or open her eyes.

Unable to go back to sleep, he padded to the
kitchen. He turned on the light to see Sergei slumped over
the table, holding his handkerchief over his mouth. He
pressed his other hand against his chest. A coughing fit
wracked his frail shoulders.

"I don't like the sound of that." Nikolai held his
hand to Sergei's forehead. "You feel feverish."

Wadding up his handkerchief, Sergei crammed it
into his dressing gown pocket, but not before Nikolai saw
the red stain on it. "Nonsense. I'm in fine fettle, Dr.
Derevenko."

To avoid an argument, Nikolai went to the ice box
and took out a bottle of milk. He poured it into a pan on the
stove and stirred in a lump of butter and some sugar.

"Did you have a nightmare, Kolyah?"

"Why do you ask?"

"I used to make the same concoction for you and
Bodrik when one of you had a bad dream."

Once the butter had melted, Nikolai turned off the fire and poured the milk into two cups. He set them on the table and sat across from Sergei.

Sergei took a sip. "Perfect, feels good on the throat."

Oxana entered the kitchen and yawned. She poured the remainder of the mixture into a cup and took a seat between the two men. "How can anyone sleep with all this racket?"

"Forgive me, daughter. I didn't mean to wake you with my barking. It seems the doctor here thinks I've taken cold." Sergei coughed again and his face went from pink to crimson.

"Must you?" Nikolai started to point out that he had never said anything about a cold, but something in his father's demeanor stopped him. Instead he said, "I'll have Oxana make a hot toddy for you. No one makes them better."

"I will be happy to," said Oxana, her eyes trained on Nikolai. "Kolyah, ever since Ulrich's party last week, you cry in your sleep every night. And I wonder, are you really asleep? I'm your wife. Why haven't you ever told me about your own brother?"

"I'm the one at fault." Sergei took a labored breath. "After Bodrik died, I became a selfish recluse and cut off my living son. I slapped him for even mentioning Bodrik's name. I fear it's become a habit for Kolyah."

"Bodrik always had to be first, the best at everything. Life was a competition to him." Protracted memories zipped through Nikolai's mind. The frozen Neva River ran like a ribbon through St. Petersburg. Sunlight glinted off Bodrik's skate blades. "I can still hear his voice. 'Race you to the bridge. The loser makes the winner's bed for a week.' I tried to catch him, but he took off before I could start." Nikolai trembled. "Suddenly he stopped and stuck out his foot. Why did he do such a stupid thing? We collided and our skates tangled. The next thing I knew I was sprawled out on the ice in a puddle of my own blood."

Sergei's eyes filled. "You never told me it was Bodrik's fault."

"Would you have listened, Tatko?"

"Dear God, I chastised you for your clumsiness."

"That's how you got that horrid scar on your leg, isn't it Kolyah?" Oxana snapped her fingers. "You made something up about being mauled by a bear."

"He did look like he'd tussled with one," said Sergei. "Bodrik's skate sliced right through Kolyah's stocking. He was a mass of bruises, cuts and scrapes. Bodrik had one little bump on his forehead. That's all. I put my children to bed that night, worried sick about Kolyah."

The cracks in the tile floor blurred as the memory of that night crashed in on Nikolai. He remembered how relentlessly his leg smarted and how he ached all over. *Bodrik sat in the chair clutching his hand. "Forgive me, Kolyah. Please don't die, Kolyah."*

"Only if you promise to make my bed for a week."

"I promise." Bodrik grinned. "I'll even polish your silly little old lady flute."

"Go to bed you dumb durak *and let me sleep."*

Before Bodrik could stand, his eyes rolled back in his head and he fell sideways to the floor. Nikolai kicked Bodrik's ribs with his big toe. "Aw, stop clowning around."

Nikolai's extremely ticklish brother did not move. Nikolai dropped to his knees and slapped his face. Bodrik's head lolled to one side like a rag doll.

Sergei buried his face in his hands. "I still hear Kolyah crying, 'Tatko, do something!' Merciful Lord, what could I have done?"

Chapter Six

Two electric fans only circulated hot air, thick with machine oil and chalk dust, in the tailor shop. Arel's rigid collar irritated his neck and he pushed his wet hair from his forehead. His sewing machine hummed and afternoon light glinted off the bobbing needle as he guided a shirtsleeve under the presser foot. A drop of sweat rolled down his cheek and dripped onto the cuff.

Whipping the linen shirt off the table, he hurried to wash it before the stain could set in. A wave of nausea swept over him and a sharp pain seared his chest. He dropped to his knees in front of the commode.

Arel's pulse pounded his temples. Evron's mouth gaped open and blood spurted from his neck. A crowbar slammed across Arel's head. Crimson spatters hung in the air like raindrops. Another blow crushed his cheek and he choked on his own blood. Havah screamed his name.

"Arel?"

A wet washcloth covered his face. Reaching for it, Arel coaxed open his eyes and tried to sit up. "Itzak...I'm oh...kay."

"Don't move." Itzak pressed his hands against Arel's shoulders. "Looks like you clocked yourself good on the toilet. I called the doctor."

***

Dr. Florin slipped off his stethoscope and put it in his medical bag. "Your heartbeat is strong, as strong as a young man's should be. The symptoms you described are those of a heart attack, but I don't detect coronary arrhythmia. None whatsoever."

In their five years of marriage, Arel had never contracted a cold that Havah could remember. She held his palm against her cheek. Although relieved at Dr. Florin's report, she doubted her husband's claims. "He's so pale and clammy, could it be influenza?"

"His temperature is normal."

"But what about his stomach distress?"

"It could be something he ate or any number of reasons." Dr. Florin patted her growing tummy. "You know the truth of that as well as anyone."

"*Oy gevalt!* Do I look like I'm with child? There's no reason to keep me in bed." Arel ripped his hand from Havah's grasp. "I feel fine. It was just the heat."

"Your shop is warm, my boy, but not warm enough to bring on heatstroke. You're not at death's door...that I can tell. Nonetheless, I'm ordering a few day's bedrest for you."

"This is ridiculous. I have customers depending on me." Arel raised his voice with each statement. "I can't afford to lose business."

"How much business will you do from six feet under?"

Havah's eyes filled. "But you said he's *not dying* and his heart's strong."

Dr. Florin's jovial smile dissolved and he turned back to Arel. "Even the healthiest heart can be overtaxed. Surely there's another tailor in this fair city in need of employment. Yes indeed, I would put an advertisement for an assistant in *The Kansas City Times.*"

"I don't know how I feel about that." Havah pinched Arel's cheek. "Isn't that how you found Dr. Eleanor? What if Arel finds a replacement for me?"

"No one could replace you, my dear." Dr. Florin grinned and opened his watch. Snapping it shut he slipped it back into his pocket with one hand and adjusted his necktie with the other. "Speaking of the good doctor, she's waiting dinner for me."

***

The feather mattress under Arel's back was a delicious change from his office sofa, and he relished his wife's softness beside him. While the idea of a few days of rest appealed to him, it riddled him with guilt.

"What do you think about Dr. Florin's idea, Havah? Should I hire an assistant? It would be one more expense."

Havah snuggled against him and laid her head on his chest. "Better than a funeral expense. Look at yourself, Arel. You're exhausted."

"I feel like such a failure."

"You know better." She stroked his neck with her fingertips. "Didn't Evron say you had a rare gift for tailoring? And Wolf agrees with him."

"He's the best in the business."

"Right, and even he never tried to run that business alone."

"You win. First thing in the morning, I'll call *The Times.* There's a lot to think—"

"Hush!" Pressing her hand over his mouth, she brushed her lips across his cheek and whispered in his ear. "Forget about tomorrow. Think only of this, 'Let him kiss me with kisses of his lips, for your love is better than wine.'"

Her hot breath sent shivers of delight through him and her rosewater perfume intoxicated him. "Havah, the mother of life." He cupped his hand around her belly. "'Oh, prince's daughter, the curves of your thighs are like jewels…your navel is a rounded goblet.'"

Chapter Seven

Glossy woodwork adorned the dining room of the King Joy Lo restaurant with its polished tile floor. A gas burning chandelier hung from the filigree ceiling. Havah gazed at the paintings of flowers and the calligraphy gracing the walls.

Instead of Grand Avenue in Kansas City, she imagined herself in Shanghai. Perhaps if she peeked out the window, she would see fishermen paddling sampans along the Yangtze River. Or she might see dainty ladies tottering on bound feet carrying their babies on their backs. Havah's own mutilated foot ached for them.

Ulrich's voice cut into her musing. "Havah, where are you?"

"China, of course."

Catherine sipped hot tea from a tiny cup with no handle. "Isn't this the most wonderful establishment? Vasily told us about it. He and his artist friends like to come here in the middle of the night."

Havah picked up an egg roll and studied it for a moment. "It looks like a cheese blintz, doesn't it?"

She dipped it in the bowl of mustard. When she bit into it, the spicy condiment seared her nasal passages. She grabbed her glass of water and gulped it down.

Dabbing her eyes, she sniffed. "Oh that's good. Like horseradish."

"I like the sweet and sour sauce better." Catherine took another sip of her tea. "I can't believe you actually like that dreadful concoction, Havah."

Ulrich mopped his brow after swallowing a bite of egg roll with a healthy dollop of hot mustard. "Our Havah's made of sterner stuff."

Two waiters set covered plates of food on the table. Fragrant steam rose as they lifted the lids and rattled off the strange names, "Egg Foo Yung, Chow Mein, and Moo Goo Gai Pan; no pork, no shellfish."

Picking up a pair of ivory sticks beside her plate, Havah studied the Chinese calligraphy etched into them. "What are these for?"

"Chopsticks. For eating." The waiter placed them in her hand. "You try?"

"Yes." Havah watched a patron one table over. "If she can do it, so can I."

Try as she might, the chopsticks slipped between Havah's fingers and fell amid the noodles on her plate. "How can anybody eat with these things?"

"I show you." The waiter picked up a piece of chicken with the chopsticks. "So easy. Even babies in China use."

"How on earth do they do it?"

"Like American babies. Very messy."

With a wink, the waiter bowed and went back to the kitchen.

"What a pity Arel couldn't join us tonight," said Ulrich.

"Is he feeling better?" asked Catherine.

"He says he is," said Havah.

Although still under doctor's bedrest orders, Havah suspected Arel would have bowed out of the evening anyway. Despite the fact that he had given in and agreed to allow Rachel to go on tour with Ulrich, Arel looked for reasons to avoid him. Even at the graduation party, Arel had kept a polite distance.

"At any rate, he has plenty of company. Rachel insisted on crawling into bed with her 'poor sick Poppy', which means the dog will join them. He won't admit it, but I think Arel is rather enjoying the attention. He dotes on his little princess."

"It's not too late to change your minds, Havah." Ulrich leaned back and sipped his tea. "Rachel is still your child."

"And break my daughter's heart? The tour is all she talks about. Arel will get used to the idea."

"He hasn't yet."

Chapter Eight

"All aboard!" cried the conductor from the train at Union Depot.

Arel handed Ulrich Rachel's suitcase. Sitting on Havah's lap, Rachel leaned her ear against Havah's belly. "Don't come out until I get back, baby brother, okay?"

Havah's tearful reflection blinked at her in Rachel's dark glasses. Although Havah abhorred the idea of them, Dr. Eleanor had strongly suggested the glasses, saying that they would cause others to be mindful. Once the doctor explained this to Rachel, she accepted the glasses as part of her attire.

A shrill whistle signaled the train's imminent departure. Catherine lifted Rachel into her arms and kissed Havah's cheek. "I'll treat her as my very own."

Havah curved her hand around Catherine's arm. "You mean you'll spoil her rotten."

Ulrich shook hands with Arel. He bent to kiss Havah's forehead and, without a word, slipped his arm through Catherine's.

Watching them board, Havah felt weak and empty. She reached for Arel's hand. His mouth set in a taut line as the train pulled away from the depot.

After a few moments, his jaw relaxed. He sniffed, took his handkerchief from his pocket, and blew his nose. "Why don't I treat you to breakfast?"

Havah's stomach growled. "I am hungry at that."

"How about the Café Valerius? It's the new one the *Kansas City Journal* is calling 'the swellest.'"

"Aren't you going back to work today?"

"Later. I'm interviewing a new tailor this afternoon."

***

Arel opened the shop for the first time in a week. Fortunately, he had no orders that needed immediate attention. Grateful for the lull, he went about catching up on orders for the following month.

Sol Mayer's tuxedo for his nephew's wedding in August was at the top of the list. Sol was a wealthy shop owner and his wife Zelda fancied herself a socialite. "Nothing's too good for our Barry," she said when she chose the fabric for Sol's suit. "That's Barry Mayorovich, MD."

Arel smiled inwardly at Barry's refusal to Americanize his last name.

Holding a cluster of pins between his teeth, Arel marked the shoulders on the woolen vest. The front door opened and slammed with a ringing crash.

"Arel, watch out!" Havah screamed. "Behind you!"

Arel yelped. The pins fell from his mouth and scattered across the floor. Chest heaving, he dropped to his knees to retrieve them.

"Are you okay, Chief?"

"Just clumsy." Arel searched the shop. Havah was nowhere to be found, only a gangly young man with a hooked nose, thick-lensed glasses, and an engaging smile. Jumping to his feet, Arel wiped his hands on his apron. "May I help you?"

"I'm here about a job. Are you Mr. Gitterman?"

Arel nodded and extended his hand. "And you must be Sam Weiner."

"The one and only." He gripped Arel's hand and pumped it up and down. "Sammy at your service. If I may say so, sir, you don't look at all like the old fuddy-duddy I expected."

Arel pulled his hand out of Sam's crushing grip and flexed his fingers. He sat and pointed to another chair. "Have a seat, Mr. Weiner. Do you mind answering a few questions?"

"Ask away, kiddo." Sitting on the bentwood chair, Sam draped one arm over the back and pointed at Arel's yarmulke with the other. "Orthodox I see."

"Are you Jewish?"

"*You* might question it. My mom and I go to the Reform Temple."

"Where were you born?"

"I'm a Yankee Doodle Dandy."

"Excuse me?"

"Y'know, like the song. Born in the U S of A, red, white and blue, through and through."

Although Arel liked the young man's free and easy manner, he hesitated. *How much experience can Sam have? He doesn't look much older than Lev.* "*Nu?* You're a tailor, Mr. Weiner?"

"Not yet. That's where you come in." Sammy crossed one lanky leg over the other and folded his hands on top of his head. "I've been working in the shirt factory with my mom since I was thirteen—five years, in case you're wondering—so I know which end of a needle is which. Mainly I've sewn cuffs, button holes, and whatnot. I'm willing, able, and ready to learn."

"What about school?"

"Dropped out in the 8th grade. Pop died in the war and my sister got married, then moved away. Mom needed help."

"All right then." Arel handed him the vest he had been working on. "Show me what you can do, Mr. Weiner."

"You got it, Chief." He took the garment and sat at Arel's sewing machine. Slipping the fabric under the needle, he dropped the presser foot and started the motor. He quickly finished the shoulder and side seams, snipped the ends of the threads and tossed the vest back to Arel. "Call me Sammy."

The seams were as straight as any Arel had ever seen. He turned the piece over to scrutinize the underside for knots and puckers. "You know what is *shleymesdik*, Sammy?"

"Whoa, horse." Sammy scratched his head. "The Weiners haven't spoken Yiddish in years, but from the look on your face I'm guessing it's something pretty okay."

"Better than okay—perfect. What would you say to nineteen cents an hour to start with and weekends off?"

Chapter Nine

Something Havah had never stopped to consider was the effect of Rachel's absence on her dog. For two days after Rachel's departure, Kreplakh wandered about the house sniffing corners, whimpering, and scratching at the doors. Havah's extra affection did nothing to console her. Reuven and Bayla tried to play games with her and offered her treats, but the dog refused to have anything to do with either of them. How did one make an animal understand that her mistress would only be gone for a little while?

By the third day, Kreplakh stopped whining but shadowed Havah everywhere. If Havah had to use the water closet the dog would stand outside and howl until she came out. Havah could hardly sit down without the dog leaping into her lap. The most frustrating thing of all was the dog's insistence on sharing Arel and Havah's bed. No matter how many times Arel shoved her off Kreplakh would merely wag her tail and jump back up. Finally, he gave in.

On the fourth night, she woke them with a sharp yap. Arel wrapped his pillow around his head and moaned. "*Farshiltn hunt.* Havah, do something about that damn mutt."

Havah patted one of her floppy ears and tried to hush her. Instead, the dog pawed at the Havah's nightgown and licked her face. Rising up on all fours Kreplakh turned in circles.

Sitting up, Havah heard someone softly playing the scales on the piano. Since Lev was spending the night with Vasily and Reuven had no interest in learning to play, it left only one of the children.

Havah fumbled for her cane and hobbled to the living room, Kreplakh at her heels.

The streetlight cast a halo around Bayla. Tears glistened on her cheeks.

Lowering herself onto the bench, Havah curved her arm around the child. "What's the matter, sweetheart? Did you have a bad dream?"

Bayla sniffed and her lower lip quivered. "I miss Rachel."

"But you're always complaining that she hogs the covers and snores too loud."

"She does." Bayla rubbed her eyes and yawned. "And she kicks like Pora used to. Now it's too quiet."

Havah stood and led Bayla to the sofa. "You've never had a bed to yourself, have you?"

Bayla curled up and laid her head on Havah's tummy. At the same time the baby kicked. "Mommy, will the baby be blind like Rachel or boring like me?"

"Who says you're boring?"

"Rachel can't see, but she can play the piano almost as good as Uncle Ulrich. Reuven writes stories and wins prizes, and Lev's really, really smart. And I'm—"

"Hush, little bird." Havah pinched Bayla's lips between her thumb and forefinger. "As my Papa of blessed memory used to say, 'every pot finds its own lid.'"

Chapter Ten

When Florin telephoned Sunday afternoon to invite him to the clinic, Nikolai doubted it was for a friendly visit. Bracing himself for the inevitable, he apprised Oxana and headed for the front door.

"Your father and Vasily are cooking up a special treat." She followed him. Her expression told him she understood. "What shall I tell them?"

"Tell them I went to visit...a sick friend."

On the way to Florin's office, the streetcar seemed more crowded and smellier than usual. The motorman had to stop at least three times. Nikolai's impatience knew no bounds.

Once he arrived at the clinic, he sat on the examination table and folded his arms across his chest. "What's with the cloak-and-dagger routine, Florin? Why couldn't you tell me on the telephone? Even a first year med student could diagnose consumption."

Florin hung his head. "His sputum culture showed no tuberculosis bacilli."

"But that's good news."

"I wish it were." Florin held the x-ray up to the overhead light. "No matter how much you deny it, Kolyah, you're a physician and you know exactly what this means."

Nikolai's heart cratered to his stomach as he studied the large mass obscuring the left side of his father's ribcage. He flung the film to the table.

***

Swallowing hard, Nikolai entered the kitchen. Sergei sat at the table puffing on his pipe, intent on Vasily's latest masterpiece.

On the canvas, Sergei with his bow poised over his violin, exuded enthusiasm and passion, the father of Nikola's youth.

Unlike his portrait, Sergei's eyes were dull with fatigue. Pulling a blanket around himself, he shivered despite the steamy air. He took a drag from his pipe and wheezed until Nikolai feared he would expire on the spot.

Nikolai yanked the pipe from him and emptied the tobacco into the waste bin. "Enough! Do you have any idea what—?"

Sergei pressed his shriveled finger to his lip and then pointed at the painting. "Incredible likeness, isn't it Kolyah?"

Stuffing the Meerschaum into his coat pocket, Nikolai sat. "I miss that look, Tatko. I can almost hear you saying, 'Bodrik, don't poke your brother with your bow.'"

Sergei chuckled. "Or, 'Kolyah that flute is a classical instrument, not a weapon.'"

Vasily set his brush aside and joined them at the table. "You hit Uncle Bodrik with your flute, Tatko?"

"Not just hit, *stabbed*. They staged sword fights."

Happy memories rushed to Nikolai's mind. "Do you remember the pillow fight, Tatko?"

"Like yesterday." Sergei's face lit up. "My head still aches at the thought of it. You two rapscallions got the best of your Tatko that night." Smile fading Sergei grasped Nikolai's arm. "Lay it on me, Dr. Derevenko. How much time do I have left?"

Chapter Eleven

Florin yawned and opened the appointment book on Oxana's desk. Row upon straight row of names and times reflected her organization. She ran the office with the discipline of a general, yet she was kind and gentle with every patient. When it came to cleanliness, she could be quite the martinet, endearing her greatly to Eleanor.

Sipping his coffee, he read the list. Mrs. Weinberg and her brood at 9:30 were the first for routine physicals. He looked forward to a pleasant start to the day. No woman was better suited for motherhood than Nettie. Since she had taken in the Berkovich girls, they had blossomed. Liba finished the school year with straight A's and Malka enjoyed helping Nettie take care of Benjamin and Bernie. What a shame that Nettie and George could not legally adopt the girls as long as their father was alive.

"Such a waste of human skin," Florin muttered.

The next appointment was not until 11:00, then no more after that. Mondays were generally slow days, barring any unforeseen emergencies. The clock on the wall read 7:15, leaving him plenty of time to grab breakfast at the Valerius.

However, he had little appetite this morning and the storm that began last night continued to rage.

Closing the ledger, he rose and stretched his arms overhead. The door chimes and thunder crashed in unison.

Eleanor entered with a dripping umbrella. She shook it and propped it beside the door.

Slipping off her hat with one hand, she smoothed her hair with the other. "Criminelly! If this keeps up, we're sure to have some cancellations." She walked to the desk and picked up the ledger. "Where's Oxana this morning? She's usually here by now."

"She telephoned to ask for the day off so she could spend some time with her family." Florin gulped the last of his coffee. "Vasily's taking the news pretty hard."

Eleanor curved her hand around Florin's. "Methinks the doctor is taking it hard as well."

"I know it's part of the job, Ellie, but I'll never get used to it." His eyes stung. "No, I'll never get used it."

The telephone rang and Eleanor answered it. "Doctor's office." She paused. "Good morning, Mrs. Weinberg." Eleanor's lips curled upward at the corners as she listened. "Oh yes, I completely understand. Four youngsters in this squall is a recipe for disaster. Stay nice and dry now. Goodbye." She set the earpiece back on the hook. "That's one down. Care to place any bets on the next?"

Florin felt his spirits lift. "You're pretty sure of yourself, aren't you, doctor?"

A bolt of lightning preceded a resounding crash of thunder. The room went dark. Eleanor shrieked and threw her arms around him, mashing his face into her neck.

The lights flickered and came back on. She dropped her arms and stepped back. "Loud noises, I...I don't like them."

"Your perfume, it's different."

"It's called White Roses."

"Very nice I—"

Once more the telephone rang. She spun around and whisked it off the desk. "Good morning, Doctor's office." She stopped to listen. "I quite agree, Mrs. Galloway. This weather is nasty, isn't it?" Dropping the earpiece onto its hook, Eleanor turned back to Florin. "The day is ours, Dr. Miklos."

Taking him by the hand, she led him up the back stairs. "I'll bet you haven't eaten breakfast, have you? I prescribe steak and eggs."

As they stepped into the kitchen, the lights went out again. Florin fumbled around for a box of matches. Once he found it, he lit the two candles he kept on the table. "A certain doctor told me once that candlelight is good for digestion."

Eleanor ignited a burner on the stove and set a large skillet on it. She took a wrapped package from the icebox that George Weinberg had brought by the day before in exchange for liniment for his back. Tearing off the paper, she dropped two steaks into the pan. They sizzled.

"Florin, there's something I must discuss with you. It's a matter of utmost importance."

He took an onion from the pantry and chopped it on the counter. "Yes?"

"Um, tongue depressors. We're almost out."

"Minor problem. I'll send Oxana to the drugstore for them tomorrow."

"And, I dropped a thermometer yesterday." She jabbed a fork into the steak and left it standing. "Oh for crying in the bucket! We don't need tongue depressors and we have three good thermometers. Florin Miklos, will you marry me?"

The knife fell from his hand, narrowly missing his big toe. Words stuck to his throat like wallpaper paste. "I...that is...I never—"

Clapping her hand over her mouth, she burst into tears. "I did it again. I've only been here a few months and I've already made a total fool of myself. How could I expect you to feel the way about me that I feel about you in such a short time?"

"Ellie, Ellie, my dear, dear girl." Stroking her hair, Florin drank in her perfume and held her close. "I always thought I'd be the one to do the asking. But it doesn't mean—"

She raised her head, her brown eyes round and shining. "Then you accept my proposal?"

"I do."

Chapter Twelve

When the captain of the ocean liner heard he had a celebrity aboard, he invited Ulrich to give an impromptu concert in the ship's music room. Ulrich accepted, seeing it as an opportunity to share Rachel's talents.

A small crowd of passengers converged on the baby grand, which took up most of the space. A mixture of perfume and cigar smoke assaulted Ulrich's nose. Ornately carved posts were interspersed with panels of red-flocked wallpaper, reminding him of Havah and her chair. Through one large window, he enjoyed the moon's reflection glittering on the waves while Rachel sat on his lap, regaling her enraptured audience with pieces by Mozart and Chopin. After each one, she clapped her hands along with them.

Following her performance, she yawned and said in a stage whisper, "Uncle Ulrich, isn't it past my bedtime?"

Oblivious to the noise around her, she popped her thumb into her mouth and lay down on the bench with her head on his lap.

She smiled in her sleep as he played a Yiddish lullaby that Havah often sang to her children called *Rojinkes mit Mandlen*. Ulrich closed his eyes and spoke over the melody. "What shall your blessings be, Rukhel Shvester? The best things that life has to offer: raisins and almonds. *Shluf jeh yiddeleh, shluf.* Sleep, little one, sleep."

After he finished, Catherine lifted Rachel and gathered her into her arms. He could not help but notice how natural she looked with a child. She kissed his cheek and whispered, "We'll see you in the morning, dearest."

The people stepped back, making a path for her and slumbering child. Some reached out to touch Rachel. Over the general chatter, Ulrich caught bits and snatches of conversations.

"So much talent for such a little one."

"Like a monkey in a circus."

"I'll bet she's really a full-grown midget."

Ulrich opened his mouth to set the last one straight, but stopped when a woman caught his attention by speaking to him in German. "*Bitte noch eine speilen, Herr* Dietrich."

It had been a long while since he had spoken the language of his youth with someone from his homeland. Her crown of braided hair reminded him of his mother.

"Are you going home to Austria, *Fräulein?*"

Her blue eyes widened. "*Ja*, how did you know?"

"The accent. I was born and raised in Vienna." He placed his fingers on the keys. "What would you like to hear? Strauss' 'Blue Danube' perhaps?"

"Could you play something by Richard Wagner? And, please, no more of that *Juden* music."

Gall boiled up in Ulrich's throat and the woman's beauty transformed into something monstrous before his eyes. "I'm sorry, I haven't included *Herr* Wagner in my repertoire. Perhaps you know this one, *Fräulein.*" He pounded out a rousing chorus of "*Khosid* Dance." "It's a favorite of my *gut freund* Itzak."

"*Und* you call yourself an enlightened *österreichisch*. You are no Austrian." Skirts swishing, she spun on her heel and left the room.

"*Nein*! I call myself a Christian and *ein menschliches Wesen*, a human being." Ulrich's jaw relaxed as he turned back to those who still surrounded the piano. "Are there any more requests? I've time for one more before we call it a night."

***

The next morning at breakfast, munching a sweet roll, he leaned back in his chair and studied the dining room's ceiling dome. Sunshine streamed through the sparkling, leaded glass panels. Gazing out the window, he tried to clear his mind of the social circus of the past few days by contemplating froth on waves.

"Am I doing the right thing, Catherine? Maybe it's a mistake to exploit a small child like this."

Across the table Catherine looked up from a stack of postcards. "Rubbish. You're hardly exploiting her. She's a natural performer."

In between bites of porridge, Rachel tapped her fingers over an imaginary piano. The sunlight glinted off her dark lenses as she rocked her head from side to side in time to her inner music. Picking up her spoon, she turned her face toward him.

"Uncle Ulri, what's a sideshow freak?"

Chapter Thirteen

A few days after the confirmed diagnosis, while strolling with Nikolai, Sergei's legs gave way and he toppled to the sidewalk. Florin commandeered a wheelchair from General Hospital. Instead of the vociferous protests Nikolai expected, Sergei accepted the chair with docile resignation.

"I hope you rented this contraption rather than buying it, Dr. Miklos." Sergei eased his fragile frame into the wicker chair. "It's for certain I won't be in need of it for long."

Up until then his mind had remained sharp, but over the past week, Nikolai had noticed the signs of dementia. Two days ago, he called Vasily, Bodrik and asked if he had been practicing for his cello recital.

Although noticeably upset, Vasily laughed it off by tickling Sergei's nose with a dry paintbrush. "I'm the artist, *Dedushkah.* Have you forgotten me so soon?"

Sergei blinked and seized Vasily's hand. "Of course I know who you are, *Solnyshko.* How could I not?"

At breakfast that morning, Sergei told Oxana he wanted to introduce her to his son the doctor. Rather than contradict him, she replied that she would like that very much.

Not sure his father would recognize him these three hours later, Nikolai prepared a dish of salted herring covered with potatoes, carrots, and beets bound together with mayonnaise. He set a cup of Russian tea beside it and went to the bedroom to fetch Sergei, but stopped short in the doorway.

The wheelchair engulfed Sergei as he gazed out the window seemingly unaware of the unkempt hair hanging in his eyes. He lifted his violin from his lap and played the opening of Beethoven's "Romance in D Major." Halfway through, his face red with exertion, he wheezed and let the bow slip from his fingers.

Gently, he caressed the violin's neck. "Farewell, my friend and lover." He laid it in the velvet-lined case on the bed and turned away from it. Head bowed, eyes focused on his lap, Sergei beckoned Nikolai with a wave of his hand. "Don't just stand there, Kolyah."

Nikolai gripped the back of the chair and wheeled it to the kitchen table. "Your lunch is ready, Tatko. Your favorite: dressed herring."

Sergei grimaced and took a sip of tea. "Business first. Bring paper and a pen. With Bodrik dead and you gone from my life, it never occurred to me to make out a will."

"Tatko, you should wait and do this in the presence of a lawyer. Tomorrow—"

A coughing fit wracked the older man. When it subsided, he whispered, "Tomorrow? I may forget who you are tomorrow. Bloody Hell, I could very well be dead tomorrow." He spat a glob of blood into his napkin. "Write it for me, Kolyah, please, whilst I have some presence of mind."

Nikolai went to his desk in the parlor and rummaged through the drawer to find a few sheets of stationery and a fountain pen. Returning to the kitchen he positioned a chair next to Sergei and sat. "Your wish is my command, Tatko."

"The bulk of my worldly goods, of course, goes to you and Oxana. I made a fortune off the sale of the mansion and properties in St. Petersburg. I've opened an account in your name at the Fidelity Trust Company."

"You've known all along, haven't you?" Nikolai's pulse thudded in his neck. "Why the charade, Tatko?"

"My doctor in Russia didn't offer much hope. Inoperable was the word he used."

"How long ago?"

Sergei counted on his brittle fingers. "It was in February...last year."

"When were you going to tell me?"

"Never. My plan was to sell everything and open a Swiss bank account in your name. I wrote a letter begging your forgiveness that I was going to have sent posthumously by my lawyers." Sergei picked up a spoon and stirred jam into his tea. "Then I received Vasily's first letter. Bless that boy."

Nikolai fought to keep his voice calm. "Go on, Tatko."

Setting down the spoon, Sergei shoved his plate aside. "My violin, my Stradivarius, I know of only one man worthy of her: Itzak Abromovich."

"Good choice." Nikolai bit his lip as he wrote. "He'll cherish her."

"In my bottom bureau drawer there's a music box. I want Havah to have it."

"The one shaped like a piano?"

"You remember it?"

"Of course. It plays 'Für Elise.' Bodrik and I were fascinated by it, but you'd never let us touch it. You said it was a gift from someone in the orchestra."

"Not just any someone, Alexei Baline, one of the greatest pianists the world has known." Sergei pressed his hand against his chest and winced. "He was only sixteen when he fled the country to avoid conscription into the Russian army. It never went well for those Jewish boys, especially a cripple like Alexei who was born with a club foot. He sent me the music box from Vienna."

"To Mrs. Havah Gitterman," Nikolai said as he wrote. "One Austrian enameled music box of great sentimental value."

"What a shame such an exquisite woman should have to suffer so. She belongs in a palace with—" Sergei paused to catch his breath. "She says you saved her life."

"She gives me too much credit. If she hadn't been such a fighter, there would've been nothing I could've done to save her."

"That's not the story she tells." Sergei reached over and gripped Nikolai's arm with unprecedented strength. "You're her knight in shining armor, Kolyah."

Pain seared Nikolai's shoulder and he let out an involuntary groan. "Vasily told me about that wound." Sergei's grip tightened as his electric glare shot through Nikolai. "No doubt there are countless others who owe their lives to your skill and courage."

"You were against my going into medicine. Why the sudden change of heart?"

"Let's say I was never more *wrong* about anything." Sergei released Nikolai's arm. "Enough of that. Let's talk about Vasily."

The topic of conversation entered with a painting under one arm and his color box in the opposite hand. "What about Vasily?"

"You're just in time to receive your inheritance, *Solnyshko.*"

After a prolonged embrace with his grandfather, Vasily set the box on the table and held up the painting. "I finally finished it. Your photographs really helped, *Dedushkah.*"

The picture sent Nikolai back in time. On the canvas, Sergei, much younger and brimming with vigor, smiled over his violin. Two little boys, Nikolai and Bodrik, mirror images of one another, flanked him. They must have been about eight. Nikolai recognized the white shirts with sailor collars and blue bow ties. To Sergei's right, Bodrik, perched on a high-backed chair, braced the unwieldly cello between his legs. His sidelong glance taunted Nikolai even now. On Sergei's left, standing erect with his flute pressed to his baby pink lips, Nikolai's pale face bore a similar expression.

"Magnificent, *Solnyshko*." Tears lined Sergei's face, his lips quivered, and he folded his hands together. "This...this is why my grandson is going to...to the Academie Julian."

Vasily flushed. "In Paris?"

Nikolai opened his mouth to protest, but Sergei held his palm flat against the air. "The details are worked out. I took the liberty of making sure his passport's up to date. All travel arrangements are made and I've secured a place for him to stay in Paris. Unless you don't want to go, *Solnyshko*."

"Yes, oh yes. I've never wanted anything more."

"Can you be packed by Thursday?"

"Are you serious? That's the day after tomorrow."

"Your train leaves at 2:00 and your ship sets out to sea next week."

"Tatko, are you—?" Nikolai sputtered.

"In my right mind? For the moment, I am. Kolyah, if I've overstepped, I'll rescind the offer."

"It's all my son's ever wanted, but this is so sudden. Why not wait until—?"

"Until what? My funeral?"

Chapter Fourteen

Three weeks had passed since Rachel's departure with the Dietrichs. While Catherine had been diligent to send frequent postcards, today the first letter finally arrived. When Havah found it in the mailbox in the morning, she stuffed it into her pocket to savor in the quiet of the evening after the children went to bed.

Hours later, after he tucked the kids in, Arel sat on the porch swing, stretched his legs, and propped his feet on the railing. "Bayla begged me to let her sleep on the back porch. That might not be a bad idea. Those upstairs rooms are hot, even with the windows open and fans blowing."

Lowering herself down beside him, Havah wiped her wet forehead with her sleeve. "If it's this hot in June, can you imagine what it will be like in August?"

Fruma Ya'el and Yussel stepped outside. "Mind if we join you?" she asked.

Not waiting for an answer, they sat in the two wicker chairs on the other side of the porch.

Havah slipped Catherine's letter from her pocket and tore open the envelope. "You're just in time to hear the news from our little world traveler." She unfolded the lavender-scented stationary.

Yussel sniffed and nodded. "I'd know Catherine's perfume anywhere."

Havah cleared her throat and read aloud.

"'21 June 1908, Sunday
"'Dear Mishpokhah,

"'I hope I spelt that right. Ulrich told me it means family in Yiddish. And indeed you are my family, my only family.'"

"Those two should be blessed with a houseful of children," said Fruma Ya'el. "After all, they have been married for three years. *Nu*? Where are the babies?"

Yussel shook his head. "Since when is this our business? Read, Havah, before Mama decides to solve the rest of the world's troubles."

"'I do wish you were here to see how your daughter is enchanting audiences, Havah. Last night, she and Ulrich played to a sold-out house at *Bechstein Hall*. Ulrich says he feels like the second fiddle, but he truly doesn't mind. Rachel is positively brilliant. Tomorrow night, they play The Royal Opera House. Rumor has it King Edward himself may make an appearance.

"'We'll be staying at the Ritz for a few days in the Royal Suite, which has its own lavatory, a sitting room, and two bedrooms with brass beds. The staff has even provided Ulrich with a piano so he and Rachel can rehearse in our private suite. As you'd expect, the décor is sumptuous: marble fireplace, curved walls with baroque carvings... I feel like a duchess in her castle.

"'I've purchased a few trinkets for the children and some lovely frocks for Bayla and Tikvah. Shopping is so much fun with Rachel. Her favourites are the perfumers and sweet shops. And I picked up some of the prettiest gowns and bonnets. I can't wait to see your baby in them.'"

Fruma Ya'el's brows furrowed and she pursed her lips. "It's bad luck." She spit three times between her fingers. "Pooh, pooh—"

"Wife. Enough of your silliness." Yussel reached over and pressed his hand over her mouth. "What else does our Catherine say, Havah?"

"'Being in London brings back so many memories. I find myself thinking of Quinnon. I'll never forgive myself for...'"

Havah stopped. Her own memories of Catherine's brother with his smoldering yellow eyes and copper hair crashed in on her in a waking nightmare. She would never forget the way he laughed as he crushed his thumbs into her windpipe.

As if Arel could read her thoughts, he drew her into his arms. "He's dead, Havah. He can't hurt you or anyone else ever again."

Havah massaged her throat. "I feel sorry for Catherine. My brothers were such good men and their memories are sweet. All her brother left was murder and cruelty to remember him by."

***

The tiny infant, perfect in every detail, floundered on a blood-soaked towel. His mouth opened as if to wail, but made no sound. An ogre of a man wearing a spattered apron bashed the child's head with a mallet and dropped his lifeless body into the rubbish bin.

"Please don't take my baby," Catherine cried.

Looming over her, brandishing his whip, her husband Sherman bared his teeth like a hyena stalking its prey. "Shut up, you bloody whore." The whip slashed her stomach.

Catherine bolted upright in bed, drenched with sweat. Beside her, Ulrich moaned and opened his eyes. "I'm sorry. I woke you," she whispered. "It was only a dream."

He sat up and gathered her to his chest. "It was more than that, wasn't it?" His steady heartbeat calmed her. He riffled his fingers through her tangles. "Forgive me, Cate. If only I'd realized how coming here would dredge up the past for you."

"I'm glad Quinnon killed Sherman. Does that make me a monster, like my brother?"

"You're my angel. That husband of yours was the monster." With his arms tight around her, he laid back taking her with him. "For what Sherman did to you and his own son, I hope he's suffering eternal torment."

"He denied it was his." Catherine could not stem her tears. "I wanted that baby. Not because he was Sherman's, but because he was mine. Now, I'm not even a woman."

"Are you sure?" Ulrich smoothed her hair back from her face and kissed her. "Hmmm. Nice and soft. They feel like a woman's lips."

Overcome with sudden desire for him she melted in the circle of his arms. "Ulrich, you're daft."

He slipped his hand under her nightgown. "I've never seen these on a man."

Chapter Fifteen

A knock on the door of the suite woke Ulrich. He switched on the bed table lamp and looked at the clock. "It's seven-thirty. Who on earth is even awake at this time of the morning, let alone out and about?"

The knock grew louder. Catherine stretched beside him and sat up. "How they got past the front desk is what I want to know. As soon as I'm dressed I'll give the management a piece of my mind."

"I'm coming." Ulrich threw on his dressing gown and hurried to the sitting room. "Patience!" He pushed back his hair and swung open the door.

A young woman stood in the hallway, a child in her arms. A blanket covered the child so only its feet were visible. The woman glared at Ulrich. *Where have I seen her before?*

Ulrich clicked his slippered heels and bowed. "Good morning. May I help you?"

"I believe you can. I'm looking for my daughter's father."

"I'm sorry, *Frau.* You must have the wrong room."

"*Fräulein* Helen Meredith. Don't you remember me, Professor Dietrich? I was one of your students at the Royal Academy."

Catherine entered the room. "Ulrich, where are your manners? Please come in, Miss Meredith." She extended her hand. "Haven't we met?"

"Only in passing. You brought Quinnon's violin to class for him one morning when he'd forgotten it." The woman sank into a chair, her eyes darting from Ulrich to

Catherine. "When Quinnon told me you married his sister, Professor Dietrich, I thought he was joking." She fixed her eyes on Catherine. "You know what a scoundrel your brother can be. He makes up the most fantastic stories. He once told me he was a strangler, but that he only killed prostitutes. Can you imagine? He said he bound their hands with his violin strings. Preposterous. He should be a novelist."

Catherine's lips paled. "Then you don't know, do you?"

"What's to know? He ran out on me and sailed off to America. Did he come back with you perchance?"

"Those 'fantastic stories' he told you are true. My baby brother was a murderer."

"Was?"

"The last one he had a go at kept a derringer under her pillow. She blew his bloody liver to kingdom come. A fitting end don't you think?"

Helen blanched so white Ulrich feared she would faint. "Is there anything we can do?"

She hugged the bundled child in her arms. "When I heard you were in London, I thought perhaps he had returned to keep his promise."

Catherine scowled. "My brother's promises were little more than words he used to manipulate his victims."

Color returned to Helen's cheeks. "I've had nearly three years to figure that out for myself. But I'd hoped—"

"I'm sorry, Miss Meredith. It's for certain he had no intention of marrying you."

"Nor I, him." Helen smirked. "If he were alive, I wouldn't have him if he crawled to me through broken glass. But I can barely feed myself these days, let alone a child. I told Olive her daddy was here for her. What do I tell her now?"

The child woke and wriggled out from under the blanket. If there had been any doubt in Ulrich's mind of

Quinnon's paternity, it vanished at that moment. Olive was a two-year-old miniature of Catherine with strawberry ringlets and green eyes.

She held out her arms and cried, "Daddy!"

Chapter Sixteen

Although Aunt Havah protested and said family doesn't charge family, Lev argued that as an adult, he needed to be responsible and pay rent. With three growing children and a baby on the way, she and Uncle Arel could use the help. In the end, she accepted with a hug and a kiss.

Daniel Kaminsky hired Lev on the spot, paid him fifteen cents an hour, and allowed him two bottles of soda pop per shift. Giving Uncle Arel a dollar a week left Lev enough for text books, paper, and pencils he would need in college.

Wednesday in the grocery store was the slowest night of the week. This explained why Mr. Kaminsky took it off and left Lev in charge. With few interruptions, Lev swept the floor, tidied shelves, and polished the glass showcases. He looked forward to the hour before closing, when after he finished his work, he could read and enjoy a cold soda.

Tonight, for the fun of it, Lev had borrowed Bayla's copy of *The Wonderful Wizard of Oz*. He sat cross-legged on a sack of flour, leaned back against the wall, and opened the book. After months of intense study, he enjoyed the escape into fantasy.

The sound of clinking glass startled him and brought him back from the "brightness and glory" of the Emerald City. He looked up to see Jamie Flynn with his hand in the candy jar.

"Well, what do ya know? Tis himself, Lev Gitterman, in the flesh."

"Oh, no you don't." Dropping the book, Lev rushed to the counter and grabbed the jar. "I can't let you steal from Mr. Kaminsky."

Jamie's genial smile dissolved. "Ya didn't seem to mind it back in the day when you was hungry now didja, Mr. High and Mighty?"

"I heard you'd been sent to the workhouse."

"I done me time and I ain't going back, y'hear? You call your nigger police friend on me and I swear by the Blessed Virgin, I'll kill ya."

"Calm down. No one's calling anyone." Lev filled a sack with a loaf of bread, a block of cheese, and a couple of apples. He dropped two coins in the cash register, walked around the counter and handed the bag to Jamie. "I wish it could be more, but it's all I can afford."

"I don't need your charity, ya stupid kike."

Jamie balled up his fist and slammed his knuckles into Lev's stomach. Stunned, Lev doubled over and went to his knees, helpless to do anything but watch Jamie run from the store, sack in hand.

When he finally caught his breath, Lev retrieved Bayla's fallen book and stood. "Dumb Irish Mick."

Carrying a flat package under one arm Vasily entered the store. "Where was that goop going in such a hurry?"

"The penitentiary." Lev locked the door behind Vasily. He took a bottle from the refrigerator. "Closing time. Have a Coca-Cola, for old time's sake. It's on the house."

"You've heard already?"

"Yeah. Your grandfather telephoned to invite us to see you off at the station tomorrow."

"I wanted to tell you myself." Vasily took a swig of soda and gave Lev the package. "This is for you. I believe they're smiling down on you from Heaven."

Ripping off the paper, Lev gasped. Leah's face glowed over the Sabbath candles. Behind her, with his burly arms around her waist, Gavrel did seem to be smiling at Lev.

He set the painting on the counter and crammed his hands into his pockets. "I don't know what to say."

"What's the matter, Jew?" Vasily held out his hand. "Afraid to shake hands with a *shaygitz?*"

Taking his hands out of his pocket, Lev seized Vasily's hand and pulled him into an embrace. "It won't be the same without you, Vasya."

Vasily and Lev discussed their futures and reminisced long into the night. They had been through so much together; it did not seem possible they had only known each other for three short years.

At half past midnight, Vasily embraced Lev once more. "I've learned a lot from you...and your family."

"I'll look for your paintings in the Louvre."

"Take care of the Buick." Vasily pulled back, took off his glasses, and wiped his eyes on his sleeve. "See you tomorrow?"

Lev gave him a gentle shove. "Would I miss the chance to get rid of you?"

After Vasily left, Lev made sure all lights were off and things put away. He stepped outside into the steamy air and locked the door behind him. Taking off his cap, he fanned himself with it as he walked the deserted sidewalk.

A cry that sounded like a wounded animal came from a nearby alley. As he inched closer Lev realized it was human. Not sure whether to run toward the cry or away from it, Lev chose the former.

Sprawled out on the pavement, a young man groaned. Lev hurried to him. "Jamie?"

"Himself in the...flesh." Jamie sputtered through bloody lips. "What's left of it."

Lev sank down beside him and cradled his head on his lap. "What happened?"

"I…went…home. Dad…welcomed me with his fists."

"Don't talk." Lev tried to lift him. "Let's get you to the hospital."

"No. Stay…here…sorry…Lev…didn't mean those things I said…it was…safer in the workhouse…" Jamie shuddered, arched his back and gasped. "Mother of God, it's cold."

***

Heartsick and fatigued, Lev unlocked the front door and pushed it open. Trying to be as quiet as he could, he hung his cap on the hall tree. He shut the door and rubbed his stomach, still tender where Jamie had slugged him.

The past two hours replayed in his head, from finding his former cohort in the alley to accompanying his body to the undertaking rooms. Lying on the table, with his cherubic round cheeks and turned up nose, Jamie looked more like a slumbering child than a twenty-year-old tramp.

There would be no funeral for him. Instead, his body would be tossed into potter's field, without a prayer spoken over him, and forgotten.

Aunt Havah's whispered voice startled him. "It's four-thirty, Lev. I thought you went to bed hours ago." She lay stretched on the sofa with a book perched on top of her belly. "Makes a nice shelf don't you think?"

Wisps of dark hair clung to her face and her cheeks flushed cherry red. Aside from her rounded bulge, resembling a basketball inflated under her robe, she was still waif thin. She shut her book and let out a soft groan.

"This kid won't let me sleep."

He eased down into an overstuffed chair and leaned his head back against its wing. "Aren't you going to ask where I've been?"

"You're a grown man." Her gaze traveled from his soiled shirt to his bloodstained trousers. "Where in heaven's name *have* you been?"

Chapter Seventeen

For the second time in two months Nikolai found himself at Union Depot waiting for a train. He dreaded the locomotive that would soon carry off his son. After being cheated out of seven years of Vasily's life, a paltry four years, fraught with heartache and tragedy, did not make up the difference.

Vasily's hair, plated into a braid, hung from under the straw hat that matched his light beige suit. At seventeen, he stood two inches taller than Nikolai, and his square jaw showed signs of maturity.

Sitting in his wheelchair next to Havah in hers, Sergei had rallied from his decline of two days ago. With his silver hair combed and his moustache curled at the ends, he was every inch the dapper gentleman.

She blushed as he flirted with her. "Mr. Derevenko, shame on you, I could be your daughter."

He kissed her hand. "I dare say, you could be my granddaughter. No matter. You're more ravishing than the sum total of prima donnas I've encountered in theaters around the world."

"Photographic opportunity knocks," said Itzak, Brownie camera in hand. "Who knows when the Derevenkos will be together in one place again? Dr. Nikolai, you stand behind Mr. Derevenko. Oxana and Vasily, you two get on either side of the good doctor—pardon me—flautist. Everybody act like you're happy, and smile."

"As you wish, Mr. Abromovich." Nikolai maneuvered Sergei's chair and stood behind it. "Never cross a man with a new toy."

"Toy? This is cutting edge technology." Itzak rotated the film advance on the side of the box-shaped camera. "Snapshots are in and tintypes are out. Like the advertisement says, 'Anybody can Kodak.'"

"Then take a picture of Mrs. Miklos and me," said Florin, his arm tight around Eleanor. "Isn't she the most gorgeous bride you've ever laid eyes on?"

The epitome of reserve, Eleanor wore a leghorn straw hat with a single purple band. Her white blouse with embroidered violets boasted Oxana's skill and complimented a simple lavender skirt. She turned in Florin's embrace and planted a loud kiss on his cheek.

"No contest, Florin," said Nikolai. "As beautiful a bride as I've ever seen."

Itzak snapped three pictures of the newlyweds. "Who's next?"

"Vasily, that suit looks wonderful on you," said Oxana. "Arel, you are better and better tailor than ever."

Arel grinned. "Thank you, but the credit goes to my assistant, Sammy. He's a born tailor."

"He's a godsend," said Florin. "You're looking much better, Arel. Much healthier indeed."

"Hey, Uncle Itzak." Vasily curved his arm around Lev's shoulder. "Take a picture of us."

Lev pulled his cap down over his disheveled hair. "Aw, get off it, Vasya. Can't you just remember me the way I looked when I was alive?"

"Smile, boys." Itzak winked at Lev and held up the camera. "Come on, Lev, show me some teeth."

The depot bell rang and the train whistle sounded in the distance. Nikolai's pulse raced. There were so many things he wanted to say.

"Do you have Mr. Baline's address, *Solnyshko*?" asked Sergei. "He's with the New York Philharmonic. You'll be staying with him for a few days."

Vasily hugged him. *"Da, Dedushkah."*

The train rumbled closer.

Oxana's eyes brimmed. "You'll write?"

"Yes, Mother. Of course." He wrapped his arms around her and she whispered something in his ear that made him laugh. "Be sure to write and tell me what he says."

All of the children clamored around Vasily to say their goodbyes. He kissed each one and swept Bayla up into his arms. "Don't forget, you promised to save your heart for me."

Setting her back on her feet, Vasily shook hands with Reuven. "Careful not to break any more bones, okay? And you'd better write to me, Mr. Author."

The ground vibrated beneath Nikolai as the train juddered to a stop. "*Solnyshko—*"

Before he could utter another word Vasily grabbed him, kissed both of his cheeks and threw his arms around his neck. "*Yah tehbyah lublu, Tatko.*"

"I love you, too, son."

Vasily stepped back, collected his luggage, and disappeared among other boarding passengers. A few minutes later, he waved from the window.

Hand in hand with Oxana, Nikolai watched the train chug from the depot until it disappeared over the horizon.

Sergei slumped to one side of his wheelchair. "Take me home, Kolyah."

Chapter Eighteen

The week culminating in Sergei Derevenko's funeral sped by in a haze. Within hours of Vasily's departure on Thursday, Sergei bade Nikolai and Oxana farewell and breathed his last. That night Nikolai steeled himself for the task of carrying out Sergei's final wishes.

Friday afternoon, he saw to the burial arrangements, which, for the most part, Sergei had made in advance down to his unadorned casket. Every expense he had paid in full.

Saturday afternoon, the hot summer sun beat down on the sparse circle of mourners. The memorial was a simple graveside service which Nikolai found odd for someone who had lived his life for his adoring audiences. Nonetheless, Sergei's written directions: "no frills, no fanfare, just plant me."

Later that evening, the people Nikolai considered more than friends congregated in his bright yellow kitchen, offering comfort and food. While the aromas of the latter filled the air, the smells he missed most were those of pigment and pipe tobacco.

Eleanor set a pie piled with meringue on the counter next to the samovar. "It's an old Amish recipe called funeral pie; full of eggs, cream, and raisins."

Havah sliced a round loaf of dark rye. "I love raisins. I put some in the bread, too."

Fruma Ya'el ladled steaming lentil soup from a kettle until she had filled bowls for everyone. "Havah puts raisins in everything. I swear she'd have put them in with the lentils if I'd let her. Lentil soup and round bread, it's our tradition for mourning."

Yussel popped a piece of bread in his mouth. "The shapes of the lentils and the loaf remind us of the circle of life."

"Maybe we should call it funeral soup." Itzak downed his in three gulps.

"You haven't touched your soup, Dr. Nikolai," said Shayndel with a worried frown. "Is something wrong with it?"

"It's perfect." Nikolai shoveled a spoonful into his mouth and swallowed. "Maybe later. I'm not very hungry."

"You look tired, Dr. Nikolai. We should leave so you can get some rest." Fruma Ya'el clucked her tongue and buttered a slice of bread. "At least eat some of this."

"No thanks."

"I'll eat it." Oxana grabbed it and wolfed it down. "Kolyah, you don't know what you're missing. It's delicious."

Until then, he had not noticed how much her face had filled out. No longer sunken and pale, her cheeks were ruddy and round as the bread. He tweaked one of her long braids.

"Don't eat too much, *zaichik*. Nothing's less appealing than a fat wife."

Sudden tears welled up her eyes. He put his arms around her as her tearful sniffs heightened to sobs.

"I'm joking," he said. "You've never looked healthier. You were too skinny."

Oxana wailed louder and shoved him away. "There's no pleasing you."

He followed her to the bedroom where he found her face down on the bed. Lying beside her, he massaged her back.

Emotions washed over him in waves. The stoic barrier he had built around his heart for the past month crumbled and surged forth in choking torrents.

She turned and held his head against her shoulder. "Let it go, Kolyah."

Relief and exhaustion whelmed him and her warmth comforted him. "I'm a physician. Why didn't I see it?"

"You said yourself your father was a dead man before he came here. There was nothing you could've done."

"I'm not talking about my father." He laid his hand on her stomach. "I should've paid better attention to the mother of my unborn child."

Chapter Nineteen

With Catherine being the next of kin, adoption with Helen's consent had been a simple matter of filling out the legal documents. Once Ulrich paid the lawyer's fee, the deal was sealed. Nonetheless, the despair in Helen's eyes as she relinquished her daughter tormented Catherine.

How horrid for Helen to learn in an instant that the father of her child was not only dead but also a murderer. *How many more victims suffered in the wake of Quinnon's deadly rampages? How many other destitute nieces and nephews do I have? Oh, the shame!* Catherine's anger at her brother burned white hot.

"You don't have to give her up, Helen," said Catherine. "She is our niece, let us help you financially."

"She'll be better off with you." Helen's mouth set in a rigid line. "Don't you see? No man wants a woman saddled with another man's brat."

"You can't mean that."

"I don't want her anymore, do you hear?"

Olive clutched Helen's skirts and followed her to the office door. "No go, Mummy. Olive go with you!"

Helen's tears betrayed her as she knelt and pried off the girl's fingers. "I can't take you where I'm going." She picked her up and shoved her into Catherine's arms. "This nice lady's your mum now. Be a good girl." Eyes brimming, she lowered her voice to a choked whisper in Catherine's ear. "Make her forget me."

The door closed behind Helen. Olive kicked her way out of Catherine's embrace. Collapsing in front of the door, she drummed her feet on the floorboards and screamed, "Mummy! Mummy! Mummy!"

Catherine swept her up in her arms to comfort her. Olive squirmed and hollered. Then she smacked Catherine's cheek so hard with her little fist Catherine nearly blacked out.

The next day, in the hotel suite, she would only go to Ulrich. She refused Catherine's affections. Every effort Catherine made was met with a tantrum.

Catherine had hoped having another child around who was close to her own age would help Olive acclimate. Alas, her hopes were short-lived. Not only did Olive shun Rachel, but Rachel was not too keen on the new playmate either.

During rehearsals, Ulrich suggested Rachel show Olive how to play the scales on the piano. "You're the big sister now."

Instead of her usual sunny disposition, Rachel scowled and pushed Olive off the bench with a resounding, "No!"

Ulrich smacked Rachel's bottom and whisked the squalling Olive up into his arms. "Shame on you, Rukhel Shvester."

Rachel huddled under the bench and curled up like a puppy. She jutted out her lower lip. "I don't like you anymore. I want my poppy."

Things did not improve the second day. Olive still would not let Catherine near her. Rachel, on the other hand, pouted, refused to play a single note, and clung to Catherine.

The third night, after the girls were finally asleep, Catherine fell into bed beside Ulrich. "This isn't working, is it?"

"Don't worry. Olive will adapt."

"It's not just her, it's Rachel. I've never seen her behave like this. She's acting like a...a..."

"A four-year-old?"

***

A jumble of conflicting emotions riddled Catherine as she watched the German countryside zip by. Although she had yearned for a child, she hated how this one came to her at another woman's expense.

Settling back against her seat on the train, she cuddled Olive, who slept on her lap, clutching a handmade rag doll. *Will she wake up and scream when she sees where she is?* Catherine tried not to let it bother her that Olive already called Ulrich Daddy. She'd never even seen her *real* father. Nonetheless, it worried Catherine that Olive would have nothing to do with her. *How can I possibly be a mother to a child who hates me? Ulrich said to give it time...but what if that time never comes? What if Olive never warms up to me?*

Olive stirred and opened her eyes. Sitting up, she dropped her doll and reached for Catherine's face. Catherine flinched for fear the child would strike her again. Instead, Olive cautiously touched the bruise on Catherine's cheek with one finger. "Does it hurt?"

"Yes."

Olive gently pulled a wayward lock of Catherine's hair and held it against one of her own curls. "Mummy says it's orange. Just like mine." Her brows furrowed in the middle and she pursed her lips like a scholar deep in thought. "Mummy went away."

"May I be your mum?"

Olive looped Catherine's curl around her pudgy forefinger and yawned. "No, not today." She laid her head on Catherine's breast.

Catherine stroked Olive's cheek and kissed her forehead. "What about tomorrow?"

Olive's eyes drooped and she smiled. "Yes...tomorrow."

Chapter Twenty

Strings of lights, 100,000 of them the newspapers boasted, outlined the Electric Park's archways and pillars. Havah gazed at them in amazement. They illumined the dark sky and reflected in the water on the lagoon aptly called Mirror Lake.

Bayla sat next to Havah on a blanket in the grass. "It's like a fairyland, isn't it, Mommy?"

Nettie stopped her wicker pram with Benny and Bernie sound asleep inside. "Oh good, we're not too late. This place is so big, I was afraid we wouldn't be able to find you."

"We saved you a spot." Bayla leaped up to greet Malka, who cradled Miss Tova in one arm. "Happy Fourth of July!"

Malka held out the doll. "I thought you might want her back."

"Nope." Bayla shook her head making her curls shake. "She's all yours."

Malka grinned and hugged Miss Tova and Bayla at the same time. Malka had filled out since Havah last saw her. In fact, one could almost call her plump.

On Nettie's other side, Liba had grown at least three inches. Not what one would call a beauty, she was pleasant to look at nonetheless.

George appeared carrying a huge tub of popcorn. "Happy Fourth, everyone." He plopped on the ground beside his boys. "Getting four children ready to go anywhere is a tougher job than cutting steaks for the Governor's ball." He reached over the baby, squeezed

Malka's hand and added, "Children are the Almighty's reward, no matter where they come from."

Four-month-old Bernie whimpered and rolled over. Sitting on the blanket, Nettie picked him up. He nuzzled against her breast. "It's always mealtime for this little fatty. Speaking of children, is it true what I've heard about the Dietrichs? Did they really adopt a little girl?"

"Yes," said Havah. "We got the telegram a few days ago. I can't wait to meet Olive."

"Mama," whispered Liba, her eyes wide with terror as she pointed toward one of the pavilions. "Papa's over there...behind a wall."

Nettie stroked Liba's hair. "Nonsense, he's sitting with Benny, stuffing his mouth with popcorn."

"No, no, not Dad. Papa. The terrible one who—" Liba buried her head in Nettie's skirts.

"It's only your imagination." Nettie laid her hand on the girl's back. "He's locked up far away from here where he can never hurt you again."

Malka hugged Miss Tova and pointed. "There he is! It *is* him." She scooted next to Havah and hid her face in the folds of Havah's sleeve.

Havah looked back over her shoulder to see the bent figure of a man. The lights cast a glow on his leering eyes. He flashed a smile and disappeared behind a tree. She assured herself he could not possibly be Zalman. *Did I not see him taken away in chains?*

Tempted to spit between her fingers to ward off the Evil Eye, she huddled against Arel and wrapped a protective arm around Malka. "It's just the night playing tricks on us."

To shake off her gnawing fear, she concentrated on the flags posted on every pillar and column. The way they snapped and rippled in the wind was music to her. They reminded her of the first American flag she had seen flying high above Ellis Island. She held her hand over her palpitating heart and recited the "Pledge of Allegiance" under her breath.

"I love the Fourth of July, don't you, Arel?"

"Red, white and blue through and through, I do."

In the music pavilion behind them a brass band played "You're a Grand Old Flag." Arel helped Havah to her feet as everyone around them stood. The first fountain of sparks flew and blossomed against the dark sky. Another rocket spun like a fiery pinwheel, shooting stars in all directions.

A tenor voice behind her sang with to the band's tune.

"You're a grand old flag, you're a high flying flag
And forever in peace may you wave…"

Havah turned to see Bayla jump into Sammy Weiner's arms. He hoisted her onto his shoulders and she sang along with him.

"You're the emblem of the land I love
The home of the free and the brave…"

After singing the song through twice, Sammy twirled Bayla around in circles. "You got a nice set of pipes there, kiddo."

Setting her back on her feet, he grabbed Arel's hand. "Happy Independence Day, Chief."

Arel opened his mouth to respond, but before he could, a line of firecrackers exploded at his feet. Knocking Sammy to the ground, he dropped to his knees, covered his head with his arms and hollered. "Evron! Cossacks! Look out!"

Chapter Twenty-One

Arel took a swig of schnapps from the bottle on his desk. He set a clean sheet of stationery on it. Blotting the point of his pen he wrote,

> "My Dearest Havah,
>
> "You are the fairest of ten thousand and worthy of so much better than I. Please don't waste your tears on a miserable coward. Someday you'll—"

An arm reached around him and seized the letter. Dropping the pen, he turned and faced Itzak's menacing scowl. "What are you doing here?"

"Someday she'll what, Arel? Have you gone completely mad?"

"Go home and put your own family to bed."

"Your wife asked me to look in on you."

"She's better off without me."

"You lunkhead." Itzak crumpled the paper in his fist and lifted the revolver that lay beside the bottle. "Will she be better off finding her husband's brains spattered everywhere? Use that matzo ball between your ears. Hasn't she suffered enough?" Itzak brandished the gun under Arel's nose. "Is this the legacy you want to leave your children?"

"It's my fault."

"What's your fault, little brother?"

"If I had done something, they might have lived."

"Enough talking in riddles. Who might have lived?"

"Evron, Katya, the children."

Arel hunched over and banged his head on the desk. No matter how many times or how hard he hit, he could not blot out the images flooding him.

"I did nothing when they slit Evron's throat. I did nothing when Katya put out the beast's eye with her knitting needle. I did nothing when he broke her neck. Nothing, nothing, nothing that's what I did."

"Arel, stop it!" Itzak's voice cracked.

Arel cupped his hands over his ears as if to prevent the screams that reverberated like a howling wind. "Innocent babies...they swung them by their feet and bashed their heads against the wall. I did nothing when Ruth and Rukhel—those beautiful twins— begged for their lives only to be...be ravaged by animals. They—my Havah fought like a lioness until he plunged a knife in her side. And, like the coward I am, I just *laid* there."

"But you were—"

"Unconscious?" Arel wailed. "Noooo! My God, I saw everything."

Itzak seized Arel's shoulders. "What could you have done?"

Arel collapsed against Itzak's chest and released five years of buried anguish and guilt. "I...I played dead so the Cossacks would stop beating me."

"I'm glad you did," said a tearful voice behind him.

Arel whipped around to see Havah, her nightgown fluttering in the wind gusting through the open window. Her ivory cheeks glistened in the lamplight.

"Don't you see, my beloved? If you hadn't feigned it, it would have meant certain death—" she knelt and laid her head in his lap "—for both of us."

***

Itzak refused to leave until Arel promised to get rid of the gun. Before he left, Itzak embraced Arel once more.

"Never, never let me hear the word 'coward' from your lips again, understand?"

Havah held her breath and waited for Arel's answer.

Arel hung his head and mumbled. "Understood."

Itzak's tense lips relaxed into a wry grin. "You're a little *farshimmelt,* perhaps. But you were never a coward."

For a few moments after Itzak left, Arel sat at his desk and stared at nothing as if in a trance. He picked up the revolver. "If Itzak hadn't—"

"But he did." Havah plucked the gun from his hand and set it on the desk. "It's late Arel, come to bed. Tomorrow, you'll call Sammy and tell him you're not well."

Awash with relief and filled with love for him, she sat on his lap and kissed the scars that cobwebbed from his forehead to his chin. "Arel, my beloved, you have always been and always will be the fairest of ten thousand to me."

Chapter Twenty-Two

Dr. Florin slapped Arel on the back. "Congratulations, Papa, it's a boy, and another boy and two girls."

"Four babies?" Arel's forehead crinkled in a worried frown. "She's so small. Is she going to be okay?"

"See for yourself." Dr. Eleanor sat on the floor beside a blanket-lined basket where Kreplakh licked and nursed her newborn puppies. "Mother and babies are doing fine."

Havah lay back on the bed and rested her hands on her belly. The baby pressed his feet against them. "I hope I do as well as Kreplakh when my time comes."

"At least you won't have to eat the afterbirth," said Lev.

Fruma Ya'el scowled. "Lev Gitterman, watch that mouth."

Yussel cocked his head to one side. "Our future doctor speaks the truth."

"He shouldn't speak it in front of the children."

"But, *Bubbe*," said Reuven, "we all watched Kreplakh eat it. Ugh. It made me want to puke."

"Listen to the way these modern children speak." Kneeling beside the basket, Fruma Ya'el stroked Kreplakh's head. "I've delivered many a baby, but never a dog. Such a good mama."

"How fortuitous the missus and I happened by this morning." Dr. Florin eyed Dr. Eleanor with the unabashed affection of a newlywed. "There's nothing like good coffee, fresh bagels, and a blessed event to start the day."

Sitting cross-legged on the floor, Reuven looked up from his journal. "This will make a good story for 'What I did over the summer.' Teachers always ask us to write papers about it."

"You might want to leave out the gory details," said Dr. Florin as he washed his hands in the basin on the stand.

Arel knelt beside Reuven. "My guess is our little apple will give his classmates an education about puppies they'll never forget."

"Nah, half those kids have seen cows born on the farm." Reuven reached into basket and petted one of the puppies. "Can we keep one?"

Without warning, Havah's unborn kicked so hard it made her blouse flounce. "Ouch! This baby is running a footrace in there."

Dr. Florin put the earpieces of his stethoscope in his ears. "This one's going to be bigger than Rachel. Much bigger." He pressed the bell against Havah's stomach. "Good strong heartbeat."

"May I listen, too?" Bayla jumped up from the floor where she had been trying to choose her favorite puppy. "Can you tell if the baby's a boy or a girl by its heartbeat?"

Dr. Eleanor put her stethoscope ends in Bayla's ears. "I'm afraid the only way to tell is after he or she is born."

Bayla's mouth formed an *o* as she listened. "It's so fast. I hear sloshing, too."

"That's the baby swimming in his bag of water," said Lev. "It's not really water, though." He shot Havah a sly grin. "It's amniotic fluid and it protects him from accidents like when his mama runs into walls."

Handing Lev his stethoscope, Dr. Florin beamed. "I can tell you've been studying hard, my boy. I predict you'll be a credit to the medical profession. Perhaps you'll specialize and take up obstetrics."

With dignified posture Lev sat on the bed and positioned the stethoscope. "Actually, I'm seriously considering it, sir." A serene smile lit his face. "I like the idea of being part of a miracle."

Despite Dr. Florin's upturned lips, the dull edge to his voice did not escape Havah's notice when he said, "Yes, son, childbirth is a miracle indeed."

***

Nikolai pushed his empty plate away and looked around Florin's apartment. He recognized Oxana's handiwork in the ruffled curtains and tatted doilies on the end tables. One of Vasily's paintings of Union Depot hung above the sofa.

"You've really turned this place into a home, Eleanor."

"It's kind of cramped for two people." She dabbed her lips with her napkin and sent a sidelong glance to Florin. "We're talking about buying a house and making this into a short term hospital ward for emergency patients."

"Sounds like the arrangement I had in Kishinev. Ulrich was gracious enough to let me use a third of his home for a clinic."

"No doubt you performed an operation or two there." Florin's ice-blue gaze seared Nikolai. "And they were successful, I'm sure."

For most of the dinner, Oxana and Eleanor had carried the bulk of the conversation. Florin, uncharacteristically silent, poked at his chicken, taking only an occasional bite. Every so often, he would open his mouth only to clamp his lips shut.

Eleanor pressed her palm against his forehead. "I hope you're not coming down with something."

"I'm quite well, my dear." He lifted her hand from his forehead and brought it to his lips. "Indeed, I'm in optimum health thanks to my doctor, my bride."

He rose from the table and gestured for Nikolai to follow. When they reached his office downstairs, Florin lowered himself into his armchair and folded his hands on the desk. Nikolai sat in the chair on the other side of it and braced himself.

After a few tense moments, Florin cast an imploring glance at Nikolai and cleared his throat. "I advised her against conception, you know."

"Why? She's never looked or felt better."

"I agree. Pregnancy agrees with Oxana." Florin twirled his thumbs around each other. "But I'm talking about Havah. We saw her this morning. Eleanor gives Havah's gestation one more month, perhaps less." Florin's eyes filled. "Frankly, Kolyah, I'm afraid she won't survive it. No, I don't believe she will."

"You can't know that. She came through fine with Rachel."

"You didn't see what I saw, Kolyah. Rachel was two weeks old when I first saw her. At the most I'd guess her birth weight at five pounds. When I examined Havah two months later, her insides were still raw. This baby is already bigger and she's not yet full term."

Florin's words confirmed suspicions and concerns Nikolai had held four years ago when Havah's birth announcement reached him and Ulrich in London. "She assured us she and the baby were in splendid health."

"Then you'll understand. My wife says I've no right to ask, but I'm going to ask anyway. I beg you, Kolyah, renew your medical license."

"Florin, are you suggesting what I think?"

"If you think I'm suggesting a Caesarean section, you'd be correct."

"Just because this child's larger, doesn't mean Havah won't be able to—"

"Do you really believe that?"

"Florin, I haven't touched a scalpel in over three years." Nikolai stood and paced the parameter of the office. "Have you discussed the dangers with Havah and Arel?"

"Do you remember Klara Ivanov?"

"The name sounds familiar."

Florin leaned back and linked his hands behind his head. "She labored twelve hours and never dilated. As I recall, she was no bigger than Havah. I wouldn't have given her *half* a chance in a thousand, yet you pulled her and her nine-pound son through." Sitting up straight, Florin held Nikolai in his incisive gaze. "Havah's chances will be far better than Klara's if we don't allow her labor to commence."

Nikolai stopped pacing. "There's always the risk of postoperative infection to consider."

"Careful, Kolyah, you're starting to sound like a physician."

Chapter Twenty-Three

Havah still missed her upstairs window overlooking the street, but this downstairs bedroom did have its advantages. While she could no longer observe the early morning activities of the milkman and his horse, she basked in the sunrise.

The original owner and builder had added this room onto the back of the house to be his library. One wall boasted built-in cabinets, bookshelves and even a dropdown writing desk. Arel and Havah's bed, armoire, and bureau only took up a quarter of the room. The additional furniture, including a settee, two upholstered chairs, an end table, and Havah's wheelchair, fit comfortably. Rich oak wainscoting, blue flowered wallpaper, and a stone fireplace made it a cheerful haven.

Sitting in her chair beside the bay window, Havah watched Kreplakh and her puppies. The rising sun bathed them in rose-tinted light. As if she could feel Havah's uneasiness, Kreplakh jumped from the basket onto her lap long enough for a pat and a lick. Then she jumped back into the basket where her offspring mewled and blindly foraged for her teats.

"Won't Rachel be surprised when she comes home?" whispered Havah.

At the mention of Rachel's name, the dog let out a plaintive whine.

With a groan, Arel rolled over in the bed, shielding his eyes from the sun with his hand. "Havah, did you sleep at all last night?"

"They're precious, aren't they?"

Crouching beside the basket, Arel gingerly scooped a puppy into his hand and held it against his cheek. "Not one of them looks like her. I suspect our unwed mother committed adultery with Mrs. Hutton's beagle."

Under Kreplakh's watchful eye, he stroked the puppy with his index finger and set it back down. Scratching her behind her furry ears, he chuckled. "Good girl. Of course I'd never say that to our daughters under the same circumstances."

Havah flexed her shoulders in an attempt to find a comfortable position. "Do you think Rachel will marry and have children?"

"I don't see why not. Nothing stops her. She's so much like her mother." He pressed his ear against Havah's belly. "Who knows? This one might be the first Jewish president of the United States."

"I won't live to see it."

"Havah, don't."

"I've had the same dream twice. My mother floated on the clouds like an angel and bade me come to her. I could almost touch her. Perhaps it's a sign."

"No!" Arel shouted, and then lowered his voice to a whisper. "Since when did you start believing in signs and omens?"

Havah's enflamed legs thrummed and the weight of her unborn baby made her back convulse with painful spasms. "What about the sign in Dr. Florin's eyes?"

***

Opening the oaken case containing the surgical tools Florin had given him last November, Nikolai lifted the scalpel. He skimmed his fingertip across its honed edge. A drop of blood oozed from the minute incision. He held up his finger and watched the thin stream flow to his palm.

Oxana entered the parlor, dressed for the day, and opened the window. Silhouetted against a backdrop of orange and golden light, her slender form accentuated her small bulge. "It's a lovely morning, isn't it?"

Wiping his hand on his dressing gown, Nikolai set the case on the end table and encircled her in his arms. "I've never seen anything more beautiful."

"You didn't come to bed last night."

"I couldn't sleep."

She leaned her head on his shoulder and whispered in his ear, "I know in my heart my husband will do the right thing."

Chapter Twenty-Four

Never was Ulrich prouder of Rachel than this night as she sat on his lap and performed for over 2,000 people at the *Musikverein*. Perhaps if she could see them, she might be frightened, but Ulrich had his doubts.

She played Beethoven's "Für Elise" and Mozart's "Turkish March" without missing a note. When she finished, he sat her on a cushion beside him.

The conductor of the Vienna Philharmonic, baton at his side, bowed. "Next, *Herr* Dietrich and *Fräulein* Gitterman will perform a particular favorite of mine, Johann Strauss' 'Vienna Waltz Number Four'."

After they finished the duet, the audience burst into applause and shouts of "Brava!"

Rachel, holding tight to Ulrich's hand, followed him to center stage where she let go, curtsied and blew a kiss to the audience. Another round of applause reverberated through the hall.

Sweeping her up into his arms, Ulrich shook hands with the conductor. "*Herr* Weingartner, thank you for sharing the stage with us. I hand it back over to you and your wonderful orchestra."

Ulrich found his seat beside Catherine on the front row of seats. Olive reached up for him. "Daddy."

"I'll never tire of being called daddy." He picked up Olive and helped Rachel find Catherine's lap. "I'll trade you, Cate."

Catherine's green eyes shone like the *Musikverein's* crystal chandeliers. "Our girls are adorable, aren't they? I'm going to hate to give Rachel back."

The hall resounded with Strauss' "Blue Danube Waltz." Olive swayed to and fro on Ulrich's lap. After a few moments, her eyes drooped and she laid against his chest, her fiery curls tickling his nose.

Leaning back his head, he studied the paintings inset between the carvings adorning the high golden ceiling. Everything was as he remembered it. Most of the décor in the *Musikverein* was painted gold accented with crimson.

His mind traveled to the first time he saw the palatial theater with its statues and balconies…

He was five years old. Grandfather brought him to hear the Philharmonic to comfort him after his parents' death from cholera.

Ulrich fell in love with music and begged his grandparents for a piano. At Grandmother's urging, Grandfather grudgingly purchased a secondhand upright. Since Grandfather refused to waste more money on an expensive teacher, Grandmother dug out her old music books.

Her lavender cologne filled his nose as she placed his hands on the keys. "This is middle C, *liebling*. It's where it all begins."

Ulrich plowed through Grandmother's books and had mastered every page by the time he was five and a half. When she insisted he needed a more suitable teacher, Grandfather scowled. "What does a banker need with music?"

Ulrich stomped his foot. "I don't want to be a stuffy ol' banker."

To this day, Ulrich could still feel the sting of Grandfather's razor strop across his bare buttocks. While he continued to practice the piano diligently, Ulrich never again broached the subject.

Ulrich's eighth birthday was a day he still recalled with wonderment. In the morning, strange men delivered a grand piano. At the sight of it, he jumped up and down, his squeals of delight resounding throughout the house.

In a rare playful mood, Grandfather wagged his head from side to side. "There must be some mistake. Take it away."

Ulrich threw his arms around Grandfather's waist. "No! No, please, please, please, let's keep it!"

Grandfather feigned dramatic surrender and tweaked Ulrich's ear. "Very well then, we'll keep it."

That night, Ulrich's second birthday present came in the form of one of Grandfather's dinner guests. The man arrived late and made no apologies, regarding the Dietrichs' aristocratic company with mild disdain.

Shorter than most of the grownups, his clothes were somewhat shabby. His shaggy hair and bushy beard fascinated Ulrich.

"Hello there, young man. If I'm not mistaken, it's your birthday. They wouldn't lie to me, would they?" He knelt to Ulrich's level, his blue eyes twinkling beneath his unruly eyebrows that slanted in a perpetual frown. Taking a handful of candy from his pocket he gave it to Ulrich. "This should be enough to spoil your dinner."

"Thank you, *Herr*—," Ulrich stammered. "I don't know your name, sir."

"*Herr* Brahms, ever hear of me?"

"No, sir. I mean, yes, sir."

"Which is it?" Johannes Brahms ruffled Ulrich's neatly combed hair and sat beside him on the bench. "Now let me judge whether or not your grandparents wasted their ill-gotten gains on this pretentious monstrosity. Play something."

Ulrich's heart fluttered to his throat as he played Brahms' own "Hungarian Dance Number Five." A group of guests thronged the piano. Ulrich closed his eyes to shut them out.

When he finished, the guests applauded enthusiastically, but the composer merely shook his unkempt head. "How did you come by that piece of rubbish?"

"At the *Musikverein,* sir. Someone dropped the sheet music." Ulrich searched the gathering for his grandfather and lowered his voice to a tremulous whisper. "When no one was looking, I...I stole it."

"I'm highly flattered, *Herr* Dietrich." Brahms' laughter echoed off the walls of the mansion's great room. "I'm also sorry to be the one to tell you that you're destined to become a renowned pianist. May God have mercy on your tender soul."

Chapter Twenty-Five

By their fourth day in Vienna, Ulrich and Rachel had fulfilled their concert obligations, freeing-up a day or two for sightseeing. Ulrich sat between Rachel and Olive at breakfast and stirred cream into his coffee. "I've missed strong German coffee. What shall we do first, m'ladies?"

"We simply must take the children shopping," said Catherine.

Ulrich twisted his face into an exaggerated grimace, making Olive giggle. "As it is, I'm going to have to buy another trunk for your purchases alone."

There was some truth to his complaint, for Catherine delighted in providing their new daughter with a suitable wardrobe: dresses, petticoats, stockings, shoes, and hats.

"Before we do any more shopping," Ulrich snapped his fingers, "let's take in the Vienna Zoo. You've never seen such a zoo. I think these two little monkeys will enjoy their own kind."

Rachel twittered as she rocked her head from side to side and played her imaginary piano. "Silly Uncle Ulrich."

He laid his hand over hers. "What are you playing, Rukhel Shvester?"

"'Nocturne in C-Sharp Minor' ...for Mommy."

"You miss her, don't you?"

"Yes."

"We'll be home soon, *schatzi*, I promise." Ulrich downed his coffee. "Now that I think of it, there's an important place you need to see before all else."

***

Two hours of dressing children and settling a squabble or two later, Ulrich pointed to a block of houses on *Seitenstettengasse*. "That's my grandmother's synagogue."

"How can you tell?" Catherine waved her hand. "They all look alike to me. Oh, there's Hebrew lettering over the door. Can you read it, Ulrich?"

"My mommy can," said Rachel. "And my *Zaydeh* and Poppy and—"

Pressing his hand over her mouth, Ulrich knelt on one knee and sat her on the other. " '*Bo-oo sh'arahv v'todah, khatzrohtahv beetheelah,* Enter His gates with thanksgiving and his courts with praise.' How'd I do, Rukhel Shvester?"

She applauded. "Bravo!"

He set her back on her feet and stood. "On the outside, *Stadttempel* looks the same as all the others, but inside it's a magnificent piece of architecture. The sanctuary is oval-shaped with a high domed ceiling and balconies circle all the way around. In my opinion it's every bit as elegant as the *Musikverein*. As for its plain exterior, it was designed like this to hide it from Emperor Joseph in 1825."

"Why did they have to hide it, Uncle Ulrich? Was it because the Emperor didn't like Jews? Did he want to hurt them like the Russians hurt Mommy and Poppy?"

"Hush. You know too much." Catherine squeezed Rachel's hand. "I'll never understand such ridiculous bigotry."

Ulrich's chest vibrated with sudden indignation. "Nor will I."

"I forgot your grandmother was Jewish."

"She was, but I didn't know it until she brought me here to my uncle's *Yizkor,* rather, memorial service in 1879.

I was eleven and it was the first time I'd ever seen the inside of a synagogue.

"'Am I a Jew?' I asked Grandmother that day.

"'*Ja,* but you must not mention this to your grandfather, do you hear?' I can still see her brown eyes, full of tears. Even then, she was a handsome woman. 'Never tell him I brought you here.'"

"Why?" asked Catherine. "It's your heritage."

"Grandfather was a staunch Lutheran who despised the Jews."

"Then why did he marry one?"

"When my grandparents met, he only knew she was a desirable woman. He wasn't one to be denied. When she refused his advances—"

"Ulrich, the children."

"Let me put it this way. My father was four months premature and, according to Grandmother, weighed nearly eight pounds. Grandfather cut her off from her family and forced her to be baptized into the church.

"Nonetheless, she spoke to me in Yiddish, which I thought was 'our secret language' until my uncle's *Yizkor.* And, she lit her *Shabbes* candles every Friday night until the day she died."

Chapter Twenty-Six

The following day, Ulrich's boyhood acquaintance, a member of the Philharmonic, loaned the Dietrichs his horse and carriage, simplifying matters. Since they didn't have a pram, Olive usually needed to be carried. Even Rachel would tire easily and beg for piggyback rides.

After a full day of touring the *Ringstrasse* with its theaters, palaces and museums, the girls had nodded off in the back seat. The sight of them, sound asleep with their arms around each other, filled Ulrich with a sense of peace and happiness.

Catherine cuddled up to him and yawned as he steered the horses. "I do hope you're directing them back to the hotel, dearest."

"*Nein,* we're going to the *Schwarzenbergplatz* where the *Hochstrahlbrunnen* lights the night.

"To the *what's*-in-berg? Honestly, I don't know how you pronounce those impossible words. I'm not sure what's more daunting, Russian, German, or Yiddish. And you speak English and Hebrew as well, how on earth do you keep them all straight?"

"German's easy. I learnt it as a baby." He winked at her and flicked one of her fallen curls. "Let's take in this one last spectacle, after which I shall take you back to the hotel for a sumptuous dinner and *Spätlese,* the wine of princes and kings, before retiring."

The steady clop of the horses' hooves along the cobblestones and cooling breeze after a particularly warm day lulled Ulrich. He fought to keep his eyes open as they made their way past classic statues and gardens.

Catherine's exclamations roused him from his drowsy stupor. "Oh Ulrich, darling, it's simply gorgeous!"

"This must be the place."

Before them in a circular courtyard was the phenomenon he had heard so much about. In the midst of a large round pool, a geyser-like fountain spotlighted from below illuminated the night sky, by turns, with purple, blue, yellow, green and red.

Reining in the horses, he stopped the carriage and reached over the seat back to wake the children. "Girls, you won't want to miss this."

He helped Catherine and the children descend the carriage. Holding hands, the four of them walked to the water's edge.

Olive pointed and clapped her hands. "Rachel, looky look. Pretty water. Oh." Olive's smile faded. "Sorry. Rachel can't look."

Rachel dipped her hand into the fountain and splashed. "It's okay. I can hear and feel it."

"If only everyone understood each other like these two," Catherine dabbed her eyes with her gloved fingertip, "the world would be a better place."

A strident voice caught Ulrich's attention. He turned to see that it came from a rail-thin man who appeared to be in his early twenties. He gestured with the fervor of someone speaking to thousands rather than one other equally scrawny youth. Ulrich inched closer to hear what he said.

"The end of the Hapsburg state is inevitable, Gustl. And do you know why? It's because it allows Austria to be overrun with Czechs, Romanians, and Jews." The last word he spat out as if it were poison on his tongue. "These strange ones with their ugly language that sounds like snuffles and squeaking and their odd dress have no place here. We are Germans. We ascribe as all Germans should to the words of the great German poet, August Heinrich Hoffman, '*Deutschland über alles!*'"

Ulrich could not bear another word. "Pardon me, sir, I couldn't help but overhear. What makes you think Germans are superior to Czechs or Romanians?" Offering his hand, he added, "Ulrich Dietrich at your service. I didn't catch your name, *Herr*—"

Hands at his sides, the young man stiffened and glowered at Ulrich. "Nor shall you catch it, *Herr* Dietrich."

"I'm August Kubizek." The other youth offered his hand. "You must excuse my friend's rudeness. It's just the way he is. We do know who you are, sir, as we saw you and your little girl Sunday afternoon at the Opera House."

Something about the first young man ensnared Ulrich. Impeccably dressed in pressed suit and tie, he stood erect and aloof. His dark side-parted hair contrasted his pallid face which boasted a high forehead and a pointed chin. Beneath his slender nose, his black moustache fringed spare lips. However, what mesmerized, even frightened Ulrich, were his eyes. Something sinister lurked behind his penetrating blue glare.

"*Herr* Dietrich, you didn't play anything by Wagner," he said.

"I'm neither fond of his music nor his Anti-Semitic notions."

August shook his head as if to warn Ulrich against pursuing the subject any further. "Your duet with the child was wonderful, *Herr* Dietrich. We enjoyed it very much, didn't we, Adolf?"

"Speak for yourself, Gustl. Her kind has no place here." Adolf cast a scorching glance in Rachel's direction. Turning back to Ulrich, he clicked his heels and bowed. "*Guten nacht, Herr* Dietrich."

Walking back to Catherine and the girls, Ulrich muttered under his breath. "Someone should put a stop that lunatic's ravings."

A passerby shrugged. "*Herr* Hitler? The lad's harmless."

***

Try as he might, Ulrich could not sleep. Every time he shut his eyes, he saw the young man whose bewitching mien could disintegrate stone. Turning on the lamp beside the bed, Ulrich opened his Bible to the Psalms and searched for words of comfort.

"'Even though I walk through the Valley of the Shadow of Death...'" he read in a soft whisper.

Catherine rolled over and blinked. "What is it, darling? You've tossed and turned all night."

"I can't shake him."

"You mean that dreadful boy at the fountain? What did he say that's vexing you so?"

"His words were of little consequence. Do you know who he reminded me of? Quinnon."

"My brother? Good heavens, do you suppose this one's a murderer, too?"

Before Ulrich could reply, Rachel padded into the room, sniffling and finding her way with her outstretched hands.

"What wrong, sweetie?" Catherine picked her up and tucked her in between herself and Ulrich. "Did you have a bad dream?"

"Can we go home right now? Mommy needs me."

Chapter Twenty-Seven

Havah watched Fruma Ya'el bustle around the kitchen preparing her kugel to take to the Weinbergs. Nettie had invited them for a dinner party this evening and Fruma Ya'el was not about to go empty handed.

"I should stay home." She clucked her tongue as she wrapped a dishtowel around the pan. "Havaleh, I don't like the idea of leaving you alone. What if your time should come?"

The extra weight of her unborn added to the pain Havah already suffered, making it difficult for her to be sociable. Not to mention, the thought of a few hours without Fruma Ya'el fussing over her appealed to her.

"The Weinbergs only live two blocks from here." Havah handed Fruma Ya'el a serving spoon to return to Nettie. "If this baby's anything like his or her sister, you'll have time to walk to St. Louis and back first."

Drumming her fingers on her wheelchair's armrest, Havah tried not to be impatient. She wanted nothing more than to go to bed and read the English novel Catherine had sent from London entitled *Far From the Madding Crowd*. In it the heroine, Bathsheba Everdene, had sent an anonymous Valentine to the standoffish Farmer Boldwood. Havah could not wait to see what would happen next.

Yussel slipped his hand around Fruma Ya'el's arm. "She's not alone. Lev's here."

"*Nu*? He's already gone to bed." Fruma Ya'el picked up the pan and headed for the door. "He's such a sound sleeper. What if something happens and he doesn't hear?"

Havah wheeled her chair behind them to the living room to see the family off.

"Can we take a puppy to show Malka?" asked Bayla.

"They're not old enough to leave their mother." Arel smiled, but his eyes, filled with concern, were fixed on Havah. "Malka's coming over tomorrow to see them."

Shayndel burst into the room from outside. "Havah, are you all right? Mama called and said you're not coming with us. Nettie will be so disappointed."

"I telephoned Nettie this afternoon," said Havah. "Of all people, she understands. Please, Shayndel, don't fret over me so."

"I can't help it. You're my sister and my best friend. I wish you hadn't—"

Itzak came behind her and clapped his hand over her mouth. "What's done is done. It's not like she could've taken a pill to prevent it. Let's go. I'm famished."

Havah watched the children race down the sidewalk with David in the lead. "Last one there's a rotten egg!" he yelled.

Reuven, who cared nothing for athletics, walked beside Yussel. Havah could not hear what he said, but she guessed by Yussel's expression Reuven was entertaining him with a new story.

At long last, the house belonged to her. She closed her eyes for a moment and relished the silence, save Lev's snoring from his room upstairs. He had been working late nights at Kaminsky's Grocery and helping at the tailor shop in the morning. Tonight was his first off in a week. Although he could usually sleep through anything, it amazed her that he slept through this last bit of commotion.

She wheeled to the bedroom where she changed into her nightgown and slipped into bed. Piling pillows behind her, she settled against them. Opening her book, she read aloud, mimicking Catherine's accent. "'Chapter Fourteen, Effect of the Letter—Sunrise.'"

Between the warm air and exhaustion from not having slept the night before, Havah managed to read only a few sentences before nodding off.

Arms outstretched, Miriam Cohen stood at the foot of Havah's bed. "Daughter, come to me."

Havah's brother, David, held a puppy in his arms. "We miss you, Bubbe *Fuss Bucket."*

Kreplakh barked and scratched at his leg. David taunted her and swung the pup over his head by its tail. Kreplakh's barking faded into whimpers. A stench filled Havah's nostrils, that of unwashed flesh and putrid breath.

"Wake up, you *nafka!*"

Havah started and woke to find herself looking into a familiar pair of red-rimmed eyes. "Mr. Berkovich. What are you doing here? You should be—"

"Where? In Osawatomie with the other *lunatishin?*"

Why had Kreplakh not barked to warn her? She peered at the basket where the dog slept. "Here, Kreplakh. Here girl."

The dog did not move. "What have you done to her?"

Zalman sneered. "I gave her a little doggy treat."

Pulling the blankets around herself, Havah sat upright. She took a deep breath and hollered as loud as she could, hoping to wake Lev. "Get out of my house!"

"I'm not going anywhere until you give me back my girls."

"They're not here."

"Liar. Now get up and take me to them."

He pulled a revolver from his pocket and trained it on her head. She recognized it as the one Arel brought home to use on himself, the one he promised to take back.

Her lips and tongue tingled. "I can't. They're really not here."

"You expect me to believe you?"

Trembling, she swung her legs over the side of the bed and stood. Her knees buckled. He grabbed her arm and rammed the muzzle of the gun into her back, forcing her through the kitchen, down the hallway to the living room.

Stopping at the foot of the stairs, he pointed. "That's where you're hiding them, isn't it?"

"Listen to me." Havah tried to keep her voice calm. "Liba and Malka are—"

He shoved her with gun. "Upstairs, witch!"

"I...I can't..."

"Move!"

***

For the past couple of weeks Lev had suffered from insomnia. His troubled sleep was filled with visions of Jamie lying in the alley, which precipitated nightmares of his own brutal father. Without Vasily to confide in, Lev felt alone. The summer heat did not help matters any.

At least Vasily gave him the car. Lev pulled on his trousers and shirt thinking a short drive might clear his head and help him sleep. Grabbing his cap, he reached for the doorknob.

On the other side of the door he heard Aunt Havah's quavering voice. What was she doing upstairs? When a man's voice answered her in slurred Yiddish, Lev opened his door a crack.

On the edge of the top step, Aunt Havah leaned against the banister, gripping a balustrade. "You have to believe me, Mr. Berkovich. Your daughters aren't here." Her wide eyes darted from the man to Lev. Her lips formed the words, "He has a gun."

Lev lunged at Zalman and grabbed him from behind. Zalman swung around in Lev's stranglehold. A shot exploded in Lev's ears. He stumbled backward.

Aunt Havah screamed and tumbled feet over head down the stairs. She landed at the bottom. Under his breath, Lev begged her to move.

Zalman's crusted lips parted in a decaying sneer. "Give me my girls or you're next, you skinny little *momzer*."

Regaining his balance, Lev seized Zalman's hand. "They aren't here and if they were, I wouldn't give them to you."

Grasping Zalman's forearm Lev shoved him and banged his wrist against the banister. Zalman held tight to the gun and dislodged his hand from Lev's hold. "Liar!"

Lev caught Zalman's hand, lowered it and fought to wrench the gun from it. In desperation, he coiled his fingers around Zalman's.

Zalman's index finger went for the trigger. Lev was not quick enough to stop him. The blast deafened Lev. Zalman's body jerked. He clutched his chest and tottered backward. Blood seeped between his fingers and soaked his grimy muslin shirt. Choking and gasping, he dropped to his knees, rolled down the stairs and stopped, face down next to Havah.

The floor tilted beneath Lev and the weapon fell from his hand.

PART IV

GO ON LIVING, EVEN IF IT KILLS YOU

Chapter One

Lev writhed and tried to free his arm from someone's firm grip. "Let go of me."

A hand covered his eyes and held his head still. "Sorry, son, this is gonna hurt like the dickens, but the wound's infected," said a husky voice. "Gotta get that slug out or you could lose the arm. Winona, put him out."

A smaller pair of hands laid a handkerchief over his nose and mouth. "Breathe deep," said a feminine voice, that reminded him a little of Aunt Shayndel's. "Do you think he understands you, Doc?"

"Hard telling, not knowing. He's delirious and I've no idea what language he's spouting. I hope he understands I mean him no..." The voices faded and Lev drifted off as the chloroform took effect.

***

Lev coaxed open his swollen eyes. Colors swirled and strangers hovered, then melted into the ceiling.

A cold hand brushed his cheek and a gentle voice whispered in Yiddish, "You're on fire like your hair, Red Bird."

He tried to focus on the face...but could not. "I killed her. I'm a murderer...murderer..." Shutting his eyes, he drifted into oblivion.

***

A warm breeze wafted over Lev. He blinked open his eyes to see pink and white gingham curtains riffling around the open window over the bed. The air smelled of fresh-cut hay, manure, and roses.

"Good morning, Red Bird," said a cheerful voice.

Lev burrowed his throbbing head in the pillow. "Go away and let me die."

"No one's dying in my bed. It's a bad omen."

"You sound like my grandmother."

"She must be a wise woman."

Curiosity piqued, Lev turned toward the voice. A slender boy wearing denim overalls, and Lev guessed, no more than twelve, sat beside the bed. His almost lavender eyes looked out of place next to his copper skin under a fringe of black hair. Nor did the softly spoken Yiddish pouring from his lips seem to fit.

Lev surveyed his surroundings. Colorful rag rugs adorned the floor planks and animal pelts hanging on the wall struck him as odd against a background of floral wallpaper.

A photograph of a man and a woman in an oval frame between the skins intrigued him. The bearded man in the picture had thinning salt and pepper hair with a yarmulke and pale eyes. He wore an old fashioned suit and tie. The girl beside him, with dark braids to her waist, wore a dress ornamented with fringes and beads. Except for his eyes, the boy bore a striking resemblance to her.

Lev pointed. "Are they your parents?"

"They were, *fun brukh zikorn.*"

"My parents are of 'blessed memory,' too." Switching to English, Lev gestured toward man in the photograph. "Your father was Jewish?"

The boy applauded. "You're pretty smart, Red Bird. Pa came from the Ukraine in 1870 to open a store and try his hand at homesteading. Nitya, my mother, was born on the Black Bob reservation in Kansas. My grandparents stayed when the rest of the tribe moved to Oklahoma. One day, Nitya and Pa met at the dry goods store in Belton. Do you believe in love at first sight?"

"My aunt and uncle say they fell in love at first sight, but sometimes I wonder."

The boy stared into space as if he could see his parents in the sky. "Pa was old enough to be her pa. People in town made fun of them. If it wasn't bad enough he was a Jew, he went and married a 'squaw'. So he sold the store and bought the land from my grandparents. This was good for them since they missed the tribe. Nitya learned to be Jewish in a Shawnee kind of way. And she loved Pa with all of her heart until she passed away four years ago, right before my fourteenth birthday. It's been just Pa and me until six months ago, when he up and died in his sleep. Doc says it was probably old age. He was over seventy-six. I'm the only one left to say *Kaddish* for him."

"Wait a minute. You're eighteen? I thought—" Pain seared Lev's arm. "*Oy vey iz mir* it hurts."

"Try not to move it too much for a few days. Doc dug a bullet out of it. I wasn't sure you'd live through the night." Leaning forward, the boy put his elbows on the bed and propped his chin on his hands. "How'd you get shot anyway? Was it in a shootout?"

"You've been reading too many cowboy stories, kid." Lev fingered the bandage around his right upper arm. "I only remember two shots."

The image of Aunt Havah's body lying in a pool of blood next to her attacker plagued him. Despite his most valiant effort, he could not rescue her. The events of the other night and the reality of her death crashed over him with the intensity of a tidal wave.

He had telephoned the police to report a double murder. Then, in a panic, he jumped in the car and headed south on Holmes Street until it turned into a dirt road.

Feeling faint, he stopped under a tree. The last thing he remembered was his smarting arm and wet sleeve. Everything after that dissolved into haze and shadow.

Back in the present, bile scorched his raw throat. *HasUncle Arel sent the police after me?* No doubt he was the suspected killer. However, if there were only two shots fired, it meant Aunt Havah had not been hit. *Could all the blood on the floor have been Zalman's and Zalman's alone?* Nonetheless, she might have broken her neck in the fall or sustained a fatal blow to her head. Either way, it did not bode well for Lev.

Being careful not to bump his right arm, Lev sat up and stretched his left. "Where am I and how did I get here?"

"Jesse and I found you night before last in your automobile, talking out of your head in Yiddish. Where you are, is the Minkowski farm, four miles south of Belton. Now it's my turn. Where are you from?"

"Kansas City."

"No, no, where did you come from before that?"

"Odessa."

The boy's face fell and his eyes welled up. "You mean the one in Ukraine and not in Missouri, don't you? I hope you got out before all the ruckus."

"What do you mean by ruckus?"

"You know, the horrible pogrom nearly three years ago. My uncle was killed before he could immigrate. I never got to meet him, but Pa wept for days and recited the *Kaddish* for him and his children every morning for a month."

"Yes, *that* Odessa."

"Is that where you got that scar on your mouth and the ones on your back? It looks like you've been horsewhipped a time or two."

"I'd rather not talk about it."

"Do you have a name or should I keep calling you Red Bird?"

"Lev Gitterman."

"Pleased to make your acquaintance, Lev Gitterman. I'm Winona Minkowski, but you may call me Winnie."

"Winnie?" Lev slunk black under the covers. "You're a girl?"

"From top to bottom."

"But…but you undressed me."

"Relax. The fellas did the honors. Jesse lives on the next farm over. He's been helping me out with chores and such since Pa passed away. Truth is, he's kinda sweet on me. Even asked me to marry him."

Lev's pulse raced. It made sense—her dainty hands, her voice, and those incredible eyes. "Why do you dress like a boy?"

"Ever try to plow a field in skirts?"

Chapter Two

For the sake of Malka and Liba Berkovich, George Weinberg paid for their father's burial and a plot in the Jewish cemetery. Nettie did not want to let the girls see Zalman's body or attend the funeral.

"That sorry excuse for a man has done enough damage," she said. "Plant him like an onion and forget him."

George's stomach roiled when Malka only giggled and said Zalman was never really her father but an evil golem sent by the devil himself. Nonetheless, George pitied a man for whom no one would observe even one hour of *Shiva*, the seven days of mourning. On the other hand, no one was less deserving of his pity than Zalman Berkovich.

George refused Liba when she, of all people, begged to be taken to the morgue until she said, "I have to see for myself the ogre's really dead."

***

To lift some of the burden off the Gitterman family, Nettie offered to take in not only Havah's children, but Shayndel's as well.

Shayndel protested, even as she marched the children into the Weinbergs' living room. "Nettie, you have your hands full enough with your own four, and Bernie's an infant. You need six more like you need a hole in the head."

"It's a *mitzvah* for me. For so long, I was denied even one child, now my house and my heart are overflowing."

"All right then, but keep your knickknacks out of Elliott and Tikvah's reach." Shayndel handed Nettie two suitcases full of clothes. "Mendel refused to leave his clarinet at home. Elliott's teddy bear is with his pajamas. He won't sleep without it and Tikvah won't sleep without her bunny."

"George is taking some time off for a while, so he'll be a great help with all these boys. You know how he loves roughhousing with them. We'll have a good time, won't we?" Nettie knelt and wrapped her arms around Bayla and Reuven who stood in the doorway like glass-eyed statues, refusing to go inside. "You shouldn't worry about them, Shayndel. We'll take care of them. You do what you need to do." Standing, she whispered, "Have the police found Lev?"

Shayndel's resolve not to cry in front of the children crumbled. All of her anger, fear and grief gushed from her. When she regained her composure, she mopped her eyes on her sleeve.

Bayla threw her arms around Shayndel's waist. "Don't leave me here, Auntie. Take me to the hospital to see Mommy, please, please, please."

***

"It's a miracle." Dr. Florin had said when he examined Havah upon her admittance. "The baby's alive. Yes, it's a miracle indeed."

Despite the doctor's joyful proclamation, his voice was devoid of emotion and his shoulders drooped. "Our little mother's in a coma, which she may or may not come out of. No, I can't make any promises."

Arel dropped his head in his hands. "If I hadn't brought that miserable gun home, none of this would've happened."

Fruma Ya'el covered her face. "I should never have left her alone."

"Enough with the blame. What's done is done. Let's not make funeral arrangements yet." Yussel's voice sounded flat and empty. "As long as she's breathing there's hope, yes?"

Five days passed and the only sign of life on Havah's bed was the baby's constant movement. The hospital room's bare walls and antiseptic odor added to the desolation mounting in the pit of Arel's stomach. His head ached from lack of sleep. Kneeling beside the narrow bed, he laid his head next to Havah's. He pressed his cheek against hers and listened to her rhythmic breathing. "Arise, my love, my fair bride…please."

A nurse entered carrying a clipboard. Arel stood to make room for her. She held Havah's wrist between her thumb and middle finger while counting the beats with the watch pinned to her apron. Setting Havah's limp hand on the blanket, she spoke as she wrote. "Respiration normal. Strong pulse. No change."

A muscular woman with sharp cheekbones and thick eyebrows, the nurse scowled. "This hospital has rules against too many visitors. And children are never allowed."

Until then, Arel had taken little notice of anyone else in the room. He raised his head to see Reuven, between Yussel and Fruma Ya'el, writing furiously in his journal. Shayndel sat opposite Arel on the other side of the bed. On her lap, Bayla clung to Havah's hand. Itzak stood at the foot of the bed, playing a lullaby on Sergei's Stradivarius.

Shayndel shot the nurse a glare that could have set fire to bricks. "We're not 'visitors' we're family."

Bayla slid off Shayndel's lap and tugged the nurse's uniform. "Dr. Miklos says nurses are angels of mercy. Are you really an angel? Can you make Mama well?"

The nurse's expression softened. "I wish I could, little one. She's in God's hands now."

Chapter Three

Rachel curled up in bed beside Olive, who had already fallen asleep. "Will this ship take us home tonight?"

Ulrich tucked the blankets around them. "You're a smart girl. Remember how long it took to reach Europe?"

"Yes."

"Well, it takes the same amount of time to go back. This is only our first night on this boat."

Heaving a sigh, Rachel jutted out her lower lip. "It's gonna be a hundred years before I see Mommy and Poppy."

Any other time Ulrich would have laughed at her melodramatic outbursts. But tonight, it only added to his own impatience and anxiety. He had memorized Florin's telegram that came almost a week ago. The words drummed against his forehead and reechoed in his every thought.

"Terrible accident. Havah's condition is critical. Come home soon.

Godspeed,
Florin and Eleanor Miklos"

After Rachel fell asleep, Ulrich tiptoed out of the stateroom and joined Catherine on the deck. The half-moon reflected on the waves that shimmered like sequins under a spotlight. Breathing in the salt spray, he gazed at the stars overhead. One of them streaked the sky, radiant against the blackness.

"Wishing on a falling star's good luck," whispered Catherine. "It's the second one I've seen tonight. Havah might already be on the mend."

"Or she might be dead."

Chapter Four

With a brightly colored shawl covering her head, Winnie lit the candles and circled her hands around them three times to usher in the Sabbath light. Pressing her fingertips against her eyelids, she uttered the same blessing the women in Lev's family had recited every Friday night since he could remember...yet it did not sound the same.

Keeping her eyes shut, Winnie picked up a wooden hoop with rawhide stretched over it and a leather mallet. "Now I sing it the way Nitya taught me in the Algonquin language."

The rhythm of her drumbeat coupled with the mystical intonation of her voice sent pleasurable shivers through him.

She opened her eyes and smiled. Her teeth shone like polished seashells against her flawless complexion. *"Gut Shabbes.* Will you say the prayers over the wine and the bread, Lev? My ears have itched to hear a man recite them since Pa died."

"I'll do my best."

"Sit down. I shouldn't have let you out of bed so soon, but it's so nice to have company who understands *Shabbes.* Jesse thinks it's gibberish and a 'waste o' good eatin' time.'" Taking a yarmulke from her pocket, she fondled it between her fingers. "This belonged to Pa. Let me put it on you, you need to keep your arm in the sling."

Her blue calico dress accentuated the violet of her eyes. Cinched at the waist it revealed her curves, unhampered by a corset. The fragrance of summer blossoms emanated from her as she bent to place the skull cap on his head.

His hand trembled as he raised the wine glass and sang, *"Barukh asah, Adonai Eloheynu, Melekh HaOlam*...Blessed are you *Adonai Eloheynu,* ruler of the world... *"* He caught a glimpse of Winnie, her eyes trained on him. With a dry cough, he swallowed and continued. *"...boray p'ree,...*who created the fruit..." Sweat trickled down the side of his face and dripped between his neck and shoulder top. *"...ha gahfen...*of the vine. Amen." He took a sip of wine and offered her the cup.

Her delicate mouth hugged the rim as she drank. When she gave it back to him, she held his hand in both of hers and leaned into him, her warm breath on his face

His lips grazed hers ever so slightly. "Winnie?"

"Yes, Red Bird?"

"I'm...I'm glad you're not a boy."

***

Whether from the August heat or his spinning thoughts, unsure of either, Lev spent the night in sleeplessness. *Have I been too hasty? I've only known her less than a week.*

Yet the taste of her lips persisted long past midnight. The softness of her body against his in the water made him ache with longing. Her silhouette in the moonlight haunted him.

He rolled out of bed and pulled on the shirt and coveralls that had belonged to Anshel Minkowski. Lev's own clothes were stained and torn beyond repair.

Tiptoeing past Winnie's bedroom, he headed for the front door. Once outside, he picked an apple and watched the sun rise over the trees. He took a bite of the fruit. The juiced dribbled down his chin as he savored its tartness.

Winnie emerged from the barn carrying a pail. "Good morning, Lev! I didn't expect you up this early."

The denim overalls no longer fooled him. Her short black hair gleamed under the blush of dawn. She walked up the hill to his side, rose on the balls of her moccasin clad feet and kissed his lips.

He stiffened and looked down at his bare feet half obscured in the tall grass. His tongue felt as dry as the dirt under his toes. He fought for words, but they eluded him.

Taking a step back, she lowered her eyes. "After last night, I thought—"

He took the pail from her and set it on the ground. Surely she could hear his heart banging against his ribs. Any moment it would leap from his chest. Tucking his finger under her chin, he raised her face and looked into her eyes.

"Forgive me, Winnie. I shouldn't have—"

"We went swimming in the pond, that's all." She snatched the apple from his hand and bit into it. "It's not like we 'knew' each other like Adam and Eve."

"Oh, but I wanted to."

Throwing her arms around Lev's neck, she burrowed her head into his chest. "So did I, Red Bird."

He winnowed his fingers through her hair. "I've got to go back and turn myself in and I can't ask you to wait until I'm out of jail."

"But it was self-defense."

"There weren't any witnesses. All the police saw were two bodies and a gun with my fingerprints all over it." He pried her arms from his neck and kissed her forehead. "I'm going back...today."

Picking up the pail, she frowned, turned on her heel, and walked toward the house, peering at him over her shoulder. "Okay then. Let me fix breakfast and change my clothes."

"Why do you need to change?"

"You're not driving with that arm and I can't meet your family looking like this, can I?"

Chapter Five

Havah woke to violin music, whispers, and prayers. A tiny foot kicked her rib and the baby flipped. She laid her hand on her tummy. "Settle down, little one. How can anyone sleep with all this commotion?"

Opening her eyes, she studied her unfamiliar surroundings. Groggy and confused, she fingered a tender bump on her forehead and turned to see Arel asleep in a chair beside the bed. His contorted position made her neck ache. She reached over and tapped his knee.

"Arel, wake up."

Eyes closed, he murmured. "Shayndel, I just had the most incredible dream that Havah touched me…"

To Havah's other side, Shayndel smiled through her tears. "It's not a dream."

Arel opened his eyes. "Havah!" Sitting on the bed, he caressed her cheek. "My love, you are as beautiful as Tirzah."

"Where's Lev?" Havah struggled to sit up, counting the faces around her. Weak and dizzy, she fell back against the pillows. "He's dead, isn't he?"

"He's run away," said Arel. "But what makes you think he's dead?"

"Zalman shot him."

Fruma Ya'el sank into a chair. "Are you sure, Havah?"

"I saw it." Havah chewed her quivering lower lip and fought the tears stinging her eyes. "The last thing I remember is Lev bleeding. I'm sure of it. Zalman shot

Lev and he...he poisoned Kreplakh. Oh dear, what can I tell Rachel?"

"You'll tell her she has not one dog but five. I'm happy to report the logy mama and her furry children are alive and well." Dr. Florin entered the room with Dr. Eleanor at his side, flashing a wide smile beneath his curled moustache. "He gave her just enough laudanum to put her to out for a while, my dear."

Dr. Eleanor sat on the bed and took Havah's hand in hers. "That was quite a tumble you took. Your pain must be unbearable. The nurse is on her way with a morphine injection."

Havah looked at Dr. Florin and then back at Dr. Eleanor. "I have a headache and my back hurts a little, but my legs don't hurt at all for a change."

Dr. Eleanor's lips paled. "Do you feel that?"

"Feel what?" Propping herself up on her elbows Havah saw Dr. Eleanor's white-knuckled hand around her ankle. "Squeeze harder."

Dr. Florin seized a pin from Dr. Eleanor's hat and jabbed Havah's calf. "Surely you felt this."

"No."

Dr. Florin poked her thigh. "This?"

"No."

***

"The baby could be pinching a nerve," Dr. Miklos had told Havah, feigning his most cheerful bedside manner as he positioned the X-ray machine. "Your spine could be bruised from the fall. Sensation might return at any given moment."

Later that night he sat up in bed, staring at the film in his hands. He held it up to the light and turned it upside down. No matter what the angle, the verdict did not change.

Taking the sheet from him, Eleanor stuck it back in its folder and laid it on the bed stand. "Florin, you can't let this destroy you. Isn't that what you keep telling Nikolai?"

Shutting off the lamp, he lay down beside her and draped his arm across her waist. "I don't know how I'm going to tell her, Ellie."

"You hold her hand, look her in the eye, and tell her what she's most likely figured out for herself."

Chapter Six

Certain the family would be sitting *Shiva* for Aunt Havah, Lev decided to stop at home first. He had to beg their forgiveness. Clinging to Winnie's hand, he pushed open the front door with his foot.

Barking and wagging her tail, Kreplakh ran to him. He knelt and scratched her behind her ear. She sniffed Winnie's skirts and growled.

Winnie laughed and held out her hand. "She probably smells barn cats." Switching around, Kreplakh yipped and scurried off. "I think she wants us to follow her."

Lev stood and followed the dog. "I'll bet she wants to show us her puppies." He studied the empty house. "They must be observing *Shiva* next door at Uncle Itzak's house, although it looked awfully empty, too."

When they entered his aunt and uncle's bedroom, Lev noted the bed had been made and the furniture dusted. Fresh newspapers had been spread under the dog's basket and her food and water bowls replenished.

Winnie tossed her straw hat on a chair and plopped down beside the basket. Reaching into it with one hand, she petted Kreplakh with the other. "May I, Mother Dog?"

Kreplakh licked her. Scooping one of the pups into her hand, Winnie lifted it to her cheek. "*Azoy zis,* so sweet. They're about five weeks old, aren't they?"

"You know a lot about animals, don't you?"

"What do *you* think, Red Bird?" Her lilac eyes had a roguish twinkle. "I grew up on a farm. Doc kind of took me under his wing. He says I have great potential as a veterinarian."

A sudden twinge shot through Lev's arm. "Doc? The same Doc who performed surgery on me? He's a veterinarian?!"

"Down, Fluffy. You were in good hands." Her laughter reminded Lev of jingling sleigh bells. "It's kind of hard to find an MD between Belton and Harrisonville on short notice."

The front door opened and shut. Nikolai's voice called, "Lev? Are you here?"

Lev shuddered. "Here it comes. Meet Lev Gitterman, the jailbird."

He started for the door. Winnie put the puppy back in the basket, jumped up, and grabbed Lev's hand. "No you don't, Red Bird. We're in this together."

Lev's feet felt like lead as they walked to the front room. Nikolai stood in front of the picture window, arms folded across his chest with a newspaper under one of them. "I saw Vasily's car. Where have you been, son?"

Lev hung his head. "I...I've come back to turn myself in."

"For what?"

"Murder, of course. Zalman...and Aunt Havah."

"Are you nuts?" Nikolai handed him the paper, opening it to the second page. He pointed to an article halfway down. "You're big news."

"'No trace of missing—hero'?" Lev read the headline twice. "I don't understand."

"Keep reading."

"'Last Sunday Zalman Berkovich, who escaped from the Osawatomie State Treatment Hospital a month ago, broke into the home of Mr. and Mrs. Arel Gitterman at 1304 Cherry Street. Mr. Berkovich, who has reportedly been seen eating out of garbage cans at Electric Park and sleeping in back alleyways, was of the notion that the Gittermans were holding his daughters hostage. In reality, Judge McCune ordered the poor abused girls to be taken away from the crazed monster. Upon entrance to the home, the unwashed vagrant— '"

Lev blinked. "I can't."
Winnie took the paper. "Here. Let me.

"'Upon entrance to the home, the unwashed vagrant found a 38-caliber revolver that is alleged to belong to Mr. Arel Gitterman. According to his pretty wife, Mrs. Havah Gitterman, the man forced her to climb the stairs to where he believed his daughters to be imprisoned.'"

Pulse racing, Lev stared at the page. "According to Mrs. *Havah* Gitterman?"
"That's what it says, Red Bird." Winnie grinned. "It gets even better. Listen to this.

"'She told police that her eighteen-year-old nephew lunged at the intruder who turned and fired. Mrs. Gitterman asserted that when she saw blood pouring from young Mr. Gitterman's wound, she fell down the stairs in a swoon.
"'From all evidence, the police have ascertained that somehow the youth wrested the weapon from Mr. Berkovich and shot him through the heart. Mrs. Gitterman fears the young hero is himself deceased from his injuries. Police continue to search for him.'"

Sinking down on the sofa, Lev tried to soak it all in.

Nikolai reached into his waistcoat pocket and took out his handkerchief. He unfolded it and pointed to a bullet. "Here's the slug the coroner removed from the old buzzard. I know how you are about souvenirs." Sitting beside Lev, Nikolai dropped it onto Lev's palm. While Nikolai's lips smiled, his eyes did not. "How does it feel to be a hero?"

Chapter Seven

"Wake up, sissy boy."

Nikolai recognized the voice, loud and playful as ever. He bolted upright in the bed and rubbed his eyes. "Oxana, did you hear that?"

Asleep beside him, she did not appear to have heard anything, including his question. Sitting on the side of the bed, he searched the darkened room. He looked at the alarm clock on the night table. Two-forty-five.

Donning his dressing gown and slippers, he stood. Careful not to wake his wife, who had been having trouble sleeping of late, he tiptoed from the room and went to the kitchen. After pouring a glass of lemonade over chipped ice, he headed for the front door.

He eased himself onto the porch swing and looked up at the star-studded sky. The full moon kissed the rooftops. *This scene would make a wonderful painting.* Nikolai sipped his drink and blinked as his thoughts turned to Vasily. Chiding himself for his tears, Nikolai reminded himself the boy sent a letter accompanied with sketches of Paris every week. *How could I ever deny my son the pursuit of his calling?*

"Why aren't you pursuing your own calling, brother?"

Nikolai snapped his head around to see a boy in a sailor top and knickers sitting beside him. "Bodrik?"

The boy grinned. "You do remember me! I was beginning to wonder, you know."

"Rubbish. You're dead."

"I still have feelings."

Nikolai jumped to his feet. "This is an absurd dream. That's all."

Bodrik yanked Nikolai's robe and jerked him back. "Not so fast, sissy boy. You and I have unfinished business."

Mesmerized by Bodrik's cerulean eyes, Nikolai sat. "Go on."

"Do you remember why you became a doctor?"

Stopping his ears, Nikolai shut his eyes. "Don't, Bodrik, please."

"'Don't, Bodrik, please.'"

His brother's mocking falsetto chilled Nikolai. He opened his eyes to see Bodrik standing in front of him, fists on his hips. "Let me refresh your memory, Kolyah. It was because I died from a bump on the head and you wanted to know why. You were going to make sure it didn't happen to another kid." Bodrik flopped down and made the swing go higher than a normal porch swing. "But it did happen, over and over again. You couldn't save the kids in Kishinev and you couldn't save the ones in Odessa."

"Please—"

"Don't you get it, you dunderhead? This is your chance to make it up to them...and to me." Bodrik thumped Nikolai's forehead. "You are Havah's only hope."

Folding himself into a fetal position, Nikolai pulled his robe over his head.

Oxana's whispered voice startled him. "Kolyah, wake up."

He sat up to find himself in bed. Looking to his left and then to his right, he pushed his damp hair off his forehead. "Where is he?"

"Who?"

"No one. Did I wake you?"

"No, the telephone did. It's for you. Florin, he says it's urgent."

***

"Havah's water broke at 2:30. She didn't even know it. The nurse called me. She's not in labor, Kolyah, but it won't be long." The mounting panic in Florin's voice had crackled through the telephone static. "If she can't feel her contractions, she certainly won't be able to bear down."

***

Five hours later, Havah still had not begun to labor. This allowed Nikolai to wait until daylight. Scrubbing his hands, he studied them. *Do I still possess the ability? Have my fingers lost their dexterity?*

At the sink across from him, Florin washed, his eyes trained on Nikolai. "The instruments are sterilized to your specifications, Dr. Derevenko. Our precious patient awaits your skill."

Nikolai returned his gaze and managed to croak out a "thank you." He turned toward the operating theater. The double doors loomed before him.

Bright light pouring from the ceiling fixture and the skylight overhead blinded him. Once his eyes adjusted, he surveyed the amphitheater seating where medical students and other physicians would observe the surgery. Nikolai nodded to Lev who sat among them with Winona at his side.

Stepping up to the table, Nikolai noted Fruma Ya'el, in a nurse's uniform and apron, held Havah's hand beneath the sheet. Eleanor answered his unspoken question with a muted whisper. "I won't tell if you don't. She should have been a surgeon herself and is a comfort to her daughter."

Nikolai smiled at Fruma Ya'el. "I couldn't agree more."

He turned his attention to Havah. Her eyes, dark and round, held him in their gaze. Hunching over the table, he kissed her forehead. "Havah, I've never really said it, but I want you to know—"

"Not now, Dr. Nikolai." She reached up and pressed her clammy palm against his cheek. "Tell me after you deliver my baby."

***

The Dietrichs' train had been detained in Jefferson City and did not make it to Union Depot until after midnight. When they finally arrived home, neither Ulrich nor Catherine bothered to unpack or undress, but fell into bed with the girls.

After a hasty breakfast of cinnamon buns, Nettie left for them the day before, Ulrich prepared to go to the hospital. Catherine opted to stay home with Olive.

An hour later, afraid of what he might find, Ulrich followed the nurse down the long corridor with Rachel in his arms. Rachel, who had not uttered a word since they entered the building, clung to Ulrich's neck and sniffed. "I heard a man on the train say people only go to hospitals to die. Is my mommy dead?"

The nurse's eyes darted from Rachel's glasses to Ulrich. "The last I saw her, she was very much alive, sweetheart." She stopped and indicated the waiting room with a wave of her hand. Dabbing her eyes with her apron, she pivoted and rushed off.

Arel leaped from his chair and hurried to the doorway. "Rukhel Shvester."

Nearly falling out of Ulrich's grasp, Rachel reached for Arel. "Poppy!"

He hugged her against his shoulder, burying his face in her hair and burst into tears. Itzak and Shayndel wrapped their arms around each other and Arel and Rachel. Yussel rose from his chair and held out his arms. "Ulrich, my brother, Havah will be so happy to see you."

After Ulrich embraced Yussel and Itzak, he sat in an empty chair next to Arel and studied his friends' faces for answers before daring to ask.

Shayndel's strained voice broke the tense silence. "The doctors give her less than a thirty percent chance."

***

Among the surgeons and nurses marshaled around the operating table, one Nikolai did not recognize scowled at him. "Dr. Derevenko, I don't believe we've met."

"Dr. Jenkins, may I introduce my friend and colleague, Dr. Nikolai Derevenko," said Florin. "Dr. Derevenko, this is Dr. Jenkins, our house surgeon."

Holding his hands aloft, Nikolai forced a stiff smile. "I'd offer you my hand, but I'm sure you understand."

Dr. Jenkins folded his arms. "Are you board certified, Doctor?"

"I sent in my application last week." With a sidelong glance Nikolai watched the nurse at the head of the table put the ether mask over Havah's nose and mouth. "I'm afraid I didn't take an emergency into consideration." Havah's sunken eyes closed and her cheeks drained of what little color they had to begin with. "I'll be happy to discuss this after the operation."

"Is this your idea of a joke, Miklos?" asked Dr. Jenkins. "Do you think because you're on staff you're entitled to do whatever you damn well please? How do I know this man isn't an osteopath or a veterinarian?"

Florin pursed his lips. "I know of no surgeon more qualified for this procedure than Dr. Derevenko."

"So you brought him in without running it by me first. Are you familiar with the proper channels, Miklos?"

Dr. Jenkins's nostrils flared. "If this woman dies in my hospital, I'll have both you and your precious Dr. Derevenko incarcerated for malpractice for life."

The back of Nikolai's neck prickled. Taking a scalpel from the tray of instruments to his right, he offered it to Dr. Jenkins. "Feel free to take over if you wish." Dr. Jenkins's frown deepened. "I'm not scrubbed. Proceed."

With one deft stroke, Nikolai sliced through Havah's abdomen while Florin recounted his actions to the audience. "Dr. Derevenko has made a transverse incision in the lower segment of the uterus."

Nikolai's mind flashed to Odessa and Devorah's lacerated belly, pieces of her decapitated newborn surrounding her like so much detritus. He shook his head and blinked. He had to concentrate on the present.

Using surgical scissors, he cut through fat, subcutaneous tissue and into the womb. Reaching into the incised uterus, he found the baby's head. Flexing it from side to side, Nikolai worked to slide the child closer to the opening. All the while Florin intoned his every move to the students.

"Forgive me, Havah," whispered Nikolai. "You don't deserve this circus."

A nurse with a stethoscope in her ears held the bell against Havah's chest. "Her heartbeat's erratic, Doctor."

After two long minutes, Nikolai managed to inch the baby's head out into the open and unwrapped the cord from its neck. With a few gentle tugs, he pulled the baby from the womb. The infant let out a hearty squall.

"It's a boy. Do the honors, Nurse Fruma."

She snipped the cord. "I've seen a miracle."

Blood gushed from Havah's open belly. Florin's brow furrowed. "Bleeder."

"Suction," said Nikolai.

A nurse inserted the hose into the abdominal cavity and cranked the machine, siphoning the blood from Havah's uterus so he could see. He gritted his teeth. "Dammit. Placenta accreta."

Fruma Ya'el blanched. "What does that mean?"

"It means the afterbirth won't let go of her womb." Eleanor curved an arm around her waist and hurried her out of the door. "Let's give your grandson his first bath."

"Her pulse is weak and thready," said the nurse.

Feeling Dr. Jenkins's searing glare, Nikolai cut the blood vessels and scooped out the ragged placenta. "Blood pressure?"

The nurse bit her lip. "Dropping."

Nikolai mopped excess blood while the nurse continued to crank the suction machine. "Don't give up on me now, Havah. We're almost home."

"Steady, Kolyah," whispered Florin as he stitched the placental bed.

The nurse's distressed expression gradually changed to one of relief. "Blood pressure's rising."

Nikolai sutured the outer uterine wall and finally the skin. "That's our little Spartan-ette."

The nurse grinned. "Heartbeat's strong and steady. Congratulations, Dr. Derevenko."

Turning to Dr. Jenkins, Nikolai wiped his hands on his apron and held them at arm's length. "If you still want to carry me off in shackles, proceed."

A hush fell over the amphitheater. One by one, the students and doctors in the audience stood and applauded.

"Dr. Derevenko, that license of yours damn well better be here by the end of the week." Dr. Jenkins chuckled. "I need you on my staff. Meanwhile, the next gaping wound you suture shut should be my mouth."

Chapter Eight

In a state between euphoria and exhaustion, Nikolai headed toward the waiting room. When he walked through the doorway, Shayndel leaped off her chair and screamed, "Oh God, no!"

He puzzled at her reaction until Ulrich pointed to Nikolai's blood-spattered apron. Taking it off, he wadded it under his arm. "Forgive me, in my haste I forgot to toss this in the laundry."

"*Nu?*" Itzak curved his arm around Shayndel. "Now that you've given my wife a heart attack, what's the word?"

Nikolai walked to where Arel sat with Rachel on his lap. Arel's fearful expression asked the question. Squeezing his shoulder, Nikolai smiled. "Your son weighed in at 8 pounds, 3 ounces and your wife is in the recovery ward asking for you."

***

"He's so big." Havah cradled her newborn son. "What do you think he'll be when he grows up, Arel?"

Arel's grey eyes fixed on her, swam, then spilled over. "A miracle like his mother."

She reached up and stroked his scared cheek. "I hope he'll be a strong man like his father."

Placing his hand over hers, he whispered, "You are my strength, Havah."

The baby nuzzled against her breast. Taking back her hand, she opened her gown for him. As his tiny mouth clenched around her nipple, she lay back and welcomed a wave of happy exhaustion.

After sucking for a few seconds, the newborn nodded off. Havah caressed his downy hair. "He's such a sleepyhead."

Dr. Eleanor pushed aside the curtain surrounding the bed and pulled up a chair. She held out her arms. "May I?"

"Yes."

"Come here, big fella." Taking the infant, Dr. Eleanor laid him on her lap. She held the bell of her stethoscope against his chest and grinned. "Stalwart. I suspect—although not all of my colleagues agree—the same ether that sent you off to the land of Nod put your son to sleep as well." She returned him to Havah. "He'll soon be filling your nights with song."

"And soiled diapers." Dr. Florin's laughter preceded him. "How is our little mother?"

Reaching up, Havah squeezed his hand. "I've never felt better. When can I go home?"

"If all goes well and there are no complications, I'd say two, maybe three weeks."

Havah fought tears. "I've already been here over two weeks."

Dr. Florin's smile vanished like a cloudburst in summer. "My dear, I've put this off long enough." He paused to clear his throat with a rumbling cough and lowered himself into a chair. Encircling both of his titan hands around hers, he lowered his eyes. "Your…um…accident…the paralysis…"

Slipping her hand out of his hold, she curved it around his forearm. "I know."

Chapter Nine

Olive peeked out from under the piano. "Daddy, find me!"

Dropping down on all fours, Ulrich crawled to her and enveloped her in a bear hug. He let out a loud growl and pretended to chew on her neck. "Num, num, num."

She cackled with glee and squealed. "Mummy, help! Daddy's eating me."

Catherine rushed to the piano. She went to her knees beside them and chomped his earlobe. "There. That will teach ferocious Daddy a lesson."

Ulrich flinched and slapped his hand over his throbbing ear. "Ouch! These redheads are treacherous, Kolyah, two against one."

Sitting on a wingback chair, Nikolai looked up from his newspaper and grinned. "It looks like a fair fight to me. Besides, I learned a long time ago never to bite the hand that feeds me. Catherine, I've missed your cooking."

"My pleasure. I've fixed a plate for Oxana. Don't forget to take it to her." Catherine scooped Olive into her arms and stood. "Bedtime."

Olive rubbed her eyes and yawned. "I'm not sleepy."

"So I see. Shall I tell you a bedtime story?"

"Yes."

"Give Daddy a kiss."

Brushing off his trousers, Ulrich jumped up from the floor. He thrilled to the touch of the girl's soft lips, blithe as dragonfly wings, on his cheek.

Laying her head on Catherine's shoulder, Olive waved. "Night, night, Uncle Nicky."

Watching them leave the room, Ulrich listened to their chatter. "Chopin never wrote a sweeter note." Ulrich stretched out on the sofa and linked his fingers behind his head. "Is there anything of significance in the news, Kolyah?"

"Nothing to speak of." Nikolai folded the paper. "Fatherhood becomes you, Ulrich."

"So it does. Speaking of fathers and mothers, it's a pity Oxana couldn't join us tonight."

"With a cold on top of her condition, we're all better off if she stays in bed with Fruma Ya'el's chicken soup and a hot toddy."

"Are those her doctor's orders?"

"Her doctor..." A slow smile spread Nikolai's lips. Letting the newspaper fall to the floor he held his hands up to his face. "Ulrich, I've never been more frightened in my life."

Ulrich rolled off the couch and proffered his hand. "Congratulations, Kolyah. You beat the odds. Even Florin wasn't sure you could carry it off."

"I did carry it off, didn't I?" Nikolai leaped off his chair and spun in a clumsy pirouette. "I did it, Ulrich." Nikolai's laughter ricocheted off the high ceiling. "I jolly well did it!"

Ulrich kissed both of Nikolai's cheeks and embraced him, laughing and crying at once. "Welcome back, Doctor."

Chapter Ten

During the three weeks of Havah's confinement, Shayndel and Fruma Ya'el had done their best to make the stark hospital room homey with braided rugs and colorful quilts. The bed stand was stacked with books and beside them sat the piano-shaped music box from Sergei. Even one of Vasily's paintings hung on one bleak wall.

Havah smiled at the nurse as she plumped her pillows. "Won't you please stay for the ceremony, Nurse Charlotte?"

The nurse knit her heavy brows into a *v*. "This is highly irregular." Her frown gave way to a smile. "Mrs. Gitterman, you and your family are such a sweet diversion. I'll hate to see you leave."

"Dr. Miklos says I still have two more weeks to go."

Nurse Charlotte looked at her watch. "I don't suppose it would hurt anything if I stay for a little while. I'm due for my morning break anyway."

Havah, with Rachel in the bed on one side of her and Bayla on the other, grinned at the throng in her room. Every inch of wall space was covered and some stood out in the hallway.

Arel sat beside the low table at the foot of Havah's bed, his *tallis* draped over his shoulders and his *tefillin* strapped about his head and arm. Yussel stood behind him, ready to conduct the commandment of *Bris Milah*, the circumcision. An empty chair, left for the prophet Elijah, sat on the other side of the table.

Next to Yussel stood a man who appeared to be in his early thirties with bright eyes and a black beard whom Dr. Eleanor introduced as Dr. Weisman. "Max is not only a physician here at General but a *mohel,* too."

Dr. Weisman chuckled. "It's not often I have the opportunity to mix business with pleasure."

"Snip it and get it over with before the kid's *bar mitzvah,*" said Itzak. He added, "He's a beautiful boy, little brother."

"As my esteemed brother-in-law would say, 'Do chickens have beaks?'" Arel's face glowed with pride. "Of course he's beautiful. He has the wisdom to look like his mother."

Dr. Nikolai stood, arms on shoulders, between Ulrich and Dr. Florin. Havah had never seen such serenity in his eyes or such a peaceful expression on his face.

"May he who cometh be blessed," sang Yussel heralding the *kvateren.*

Traditionally the *kvateren* would be the godparents, but Arel and Havah agreed the honor of bringing the baby should be given to his older brothers. Lev and Reuven, with proud smiles, entered the room carrying him on a pillow between them.

Yussel continued to chant the blessings. "Happy is he whom Thou choosest and bringeth nigh that he may dwell in Thy courts."

Lev laid the baby, pillow and all, on the table. Arel poured a drop of wine into the baby's mouth.

"*Hashem*'s presence has been waiting," said Yussel, "to bring this child, this son of Israel, into the holy covenant of circumcision."

When the actual moment came for Dr. Weisman to do the deed, Havah turned her head. She cringed at her son's shrill scream.

"It's okay, Mommy," whispered Bayla. "He's itty bitty and won't remember a thing."

Arel wrapped the infant in his prayer shawl and laid him in Fruma Ya'el's waiting arms. She pressed her cheek against the baby's as she carried him to Havah. Placing him in her arms, Fruma Ya'el's eyes glistened. She smiled over her shoulder at Dr. Nikolai. "I've truly seen a miracle."

Rachel grazed her fingers over his tiny nose. "Can my baby brother see, Mommy?"

Havah studied her son's round cheeks and black hair and asked herself the same question. In the past eight days, the baby had hardly opened his eyes. As though he understood his sister, he opened them and squinted at the sunlight streaming through the window.

Havah heaved a sigh of relief. "Yes, Rukhel Shvester, your baby brother can see."

Reuven turned the pages of his journal and poised his pencil. "Does he have a name?"

Yussel cocked his head and turned his face toward Havah. "The honor goes to his mother."

"His Hebrew name shall be known in the House of Israel as Shimon, for my father, Shimon Cohen, of blessed memory." Havah bundled him to her shoulder. "He shall be known in Kansas City as Simon Nikolai Gitterman."

Chapter Eleven

Sitting beside her bedroom window with Simon asleep on her lap, Havah watched red and gold leaves flutter to the ground. How could it be October already? The High Holidays had passed and Reuven and Bayla had gone back to school.

"Autumn comes to Kansas City," whispered Havah.

She remembered Miss Kline's assignment to the fifth grade. Havah did not think her son would shock his new teacher with his memories of Odessa. Thus far, most of his essays and stories were about such things as the puppies and his baby brother. Already he brought home straight A's on his compositions.

Closing her eyes, Havah listened to Rachel and Yussel as they read their Braille books to each other in the kitchen. Fruma Ya'el hummed a tune as dishes clattered in the sink. The lemony aroma of baking sponge cake filled the air.

Simon woke with a hungry squall. At two months, he weighed ten pounds and was bigger than Rachel had been at six months. Havah held him to her breast. His brown eyes—his grandfather Shimon's eyes—captivated her.

She turned and surveyed the packing boxes stacked in corners. They were filled with linens, knickknacks and dishes to take to the new house. Although she balked at the idea of moving, she could no longer fight the obstacles presented by this one.

In any case, the decision was no longer hers to make. Unbeknownst to her, during her two-month hospital stay, Itzak, Ulrich, and even Arel conspired to build a house. Two weeks ago, Ulrich had piled her and her family into his car and drove them to the southern tip of Kansas City.

The first thing Havah noticed about the new house was the ramp leading up to the porch. She wheeled herself to the door. Catherine welcomed her with a cheerful wave. "Now begins the grand tour for herself, Madame Gitterman."

Shayndel joined them in the entryway. "First, you have to see the great room. It's Itzak's triumph."

The long foyer led into the room. In one corner sat a baby grand piano beside a stone fireplace. On either side, Itzak had built book cases with shelves from ceiling to midway where he had put in glass-fronted cabinets. Bay windows faced east so she could enjoy the sunrise while she read a book or played Chopin.

From the great room, Shayndel led Havah to the dining room and kitchen. "My husband took great pains with the countertops. Easy to reach for someone in a wheelchair so she can knead her famous *holla.*"

Havah's eyes smarted. "I don't know what to say."

"Don't say anything until you see the rest of it."

Bayla skipped from room to room. "May I choose Rachel's and my room? Reuven already picked one for him and Simon."

Shayndel winked at Arel. "There are five other rooms to choose from. One of them has lots of bookshelves and a new sofa for my brother's office."

Piano music could be heard coming from the front room. Havah closed her eyes for a moment. "Rachel's found her favorite spot hasn't she?"

"Uncle Ulrich's teaching her a new piece." Bayla stopped skipping for a moment. "He says he loved it when he was a little boy. It's called 'Hungarian Dance Number Five'."

Each bedroom was spacious. The one Reuven chose had shelves built into the corner and a writing desk. Havah could tell Itzak had planned the rooms with each of the children in mind. The room next to it had pink flowered wallpaper and lacy curtains so it did not surprise her when Bayla claimed it for the girls.

Havah pondered. "Which room shall I choose? Mama and Papa should have the biggest one nearest the loo."

"And so they shall. Your room is this way." Shayndel pushed Havah's chair through the kitchen to the back of the house. "Here's the master suite, replete with its own water closet and a picture window to watch the sunset."

Tears welled in Havah's eyes as she peered up at Shayndel. "It's all so wonderful. Not a stair in sight, but...but there is one thing wrong with it."

"Oh, that." Shayndel leaned over and wrapped her arms around Havah. She pointed out the window to a half-built house on the next lot over. "You're going to love your new neighbors."

Chapter Twelve

By the end of October, the Gittermans, with the help of family and friends, completed their move into the new house. At the same time, Nikolai decided he and Oxana needed a larger home for their growing family, so he bought Arel and Havah's old house. This left the Derevenkos' bungalow vacant. In turn, Florin reasoned the small cottage was a splendid dwelling for two.

"Perfect timing," he said. "Yes, indeed, everything is falling into place."

In the process of packing, Nikolai kept a solicitous eye on Oxana. More than once she protested his admonitions to rest. "Florin says I am strong as any Romanian farmer's wife. What a sweet compliment. He says I am born for having children."

A spasm seized Nikolai's shoulder as he hefted a box of dishes. Turning to leave, he winced and nearly bumped into Oxana. She flashed a look of concern and whisked the box from him. "Who should be careful?"

Before Nikolai could take another step, Florin piled a stack of pillows in Nikolai's arms. "Take it easy, Kolyah. I don't want my new colleague injured."

Eleanor whistled as she carried a box of tableware into the kitchen. "With everyone moving at the same time it's hard to tell who's going and who's coming."

In less than a week, the Derevenkos and the Mikloses had settled into their respective homes; at least their possessions had made it to their destinations.

Amid packing crates and piles of things waiting to be put away, Nikolai and Oxana ate their first breakfast in their new kitchen. Steam rose from the brass samovar. Oxana flipped a *blin,* a Russian pancake onto Nikolai's plate and sprinkled it with sugar. He cut a piece with his fork and sniffed it before he took a bite. It melted in his mouth. "When did you learn to cook?"

Oxana's full lips spread into a proud smile. "Your father taught me his recipe. He said he used to make *blinis* every Sunday morning for you and your brother."

"I thought it tasted familiar. Bodrik and I loved them."

"Our son will love them, too." Oxana patted her belly. Her smile vanished and her eyes widened as if she had received an electric shock. "Will it be okay with you if our son turns out to be daughter?"

***

Nikolai followed Florin up the stairs to what used to be Florin's apartment. Opening the door at the top of the stairs, he flourished his hand in a beckoning gesture. "Prepare to be dazzled, Dr. Derevenko."

The three-room flat had been transformed into a four bed clinic and an infirmary complete with a table for emergency surgery. A boiler for sterilizing instruments sat on a table in one corner. The floors had even been resurfaced with new tiles.

Florin turned back to the stairs. "Now, the pièce de résistance." He led Nikolai to their office and pointed to a large painted sign leaning against the desk. "This came yesterday from Paris."

A golden Caduceus, designed with Vasily's artistic flair, took up the left side of the sign. Bold white letters painted on a black background proclaimed:

DOCTORS OFFICE
Florin Miklos, M.D.
E.W. Miklos, M.D.

Nikolai Derevenko, M. D. & Surgeon

Florin handed Nikolai an envelope. On the front, in Vasily's cramped handwriting, it was addressed to "Dr. Derevenko, Life Giver."

Nikolai rolled his eyes and tore open the envelope.

"Dear Tatko,

I always knew you were more than a flautist. You made your scalpel sing for Havah and Simon. I've never been prouder of my father.

All my love,

Vasya"

The smudged letters blurred. Nikolai folded the letter and slipped it back into the envelope. "My boy. My wonderful boy."

Florin peered over Nikolai's shoulder. "What did he say to make you weep?"

Fondling the paper in his pocket, Nikolai blinked. "Oh, you know, the usual."

Chapter Thirteen

With the low countertops in her new kitchen, it pleased Havah to be able to help prepare meals. Tonight she had roasted the chicken by herself and cut the potatoes with ease. After washing the dishes, she wheeled into the living room, leaving Fruma Ya'el to put them away.

Rachel sat at the piano and bounced her head from side to side as she played "The Entertainer." She stopped and waved her hands in the air. "See, Mommy, my hands are almost five. Uncle Ulrich says they're big enough to play Scott Joplin now."

From his spot on the sofa, Arel shot a look of sheer pride at his daughter. "That's my *Rukhel Shvester*."

On his lap, three-month-old Bagel chewed a beef bone. Arel stroked the puppy's head and scratched him behind his shaggy ear. Although he had the black, white, and brown coloring of his beagle father, Bagel's fur was as long as Kreplakh's.

Fruma Ya'el frowned as she entered the room, wiping her hands on her apron. "That mangy cur shouldn't be eating on your lap, Arel. He'll ruin your clothes."

Arel shrugged. "I'm a tailor."

Throwing her hands in the air, she sank down in her rocking chair. "Let a pig in the house and he'll crawl on the table."

Bayla, lying on her tummy in front of the fireplace, looked up from her book. "He's a puppy, not a pig, *Bubbe*."

"Close enough. First it was one dog. Now it's two. *Nu?* What's next? Shall we bring a cow in the house so we can have fresh milk every morning?"

At first Havah had balked at the idea of keeping one of Kreplakh's puppies, but she could not deny the peace Bagel gave Arel. After a nightmare or flashback, no one, not even Havah could calm him like that pup.

"Havah, here's an article that should interest you." Arel peered over his newspaper. "It's about our old friend, Judge Wallace. The headline reads, 'Life Threatened, Says Wallace.' He goes on to say, and I quote, 'Since I have taken office I have received many threatening letters on account of my attitude as to the Sunday law enforcement.'"

Havah rolled to the sofa and peeked over Arel's shoulder. "I suppose he still insists he's on a mission from God."

Moving the puppy over, Arel rose and lifted Havah from her chair. He sat back down, settling her next to him and took an envelope from his vest pocket. "Now I think it's time to read this letter from Washington D.C."

Taking it from him, her hands trembled. She ripped it open and unfolded the letter. Written on White House stationary, in the president's own hand, the words leaped off the page.

> White House, November 10, 1908
> Dear Mr. and Mrs. Gitterman,
>
> What a great disappointment to us this past August when Mr. Dietrich canceled his concert here. After his delightful concert three years ago, we had so looked forward to hearing him again and to enjoying your Rachel's talent he told us so much about.
>
> We rejoice at news of Mrs. Gitterman's courageous recovery and continued good health. It

is also our hope that you and your entire family, along with the Dietrichs, will accept our invitation to join us here on the weekend of the 5th and 6th of December.

> Sincerely Yours,
> Theodore Roosevelt.

Chapter Fourteen

Ample space between wall and railing on the rambling porch left room for Havah to wheel from one side to the other. This made it easy for her to keep an eye on the children.

With the Gittermans and Abromoviches living next door to each other once more, Itzak had built a fence to encompass both yards. He also constructed two swing sets and a huge sandbox.

"We have enough children between us to open our own school," he said. "It makes perfect sense to have our own playground."

At Shayndel and Havah's insistence, Itzak and Arel put in a large garden between the two houses. Next spring, there would be a vibrant array of crocuses and daffodils, tulips and irises. In the middle of the garden Itzak planted a young oak.

This afternoon, although it was the middle of November, it felt almost like spring. Havah took a deep breath. Tomorrow, it would probably snow.

On her lap, Simon opened his mouth wide in a toothless grin. His bright eyes held her in their gaze. He cooed as she jostled him in her arms. "We'll enjoy today. How does that sound to my big boy?"

Lev's car rumbled to a stop in front of the house. He stepped out and walked to the passenger's side. Opening the door for Winnie, he waved. "Is *Zaydeh* here? We want to ask a favor of him."

Havah missed Lev. Everyone agreed he would keep his bedroom at the old house for the time being. That way, he did not heap the stress of moving onto the stress of going back and forth to Lawrence, Kansas for college classes. Not to mention, Nikolai could help him with this homework.

She watched Lev and Winnie walk up the ramp, hand in hand. "You're just in time for lunch. Be careful not to get in *Bubbe*'s way, she's preparing for *Shabbes.*"

Lev opened the front door for Havah and Winnie. He licked his lips. "Did you bake *holla*, Auntie?"

"Of course. You're staying for dinner, then?"

Winnie's even teeth shone against her copper complexion. "If it's not an imposition."

Havah could not shake the feeling she had met the girl somewhere else, a long time ago. *But where?*

Fruma Ya'el welcomed Lev as if it had been years instead of a few days since she had seen him. "It's only soup and chicken sandwiches, but tonight there's pot roast, noodle kugel and Havah's favorite, *tzimmes* with raisins."

Sitting at the table with Rachel on his lap, Yussel reached out with his hand. "I hear someone wants to speak to the old blind man. A business proposition perhaps?"

Lev took a seat beside him. "I won't beat around the bush, *Zaydeh*, I—"

"You and Miss Minkowski want I should marry you."

"How did you know?"

Yussel grinned and pointed to his ear. "The eyes might not work, but these do. Why aren't you going to Rabbi Zaretsky? You want to get married in the *shul*, don't you?"

"He refused us because Winnie's only half Jewish on the wrong side—her father's."

"*Feh*! Rabbinic law. According to the Torah and as far as I'm concerned, Jewish blood is Jewish blood no matter whose veins it came from. But you know, legally, I'm no longer a rabbi?"

Lev's brick red cheeks matched his hair. He shot a sidelong glance at Fruma Ya'el. "We went to the courthouse Wednesday, *Zaydeh*."

Fruma Ya'el gasped. "You eloped?"

"Yes, *Bubbe*."

"You get married behind our backs and after this you expect a ceremony?" Yussel tilted his head and his voice scaled an octave. "On top of that, you want I should bless you?"

Winnie's jaw tightened and her eyes flashed blue fire. "Rabbi Gitterman, I love your grandson with all my heart and soul, with or without your precious blessing."

A chuckle rose from Yussel's throat and intensified into a belly laugh. "Welcome home...granddaughter!"

***

After a festive *Shabbes* dinner, Havah grew weary of sitting in her chair and asked Arel to put her to bed. Propped up against her pillows, she nursed Simon and smiled at Lev's bride. A cheerful blaze in the fireplace warmed the air. Winnie poked at the logs to keep the fire going. Once satisfied, she sat in a chair beside the bed.

Simon drifted off to sleep and Havah buttoned her nightgown. "I hope you don't mind visiting with me in here. I tire so easily these days. Sometimes I feel like such an old fuddy-duddy even though I'm only twenty-five."

"It's okay. I haven't had a chance to talk to you." Winnie's head swiveled as she looked around the room. "It's more like an apartment than a bedroom."

"I spend a lot of time in here." Lifting the baby, Havah held him out to Winnie. "Would you put him in his cradle for me?"

Winnie took him and hummed a lullaby as she laid him on the little bed. "The carvings on this cradle are gorgeous. Did Uncle Itzak make it?"

"Do one legged ducks swim in circles?" Havah lowered her voice to a whisper. "Winnie, you're not…with child are you? It's not why you eloped is it?"

Without a trace of offense taken, Winnie shook her head. "No, I'm not. Someday, maybe, but not for a while." She frowned. "Who knows what our children will look like? I don't want them branded half-breed like me."

Havah snapped her fingers. "Now I remember where I met you. Your father was an older man named Anshel, right?"

"Yes, did you know him?"

"No, but I met him once…at the synagogue. It was right after we came to America. My English wasn't so great and he spoke Yiddish. He told me his wife passed away and he wanted to light a *Yizkor* candle for her. Then he introduced me to you. How could I forget your stunning eyes? But they were so sad. Do you remember?"

Winnie's mouth dropped. "Not until now. All I could think of then was how much I missed Nitya. But later, I thought about the pretty lady who hugged me, and her eagle-headed cane. I was sorry she needed it."

"You and your father never returned to *shul*. Why?"

"The people treated us like unclean animals; pigs at their Sabbath table. The men shunned Pa and the other children laughed at me and called me 'Wild Injun.'"

Anger boiled in Havah's chest. "How dare they!"

"So Pa continued to be my teacher the same way he always had." Winnie twirled a lock of her shoulder-length hair around her finger. "I miss him."

"I see you're letting your beautiful hair grow out. Whatever possessed you to cut it?"

"When Pa died, I had to run the farm. I cut my hair to prove I could hold my own in this man's world."

"Men are strange beasts, aren't they? In the Old Country I refused to cut mine for the same reason."

"I don't understand."

"In our little *shtetls*, the custom was for brides to shave off their hair to show their piety and devotion to their husbands. And if that wasn't enough, we were supposed to keep our heads covered with a scarf or a wig."

"A wig doesn't make much sense to me."

"Me neither, which is why I wouldn't do it." A wave of drowsiness washed over Havah. "There's been so much going on the past few months I haven't had a chance to properly thank you for what you did for Lev."

"He's a wonderful man." Winnie took hold of Havah's hand. "Thanks to him, and all of you, I don't feel alone anymore."

Havah brought Winnie's palm to her lips. "As King David wrote, 'Adoshem puts the solitary in families.'"

Chapter Fifteen

Ulrich's great room glowed with candlelight. Under the wedding canopy, Winnie and Lev shared the marriage cup and pledged their eternal troth to one another. Yussel's face shone as he recited the blessings for them to repeat.

Havah could not keep her eyes off the bride, who wore her mother's cream-colored buckskin dress and moccasins. Adorned with colorful beadwork from shoulder to elbow, the rest of the sleeves were long fringes that went past Winnie's wrists. Her sleek hair, pulled back into two short braids tied with beaded medallions, gleamed under her lace veil.

Lev slipped the gold band on her finger. In a clear voice heavy with emotion, he repeated after Yussel. "Behold, you are betrothed to me with this ring according to the Law of Moses."

"May you rejoice forever together as did Adam and Eve in the Garden." Yussel cried out. "May the names of Winona and Lev Gitterman be shining names in Jerusalem one day when the temple is restored."

To end the ceremony, Itzak placed a wine glass wrapped in a linen napkin under Lev's foot. With a smile so bright Havah swore she could read by it, Lev stomped on the glass.

In unison, everyone in the room shouted, "*Mazel tov!*"

The musicians—Itzak, Ulrich, Dr. Nikolai, Rachel and Mendel—started off the next part of the festivities with "*Khosid* Dance." Dr. Tillman and Daniel Kaminsky led Lev to one of the red brocade chairs and, once he sat on it, hoisted him into the air. At the same time, Winnie sat on the other chair as Arel and George Weinberg followed suit. The bride and groom were paraded around the room on the chairs.

After the chairs returned to the floor, Arel and Havah accompanied Winnie and Lev to the doorway of the *yikhud*. According to tradition, it was the room where the bride and groom would share their first meal as man and wife. Havah grinned for she did not recall sharing one bite of food in their *yikhud* in Ulrich's Kishinev mansion.

Hand in hand, right feet forward, Lev and Winnie stepped over the silver spoon in front of the threshold. Arel slapped Lev on the back. "Remember, you have eight minutes to…eat."

"I'm sick of rabbi's rules and laws already." Havah kissed Winnie's cheek. "Pay tradition no mind. Take your sweet time. Tonight the stars in the heavens burn for you."

***

Havah held her slumbering son on her shoulder, his breath warm and sweet on her neck. She tapped her fingers in time to a lively Klezmer tune and watched the children dance. Joining hands with Olive and Tikvah, Bayla showed them how to skip. Malka and Liba Weinberg, with happy smiles, hopped with their brother Benny between them.

When the song ended, Winnie picked up her hand drum. "May I teach you the dance my mother, taught me?"

Ulrich rose and bowed low at the waist. "*Frau* Gitterman, the floor is yours. How may we accompany you?"

"Flute from the medicine man and clarinet from the young warrior."

Mendel puffed out his chest and wrapped his lips around his clarinet's mouthpiece. "Weddy when woo ah, Wimmie."

Winnie chuckled. "A warrior should always be prepared. Now I want all of the girls and women who will to join me in a circle. Sorry, fellas." Her periwinkle eyes held Havah in their gaze. "I sing this song in honor of my new mothers, Havah and Fruma Ya'el. Please come to the middle of our circle. The words mean 'See them dance, mothers, aunts and grandmothers. Women of all nations, you are the strength, you are the healers.'"

"I hope she's not calling down some kind of curse on us." Fruma Ya'el whispered.

"Mama, how can you say such a thing?" Havah raised her eyebrow. "Remember when Pavel Krushevan had Christians in Kishinev believing we Jews used the blood of their children to make our *matzo*?"

With a nod of agreement, Fruma Ya'el pushed Havah's chair into the center of the ring. Winnie thumped out a soft drumbeat. Moving her body to the pulsing rhythm, she stepped to the right. The women and girls, including Officer Tillman's wife and daughters, mimicked her movements. Nikolai and Mendel played the ethereal melody as Winnie sang in her mother's language. Havah savored the music's peculiar harmony and the sight of the diverse complexions dancing around her like a human rainbow.

A hush fell over the guests as the dance ended, followed by applause. Havah wheeled to the sofa where Oxana sat with Bernie Weinberg on her almost nonexistent lap.

Havah tickled Bernie's chin. "Your baby will be here before you know it. Are you excited?"

Oxana's eyes looked past Havah. "I should be happy. I have good husband who is once again good doctor. But lately, all I can think about is my brother Pasha."

"May the Almighty rest his soul. Lev's told me a lot about him. He sounds like a wonderful man."

"Everything he do—did—was for the Lord. Why is saint like Pasha murdered and dies in the street, Havah? I don't understand how, if there is a God, he does this to someone who loved him."

"My papa would say it's one of those things we have to hide away into our mystery bag." Havah took Simon from her shoulder and held him in the crook of her arm. He opened his eyes and cooed. She outlined his lips with her fingertip. "This is what I know. This is what I believe. The Almighty gives, the Almighty takes away, blessed be He."

Oxana brushed away a deciduous tear. "I will think—perhaps I will pray to the Lord on this. It's what my brother would have done."

***

As the evening progressed, the crowd thinned. Itzak, Ulrich and Nikolai played more waltzes and slower tunes. The other two musicians, Mendel and Rachel, had given up and gone upstairs with Olive and the other children where Catherine had prepared places for them to sleep.

Havah watched the few remaining couples swirling across the dance floor. Winnie and Lev looked at home in each other's arms. Dr. Eleanor and Dr. Florin, head and shoulders above everyone else, had not sat out one waltz. Officer Tillman and his wife Amy made a handsome couple. With a watchful eye on those around them, Fruma Ya'el led Yussel in an awkward turn. They giggled like young lovers.

At Havah's urging, Arel danced a few times with Catherine, Oxana, and even Shayndel. "It's not like I can dance and the musician's wives shouldn't always have to be wallflowers."

At Dr. Eleanor's request, Ulrich and Itzak played a Strauss waltz. Nikolai rose from his chair, leaving his flute on the cushion. Approaching Havah, he bowed and offered his hand. "Madame, may I have the honor of this dance?"

Havah looked over her shoulder to see Oxana stretched out on the sofa, sound asleep, and back up at him. "Don't tease me, Dr. Nikolai."

"I never tease." He nodded toward Arel. "With your permission, sir?"

Arel returned the nod with a smile. "Her life is in your hands."

Scooping her up into his arms, Nikolai carried her to the middle of the room. She wrapped her arms around his neck. "But Dr. Nikolai, your shoulder."

"You're no more stress on my shoulder than a humming bird, Havah. And please, call me Kolyah."

"But, you are—"

"How long have we been friends?"

"Six years, but I didn't like you at first. I thought you were rude and arrogant."

"And too gentile?"

A warm flush rose from her neck and spread to her cheeks. "I was a silly little girl."

"No, you had valid reasons, Havah. Better reasons than I in my animosity toward women."

She laid her head against his shoulder as he dipped, swayed and turned. The lights sparkled in dizzying array. "You're very graceful, Dr.—Kolyah. I've never seen you dance."

"It's been a great while. Long before we met, I'm afraid."

After the dance ended, he lowered her onto her chair and knelt before it. His effervescent smile vanished like smoke. "Havah, I have to tell you—that is—what you mean to us...to me—"

"Shush." She pressed her fingers against his lips. "I owe you my life."

He caressed her hand and kissed her fingertips. "It's the other way around, Havah Cohen Gitterman. I owe you mine."

Chapter Sixteen

Tonight, Havah had dined at the president's table. Tonight, her children had joked and roughhoused with his children. How far Rabbi Cohen's orphaned daughter had come in less than ten years!

She could scarce take it all in. Tent and bowl chandeliers crafted of Bohemian crystal flooded the East Room with sparkling light. Red marble tables sat between long windows that were adorned with golden drapes and gilded cornices. The highly polished oak parquet floor reflected it all like a mirror.

Havah's mind traveled back to the fateful day at Ellis Island when she had lost her place in line for train tickets. She would never forget how rude the concessionaire at the ticket window had been and how hard to understand in her new language.

"Listen, sis, it ain't my fault you lost your place in line. You're gonna have to wait like everybody else."

Resigned to a long wait, she took a book from her bag. Someone bumped into her from behind and knocked it from her hands. Her anger ignited against the clumsy stranger and she whirled about to confront him.

Instead of the impudent lout she expected, Shayndel dropped to her knees and recovered the fallen book. Then she stood, tears streaming down her cheeks.

Havah's anger dissolved. "Shayndel, what's the matter? Where were you going in such a hurry?"

"It's David. He's run off. I put the boys down for a nap. Mendel went right to sleep, but David was full of wiggles. I...only looked away for a minute."

"We'll find him."

With frustrated reluctance Havah relinquished her place in line and made a silent vow to spank three-year-old David without mercy if she found him first.

A worrisome hour of searching and questioning people, often resorting to sign language, ensued. Finally, she caught a glimpse of her nephew as he ran headlong into a stout man with a bushy moustache in a tweed suit. Rather than the irritation and tongue lashing she might have expected from such a well-dressed gentleman, he laughed and swept David up into his brawny arms.

He took a silver coin from his pocket and pressed it into David's hand. You're not much younger than my fine bad boy Quentin. I'll wager you're as mischievous, too."

After an hour of listening to Havah's story of her escape from Kishinev, Mr. Roosevelt, with tears in his eyes, instructed the concessionaire to give her eight tickets to Kansas City.

The expression on his face, as he counted out the tickets, still made Havah laugh.

Startling Havah back to the White House, Shayndel leaned over and whispered, "Have you ever seen such a grand piano?"

Havah marveled at the gilded instrument with its ornate trim. Even the underside of the lid boasted a painting of gowned ladies against a green background. However, nothing compared to the two musicians who shared the bench. Their concert for the evening consisted of alternating solos and duets in which they played everything from Beethoven to Joplin.

Rachel introduced the finale in a clear voice. "This is for my mommy. It's her favorite."

Ulrich's face glowed with pride as Rachel played "Nocturne in C-Sharp Minor." When she finished,

President Roosevelt led a standing ovation and shouted, "Bully! Bully!"

Ulrich bowed. "Thank you, Mr. President."

Havah noted how, since his return from Austria, Ulrich no longer clicked his heels before he bowed. When she asked him why, he replied he was an American now and declined any further discussion.

"I remain in the shadows of my lovely partner." Ulrich helped Rachel off the bench. "Miss Gitterman, take a bow."

With dramatic flair, Rachel held up the ends of her lace frock, and curtsied. "Thank you ever so much, Mr. President."

Ulrich gathered her into his arms and sat her back on the bench. "With your permission, sir, we've prepared an encore."

The president waved his hand. "Permission most assuredly granted."

Ulrich gestured to Itzak and Mendel to come up to the piano. "I'm confident you will agree Rachel isn't the only talented musician in the Gitterman family."

He nodded to Itzak who tucked the Stradivarius under his chin and positioned the bow. "'*Khosid* Dance.' *Eyn und Zvay und Dray.*"

Once the music began, Mendel, who had hidden behind Itzak, lost his shyness and never missed a note. Rachel's fingers danced across the keys and Itzak grinned at Havah over his violin. About the magnificent room, patent leather toes tapped. Politicians and diplomats clapped their hands to the lively *klezmer* tune.

"Everybody dance!" yelled eleven-year-old Quentin Roosevelt.

Arm in arm with his buddy Charlie Taft, Quentin led the line of kids along with David, who was still 'full of wiggles', Reuven, Bayla, Elliott, Olive, and Tikvah.

By the time the musicians played three more folk tunes, everyone in the room, young and old, including the president, did their best to keep up with the energetic hora. With a tinge of sadness, Havah realized she was the only one still sitting.

Arel scooped her up and twirled her around. "No one's calling my bride a wallflower."

After a few steps in her husband's arms, Havah found herself in the arms of none other than President Roosevelt. There she stayed until the dance's end when he addressed the crowd. "If you'll all be seated, I'd like to make a presentation to our esteemed guests. Mr. Gitterman, I return your wife, despite my clumsiness, remarkably unharmed. Now I'd like for the rest of the Gittermans to join me."

Arel lowered her back into her chair and wheeled her to the front of the room. The Gitterman family lined up before the winded audience as the president continued.

"As you know, the holiday season is upon us. Those of us who are of the Christian faith will celebrate Christmas, while Jewish folks, such as my friends the Gittermans, will celebrate Hanukkah. In light of this, my darling Edith and I have collected what we think are suitable gifts for you and yours, Havah, beginning with the children."

Quentin and Charlie took turns carrying gaily wrapped presents to the president as he presented them, beginning with David.

"You have certainly grown since we bumped into each other five years ago. I presume you speak English now. Do you still have what I gave you or have you spent it on penny candy?"

David took the silver dollar from his pocket and held it up for all to see. "I still have it, sir. I shall keep it until the day I die."

"Bully!" Mr. Roosevelt chuckled and handed him a package. "I've been told that you enjoy the all-American sport of baseball. I think you'll find this gift useful. Don't wait. Open it now."

"Wow!" David whooped as he ripped open the package to find a bat and ball. "Thanks!"

Many times Havah wiped tears from her eyes as the president went down the line and gave each child a carefully chosen gift. To Olive, Tikvah, and Simon he gave Teddy bears. To Elliott, who already had a Teddy bear, he gave a cast iron train.

Reuven joyfully opened a box containing four leather bound journals. "I shall write about today on the very first page, sir. Thank you."

Rachel sniffed her new perfume. "So pretty. It's roses like Mommy's."

Quentin handed Bayla a long box tied with curling blue and white ribbons. He bowed and grinned shyly. "Happy Hanukkah, pretty Miss."

"I believe you've made a conquest, little lady." The president patted Bayla's head. "Before you open your present, I must confess one of my informants told me about something you did."

Bayla sucked in her lower lip. "Was it good or bad?"

"Good, my dear, exceedingly good. You see, you have a gift, a very special talent, if you will."

"What talent? I don't play piano or draw or nothing."

The president knelt to her eye level and covered her hands with his. "Your tender heart, my girl, and the way you care about others is a gift not bestowed upon everyone. Acts of kindness are often a reward unto themselves. Today I have the privilege of giving you this small reward."

He kissed Bayla's forehead and stood.

She excitedly tore off the silver wrapping paper. Shuffling through layers of tissue paper, her mouth dropped open. "Mommy, look! She's...she's splendiferous!" Bayla lifted a doll with dark ringlets and grey eyes and cradled her in the crook of her arm. "Her dress is exactly like mine. How did you ever know, Mr. President?"

Catherine and Edith Roosevelt flashed knowing smiles to each other. Havah mouthed "Thank you" to them. Bayla pressed her cheek against the doll's porcelain cheek. "I shall call her Miss Me-Me."

Reuven peered at her over his stack of new journals. "Why?"

"Because she looks like *me*, silly."

He rolled his eyes. "Girls."

Holding his new velvet-lined clarinet case to his chest, Mendel beamed. "Uncle Evron's clarinet will have a proper home at last."

"No, son." Itzak knelt beside him and pointed to the name embossed on the leather case. "It's Mendel Abromovich's clarinet."

"Onto the grownups in the family." The president approached Lev and Winnie. "I'll begin with the newlyweds who have graciously agreed to share their honeymoon with us." He winked at the crowd. "They missed dinner tonight to go...um...sightseeing."

Despite the fact she was only seven years Lev's senior, Havah swelled with maternal pride. His mustache, covering some of his scar, gave him a distinguished look. Beside him, Winnie wore an ivory silk gown that accentuated her graceful curves.

Handing Lev an envelope, the president grasped Lev's hand. "The first few years can be difficult for young marrieds. Here's a small token to help. I understand you're studying to be a physician, son."

Curving his arm protectively around Winnie, Lev nodded. "And my wife is studying to become a veterinarian."

"Good for you, my dear," said the president, taking her hand. "We Roosevelts rely on our vet as much as we do our medical doctor." He grinned at Lev. "Your parents tell me you've matriculated to the University of Kansas."

"Yes, sir."

"Well then, Rock Chalk Jayhawk! All my best to you."

A twitter went through the crowd as he moved down the line giving each couple a personally signed photograph of himself. "Here's something to keep the moths away." Quentin and Charlie delivered a bouquet of roses to each of the Gitterman women. "Flowers for fair flowers," said the president.

Then he stopped beside Yussel and beckoned a servant who placed a plain box in Yussel's hands. "I didn't bother wrapping this gift. I'm most certain the recipient won't mind."

"You're a good man, Mr. President," Yussel's tremulous voice cracked, "but have you not given us enough already?"

"Indulge me. Consider this a gift from myself and your friend, Mr. Dietrich. He sent your elegant heirloom to me months ago to enlist my help. I think you'll agree we found the right silversmith."

The president lifted the box lid and Yussel reached inside. He trembled and his eyes brimmed. "Oh...my...is this...?"

Havah clapped her hand over her mouth as he lifted out his repaired and polished menorah. Yussel brushed his fingers over it. "I can't even feel the break." He smiled through his tears and reached for the president's hand. "Does not the psalmist say, 'Adoshem mends the broken heart'?"

"May the lights of this menorah shine for many generations to come." Enfolding Yussel's hand in both of his, the president pumped it up and down. "Godspeed, Rabbi."

Taking a chair from the front row, Mr. Roosevelt scooted it next to Havah's wheelchair and sat. "I have one last gift for an exceptional woman." His blue eyes caught hers in their steady gaze and he spoke to her as if no one else were in the room. "My darling Havah, my parents and my doctors doubted I would survive childhood. I was a sickly boy. Simply breathing was difficult because I had asthma, yet my father encouraged me to do calisthenics to strengthen my body." He placed a small package on her lap. "I've spoken with your physician, Dr. Eleanor Miklos, in Kansas City. An extraordinary woman. She agrees this is a splendid gift."

Havah opened the package to find a pair of metal dumbbells. She took one in each hand. "For me?"

"Yes, for you. No one can give you back your legs, but you still have your arms. It's my firm belief that women, as well as men, can benefit from weight lifting."

"That's our Havah." Itzak nudged Arel. "As strong as iron."

The president kissed her hand, still holding a dumbbell. "Never give up Havah. As you, of all people know, courage is not having the strength to go on, it's going on when you don't have the strength."

Chapter Seventeen

The fragrance of daffodils floated on the air like angel wings. Havah drank it in as she wheeled her chair to the mailbox at the end of the sidewalk. Opening it, she collected a pile of envelopes and a package. Some were the dreaded monthly bills addressed to Mr. Arel Gitterman, and the rest, with the exception of the package, were for her.

She inspected the heavy parcel addressed to Rachel. In the upper left hand corner, printed in block letters, it read, "Helen Keller, Wrentham, Massachusetts."

Three years before, when on tour, Ulrich had visited her at her home and asked how he could help Rachel. Since then, Miss Keller had taken an interest in her and after Rachel learned how to write, the two exchanged occasional letters.

Every March, Miss Keller sent Rachel a Braille birthday greeting and a new book. Havah moved the parcel to the bottom of the stack for later when Rachel came home from her piano lesson at Ulrich's.

The next envelope was postmarked Paris, France. She opened it carefully so she would not damage the contents. Holding her breath, she slipped out a hand-painted card. On it was a picture of her in her wheelchair flying through a blue sky. Vasily had painted wings on the chair and deftly written "Happy Birthday" in a rainbow behind it.

Unfolding the card, she read.

"Dear Miss Havah,

I wish I could be there to help you celebrate your birthday. You have always inspired me. I learned from you a person can overcome any obstacle, be it in the flesh or the emotions.

I will be home for Christmas this year. By then, my baby sister will be a year old. Tell Reuven I loved his story about the crazy artist across the sea. I hope he gets an 'A' on it. I know he will. Give Bayla a kiss and tell her she's still my sweetheart. Congratulations to Lev and Winnie on their new house in Lawrence and her admittance to veterinary college.

Rachel is always on my mind. Tatko tells me Uncle Ulrich is hiring a tutor for her since she's too advanced for the local blind school. She is brilliant. I look forward to meeting her brother Simon, too. Give my regards to Arel.

All my love,
Vasya"
March 1, 1909

Heaving a sigh, Havah slipped the card back into the envelope. Tonight she would ask Itzak to make a frame for it. She wheeled to the garden to read the rest of her birthday cards.

Opening the next one, she laughed at a crudely drawn cartoon of a stick man with a clown hat, glasses and hook nose that took up half the page. The message read, "Happy birthday, Chief. Love, Sammy the tailor."

Like wedding dancers, purple crocuses and yellow jonquils circled the oak in the center of the flower bed. Havah envisioned her mother picking bunches of the blossoms the way she did every year in honor of Havah's birthday, the last time exactly ten years ago.

Bagel's barking rousted Havah from her musing and announced Arel's homecoming. That dog belonged to him furry heart and soul. Arel had not even reached the porch before Bagel cavorted in circles at his feet. Kneeling, Arel let the enthusiastic pup cover his face with doggy kisses.

Strolling to Havah, Arel wiped his cheek with the back of his hand. He leaned down to kiss her and she turned from him in mock disgust. "You expect me to kiss that *punim* after it's been kissed by a dog?"

He grasped her face between his hands and planted a loud smooch on her lips. "Ah, what's a little Bagel slobber between lovers?"

She turned the chair. "Last one to the porch is a rotten egg."

Running with the dog at his heels, Arel tripped and fell in the grass. Havah raced up the ramp, wheels spinning. Once on the porch, she clasped her hands over her head and yelled. "Winner and still champion!"

Arel limped to her, rubbing his shin. "No fair taking advantage of a cripple."

"You're home early."

"Sammy made me do it."

"Good, you're in time to help me get ready for my surprise birthday party."

"We're only going to Ulrich and Catherine's for a quiet dinner." Feigning puzzlement, Arel scratched his head. "What makes you think there's a party?"

"Elementary, my dear Watson." Havah sat up straight, folded her arms and tapped her side-twisted lips with her index finger. "Mama and Papa went for a long 'walk.' They left two hours ago. Shayndel and Itzak took the kids shopping. Itzak shopping? And why would he take his violin? I've tried to telephone Oxana and no one's home."

"Maybe she took the baby to visit Nikolai at work."

"Nice try, but no one's answering at the clinic either."

Arel cast his eyes upward. "A medical emergency perhaps?"

"I suppose that could be, but with three doctors? I doubt it. I'm sure they're helping Catherine hang streamers and wrap presents."

Whistling "Yankee Doodle Dandy," Arel held his hands behind his back. Havah continued. "Bayla and Reuven told me they had to stay after school, but couldn't tell me why. Even Nettie cut our breakfast visit short this morning. She said she had important matters to attend to. She should've let George make her excuses since she's not much of an actress. But the biggest clue came with the birthday card I got from Evalyne last Friday saying she couldn't wait to see me 'next Tuesday.' Now why else would Wolf be coming in from St. Louis with his family?"

Blushing like a schoolboy caught stealing gumdrops, Arel looked down at his feet. "Don't rush me, I'm thinking."

"You're as bad as Evie when it comes to keeping a secret. At any rate, I'm looking forward to meeting Dora."

Arel opened the door and Havah rolled her chair over the threshold. Heading for the kitchen, she detoured to the boys' room when Simon cried. "His naps are getting shorter all the time."

Picking him up, Arel wrinkled his nose. "He left a present. So to show what a great fella I am, I'll change his diaper."

Simon grinned, showing off his first tooth. Arel laid him on Reuven's bed. As soon as Arel removed the soiled diaper, a surprise fountain doused him. Simon squealed and rolled over onto this tummy. Wiping his face on a clean diaper with one hand, Arel captured his wriggly son with the other. After two failed attempts to hold Simon still, Arel succeeded in diapering him.

Havah took the baby and laid him on her lap. Simon frantically tugged at her bodice. Before she could completely unbutton her blouse, he latched onto her breast. "Have you eaten lunch, Arel?"

With a sly grin, Arel pushed her chair toward the kitchen. "I'll have what he's having."

"Mashed bananas and Pablum coming right up."

Stopping her chair at the counter, Arel reached for the icebox. "Is there still leftover chicken and *holla*?"

"There was enough for a couple of sandwiches, if Reuven hasn't gotten to it first."

Simon finished nursing and Havah lifted him into his highchair. Arel let out a low whistle and squeezed her upper arm. "Your dumbbell exercises are paying off."

She peeled a banana and mashed it into the baby's cereal. He clapped his hands and bounced up and down as she fed him the first bite. "He's a heavyweight, isn't he?"

After lunch, Arel set Simon on a blanket in their bedroom. Then he lifted Havah from her chair and attended to her toilette. Helping her undress, he ran her bath and lowered her into the tub.

She luxuriated in the fragrance of Fruma Ya'el's homemade cinnamon-and-vanilla-scented soap. Kneeling, Arel scrubbed her back and brushed his lips over the nape of her neck. She shivered with delight.

"It's just the two of us," he whispered, his lips moist and warm against her ear.

Simon, who had wedged himself between the wardrobe and the bureau hollered. Havah heaved a disappointed sigh. "Make that three of us."

Once he had rescued the baby and put him back on the blanket, Arel lifted her out of the tub and wrapped her in a towel. "I don't understand why you never complain, Havah. You railed against Itzak when he suggested he make you a cane and you wept bitterly when Dr. Florin confined you to a wheelchair. Before the accident, you wouldn't let me fasten your shoes. Now you seem almost happy to be paralyzed."

He laid her on the bed and slipped her stockings over her feet and legs. With his help, she sat up and raised her arms so he could slide on her undergarments. "It's like my papa used to say, I finally realized I couldn't empty the ocean with a spoon."

"I'm not following you."

"No matter how much I denied the pain, it was eating me alive. I thought I could beat it. Granted, I'm an invalid now, but I don't hurt anymore. Being dependent on those who love me is a small price to pay for such relief."

Arel secured her petticoat and fastened her skirt while she buttoned her blouse. Once she was dressed, he picked her up. "Can you do one thing for me, Havah?"

She wreathed her arms about his neck. "Anything for you, my beloved. Name it."

"When we get to Ulrich's, act surprised."

Rochelle Wisoff-Fields

"Startlingly new! Wonderfully different!" boasted the advertisements for the 1953 Chevrolet sedan. Much to the chagrin of her brother Jeff, Rochelle made her entrance into the world the same year her parents purchased their first car. Growing up in Kansas City, she doesn't remember wanting to be anything other than an artist. Her mother would bemoan the fact with, "Thanks to Rochelle, I can't find a clean sheet of paper in this house."

Early on, Rochelle's love of the arts extended to writing. At age nine she had a poem entitled "The Girl with the Dolls" printed in a magazine. While excited to see her name in black and white, she wasn't thrilled with the way her grandmother, a widely published poet in New York, saw fit to edit it.

Wisoff-Fields is a woman of Jewish descent—the granddaughter of Eastern European immigrants—whose close personal connection to Jewish history is a recurring theme throughout much of her writing. Growing up, she was heavily influenced by the *Sholom Aleichem* stories as well as *Fiddler on the Roof*. Her novels *Please Say Kaddish for Me, From Silt and Ashes* and *As One Must, One Can* were born of her desire to share the darker side of these beloved tales; the history that can be difficult to view, much less embrace.

Before becoming an author, Rochelle attended the Kansas City Art Institute, where she studied painting and lithography. Her preferred media are pen and ink, pencil, and watercolor, which she uses in her book covers, character studies and will be used in her upcoming companion coffee table book for the series, *A Stone for the Journey* (Argus spring 2017).

Rochelle's short story "Savant" was published in *Voices, Vol. III;* "The Swimming Lesson," in *Echoes of the Ozarks, Vol. VI*; and "Reap the Whirlwind" in *Voices, Volume IV* Two of these are included in her own short story collection, with original artwork, *This, That and Sometimes the Other* (High Hill Press).